The Dog of the South

ALSO BY CHARLES PORTIS
FROM CLIPPER LARGE PRINT

True Grit

The Dog of the South

Charles Portis

W F HOWES LTD

This large print edition published in 2012 by
W F Howes Ltd
Unit 4, Rearsby Business Park, Gaddesby Lane,
Rearsby, Leicester LE7 4YH

1 3 5 7 9 10 8 6 4 2

First published in the United Kingdom in 1979
by Random House

A CIP catalogue record for this book is available
from the British Library

ISBN 978 1 47120 586 6

Typeset by Palimpsest Book Production Limited,
Falkirk, Stirlingshire
Printed and bound in Great Britain
by MPG Books Ltd, Bodmin, Cornwall

. . . Even Animals near the Classis of plants seem to have the most restlesse motions. The Summer-worm of Ponds and plashes makes a long waving motion; the hair-worm seldome lies still. He that would behold a very anomalous motion, may observe it in the Tortile and tiring stroaks of Gnatworms.

—SIR THOMAS BROWNE

CHAPTER 1

My wife Norma had run off with Guy Dupree and I was waiting around for the credit card billings to come in so I could see where they had gone. I was biding my time. This was October. They had taken my car and my Texaco card and my American Express card. Dupree had also taken from the bedroom closet my good raincoat and a shotgun and perhaps some other articles. It was just like him to pick the 410 – a boy's first gun. I suppose he thought it wouldn't kick much, that it would kill or at least rip up the flesh in a satisfying way without making a lot of noise or giving much of a jolt to his sloping monkey shoulder.

When the receipts arrived, they were in lumpy envelopes and the sums owed were such that American Express gave way to panic and urged me to call B. Tucker in New York at once and work out terms of payment. It was my guess that this 'Tucker' was only a house name, or maybe a hard woman who sat by a telephone all day with a Kool in her mouth. I got out my road maps and plotted the journey by following the sequence of dates and locations on the receipts. I love nothing better than a job like that and I had to laugh a little as the route took shape.

What a trip. What a pair of lovebirds! Pure Dupree! The line started in Little Rock and showed purpose as it plunged straight down into Texas. Then it became wobbly and disorderly. There was one grand loop that went as far west as Moffit's Texaco station in San Angelo, where sheep graze, and there were tiny epicycles along the way that made no sense at all.

I was reminded of the dotted line in history books that represents the aimless trek of Hernando De Soto, a brave soldier who found no gold but only hardship and a wide muddy river to which his body was at last committed – at night, they say. What a man! I was at that time fascinated by the great captains of history and I sometimes became so excited when reading about such men as Lee or Hannibal (both defeated, it occurs to me) that I would have to get up and walk around the room to catch my breath.

Not that there was space for any real strolling in our apartment on Gum Street. Norma wanted to move to a bigger place and so did I – to a bigger and *quieter* place – but I resisted going to the houses and apartments she had scouted out because I knew from experience that they would not be suitable.

The last one had been a little chocolate-brown cottage, with a shed of the same rich color in the back yard. The real-estate fellow showed us around and he talked about the rent-like payments. In the shed we came across an old man lying on a cot. He was eating nuts from a can and watching a daytime television show. His pearly shins were exposed above his socks. A piece of cotton covered one eye.

'That's Mr Proctor,' said the real-estate bird. 'He pays fifty a month for the shed and you can apply that, see, on your note.' I didn't want an old man living in my back yard and the real-estate bird said, 'Well, tell him to hit the road then,' but I didn't want to do that either, to Mr Proctor. The truth was, we couldn't afford a house, not even this cottage, living on my father's charity as we were, and Norma either could not or would not find an apartment with thick walls made of honest plaster. I had specified this as against the modern dry-wall material, which not only conducts sound readily but in many cases seems to amplify it.

I should have paid more attention to Norma. I should have talked to her and listened to her but I didn't do it. A timely word here and there might have worked wonders. I knew she was restless, and anxious to play a more active part in life. She spoke in just those terms, and there were other signals as well.

She announced one day that she wanted to give a party in our apartment with the theme of 'Around the World in 80 Days.' I couldn't believe my ears. A party! She talked about applying for a job as stewardess with Braniff Airlines. She bought a bicycle, an expensive multi-geared model, and joined a cycling club against my wishes. The idea was that she and her chums would pedal along leafy country lanes, shouting and singing like a bunch of Germans, but from all I could see they just had meetings in the damp basement of a church.

I could go on and on. She wanted to dye her hair. She wanted to change her name to Staci or Pam or April. She wanted to open a shop selling Indian jewelry. It wouldn't have hurt me to discuss this shop idea with her – big profits are made every day in that silver and turquoise stuff – but I couldn't be bothered. I had to get on with my reading!

Now she was gone. She had gone to Mexico with Guy Dupree, for that was where my dotted line led. The last position was the Hotel Mogador in San Miguel de Allende, where I drew a terminal cross on the map with my draftsman's pencil and shaded it to give an effect of depth.

The last receipt was just twelve days old. Our Mexican friends have a reputation for putting things off until another day and for taking long naps but there had been no snoozing over this bill. I looked at Dupree's contemptuous approximation of my signature on the receipt. On some of the others he had signed 'Mr Smart Shopper' and 'Wallace Fard.'

Here he was then, cruising the deserts of Mexico

in my Ford Torino with my wife and my credit cards and his black-tongued dog. He had a chow dog that went everywhere with him, to the post office and ball games, and now that red beast was making free with his lion feet on my Torino seats.

In exchange for my car he had left me his 1963 Buick Special. I had found it in my slot at the Rhino Apartments parking lot, standing astride a red puddle of transmission fluid. It was a compact car, a rusty little piece of basic transportation with a V-6 engine. The thing ran well enough and it seemed eager to please but I couldn't believe the Buick engineers ever had their hearts in a people's car. Dupree had shamefully neglected it. There was about a quarter-turn of slack in the steering wheel and I had to swing it wildly back and forth in a childlike burlesque of motoring. After a day or two I got the hang of it but the violent arm movements made me look like a lunatic. I had to stay alert every second, every instant, to make small corrections. That car had 74,000 miles on it and the speedometer cable was broken. There was a hole in the floor on the driver's side and when I drove over something white the flash between my feet made me jump. That's enough on the car for now.

This business came at a bad time. Just a month earlier – right after my twenty-sixth birthday – I had quit my job on the copy desk at the newspaper to return to school. My father had agreed to support me again until I had received a degree of

5

some sort or at least a teaching certificate. He had also presented me with the American Express card, he having had a good business year sprucing up old houses with Midgestone. As I say, the birthday was my twenty-sixth, but for some reason I had been thinking throughout the previous year that I was already twenty-six. A free year! The question was: would I piddle it away like the others?

My new plan was to become a high-school teacher. I had accumulated enough college hours over the years for at least two bachelor's degrees but I had never actually taken one. I had never stayed long enough in any one course of study. I had no education hours at all but I did have some pre-law at Southwestern and some engineering at Arkansas. I had been at Ole Miss too, where I studied the Western campaigns of the Civil War under Dr Buddy Casey. Don't talk about Virginia to Dr Bud; talk about Forrest!

For a long time I had a tape recording of his famous lecture on the Siege of Vicksburg and I liked to play it in the morning while I was shaving. I also played it sometimes in the car when Norma and I went for drives. It was one of those performances – 'bravura' is the word for it – that never become stale. Dr Bud made the thing come alive. With nothing more than his knuckles and the resonating sideboards of his desk he could give you caissons crossing a plank bridge, and with his dentures and inflated cheeks and moist thick lips he could give you a mortar barrage in the distance and rattling anchor chains and lapping water and hissing fuses and neighing horses. I had heard the tape hundreds of times and yet each time I would be surprised and delighted anew by some bit of Casey genius, some description or insight or narrative passage or sound effect. The bird peals, for instance. Dr Bud gives a couple of unexpected bird calls in the tense scene where Grant and Pemberton are discussing surrender terms under the oak tree. The call is a stylized one – *tu-whit, tu-whee* – and is not meant to represent that of any particular bird. It has never failed to catch me by surprise. But no one could hope to keep the whole of that lecture in his head at once, such are its riches.

I say I 'had' the tape. It disappeared suddenly and Norma denied that she had thrown it away. After making a few inquiries and turning the apartment upside down I let the matter drop. That was my way. I once read about a man who would not let his wife know how he liked for things to be done, so that she could offend him. That was never my way. Norma and I had our squabbles, certainly, but never any scenes of rage like those on television with actors and actresses screaming at one another. It was give and take in our house. Two of my rules did cause a certain amount of continuing friction – my rule against smoking at the table and my rule against record-playing after 9 p.m., by which time I had settled in for a night of reading – but I didn't see how I could compromise in either of those areas.

Norma was married to Dupree when I met her. She had golden down on her forearms and a little blue vein or artery that ran across her forehead and became distended and pulsed noticeably when she was upset or expressing some strong opinion. You hardly ever see the wives of people who work for newspapers and I'm embarrassed to say I can't remember the occasion of our first meeting. I had sat next to Dupree on the rim of the copy desk. In fact, I had gotten him the job. He was not well liked in the newsroom. He radiated dense waves of hatred and he never joined in the friendly banter around the desk, he who had once been so lively. He hardly spoke at all except to mutter 'Crap' or 'What crap' as he processed news matter, affecting a contempt for all events on earth and for the written accounts of those events.

As for his height, I would put it at no more than five feet nine inches – he being fully erect, out of his monkey crouch – and yet he brazenly put down five eleven on all forms and applications. His dress was sloppy even by newspaper standards – thousands of wrinkles! It was a studied effect rather than carelessness. I know he had to work at it, because his clothes were of the permanent-press type and you can't make that stuff wrinkle unless you bake it in a dryer and then crumple it up. He had a nervous habit of rubbing his hands back and forth on his trousers when he was seated and this made for an unsightly condition called 'pilling,' where the surface fibers form hard little balls or

8

pills from being scuffed about. Pilling is more often seen on cheap blankets than on clothing but all of Dupree's trousers were badly pilled in front. His shirts were downright dirty. He wore glasses, the lenses thick and greasy, which distorted the things of the world into unnatural shapes. I myself have never needed glasses. I can read road signs a half-mile away and I can see individual stars and planets down to the seventh magnitude with no optical aids whatever. I can see Uranus.

For eleven miserable months Norma was married to Dupree and after some of the things she told me I was amazed that she could go back to him. His kissing frenzies! His carbide cannon! Still, there it was. I had no idea that anything was going on. How had he made his new approaches? What were his disgusting courtship techniques? Had the cycling club been a ruse? There had been some night meetings. But Dupree already had a sweetheart! A friend at the paper told me that Dupree had been seeing this person for several months – a mystery woman who lived upstairs in a gray house behind the Game and Fish Building. What about her?

Norma and I were getting along well enough, or so I thought. I have mentioned her restlessness. The only other thing I could put my finger on was a slight change in her manner. She had begun to treat me with a hearty but impersonal courtesy, something like a nurse dealing with an old-timer. 'I'll be right with you,' she would say, or, when presenting me with something, 'Here we are, Midge.' She had always called me by my last name.

I think now this coolness must have started with our algebra course. She had agreed to let me practice my teaching methods on her and so I had worked out a lecture plan in elementary algebra. I had a little blackboard, green actually, that I set up in the kitchen every Thursday at 7 p.m. for my demonstrations. It was not the kind of thing you like to ask a person to do but Norma was a good sport about it and I thought if I could teach her ninth-grade algebra I could teach just about anything to anybody. A good sport, I say, but that was only at the beginning of the course. Later on she began to fake the answers on her weekly tests. That is, she would look up the answers to the problems in the back of the textbook and copy them without showing me her step-by-step proofs. But wasn't this a part of teaching too? Wouldn't I have to deal with widespread cheating in the raucous classrooms of our public schools? I handled it this way with Norma. I said nothing about her dishonesty and simply gave her a score of zero on each test. Still she continued to look up the answers, whether I was watching her or not. She would complete the test in two or three minutes and sign her name to it and hand it to me, saying, 'There you go, Midge. Will there be anything else?'

Of course I knew she felt sorry for Dupree in his recent troubles and I suppose she must have come to see him as a romantic outlaw. I didn't feel sorry for him at all. The troubles were entirely of his own making. You can't go around bothering people and not expect some inconvenience yourself. The trouble was politics. He had lately become interested in politics and this had brought his nastiness into bloom.

That is, it was 'lately' to me. I didn't see Dupree much for seven or eight years, when he was away at all those different schools, and the change was probably more gradual than it appeared to me. He had once been a funny fellow. I don't often laugh out loud, even when I can recognize a joke as being a good one, but Dupree could always make me laugh when he did a thing called The Electric Man. As The Electric Man or The Mud Man he could make anyone laugh. And sometimes he would go out one door and come in at another one, as though he had just arrived, having moved very quickly in concealment between the two points. It wasn't so funny the first time – but he would keep doing it!

To the best of my knowledge he had never even voted, and then someone must have told him something about politics, some convincing lie, or he read something – it's usually one or the other – and he stopped being funny and turned mean and silent. That wasn't so bad, but then he stopped being silent.

He wrote abusive letters to the President, calling him a coward and a mangy rat with scabs on his ears, and he even challenged him to a fistfight on Pennsylvania Avenue. This was pretty good coming from a person who had been kayoed in every beer joint in Little Rock, often within the first ten minutes of his arrival. I don't believe we've ever had a President, unless it was tiny James Madison with his short arms, who couldn't have handled Dupree in a fair fight. Any provocation at all would do. One of his favorite ploys was to take a seat at a bar and repeat overheard fatuous remarks in a quacking voice like Donald Duck. Or he would spit BB's at people. He could fire BB's from between his teeth at high velocity and he would sit there and sting the tender chins and noses of the drinkers with these little bullets until he was discovered and, as was usually the consequence, knocked cold as a wedge.

I will have to admit that Dupree took his medicine without whining, unlike so many troublemakers. I will have to admit that he was not afraid of physical blows. On the other hand he did whine when the law came down on him. He couldn't see the legal distinction between verbal abuse and death threats, and he thought the government was persecuting him. The threats were not real, in the sense that they were likely to be carried out, but the Secret Service had no way of knowing that.

And he had certainly made the threats. I saw the letters myself. He had written such things to the President of the United States as 'This time it's curtains for you and your rat family. I know your movements and I have access to your pets too.'

A man from the Secret Service came by to talk to me and he showed me some of the letters. Dupree had signed them 'Night Rider' and 'Jo Jo the Dog-Faced Boy' and 'Hoecake Scarfer' and 'Old Nigger Man' and 'Don Winslow of the Navy' and 'Think Again' and 'Home Room Teacher' and 'Smirking Punk' and 'Dirt Bike Punk' and 'Yard Man.'

He was arrested and he called me. I called his father – they didn't speak – and Mr Dupree said, 'Leavenworth will be a good place for him.' The U.S. Commissioner had set bond at three thousand dollars – not a great deal, it seemed to me, for such a charge – but Mr Dupree refused to post it.

'Well, I didn't know whether you could afford it or not,' I said, knowing he would be stung by any suggestion that he might not be rich. He didn't say anything for a long moment and then he said, 'Don't call me again about this.' Dupree's mother might have done something but I didn't like to talk to her because she was usually in an alcoholic fog. She had a sharp tongue too, drunk or sober.

It certainly wasn't a question of the money, because Mr Dupree was a prosperous soybean farmer who had operations not only in Arkansas but in Louisiana and Central America as well. The newspaper was already embarrassed and didn't want to get further involved. Norma put it to me that I ought to lend Dupree a hand since he was so absolutely friendless. Against my better judgment I got three hundred dollars together and arranged for a bondsman named Jack Wilkie to bail him out.

Not a word of thanks did I get. As soon as he was released from the county jail, Dupree complained to me that he had been fed only twice a day, oatmeal and pancakes and other such blood-less fare. A cellmate embezzler had told him that federal prisoners were entitled to three meals. Then he asked me to get him a lawyer. He didn't want Jack Wilkie to represent him.

I said, 'The court will appoint you a lawyer.'

He said, 'They already have but he's no good. He doesn't even know the federal procedure. He'll start talking to this guy when he's supposed to be talking to that other guy. He waives everything. He's going to stipulate my ass right into a federal pen. A first offender.'

'You'll have to get your own lawyer, Dupree.'

'Where am I supposed to get him? I've called every son of a bitch in the yellow pages.'

A good lawyer, he thought, would be able to forestall the psychiatric examination at the prison hospital in Springfield, Missouri. That examin-ation was what he feared most, and with good reason, even though the finding would no doubt have provided a solid defense. In any case, he didn't really need a lawyer, good or bad, because on the following Friday night he jumped bail and ran off with my wife in my Ford Torino.

14

Since that night I had been biding my time but now that I knew where they were, more or less, I was ready to make my move. I had very little cash money for the trip and no credit cards. My father was floating somewhere on a lake near Eufaula, Alabama, in his green plastic boat, taking part in a bass tournament. Of course I had had many opportunities to explain the thing to him but I had been ashamed to do so. I was no longer an employee of the paper and I couldn't go to the credit union. My friend Burke never had any money. I could have sold some of my guns but I was reluctant to do so, saving that as a last resort. Gun fanciers are quick to sniff out a distress sale and I would have taken a beating from those heartless traders.

Then on the very day of my departure I remembered the savings bonds. My mother had left them to me when she died. I kept them hidden behind the encyclopedias where Norma never tarried and I had all but forgotten about them. Norma was a great one to nose around in my things. I never bothered her stuff. I had a drawer full of pistols in my desk and I kept that drawer locked but she got it open somehow and handled those pistols. Little rust spots from her moist fingertips told the story. Not even my food was safe. She ate very little, in fact, but if some attractive morsel on my plate happened to catch her eye she would spear it and eat it in a flash without acknowledging that she had done anything out of the way. She knew

I didn't like that. I didn't tamper with her plate and she knew I didn't like her tampering with my plate. If the individual place setting means no more than that, then it is all a poor joke and you might as well have a trough and be done with it. She wouldn't keep her hands off my telescope either. But the Hope Diamond would have been safe behind those *Britannicas*.

I retrieved the bonds and sat down at the kitchen table to count them. I hadn't seen them in a long time and I decided to line them up shoulder to shoulder and see if I could cover every square inch of table surface with bonds. When I had done this, I stood back and looked at them. These were twenty-five-dollar E bonds.

Just then I heard someone at the door and I thought it was the children. Some sort of youth congress had been in session at the capitol for two or three days and children were milling about all over town. A few had even wandered into Gum Street where they had no conceivable business. I had been packing my clothes and watching these youngsters off and on all day through the curtain and now – the very thing I feared – they were at my door. What could they want? A glass of water? The phone? My signature on a petition? I made no sound and no move.

'Ray!'

It was Jack Wilkie and not the kids. What a pest! Day and night! I went to the door and unchained it and let him in but I kept him standing in the living room because I didn't want him to see my savings-bond table.

He said, 'Why don't you turn on some lights in here or raise a shade or something?'

'I like it this way.'

'What do you do, just stay in here all the time?'

He went through this same business at the beginning of each visit, the implication being that my way of life was strange and unwholesome. Jack was not only a bondsman and a lawyer of sorts but a businessman too. He owned a doughnut shop and some taxicabs. When I said he was a lawyer, I didn't mean he wore a soft gray suit and stayed home at night in his study reading Blackstone's *Commentaries*. If you had hired him unseen and were expecting that kind of lawyer, you would be knocked for a loop when you got to court and saw Jack standing there in his orange leisure suit, inspecting the green stuff under his fingernails. You would say, Well, there are a thousand lawyers in Pulaski County and it looks like I've got this one!

But Jack was a good-natured fellow and I admired him for being a man of action. I was uneasy when I first met him. He struck me as one of these country birds who, one second after meeting you, will start telling of some bestial escapade involving violence or sex or both, or who might in the same chatty way want to talk about Christ's Kingdom on Earth. It can go either way with those fellows and you need to be ready.

He had some big news for me this time, or so he thought. It was a postcard that Norma had sent to her mother from Wormington, Texas. 'Gateway to the Hill Country,' it said under the photograph of a low, dim structure that was the Wormington Motel. Gateway claims have always struck me as thin stuff because they can only mean that you're not there yet, that you're still in transit, that you're not in any very well defined place. I knew about the card already because Mrs Edge, Norma's mother, had called me about it the day before. I had met her in front of the Federal Building and looked it over. Norma said she was all right and would be in touch later. That was all, but Jack wanted to stand there and talk about the card.

I studied the motel picture again. Next to the office door of the place there was another door opening into what must have been a utility room. I knew that Norma with her instinct for the wrong turn had opened it and stood there a long time looking at the pipes and buckets and tools, trying to figure out how the office had changed so much. I would have seen in a split second that I was in the wrong room.

I said, 'They're not in Wormington now, Jack. It was just a stopover. Those lovebirds didn't run off to Wormington, Texas.'

'I know that but it's a place to start.'

'They'll turn up here in a few days.'

'Let me tell you something. That old boy is long gone. He got a taste of jail and didn't like it.'

'They'll turn up.'

'You should have told me he was a nut. I don't appreciate the way you brought me into this thing.'

'You knew what the charge was. You saw those letters.'

'I thought his daddy would be good for it. A slow-pay rich guy maybe. I thought he just meant to let the boy stew for a while.'

'Guy has given Mr Dupree a lot of headaches.'

'I'm going to report your car stolen. It's the only way.'

'No, I can't go along with that.'

'Let the police do our work for us. It's the only way to get a quick line on those lovebirds.'

'I don't want to embarrass Norma.'

'You don't want to embarrass yourself. You're afraid it'll get in the paper. Let me tell you something. The minute that bail is forfeited, it'll be in the paper anyway and by that time you may not even get your car back.'

There was something to this. Jack was no dope. The paper didn't run cuckold stories as such but I thought it best to keep my name out of any public record. That way I could not be tied into Dupree's flight. Tongues were already wagging, to be sure. Everyone at the paper knew what had happened but what they knew and what they could print – without the protection of public records – were two different things. All I wanted to do now was to get my car back. I was already cuckolded but I wouldn't appear so foolish, I thought, if I could just get my car back without any help.

Jack stood there and reviewed the whole case again. He did this every time, as though I might be confused on certain points. When his eyes became adjusted to the murky light, he saw my suitcase on the couch and I saw him taking this in, a suitcase fact. He said, 'I don't forfeit many bonds, Ray.' I had heard him say that before too.

He left and I quickly gathered my E bonds and stowed them in the suitcase. I selected a .38 Colt Cobra from the pistol drawer and sprayed it with a silicone lubricant and sealed it in a plastic bag and packed it next to the bonds. What else now? The lower-back capsules! Norma never went anywhere without her lower-back medicine and yet she had forgotten it this time, such was her haste in dusting out of town, away from my weekly embraces. I got it from the bathroom and packed it too. She would thank me for that. Those capsules cost four dollars apiece.

I made sure all the windows were locked and I found a country-music station on my big Hallicrafters radio and left it playing at high volume against the kitchen wall. There was a rock-and-roll twerp with a stereo set in the next apartment and his jungle rhythms penetrated my wall. Noise was his joy. He had a motorcycle too. The Rhino management had a rule prohibiting the repair of motorcycles in the parking lot but the twerp paid no attention to it. One night I called him. I was reading a biography of Raphael Semmes and I put it down and rang up the twerp and asked him if he knew who Admiral Semmes was. He said, 'What!' and I said, 'He was captain of the *Alabama*, twerp!' and hung up.

Everything was in readiness. My checklist was complete. I called a cab and typed a note and tacked it to the door.

> *I will be out of town for a few days.*
> *Raymond E. Midge*

The cabdriver honked and picked his way slowly down Broadway through the little delegates to that endless convention of Junior Bankers or Young Teamsters. Their numbers seemed to be growing. I had left the Buick Special with a mechanic on Asher Avenue to get the solenoid switch replaced on the starter. The cabdriver let me out in front of a filthy café called Nub's or Dub's that was next door to the garage. Nub – or anyway some man in an apron – was standing behind the screen door and he looked at me. I was wearing a coat and tie and carrying a suitcase and I suppose he thought I had just flown in from some distant city and then dashed across town in a cab to get one of his plate lunches. A meal wasn't a bad idea at that but it was getting late and I wanted to be off.

The mechanic told me I needed a new motor mount and he wanted to sell me a manifold gasket too, for an oil leak. I wasn't having any of that. I wasn't repairing anything on that car that wasn't absolutely necessary. This was a strange attitude for me because I hate to see a car abused. Maintenance! I never went along with that new policy of the six-thousand-mile oil change. It was always fifteen hundred for me and a new filter every time.

And yet here I was starting off for Mexico in this junker without so much as a new fan belt. There were Heath bar wrappers, at least forty of them, all over the floor and seats and I hadn't even bothered to clean them out. It wasn't my car and I despised it. I had done some thinking too. The shock of clean oil or the stiffer tension of a new belt might have been just enough to upset the fragile equilibrium of the system. And I had worked it out that the high mileage was not really a disadvantage, reasoning in this specious way: that a man who has made it to the age of seventy-four has a very good chance of making it to seventy-six – a better chance, in fact, than a young man would have.

Before I could get out of town, I remembered the silver service that Mrs Edge had passed along to Norma. What if it were stolen? I wasn't worried much about my guns or my books or my telescope or my stamps but if some burglar nabbed the Edge forks I knew I would never hear the end of it. My note would invite a break-in! I returned to the apartment and got the silver chest. On my note saying that I would be out of town for a few days a smart-ass had written, 'Who cares?' I ripped it off the door and drove downtown to the Federal Building where Mrs Edge worked. She wore a chain on her glasses and she had a good job with a lot of seniority at the Cotton Compliance Board.

She wasn't in the office and no one could tell me where she was. What a sweet job! Just drift out for the afternoon! I called her house and there was no answer. I wondered if she might have found a place where she could dance in the afternoon. She was crazy about dancing and she went out almost every night with big red-faced men who could stay on the floor with her for three or four hours. I mean smoking soles! She called me a 'pill' because I would never take Norma dancing. I say 'never' and yet we had scuttled stiffly across the floor on certain special occasions, although our total dancing time could be readily computed in seconds, the way pilots measure their flying time in hours. I believe Mrs Edge did prefer me over Dupree, for my civil manner and my neat attire if nothing else, but that's not to say she liked me. She had also called me 'furtive' and 'a selfish little fox.'

I decided that she was probably out for an afternoon of city obstruction and I went to the west side of town and cruised the parking lots of the big shopping centers looking for her car. On certain days of the week she and several hundred other biddies would meet at these places and get their assignments, first having taken care to park their Larks and Volvos and Cadillacs across the painted lines and thus taking up two parking spaces, sometimes three. Then they would spread out over town. Some would go to supermarkets and stall the checkout lines with purse-fumbling and check-writing. Others would wait for the noon rush at cafeterias and there bring the serving lines to a crawl with long deliberative stops at the pie station. The rest were on motor patrol and they would poke along on the inside lanes of busy streets and stop cold for left turns whenever they saw a good chance to stack up traffic. Another trick was to stick the nose of a car about halfway into a thoroughfare from a side street, thereby blocking all traffic in that lane. Mrs Edge was a leader of this gang. Turn her loose and she would have a dancing academy in the post office!

It was dark when I gave up the search. This silver wasn't old or rare or particularly valuable and I was furious with myself at having wasted so much time over it. I didn't feel like going all the way back to the apartment, so I just left the chest in the car trunk.

I was off at last and I was excited about the trip. The radio didn't work and I hummed a little. When I reached Benton, I was already tired of driving that car. Twenty-five miles! I couldn't believe it. I had a thousand miles to go and I was sleepy and my arms were tired and I didn't see how I was going to make it to Texarkana.

I pulled in at a rest stop and lay down on the seat,

which had a strong dog odor. My nose was right against the plastic weave. This rest stop was a bad place to rest. Big diesel rigs roared in and the drivers left their engines running and made everybody miserable, and then some turd from Ohio parked a horse trailer next to me. The horses made the trailer springs squeak when they shifted their weight. That squeaking went on all night and it nearly drove me crazy. I slept for about four hours. It was a hard sleep and my eyes were swollen. A lot of people, the same ones who lie about their gas mileage, would have said they got no sleep at all.

It was breaking day when I reached Texarkana. I stopped and added some transmission fluid and put through a call to Little Rock from a pay station and woke up Mrs Edge. I asked her to call my father on his return and tell him that I had gone to San Miguel de Allende in Mexico and would be back in a few days. The silverware was safe. What? Mexico? Silver? She was usually pretty quick but I had given it to her in a jumble and she couldn't take it in. It was just as well, because I didn't want to discuss my private business with her.

The drive to Laredo took all day. Gasoline was cheap – 22.9 cents a gallon at some Shamrock stations – and the Texas police didn't care how fast you drove, but I had to keep the Buick speed below what I took to be about sixty because at that point the wind came up through the floor hole in such a way that the Heath wrappers were suspended behind my head in a noisy brown vortex. It was late October. The weather was fine but the leaves weren't pretty; they had just gone suddenly from green to dead.

I bought a quart of transmission fluid in Dallas and I stopped twice to cash bonds. The girl teller in the bank at Waco stared at me and I thought I must be giving off a dog smell. I got a roll of quarters from her and hefted it in my fist as I drove along.

Just south of Waco I looked about for some sign of the big gas line, the Scott-Eastern Line, but I could never determine where it crossed under the highway. My father and Mr Dupree had helped build it, first as swabbers and then as boy welders. The Sons of the Pioneers! They had once been fairly close friends but had drifted apart over the years, Mr Dupree having made a lot more money. My father resented his great success, although he tried not to, always giving Mr Dupree credit for his energy. The hammer and the cutting torch, he said, were Mr Dupree's favorite tools. My father's touch was much finer, his welding bead smoother and stronger and more pleasing to the eye, or so I am told. Of course he no longer made his living at it but people still called him on occasion when there was a tricky job to be done, such as welding airtight pressure seams on thin metal, or welding aluminum. Thin metal? Give him two beer cans and he'll weld them together for you!

26

In South Texas I saw three interesting things. The first was a tiny girl, maybe ten years old, driving a 1965 Cadillac. She wasn't going very fast, because I passed her, but still she was cruising right along, with her head tilted back and her mouth open and her little hands gripping the wheel.

Then I saw an old man walking up the median strip pulling a wooden cross behind him. It was mounted on something like a golf cart with two spoked wheels. I slowed down to read the hand-lettered sign on his chest.

JACKSONVILLE
FLA OR BUST

I had never been to Jacksonville but I knew it was the home of the Gator Bowl and I had heard it was a boom town, taking in an entire county or some such thing. It seemed an odd destination for a religious pilgrim. Penance maybe for some terrible sin, or some bargain he had worked out with God, or maybe just a crazed hiker. I waved and called out to him, wishing him luck, but he was intent on his marching and had no time for idle greetings. His step was brisk and I was convinced he wouldn't bust.

The third interesting thing was a convoy of stake-bed trucks all piled high with loose watermelons and cantaloupes. I was amazed. I couldn't believe that the bottom ones weren't being crushed under all that weight, exploding and spraying hazardous melon juice onto the highway. One of nature's tricks with curved surfaces. Topology! I had never made it that far in my mathematics and engineering studies, and I knew now that I never would, just as I knew that I would never be a navy pilot or a Treasury agent. I made a B in Statics but I was failing in Dynamics when I withdrew from the field. The course I liked best was one called Strength of Materials. Everybody else hated it because of all the tables we had to memorize but I loved it, the sheared beam. I had once tried to explain to Dupree how things fell apart from being pulled and compressed and twisted and bent and sheared but he wouldn't listen. Whenever that kind of thing came up, he would always say – *boast*, the way those people do – that he had no head for figures and couldn't do things with his hands, slyly suggesting the presence of finer qualities.

CHAPTER 2

In Laredo I got a six-dollar motel room that had a lot of posted rules on the door and one rubber pillow on the bed and an oil-burning heater in the wall that had left many a salesman groggy. It was the kind of place I knew well. I always try to get a room in a cheap motel with no restaurant that is near a better motel where I can eat and drink. Norma never liked this practice. She was afraid we would be caught out in the better place and humiliated before some socialites we might have just met. The socialites would spot our room key, with a chunk of wood dangling from it like a carrot, or catch us in some gaffe, and stop talking to us. This Laredo room also had a tin shower stall and one paper bath mat.

I went to a discount store and bought three quarts of transmission fluid and some food for the road and a Styrofoam ice chest and a frozen pie. I didn't want the pie but I did want the carton it came in. Back in the shadows of my room I replaced the pie with the Colt Cobra and sealed the box with tape. The cylinder of the revolver made a bulge in the carton and I regretted that I had not brought a flat automatic. Then I put the innocent-looking carton at the bottom of the ice chest and covered it with little crescents of ice from the motel dispenser. This was against motel policy, the crescents being intended for solitary drinks in the room instead of bulk use.

But I filled the chest anyway and on top of the ice I arranged cans of beer and packets of baloney and cheese in a festive display. The pie itself, lemon, I carried about in the room for a while, putting it down here and there. I couldn't find a good place for it. Finally I took it outside and left it by the dumpster for a passing rat, who would squeak with delight when he saw those white billows of meringue.

The better motel was across the wide street. I went over and scouted the place out, the magazine rack and the lounge and the restaurant. No salad bar but that was all right. I noted too that a person would have to pass through the steaming nastiness of the kitchen in order to reach the toilet. The people who were running the motel seemed to be from some place like North Dakota instead of Texas, and they all seemed to be worried about something, distracted. I could hear carpentry work going on in the kitchen and occasional shouts.

You can usually count on a pretty good chicken-fried steak in Texas, if not a chicken-fried chicken, but I didn't like this setup. All afternoon I had been thinking about one of those steaks, with white gravy and a lot of black pepper, and now I was afraid these people from Fargo would bring me a prefabricated vealette pattie instead of fresh meat. I ordered roast beef and I told the waitress I wanted plenty of gristle and would like for the meat to be gray with an iridescent rainbow sheen. She was not in the mood for teasing, being preoccupied with some private distress like the others. She brought me a plate of fish sticks and the smallest portion of coleslaw I've ever seen. It was in a paper nut cup. I didn't say anything because they have a rough job. Those waitresses are on their feet all day and they never get a raise and they never get a vacation until they quit. The menu was complete fiction. She was serving the fish sticks to everybody, and not a uniform count either.

After supper I went into the darkened lounge. It was still 'happy hour' and the place was packed with local people. I saw no socialites. I had trouble getting a stool at the bar because when one fell vacant I would wait for a minute or two to let it cool off, to let the body heat dissipate from the plastic cushion, and then someone else would get it. The crowd cleared out when the prices went up and then I had the bar pretty much to myself. I could see a man standing at the far end writing a letter with a pencil. He was laughing at his work, a lone bandit writing cruel taunts to the chief of police.

I ordered a glass of beer and arranged my coins before me on the bar in columns according to value.

When the beer came, I dipped a finger in it and wet down each corner of the paper napkin to anchor it, so it would not come up with the mug each time and make me appear ridiculous. I drank from the side of the mug that a left-handed person would use, in the belief that fewer mouths had been on that side. That is also my policy with cups, any vessel with a handle, although you can usually count on cups getting a more thorough washing than bar glasses. A quick slosh here and there and those babies are right back on the shelf!

Across from me there was a dark mirror and above that a mounted deer's head with a cigarette in his mouth. Back in the table area a woman was playing an electric organ. No one was shouting requests to her. I was the only person in the place who applauded her music – a piece of traveler's bravado. And after a while I didn't clap either. I had no character at all. If the other customers had suddenly decided to club the poor woman with bottles, with those square gin bottles, I suppose I would have joined in. Here was something new. We all know about the gentry going to seed but here was something Jefferson had not foreseen: an effete yeoman.

An old man wearing clown shoes came through the door and began to play a kind of tune on a toy trombone. He hummed into the tiny instrument, as with a comb and tissue paper. The Mexican bartender chased him out. Then another man came in and sat down beside me. I was annoyed, because there were plenty of empty stools. I stiffened and waited for him to start talking. I avoided eye contact. Any minute now, I said to myself, this fellow is going to order an Old Charter and 7-Up and tell me he had gone to boot camp with Tyrone Power. I couldn't see his face but I watched his hairy paw as it reached across me and grabbed a handful of matchbooks from the courtesy bowl. Greenish fingernails and a heavy silver ring with a black stone.

He punched me on the shoulder and laughed. It was Jack Wilkie. I couldn't believe it.

He said, 'How's the little car holding up?'

'It's doing all right.'

'Little car drives out good, does it?'

'What are you doing here, Jack?'

'It's all in the day's work.' He was windblown and his knit shirt was sagging and damp with sweat but he was pleased with the effect he had achieved and he kept punching me and laughing.

Mrs Edge had told him about the Texarkana call and he had immediately divined my plan. He had made up the lost time easily enough in his Chrysler Imperial. Tomorrow morning he would drive to San Miguel and pick up Dupree and take him back to Little Rock. It was as simple as that. He seemed to think San Miguel was right across the border.

'You should have told me where he was, Ray.'

'I was going to tell you as soon as I got my car back. I wanted to get my car without your help.'

33

'You should have told me about this Mexico thing. We could have worked something out. This is business to me.'

'I know that.'

'What difference does it make as long as you get your car?'

'It's not the same thing.'

I gave him what information I had and he wrote down 'Hotel Mogador' on a paper napkin. He said I might as well ride along with him to San Miguel in the comfort of the big Chrysler. I halfway agreed. It seemed the only thing to do, except maybe forget the whole business and go back to Little Rock like a whipped dog. There was no way I could beat him to San Miguel in the little Buick.

I said, 'How are you going to get Dupree out of Mexico? Your warrant won't be any good down there.'

Jack was scornful. '*Warrant*. That's a good one. Warrant's ass. I don't need a warrant. All I need is a certified copy of the bond. I'm a party to the action. That's better than a warrant any day. I can take custody anywhere. The dumbest person in this motel knows that.'

The woman at the organ was singing. She had been singing for some time but this was no background stuff; this song was a showstopper and we had to take notice: 'And then they nursed it, rehearsed it, . . . And gave out the news . . .'

The old man with the big shoes came back and this time he was wearing a bellboy's cap with a strap under his chin. He ran through the place waving a scrap of paper and shouting, 'Phone call! Phone call for the Sheriff of Cochise! Emergency phone call! Code ten!' The bartender ducked under the bar flap and popped a rag at him and chased him out again and I could hear the old man's shoes flopping down the hall.

Jack said, 'Who was that old guy?'

I said, 'I don't know.'

'They ought to lock that son of a bitch up.'

'I think it's Halloween.'

'No, it's not. A guy like that wouldn't know what day it was anyway. This place smells like a kennel. Did you eat here?'

'Yes.'

'Can you recommend anything?'

'I can't recommend what I had.'

'Some hot-tamale crap?'

'I had fish.'

'That's a mistake. A place like this. Let's go to some nice steakhouse. I'm hungry.'

'I've already eaten.'

'How about the track? Why don't we take a run out to the dog track and make some quick money? Let them dogs pay for our trip.'

'They don't have dog races here, Jack.'

'I think they do.'

'They don't have legal gambling in Texas.'

'I think they have dog races.'

'I don't think so. Out in the streets maybe. Among themselves.'

'Across the border then. I know they have some kind of racing in Juárez.'

'That's way up there at El Paso.'

I still didn't see how Jack could take Dupree out of Mexico without going through some sort of legal formality. He kept telling me he was 'the surety' and 'a party to the action' and that such a person could go anywhere in the world and do just as he pleased. He said, 'I don't care where they are. I've taken these old boys out of Venezuela and the Dominican Republic.'

We sat there and drank for a long time. Jack showed me his handcuffs, which he carried in a leather pouch on his belt. He also had a blackjack, or rather a 'Big John' flat sap. He didn't carry a gun. He said he loved the bail-bond business. His wife thought it was sleazy and she wanted him to give it up and devote all his time to the practice of law, which he found dull.

'I was in the army and nobody wanted to see me,' he said. 'Then I was a salesman and nobody wanted to see me. Now they're glad to see me. Let me tell you something. You're doing that old boy a real service when you get him out of jail. Sure, everybody has to go to jail sometime, but that don't mean you have to stay there.'

I asked Jack if he could help me get a job as an insurance adjuster. I had often thought of becoming an investigator of some kind and I asked him if he could put me on to something, perhaps a small shadowing job. The paper had once given me a trial as a police reporter, although hardly a fair one. Two days! Jack wasn't interested in this subject and he wouldn't discuss it with me.

He wanted to talk about his family. He had a jug-eared stepson named Gary who smoked marijuana and made D's in school and spent his money on trashy phonograph records. The boy also spent a lot of his time and money at an amusement arcade downtown and Jack said he had ugly sores in his right eyebrow from many hours of pressing his eye against the periscope of the submarine game. The thought of this boy and his smart mouth and his teen mustache made Jack angry. But he didn't hold it against his wife that she had given birth to the unsatisfactory kid and brought him to live in the Wilkie home.

He poked me with a finger and said, 'My wife is just as sweet as pie. Get that straight.' And a little later he said, 'I'm glad my wife is not a porker.' He told me she had 'firm muscles' and he told me about all the birthday presents and Christmas presents he had given her in recent years. He said she had never locked him out of the house.

I didn't see how Jack Wilkie could have a very nice wife and I was tired of hearing about her. He left to get a cheeseburger and I thought about his remarks. The insinuation seemed to be that Norma was not as sweet as pie. When he got back, I asked him if that was his meaning and he said it wasn't.

He had spilled food on his knit shirt. I told him

that I thought an investigator going on a trip should wear a coat and tie. He didn't hear me. He was looking at the mounted deer head. He jumped up on the bar and straddled the walkway behind the bar and took the cigarette from the deer's mouth and flung it down on the duckboards. Then he turned on the bartender. 'That's not right and you know it's not right,' he said. 'That's not the thing to do. Don't put another cigarette in that deer's mouth.'

The Mexican bartender was slicing limes. With his hooded eyes and his little mustache he looked like a hard customer to me. He was fed up with these antics in his bar, I could tell, and I thought he was going to do something. But he just said, 'I didn't put that one in there.'

Jack climbed down and started telling me about all the different people who had attacked him while he was just doing his job. Everybody who attacked him was crazy. He pulled up a trouser leg and showed me a pitted place on his calf where a crazy woman in Mississippi had stabbed him with a Phillips screwdriver. Then he raised his knit shirt and showed me a purple scar on his broad white back where he had been shot by a crazy man in Memphis. One of his lungs had filled up with blood and when he came around in the emergency room of Methodist Hospital he heard the doctor ask a nurse if she had the key to the morgue. A close call for Jack! Not everybody was glad to see him!

Nothing more was said about our business. I left him there drunk on the stool. He said he would see me at breakfast.

I returned to my room across the street and went to bed and lay with my head under the rubber pillow to keep out highway noise. I couldn't sleep. After a time I could hear knocking and bumping and voices outside. Someone seemed to be going from door to door. Maybe trick or treat, or the Lions Club selling brooms. Or the dumbest person in the motel looking for his room. My turn came and I went to the door. It was the old man in the big shoes. He was also wearing a white cotton jacket or smock. With his purple face up close to mine, I saw his bad eye and I had the momentary impression that I was looking at Mr Proctor. But how could that be? Mr Proctor was snug in his brown shed in Little Rock, eating canned peanuts and watching some hard-hitting documentary on television. The man gave me a card. Scriptural quotations, I thought, or the deaf-and-dumb signs.

'What is this? What are you doing?'

'I'm just fooling around,' he said.

It was my guess that he had been a veteran handyman here on motel row, known all up and down the street as Dad or Pete. Then one day he was falsely accused of something, stealing sheets maybe, and fired summarily with no pension. He was now getting back at people. This was his way of getting back at the motel bosses. But when I asked about this, he said, 'No, I'm just fooling around. It's something to do. My wife is an old shopping-cart lady. That's Mrs Meigs I'm speaking of. She picks up bottles all day and I do this all night.'

'You weren't wearing that jacket thing before.'

'This is my traffic coat. Mrs Meigs made it for me so the cars and trucks could see me at night and not run over me. It's just got this one button in the middle and these two pockets here at the bottom. How do you like it?'

'I like it all right. It looks like a pharmacist's coat.'

'It don't have near enough pockets to suit me but you can't have everything.'

'What else do you do? What else are you going to do tonight?'

'First let me tell you what I'm not going to do. I'm not going to stand here any longer and talk to you. If I gave this much time to everybody, I'd never get through my rounds, would I?'

He produced a harmonica, not a trombone this time, and rapped it against his palm in a professional way to dislodge any spittle or crumbs. He stuck it in his mouth and inhaled and exhaled, making those two different sounds, in and out, and then he rapped it again to clear the passages and put it away. I had nothing to say to that, to those two chords, and he bolted and was gone.

I took the card to bed and studied it. Tiny things take on significance when I'm away from home. I'm on the alert for omens. Odd things happen when you get out of town. At the top of the card there were two crossed American flags printed in color. Under that was the ever-popular 'Kwitcher-bellyachin' and at the bottom was 'Mr and Mrs Meigs/Laredo, Texas.' On the back of the card Meigs or his wife had added a penciled postscript: 'adios AMIGO and watch out for the FLORR.'

I couldn't make anything out of this and I turned off the light. I could hear a Mexican shouting angrily at Meigs down the way. I still couldn't sleep. I got up again and drank one of the beers from the ice chest. I looked at the card again. 'Kwitcherbellyachin'! I thought, Well, all right, I will. I decided to leave at once. I would get the jump on Jack. It was worth a try. I dressed quickly and loaded the suitcase and the ice chest in the trunk of the car.

Nothing at all was stirring in downtown Laredo. I didn't bother with the Mexican car insurance. I drove across the Rio Grande and on the other side of the bridge a Mexican officer flagged me into a parking compound that was enclosed by a high wire fence.

I was the only person entering Nuevo Laredo at that dead hour but it still took a long time to get my tourist card and car papers. The Mexican officer at the typewriter didn't believe that my Arkansas driver's license was really a driver's license. At that time it was just a flimsy piece of paper torn from a pad and it looked like a fishing license. I gave him the registration slip for my

Torino and he didn't bother to look outside to see if that was in fact what I was driving. The big problem was the typing. When you run up against a policeman at a typewriter, you might as well get a Coke and relax.

While I was waiting, an idea drifted into my head that made me laugh a little. The idea was to get this Mexican fellow and Nub or Dub on a television show for a type-off. You would have them on a stage glaring at each other from behind their big Underwoods and Nub would try to peck out 'Choice of 3 Veg.' on his menu while this Mexican was trying to get 'Raymond Earl Midge' down on his form. People would be howling from coast to coast at those two slowpokes. I slipped the man a dollar bill folded to the size of a stick of gum. I did the same with the porters and customs men outside.

This was the thing to do, I had been told, but it bothered me a little. You could look on a dollar as a tip and you could also look on it as a small bribe. I was afraid one of these fellows might turn out to be a zealot like Bruce Wayne, whose parents were murdered by crooks and who had dedicated his entire life to the fight against crime. An attempted bribe, followed by the discovery of a pistol concealed in a pie carton, and I would really be in the soup. But nothing happened. They palmed those dollars like carnival guys and nobody looked into anything. The customs man marked my suitcase with a piece of chalk and a porter stuck the decals on my windows and I was gone. I was free and clear in Mexico with my Colt Cobra.

Those boys were sleepy and not much interested in their work, it's true enough, but I was still pleased at the way I had brought it off. I couldn't get over how composed I had been, looking prison right in the face. Now I was surprised and light-headed, like a domestic fowl that finds itself able to fly over a low fence in a moment of terror. Vestigial Midge powers were rising in the blood. I was pleased too that I was in Mexico and not at home, but that works both ways because after sunrise I met Americans driving out of Mexico and they all appeared to be singing happy songs.

I waved at children carrying buckets of water and at old women with shawls on their heads. It was a chilly morning. *I'm a gringo of good will in a small Buick! I'll try to observe your customs!* That was what I put into my waves.

The poor people of Mexico were the ones without sunglasses. I could see that right off the bat. The others, descendants of the great Cortez, he who had burned his ships at Veracruz, were stealing small advantages in traffic. They would speed up and hog the center line when you tried to pass them. They hated to be passed. I say Cortez 'burned' his ships because everyone else does, but I know perfectly well that he only had them dismantled there on the beach – not that it takes away from his courage.

A few miles from the border there was a

checkpoint and an officer there examined my papers. Nothing matched! I was driving a completely different car from the one described on the form. He couldn't deal with such a big lie so early in the morning and he gave the papers back to me and waved me on.

The desert road was straight and the guidebook said it was boring but I didn't find it so. I was interested in everything, the gray-green bushes, the cactus, a low brown hill, a spider crossing the road. Later in the morning a dark cloud came up that had a green rim and then rain fell in such torrents that cars and buses pulled over to wait it out. A desert rainstorm! You couldn't see three feet! I turned on the headlights and slowed down but I kept going until the brake linings got wet and wouldn't hold.

I don't like to piddle around when I'm on the road and this stop made me impatient. If you stop for ten minutes, you lose more than ten minutes' driving time. I don't know why, but I do know why slow ships can cross the Atlantic Ocean in just a few days. Because they never stop! My ankles and my new cordovan shoes were soaked from water sloshing up through the hole in the floor. I sat out the storm there on the shoulder of the road reading *The Life and Glorious Times of Zach Taylor*, by Binder. It was not the kind of title I liked but it was a pretty good book.

After the sun came out, I drove slow and rode the brakes for a while until they were dry. I was still on the straight part of the highway north of Monterrey when a big yellow car came racing up behind me and stayed right on my bumper. More Mexican stuff, I thought, and then I saw that it was Jack Wilkie in his Chrysler Imperial. I could see him in my mirror, laughing and tapping a finger on the steering wheel, in time, I supposed, to some radio music. I could see his big silver ring and some frosty flecks of doughnut sugar around his mouth. That was how close he was.

I tapped the brake pedal just enough to flash the brake light but I kept the accelerator depressed. Jack thought I was going to stop suddenly and he braked and skidded. His right-hand wheels dropped off the ledge of the pavement onto the dirt shoulder and dust was boiling up behind him. Then he recovered and got on my bumper again, still laughing. I didn't like that laughing. The brake-light trick was the only one I knew so I just started going faster and faster. Jack stayed right with me, inches away. He was playing with me. He could have passed me easily enough but he was going to run the Buick into the ground or make me give up, one or the other. I drove the little car as fast as it would go, which I guessed to be around ninety or so. That was nothing at all for the Imperial but I had a six-cylinder engine and a little air-cooled, two-speed transmission that was squealing like a pig.

We went roaring along like this for four or five miles, bumper to bumper, two hell drivers, and I was beginning to lose my stomach for it. I didn't even know what the point of it was. The sheet metal was vibrating and resonating and it appeared fuzzy to the eye. Particles of rust and dirt were dancing on the floor. Candy wrappers were flying everywhere.

I've had enough of this, I said to myself, and I was just about ready to quit when the exhaust system or the drive shaft dropped to the highway beneath the Chrysler and began to kick up sparks. Jack was done for the day. I shot over a rise and left him with a couple of honks. *Harvest yellow Imperial. Like new. Loaded. One owner. See to appreciate. Extra sharp. Good rubber. A real nice car. Needs some work. Call Cherokee Bail Bonds and ask for Jack. Work odd hours. Keep calling.*

CHAPTER 3

I lost some more time in and about the adobe city of Saltillo looking for the Buena Vista battlefield. I couldn't find it. Binder's maps were useless and the Mexicans pretended they had never heard of Zachary Taylor and Archibald Yell. At the height of the battle, when it might have gone either way, the cool Taylor turned to his artillery officer and said, 'A little more grape, Captain Bragg.' Remarks like that were embedded in my head and took up precious space that should have been occupied with other things but wasn't.

I gave up the search and pressed on south atop a desolate plateau. It was cool up there and the landscape was not like the friendly earth I knew. This was the cool dry place that we hear so much about, the place where we are supposed to store things. The car ran well and I glowed in the joy of solitary flight. It was almost a blessed state. Was I now a ramblin' man, like in the country songs? *Sorry, lady, but I got to be ramblin' on!* Or was this just a trip? Whenever I saw a person or a domestic animal, I would shout some greeting, or perhaps a question – 'How do you like living here in

Mexico?' – just the first thing that came into my head. I stopped for the night at a camper park in Matehuala. A young Canadian couple in a van shared their supper with me.

I slept in the car again, although I didn't much like it, being exposed that way to people walking by and peering in the windows, watching me sleep. It was like lying supine on the beach with your eyes closed and fearing that some terrible person in heavy shoes will come along and be seized by an impulse to stomp on your vulnerable belly. I rose early and shaved with cold water in the wash-house. The Canadians were up too, and they gave me a slice of pound cake and a cup of coffee. I was in San Miguel de Allende by noon.

The Hotel Mogador was only a block or so from the main square, or *jardín,* as they called it, which is to say 'garden.' There wasn't one guest in the place. Dupree and Norma had been gone for a little over three weeks. I was not greatly surprised at this, and not much concerned. From this point, I thought, tracing two foreigners and a chow dog in a blue Ford Torino could be no very hard task. I had not realized there were so many other Americans in Mexico.

The owner of the hotel was an accommodating man and he showed me their room, the blocky wooden bed, the short bathtub faced with little blue tiles. I had no particular feeling about the room but I certainly didn't want to stay in it, as the man suggested. I questioned him closely. Did they say where they were going? No. Had they perhaps moved to another hotel here? Possibly, but he had not seen them around town. Was there a trailer park in San Miguel? Yes, behind the Siesta Motel on the edge of town.

It had been in my mind all along that I would find them in a trailer park. I suppose I thought it would be a suitable place for their meretricious relationship. I had a plan for that trailer. I would jerk open the flimsy door with such force that the stop-chain would snap. Dupree would be sitting down eating a bowl of cereal, holding a big spoon in his monkey hand. I would throw an armlock on his neck from behind. While he sputtered and milk drops flew from his mouth, I would remove my car keys and my credit cards from his pockets. Norma would say, 'Let him have some air!' and I would shove him away and leave them there in their sty without a word.

I drove out to the place on the edge of town but it wasn't a mobile-home community of the kind I had visualized. It was literally a trailer park, a dusty field where Mom and Dad could park their Airstream for a day or two and let their big Olds 98 cool off. The place was all but deserted. At one end of the field there was a square lump of a motor home and at the other end was an old school bus that had been painted white and rigged as a camper. The bus had been given a name, 'The Dog of the South,' which was painted in black on one side, but not by a sign painter with a straight-edge and a steady hand. The big childish letters sprawled at different angles and dribbled at the bottom. The white paint had also been applied in a slapdash manner, and it had drawn up in places, presenting a crinkled finish like that seen on old adding machines and cash registers. This thing was a hippie wagon.

I went to the Mogador and had lunch in the courtyard with the owner. I had to take two meals there with my room. There were flowers and cats all around us. I could see the pale blue sky above. We had onion soup and then some veal cutlets and rice. The hotel man fed table scraps to the cats and so I did the same. What a life!

He said he had been a bit mixed up before and had shown me the wrong room. The Norma-Dupree room was actually one floor above the first room he had shown me, and was in fact the very room he had given me. Did I wish to be moved? I said no, it made no difference. Then there was a disturbance in the kitchen and he went to investigate. When he came back, he said, 'It was nothing, the mop caught fire. All my employees are fools.'

This Mexican lunch was a long affair and before it was over we were joined by a tall bird wearing metallic-silver coveralls. He was a Canadian artist who made paper rabbits. He showed me one and it was a pretty well done bunny except for the big eyelashes. The price was ten dollars. I remarked that there seemed to be quite a few Canadians in Mexico.

He bristled. 'Why shouldn't there be?'

'Out of proportion to your numbers, I mean. It was just a neutral observation.'

'We're quite free to travel, you know. We can even go to Cuba if we wish.'

'I'm not making myself clear.'

'Do please make yourself clear.'

'Well, there are two hundred million Americans and twenty million Canadians, and my country is closer to Mexico than yours, but I get the impression that there are just about as many Canadians here as Americans. At this table, for instance.'

'You're not the only Americans. You people just stole that name.'

'Look here, why don't you kiss my ass?'

'So bright of you. So typical.'

It was my guess that this queer was having big trouble selling his overpriced rabbits. That was the only way I could account for his manner. The hotel man became jolly and tried to patch things up. But this too annoyed the artist and he got up and flounced out, stopping for a moment under the archway as he thought of something pretty good to call me, which was 'rat face.'

He thought it was pretty good but it was old stuff to me, being compared to a rat. In fact, I look more like a predatory bird than a rat but any person with small sharp features that are bunched in the center of his face can expect to be called a rat about three times a year.

We finished our meal in peace and then I went

51

downtown to trade bonds for pesos. The bank was closed for lunch until 4 p.m. Some lunch! I wandered about town on foot looking for my Torino.

There was a bandstand in the central square, and some wrought-iron benches and some noisy flocking birds with long tail feathers. I took them to be members of the grackle family. There were elegant trees too, of the kind that architects like to sketch in front of their buildings. A few gringos were scattered around on the benches, dozing and reading newspapers and working crossword puzzles. I approached them one by one and made inquiries. I got nowhere until I mentioned the dog. They remembered the dog. Still, they could give nothing more than bare sighting reports. I could get no leads and no firm dates.

Hippies interfered with my work by stopping me and asking me the time. Why did they care? And if so, why didn't they have watches? The watch factories were humming day and night in Tokyo and Geneva and Little Rock so that everyone might have a cheap watch, but not one of these hippies had a watch. Maybe the winding put them off. Or maybe it was all mockery of me and my coat and tie. The same hippies seemed to be stopping me again and again, though I couldn't be sure.

A retired army sergeant told me that he had chatted for a bit with Dupree. He said they had discussed the curious drinking laws of the different states, and the curious alcoholic beverages of the world, such as ouzo and pulque, and he made me glad I wasn't there. In all his travels over the world, he said, he had found only one thing he couldn't drink and that was some first-run brandy in Parral, Chihuahua.

'Where did you talk to him?'

'That Southern boy?'

'Yes.'

'Right here. I don't sit in the same place every day. It's not like I have my own bench but I *was* here that day. The boy sat over there and bought a Popsicle for his dog.'

I wondered if the man might be confused. The Popsicle business sounded all right but I couldn't see Dupree sitting here being civil and swapping yarns with Sarge.

'Did he say where he was going from here?'

'I don't believe he did. He didn't have a whole lot to say.'

'And the girl wasn't with him?'

'I didn't see any girl, just the dog. A big shaggy chow. The boy said he was going to trim his coat. He was worried about the tropical heat and humidity and he said he was going to give him a close trim with some scissors. He wanted to know where he could buy some flea powder and some heavy scissors.'

'When was this?'

'It's been a while. I don't know. They come and go. Did he steal your dog?'

'No. Did you see him after that?'

'I saw him once in a car with some other people.'

'Was it a Ford Torino?'

'No, it was a small foreign car. All beat up. It was some odd little car like a Simca. They were just cruising around the *jardín* here. I didn't pay much attention.'

Other people? Foreign car? Dupree was not one to take up with strangers. What was this all about? But Sarge could tell me nothing more, except that the people were 'scruffy' and appeared to be Americans. He pointed out the drugstore on the corner where he had sent Dupree for the flea powder. Then he took a ball-point pen and some glasses from his shirt pocket and I jumped up from the bench in alarm, fearing he was about to diagram something for me, but he was only rearranging his pocket stuff.

I thanked him and went to the drugstore and learned that an American wearing glasses had indeed bought some flea powder in the place. The woman pharmacist could tell me nothing else. I was tired. All this chasing around to prove something that I already knew, that Dupree had been in San Miguel. I couldn't get beyond that point. What I needed was a new investigative approach, a new plan, and I couldn't think of one. I looked over the aspirin display.

'*¿Dolor?*' said the woman, and I said *Sí*, and pointed to my head. Aspirins were too weak, she said, and she sold me some orange pills wrapped

54

in a piece of brown paper. I took the pills to a café and crushed one on the table and tasted a bit of it. For all I knew, they were dangerous Mexican drugs, but I took a couple of them anyway. They were bitter.

On the way to the bank for a second try I got sidetracked into a small museum. The man who ran the place was standing on the sidewalk and he coaxed me inside. The admission fee was only two pesos. He had some good stuff to show. There were rough chunks of silver ore and clay figurines and two rotting mummies and colonial artifacts and delicate bird skulls and utensils of hammered copper. The man let me handle the silver. I wrote my name in the guest book and I saw that Norma and Dupree had been there. In the space for remarks Dupree had written, 'A big gyp. Most boring exhibition in North America.' Norma had written, 'I like the opals best. They are very striking.' She had signed herself Norma Midge. She was still using my name. I stood there and looked at her signature, at the little teacup handles on her capital N and capital M.

The book was on a high table like a lectern and behind it, tacked to the wall, was a map of Mexico. I drew closer to admire the map. It dated from around 1880 and it was a fine piece of English cartography. Your newer map is not always your better map! The relief was shown by hachuring, with every tiny line perfectly spaced. The engraver was a master and the printer had done wonders with only two shades of ink, black and brown. It was hand-lettered. I located myself at about 21 degrees north and 101 degrees west. This was as far south as I had ever been, about two degrees below the Tropic of Cancer.

Then after a few minutes it came to me. I knew where Dupree had gone and I should have known all along. He had gone to his father's farm in Central America. San Miguel was technically within the tropics but at an elevation of over six thousand feet the heat here would not be such as to cause dog suffering. And there was no humidity to speak of. They were on that farm in British Honduras. That monkey had taken my wife to British Honduras and he had planned it all in the Wormington Motel!

I was excited, my *dolor* suddenly gone, and I wanted to share the good news with someone. *¡Misión cumplida!* That is, it was not exactly accomplished, but the rest would be easy. I looked about for a place to gloat and soon hit on a bar called the Cucaracha.

It was a dark square room with a high ceiling. Some padded wooden benches were arranged in a maze-like pattern. They faced this way and that way and they were so close together that it was hard to move about. I drank bourbon until I figured out what it cost and then I switched to gin and tonic, which was much cheaper.

The customers were mostly gringos and they were a curious mix of retired veterans and hippies and alimony dodgers and artists. They were friendly people and I liked the place immediately. *We've all run off to Mexico* – that was the thing that hung in the air, and it made for a kind of sad bonhomie. I was suprised to find myself speaking so freely of my private affairs. The Cucaracha people offered tips on the drive south to British Honduras. I basked in their attention as a figure of international drama. My headache returned and I took some more pills.

One of the hippies turned out to be from Little Rock. I never thought I would be glad to see a hippie but I was glad to see this fellow. He had a hippie sweetheart with him who was wearing white nurse stockings. She was a pretty little thing but I didn't realize it for a while because her electrified hair was so ugly. It was dark in there too. I asked the hippie what he did and he said he drank a liter of Madero brandy every day and took six Benzedrine tablets. He asked me what I did and I had to say I did nothing much at all. Then we talked about Little Rock, or at least I did. I thought we might have some mutual friends, or if not, we could always talk about the different streets and their names. The hippie wasn't interested in this. He said, 'Little Rock is a pain in the ass,' and his sweetheart said, 'North Little Rock too.'

But it didn't matter, I was having a good time. Everything was funny. An American woman wearing a white tennis hat stuck her head in the doorway and then withdrew it in one second when she saw what kind of place it was. The Cucaracha gang got a good laugh out of this, each one accusing the other of being the frightful person who had scared her away. I talked to a crippled man, a gringo with gray hair, who was being shunned by the other drinkers. He said he had shot down two Nip planes when he was in the Flying Tigers. He now owned a Chiclets factory in Guadalajara. People hated him, he said, because his principles didn't permit him to lend money, or to buy drinks for anyone but himself. He described for me the first six plays of an important Stanford football game of 1935, or I should say the first six plays from scrimmage, since he didn't count the kickoff as a play.

There were two Australian girls across the room and the Flying Tiger said they wanted to see me. He told me they had been trying to get my attention for quite a while. I went over at once and sat with them. These girls were slender cuties who were hitchhiking around the world with their shoulder bags. But it was all a hoax, the invitation, and they didn't want to see me at all. I sat down by another girl, this one a teacher from Chicago, and then I had to get up again because the seat was saved, or so she said. I watched that empty seat for a long time and it wasn't really saved for anyone. A hippie wearing striped bib overalls came in from the bar and sat beside her. She advised him that the seat was saved but that bird didn't get up. 'You can't save seats,' he said. What a

58

statement! You can't save seats! I would never have thought of that in a thousand years!

I forgot about the bank business and I sat there and drank gin and tonic until the quinine in the tonic water made my ears hum. Someone that night told me about having seen Dupree with a fellow wearing a neck brace but I was too drunk to pursue it and the thing went completely out of my mind. I began to babble. I told everybody about my father's Midgestone business, how the stone veneer was cut with special band saws, and how it was shaped and sanded. I told them about my great-grandfather building the first greenhouse in Arkansas and how he had developed a hard little peach called the Lydia that was bird-resistant and well suited for shipping, although tasteless. I couldn't stop talking. I was a raving bore and I knew it too, but I couldn't stop. It was important to me that they know these things and who would tell them if I didn't?

They fled my presence, the hippies and vets and cuties alike, and left me sitting alone in the corner. I kept drinking, I refused to leave. They had all turned on me but I wasn't going to let them run me off. There was a lot of old stuff on the jukebox and I who had never played a jukebox in my life had the waiter take my change after each drink and play 'It's Magic' by Doris Day. She was singing that song, a new one to me, when I first entered the place. I had heard of Doris Day but no one had ever told me what a good singer she was.

Sometime around midnight the hippie couple from Little Rock got into a squabble. I couldn't hear what he was saying because his voice was low but I heard her say, 'My *daddy* don't even talk to me like that and you *damn* sure ain't!' The little girl was blazing. He put his hand out to touch her or to make some new point and she pushed it away and got up and left, stepping smartly in her white stockings and brushing past an old man who had appeared in the doorway.

He was a fat man, older than the Flying Tiger, and he was looking from left to right like an animal questing for food. He wore a white hat and a white shirt and white trousers and a black bow tie. This old-timer, I said to myself, looks very much like a boxing referee, except for the big floppy hat and the army flashlight clipped to his belt.

He looked around and said, 'Where's the boy who's going to British Honduras?'

I said nothing.

He raised his voice. 'I'm looking for the boy who's going to British Honduras! Is he here?'

If I had kept my mouth shut for five more seconds, he would have gone his way and I would have gone mine. I said, 'Here I am! In the corner! I'm not supposed to talk!' I hadn't spoken for a long time and my voice croaked and had no authority in it.

'Where?'

'Over here!'

'I can't see you!'

'In the corner!'

He bumped his way across the room and took off his hat and joined me on the bench. His white pants were too long and even when he was seated there was excess cloth piled up on top of his shoes. 'I couldn't see you over all those heads,' he said.

I was still fuming, a resentful drunk, and I took my anger out on him. 'You couldn't see any normal human being over here from where you were standing. I'm not a giraffe. For your information, sir, a lot of navy pilots are five seven. Why don't you try calling Audie Murphy a runt? You do and you'll wake up in St Vincent's Infirmary.'

He paid no attention to this rant. 'My bus broke down and I need to get back on the road,' he said. 'When are you leaving?'

'They won't let me talk in here.'

'Who won't?'

'All these juiceheads. You'd think they owned the place. I have just as much right to be here as they do and if they don't want to hear about the green-house they can all kiss my ass! These juiceheads never grew anything in their lives!'

Neither had I for that matter but it wasn't the same thing. The old man introduced himself as Dr Reo Symes. He looked to be in bad health. His belt was about eight inches too long, with the end curling out limp from the buckle. There were dark bags under his eyes and he had long meaty ears. One eye was badly inflamed and this was the

61

thing that made me feel I was talking to Mr Proctor or Mr Meigs.

He said he was from Louisiana and had been making his way to British Honduras when his school-bus camper broke down. He was the owner of The Dog of the South. He asked if he might ride along with me and share the expenses. Overdoing everything like the disgusting drunk that I was, I told him that he would be more than welcome and that there would be absolutely no charge. His company would be payment enough. He questioned me about my driving skills and I assured him that I was a good driver. He said he was afraid to take a Mexican bus because the drivers here had a reputation for trying to beat out locomotives at grade crossings. He offered me some money in advance and I waved it aside. I told him I would pick him up in the morning.

I had planned on searching the sky that night for the Southern Cross and the Coalsack but when I left the bar it was overcast and drizzling rain. I bought two hot dogs from a man pushing a cart around the square. One block away the town was totally dark. I staggered down the middle of the cobbled street and tried to make it appear that I was sauntering. In the darkened doorways there were people smoking cigarettes and thinking their Mexican thoughts.

A hotel cat, a white one, followed me up the stairs to my room and I gave him one of the hot dogs. I didn't let him in the room. That would be a misplaced kindness. He would take up with me and then I would have to leave. Just inside the door there was a full-length mirror and the image it gave back was wavy and yellowish. I knew that Norma must have stood before it and adjusted her clothes. What would she be wearing? I liked her best in her winter clothes and I couldn't remember much about her summer things. What a knockout she was in her white coat and her red knit cap! With Jack Frost nipping her cheeks and her wavy nose!

CHAPTER 4

Rain was still falling when I got up in the morning. After I had paid the hotel bill, I had seven or eight dollars and around sixty pesos left. There was a terrible metallic clatter when I tried to start the car. A bad water pump or a bad universal joint will give you notice before it goes but this was some sudden and major failure, or so I thought. A broken connecting rod or a broken timing chain. Strength of materials! Well, I said to myself, the little Buick is done.

I got out and opened the hood. There was the white cat, decapitated by the fan blades. I couldn't believe it. He had crawled up into the engine compartment of this car, not another car, and there was my bloody handiwork. I couldn't handle anything. I couldn't even manage the minor decencies of life. I could hardly get my breath and I walked around and around the car.

A boy with some schoolbooks stopped to watch me and I gave him ten pesos to remove the carcass. I tried to get a grip on myself. Idleness and solitude led to these dramatics: an ordinary turd indulging himself as the chief of sinners. I drove down to the square and waited for the bank to open. My hands were shaking. I had read somewhere that white cats were very often deaf, like Dalmatian dogs. I had dry mouth and tunnel vision.

The bank manager said he could not cash the bonds but he could accept them as a deposit if I wished to open a checking account. They should clear in about a month. A month! Why had I not cashed them all in the States? What a piddler! Norma would have enjoyed this and I couldn't have blamed her for it. I was always impatient with this kind of childish improvidence in other people.

The Siesta trailer park was now a field of mud. Dr Symes was having coffee in his white Ford bus. The passenger seats had been removed from the thing and replaced by a clutter of household furnishings that had not been anchored or scaled down or customized in any way. There was a dirty mattress on the floor and a jumble of boxes and chairs and tables. It was an old man's mess on top of a hippie mess. I accepted a roll and passed up the coffee. I loved those Mexican rolls but I didn't like the looks of the doctor's cup and I've never cared for instant coffee because it has no smell.

I was frank with him. I explained the bonds problem and I showed him exactly how much money I had. It was a bad moment. I was already embarrassed by my behavior in the bar and now, after all the expansive talk of a free ride, I was making myself look like a cheap liar. I made him a proposition. I would drive him to British Honduras if he would pay for the gasoline and other expenses. When we reached Belize, I would wire home for money and repay him half of his outlay. In the meantime I would give him five of my savings bonds to hold.

He was suspicious and I could understand that, although the deal seemed fair enough to me. The bonds were not negotiable, he said, and they were of no use to him. I pointed out that they did have a certain hostage value. It would be in my interest to redeem them. He looked at me and he looked outside at the car. It sat funny because the tires were of different sizes. He said, 'All right then, let's go,' and he flung his coffee through a window.

There was a staple-and-hasp affair on the bus door and he locked it with a brass padlock. He brought along his grip and a gallon of drinking water in a plastic jug and a sack of marshmallows. We left The Dog of the South parked there in the mud.

He was wary. He had little to say. He tried the radio, longer than I would have, and then gave it up. He said, 'If a man wanted to get the news in this car, he would be out of luck, wouldn't he?'

'This is not my car. Everything works in my car.'

The skies were clearing and the morning sun was blinding. He reached up for the right-hand sun visor that had never been there. His hand fell away and he grunted.

'It runs okay,' I said.

'What's all that vibration?'

'The motor mounts are shot.'

'The what?'

'The motor mounts. They look like black jelly down there. A V-6 shakes a lot anyway. It'll be all right after we get up some speed.'

'Do you think it'll make it?'

'Yes, I do. It's a good car.' I had said that just to be saying something but I thought it over and decided it was true.

'I hope a wheel doesn't fly off this thing,' he said.

'I do too.'

He worried a lot about that, a wheel flying off, and I gathered it had happened to him once and made an impression on him.

When we reached Celaya, which was only thirty miles or so from San Miguel, I left the highway and went downtown. I drove slowly up one street and down another. I thought I might see some shell-pocked buildings or at least a statue or a plaque of some kind.

Dr Symes said, 'What are you doing now?'

'This is Celaya.'

'What about it?'

'There was a big battle here in 1915.'

'I never heard of this place.'

'I figure it was the third bloodiest battle ever fought in this hemisphere.'

'So what?'

'Some sources say the fourth bloodiest. Obregón

67

lost his arm here. Pancho Villa's army was routed. Do you know what he said?'

'No.'

'He said, "I would rather have been beaten by a Chinaman than by that *perfumado*, Obregón."'

'Who were they fighting?'

'It was a civil war. They were fighting each other.'

'I never heard of it.'

'Well, it wasn't that long ago, and it was all right here, in this very town. I'll bet there are plenty of old-timers walking around here who were in that fight. If my Spanish was better, I would try to find one and talk to him.'

'Let's don't do that.'

The doctor made a show of counting his money. He said he had only about fifty dollars. His scuffed leather wallet was about a foot long and it was chained to his clothing in some way. It was like the big wallets carried by route men, by milkmen and potato-chip men.

There were three grades of gasoline in Mexico at that time and I had been buying the top grade, the Pemex 100. Now, to save money, the doctor's money, I began using the middle grade, which was supposed to be around 90 octane. I don't believe it was that high, because on the long mountain pulls the pistons rattled like empty bottles in a sack.

This noise bothered the doctor. He said, 'The old Model A had a spark advance you could manipulate. I don't know why they got rid of it.

Well, that's your Detroit smarties. The hand choke too. That's gone. *Been* gone.'

'What's wrong with your bus?'

'I think it's a burnt wheel bearing. My right front wheel. The wheel was shaking and there was a grinding racket coming out of that hub. I had a man look at it in a garage in Ciudad Victoria.'

'What did he say?'

'I don't know what he said. He greased it. I went on and it did all right for a while. Then that wheel commenced shaking again and I was afraid that booger might fly off on me.'

But the doctor didn't talk much, except to make complaints, and I thought it was going to be a long silent trip. I made some travel observations. I said that Mexican parents seemed to be kinder and more affectionate to their children than American parents. He said nothing. I remarked on the new buildings, on the flamboyant Mexican architecture. He said, 'There's not much going on inside those buildings.'

My abrupt steering movements bothered him too. He sat rigid in the seat and watched and listened. He complained about the dog smell on the seat and the dust that came up from the floor. He drank from a bottle of B and B liqueur. He said he had the chronic bronchitis of a singer and had used this liqueur for his throat ever since the government had barred the use of codeine in cough syrup.

'Pure baloney,' he said. 'I've seen every kind of addict there is and I've never known one person who was addicted to codeine. I've taken fifty gallons of the stuff myself. Wine will drive you crazy faster than anything I know and you can buy all the wine you want. Well, that's your Washington smarties. They know everything.'

'Are you a medical doctor?'

'I'm not in active practice at this time.'

'I once looked into medicine myself. I sent off for some university catalogues.'

'I'm retired from active practice.'

'These doctors make plenty of money.'

'That's generally true, yes. I would be well fixed today if I had paid more attention to my screening methods. Screening is your big worry. I was always more concerned with healing. That was a serious mistake on my part. My entire life was ruined by a man named Brimlett. I didn't screen him.'

After a time he seemed to realize that I wasn't going to rob him and I wasn't going to wreck the car. He relaxed and took off his big hat. There was a pointed crest of hair at the back of his head like that of a jaybird. He couldn't remember my name and he kept calling me 'Speed.'

I learned that he had been dwelling in the shadows for several years. He had sold hi-lo shag carpet remnants and velvet paintings from the back of a truck in California. He had sold wide shoes by mail, shoes that must have been almost round, at widths up to EEEEE. He had sold gladiola bulbs and vitamins for men and fat-melting pills and all-purpose hooks and hail-damaged pears.

He had picked up small fees counseling veterans on how to fake chest pains so as to gain immediate admission to V.A. hospitals and a free week in bed. He had sold ranchettes in Colorado and unregistered securities in Arkansas.

He said he had had very little trouble with the law in recent years, although he had been arrested twice in California: once for disturbing divine service, and again for impersonating a naval officer. They were trifling matters. He was collared in San Diego on the last charge; the uniform was a poor fit and he was too old for the modest rank he had assumed. He said he was only trying to establish a short line of credit at a bank. A friend from Tijuana named Rod Garza bailed him out and the thing never even came to trial. The church arrest had grown out of a squabble with some choir members who had pinched him and bitten him and goosed him. They were trying to force him out of the choir, he said, because they claimed he sang at an odd tempo and threw them off the beat. One Sunday he turned on them and whipped at them with a short piece of grass rope. Some of the women cried.

I asked him if he had ever visited Yosemite National Park when he was in California.

'No, I never did.'

'What about Muir Woods?'

'What?'

'Muir Woods. Near San Francisco.'

'I never heard of it.'

'I'd like to see some of that country. I've been to New Mexico and Arizona but I never made it all the way to California. I'd like to go out there sometime.'

'You'll love it if you like to see big buck niggers strutting around town kissing white women on the mouth and fondling their titties in public. They're running wild out there, Speed. They're water-skiing out there now. If I was a nigger, that's where I would go. It was a nigger policeman that arrested me outside that little church in Riverside. Can you beat it? He put the cuffs on me too, like I was Billy Cook. You don't expect a California nigger to defer to a white man but I thought he might have shown some consideration for my age.'

'Did you go to jail?'

'Just overnight, till Monday morning. The municipal judge fined me thirty-five dollars and told me to find myself another church to sing in.'

I asked him if he was going to British Honduras on vacation and he said, 'Vacation! Do you think I'm the kind of man who takes vacations?'

'What are you going down there for?'

'My mother's there. I need to see her.'

His mother! I couldn't believe it. 'Is she sick?' I said.

'I don't know. I need to see her on some business.'

'How old is she?'

'She's so old she's walking sideways. I hate to see it too. That's a bad sign. When these old folks start creeping around and shuffling their feet, church is about out.'

He wanted to see her about some land she owned in Louisiana near the town of Ferriday. It was an island in the Mississippi River called Jean's Island.

'It's not doing her any good,' he said. 'She's just turned it over to the birds and snakes. She pays taxes on it every year and there's not one penny of income. There's no gain at all except for the appreciated value. She won't give it to me and she won't let me use it. She's my mother and I think the world of her but she's hard to do business with.'

'It's not cultivated land?'

'No, it's just rough timber. The potential is enormous. The black-walnut trees alone are worth fifty thousand dollars for furniture veneer. The stumps could then be cut up and made into pistol grips. How does fifty thousand dollars sound to you?'

'It sounds pretty good.'

'Some of those trees are whoppers. Double trunks.'

'Maybe you could get a timber lease.'

'I'd take a lease if I could get it. What I want is a deed. I don't mean a quitclaim either, I mean a warranty deed with a seal on it. So you understand what I'm telling you?'

'Yes.'

'Did you say *timber* lease?'

'Yes.'

'That's what I thought you said. Why would you want to cut the timber?'

'That was your idea. The walnut trees.'

'I was only trying to suggest to you the value of the place. I'm not going to cut those trees. Are you crazy? Cut the trees and the whole thing would wash away and then where would you be? Do you want my opinion? I say leave the trees and make a private hunting preserve out of the place. I'm not talking about squirrels and ducks either. I mean stock the place with some real brutes. Wart hogs and Cape buffalo. I don't say it would be cheap but these hunters have plenty of money and they don't mind spending it.'

'That's not a bad idea.'

'I've got a hundred ideas better than that but Mama won't answer my letters. What about a Christian boys' ranch? It's an ideal setting. You'd think that would appeal to her, wouldn't you? Well, you'd be wrong. How about a theme park? Jefferson Davis Land. It's not far from the old Davis plantation. Listen to this. I would dress up like Davis in a frock coat and greet the tourists as they stepped off the ferry. I would glower at them like old Davis with his cloudy eye and the children would cry and clutch their mothers' hands and then – here's the payoff – they would see the twinkle in my clear eye. I'd have Lee too, and Jackson and Albert Sidney Johnston, walking around the midway. Hire some people with beards, you know, to do that. I wouldn't have Braxton Bragg or Joseph E. Johnston. Every afternoon at three Lee would take off his gray coat and wrestle

74

an alligator in a mud hole. Prize drawings. A lot of T-shirts and maybe a few black-and-white portables. If you don't like that, how about a stock-car track? Year-round racing with hardly any rules. Deadly curves right on the water. The Symes 500 on Christmas Day. Get a promotional tie-in with the Sugar Bowl. How about an industrial park? How about a high-rise condominium with a roof garden? How about a baseball clinic? How about a monkey island? I don't say it would be cheap. Nobody's going to pay to see one or two monkeys these days. People want to see a lot of monkeys. I've got plenty of ideas but first I have to get my hands on the island. Can you see what I'm driving at? It's the hottest piece of real estate in Louisiana, bar none.'

'Are you a student of the Civil War, Dr Symes?'

'No, but my father was.'

'What was that about Bragg? You said you wouldn't have Bragg walking around in your park.'

'My father had no time for Bragg or Joseph E. Johnston. He always said Bragg lost the war. What do you know about these revolving restaurants, Speed?'

'I don't know anything about them but I can tell you that Braxton Bragg didn't lose the war by himself.'

'I'm talking about these restaurants up on top of buildings that turn around and around while the people are in there eating.'

'I know what you're talking about but I've never

been in one. Look here, you can't just go around saying Braxton Bragg lost the war.'

'My father said he lost it at Chickamauga.'

'I know what Bragg did at Chickamauga, or rather what he didn't do. I can't accept Joseph E. Johnston's excuses either for not going to help Pemberton but I don't go around saying he lost the war.'

'Well, my father believed it. Pollard was his man. A fellow named Pollard, he said, wrote the only fair account of the thing.'

'I've read Pollard. He calls Lincoln the Illinois ape.'

'Pollard was his man. I don't read that old-timey stuff myself. That's water over the dam. I've never wasted my time with that trash. What's your personal opinion of these revolving restaurants?'

'I think they're all right.'

'Leon Vurro's wife said I should have a fifty-story tower right in the middle of the park with a revolving restaurant on top. What do you think?'

'I think it would be all right.'

'That's your opinion. I happen to have my own. Let's cost it out. Let's look a little closer. All right, your sap tourists and honeymooners are up there eating and they say, 'Let's see, are we looking into Louisiana now or Mississippi, which?' I say what the hell difference would it make? One side of the river looks just like the other. You think it would be cheap? All that machinery? Gears and chains breaking every day? You'd have to hire two or three union bastards full time just to keep it working. What about your light bill? A thousand dollars a month? Two thousand? You'd have to charge eighteen dollars for a steak to come out on a deal like that. And just so some sap and his family can see three hundred and sixty degrees of the same damned cotton fields. I don't like it myself. Do you have the faintest notion of what it would cost to erect a fifty-story tower? No, you don't, and neither does Bella Vurro. And you probably don't care. I'm the poor son of a bitch who will have to shoulder the debt.'

'Look here. Dr Symes, I know that Bragg should have been relieved earlier. Everybody knows that today. Joe Johnston too, but that's a long way from saying they lost the war.'

'What line of work are you in, Speed?'

'I'm back in college now. I'm trying to pick up some education hours so I can get a teaching certificate.'

'What you are then is a thirty-year-old schoolboy.'

'I'm twenty-six.'

'Well, I don't guess you're bothering anybody.'

'The Civil War used to be my field.'

'A big waste of time.'

'I didn't think so. I studied for two years at Ole Miss under Dr Buddy Casey. He's a fine man and a fine scholar.'

'You might as well loiter for two years. You might as well play Parcheesi for two years.'

'That's a foolish remark.'

'You think so?'

'It's dumb.'

'All right, listen to me. Are you a reader? Do you read a lot of books?'

'I read quite a bit.'

'And you come from a family of readers, right?'

'No, that's not right. That's completely wrong. My father doesn't own six books. He reads the paper about twice a week. He reads fishing magazines and he reads the construction bids. He works. He doesn't have time to read.'

'But you're a big reader yourself.'

'I have more than four hundred volumes of military history in my apartment. All told, I have sixty-six lineal feet of books.'

'All right, now listen to me. Throw that trash out the window. Every bit of it.'

He reached into his grip and brought out a little book with yellow paper covers. The cellophane that had once been bonded to the covers was cracked and peeling. He flourished the book. 'Throw all that dead stuff out the window and put this on your shelf. Put it by your bed.'

What a statement! Books, heavy ones, flying out the windows of the Rhino apartment! I couldn't take my eyes from the road for very long but I glanced at the cover. The title was *With Wings as Eagles* and the author was John Selmer Dix, M.A.

Dr Symes turned through the pages. 'Dix wrote this book forty years ago and it's still just as fresh as the morning dew. Well, why shouldn't it be?

The truth never dies. Now this is a first edition. That's important. This is the one you want. Remember the yellow cover. They've changed up things in these later editions. Just a word here and there but it adds up. I don't know who's behind it. They'll have Marvin watching television instead of listening to dance music on the radio. Stuff like that. This is the one you want. This is straight Dix. This is the book you want on your night table right beside your glass of water, *With Wings as Eagles* in the yellow cover. Dix was the greatest man of our time. He was truly a master of the arts, and of some of the sciences too. He was the greatest writer who ever lived.'

'They say Shakespeare was the greatest writer who ever lived.'

'Dix puts William Shakespeare in the shithouse.'

'I've never heard of him. Where is he from?'

'He was from all over. He's dead now. He's buried in Ardmore, Oklahoma. He got his mail in Fort Worth, Texas.'

'Did he live in Fort Worth?'

'He lived all over. Do you know the old Elks Club in Shreveport?'

'No.'

'Not the new one. I'm not talking about the new lodge.'

'I don't know anything about Shreveport.'

'Well, it doesn't matter. It's one of my great regrets that I never got to meet Dix. He died broke in a railroad hotel in Tulsa. The last thing he saw from his window is anyone's guess. They never found his trunk, you know. He had a big tin trunk that was all tied up with wire and ropes and belts and straps, and he took it with him everywhere. They never found it. Nobody knows what happened to it. Nobody even knows what was in the trunk.'

'Well, his clothes, don't you think?'

'No, he didn't have any clothes to speak of. No *change* of clothes. His famous slippers of course.'

'His correspondence maybe.'

'He burned all letters unread. I don't want to hear any more of your guesses. Do you think you're going to hit on the answer right off? Smarter people than you have been studying this problem for years.'

'Books then.'

'No, no, no. Dix never read anything but the daily papers. He *wrote* books, he didn't have to read them. No, he traveled light except for the trunk. He did his clearest thinking while moving. He did all his best work on a bus. Do you know that express bus that leaves Dallas every day at noon for Los Angeles? That's the one he liked. He rode back and forth on it for an entire year when he was working on *Wings*. He saw the seasons change on that bus. He knew all the drivers. He had a board that he put on his lap so he could spread his stuff out, you see, and work right there in his seat by the window.'

'I don't see how you could ride a bus for a year.'

'He was completely exhausted at the end of that

year and he never fully recovered his health. His tin trunk had a thousand dents in it by that time and the hinges and latches were little better than a joke. That's when he began tying it up with ropes and belts. His mouth was bleeding from scurvy, from mucosal lesions and suppurating ulcers, his gums gone all spongy. He was a broken man all right but by God the work got done. He wrecked his health so that we might have *Wings as Eagles*.'

The doctor went on and on. He said that all other writing, compared to Dix's work, was just 'foul grunting.' I could understand how a man might say such things about the Bible or the Koran, some holy book, but this Dix book, from what I could see of it, was nothing more than an inspirational work for salesmen. Still, I didn't want to judge it too quickly. There might be some useful tips in those pages, some Dix thoughts that would throw a new light on things. I was still on the alert for chance messages.

I asked the doctor what his mother was doing in British Honduras.

'Preaching,' he said. 'Teaching hygiene to pickaninnies.'

'She's not retired?'

'She'll never retire.'

'How does she happen to be in British Honduras?'

'She first went down there with some church folks to take clothes to hurricane victims. After my father died in 1950, she went back to help run a mission. Then she just stayed on. The church bosses tried to run her off two or three times but they couldn't get her out because she owned the building. She just started her own church. She says God told her to stay on the job down there. She's deathly afraid of hurricanes but she stays on anyway.'

'Do you think God really told her to do that?'

'Well, I don't know. That's the only thing that would keep me down there. Mama claims she likes it. She and Melba both. She lives in the church with her pal Melba. There's a pair for you.'

'Have you ever been down there?'

'Just once.'

'What's it like?'

'Hot. A bunch of niggers.'

'It seems a long way off from everything.'

'After you get there it doesn't. It's the same old stuff.'

'What does your mother do, go back and forth to Louisiana?'

'No, she doesn't go back at all.'

'And you haven't seen her but once since she's been there?'

'It's a hard trip. You see the trouble I'm having. This is my last shot.'

'You could fly down in a few hours.'

'I've never been interested in aviation.'

'I'm going down there after a stolen car.'

'Say you are.'

He kept twisting about in the seat to look at the cars approaching us from behind. He examined

82

them all as they passed us and once he said to me, 'Can you see that man's arms?'

'What man?'

'Driving that station wagon.'

'I can see his hands.'

'No, his arms. Ski has tattoos on his forearms. Flowers and stars and spiders.'

'I can't see his arms. Who is Ski?'

He wouldn't answer me and he had no curiosity at all about my business. I told him about Norma and Dupree. He said nothing, but I could sense his contempt. I was not only a schoolboy but a cuckold too. And broke to boot.

He nodded and dozed whenever I was doing the talking. His heavy crested head would droop over and topple him forward and the angle-head flashlight on his belt would poke him in the belly and wake him. Then he would sit up and do it over again. I could see a tangle of gray hair in his long left ear. I wondered at what age that business started, the hair-in-the-ear business. I was getting on myself. The doctor had taken me for thirty. I felt in my ears and found nothing, but I knew the stuff would be sprouting there soon, perhaps in a matter of hours. I was gaining weight too. In the last few months I had begun to see my own cheeks, little pink horizons.

I was hypnotized by the road. I was leaning forward and I let the speed gradually creep up and I bypassed Mexico City with hardly a thought for Winfield Scott and the heights of Chapultepec.

To pass it like that! Mexico City! On the long empty stretches I tried to imagine that I was stationary and that the brown earth was being rolled beneath me by the Buick tires. It was a shaky illusion at best and it broke down entirely when I met another car.

A front tire went flat in a suburb of Puebla and I drove on it for about half a mile. The spare was flat too, and it took the rest of the afternoon to get everything fixed. The casing I had driven on had two breaks in the sidewall. I didn't see how it could be repaired but the Mexican tire man put two boots and an inner tube in the thing and it stood up fine. He was quite a man, doing all this filthy work in the street in front of his mud house without a mechanical tire breaker or an impact wrench or any other kind of special tool.

We found a bakery and bought some rolls and left Puebla in the night. Dr Symes took a blood-pressure cuff from his grip. He put it on his arm and pumped it up and I had to drive with one hand and hold the flashlight with the other so he could take the reading. He grunted but he didn't say whether it pleased him or not. He crawled over into the back seat and cleared things out of his way and said he was going to take a nap. He threw something out the window and I realized later it must have been my Zachary Taylor book.

'You might keep your eye peeled for a tan station wagon,' he said. 'I don't know what kind it is but it's a nice car. Texas plates. Dealer plates. Ski will be driving. He's a pale man with no chin. Tattoos on his forearms. He wears a little straw hat with one of those things in the hatband. I can't think of the word.'

'Feather.'

'No, I can think of feather. This is harder to think of. A brass thing.'

'Who is this Ski?'

'Ted Brunowski. He's an old friend of mine. They call him Ski. You know how they call people Ski and Chief and Tex in the army.'

'I've never been in the service.'

'Did you have asthma?'

'No.'

'What are you taking for it?'

'I don't have asthma.'

'Have you tried the Chihuahua dogs in your bedroom at night? They say it works. I'm an orthodox physician but I'm also for whatever works. You might try it anyway.'

'I have never had asthma.'

'The slacker's friend. That's what they called it during the war. I certified many a one at a hundred and fifty bucks a throw.'

'What do you want to see this fellow for?'

'It's a tan station wagon. He's a pale man in a straw hat and he has no more chin than a bird. Look for dealer plates. Ski has never been a car dealer but he always has dealer plates. He's not a Mason either but when he shakes your hand he does something with his thumb. He knows how to give the Masonic sign of distress too. He would never show me how to do it. Do you understand what I'm telling you?'

'I understand what you've said so far. Do you want to talk to him or what?'

'Just let me know if you see him.'

'Is there some possibility of trouble?'

'There's every possibility.'

'You didn't say anything about this.'

'Get Ski out of sorts and he'll crack your bones. He'll smack you right in the snout, the foremost part of the body. He'll knock you white-eyed on the least provocation. He'll teach you a lesson you won't soon forget.'

'You should have said something about this.'

'He kicked a merchant seaman to death down on the ship channel. He was trying to get a line on the Blackie Steadman mob, just trying to do his job, you see, and the chap didn't want to help him.'

'You should have told me about all this.'

'Blackie was hiring these merchant seamen to do his killings for him. He would hire one of those boys to do the job on the night before he shipped out and by the time the body was found the killer would be in some place like Poland. But Ski got wise to their game.'

'What does he want you for?'

'He made short work of that sailor. Ski's all business. He's tough. He's stout. I'm not talking about these puffy muscles from the gymnasium either,

I'm talking about hard thick arms like bodark posts. You'd do better to leave him alone.'

All this time the doctor was squirming around in the back trying to arrange himself comfortably on the seat. He made the car rock. I was afraid he would bump the door latch and fall out of the car. He hummed and snuffled. He sang one verse of 'My Happiness' over and over again, and then, with a church quaver, 'He's the Lily of the Valley, the bright and morning star.'

I tuned him out. After a while he slept. I roared through the dark mountains, descending mostly, and I thought I would never reach the bottom. I checked the mirror over and over again and I examined every vehicle that passed us. There weren't many. The doctor had given me a tough job and now he was sleeping.

The guidebook advised against driving at night in Mexico but I figured that stuff was written for fools. I was leaning forward again and going at a headlong pace like an ant running home with something. The guidebook was right. It was a nightmare. Trucks with no taillights! Cows and donkeys and bicyclists in the middle of the road! A stalled bus on the crest of a hill! A pile of rocks coming up fast! An overturned truck and ten thousand oranges rolling down the road! I was trying to deal with all this and watch for Ski at the same time and I was furious at Dr Symes for sleeping through it. I no longer cared whether he fell out or not.

Finally I woke him, although the worst was over by that time.

'What is it?' he said.

'I'm not looking for that station wagon anymore. I've got my hands full up here.'

'What?'

'It's driving me crazy. I can't tell what color these cars are.'

'What are you talking about?'

'I'm talking about Ski!'

'I wouldn't worry about Ski. Leon Vurro is the man he's looking for. Where did you know Ski?'

'I don't know Ski.'

'Do you want me to drive for a while?'

'No, I don't.'

'Where are we?'

'I don't know exactly. Out of the mountains anyway. We're near Veracruz somewhere.'

I kept thinking I would pull over at some point and sleep until daylight but I couldn't find a place that looked just right. The Pemex stations were too noisy and busy. The doctor had me stop once on the highway so he could put some drops in his red eye. This was a slow and messy business. He flung his elbows out like a skeet shooter. I held the army flashlight for him. He said the drops were cold. While I was at it, I checked the transmission fluid and there were a lot of little blue flashes playing around the engine where the spark-plug cables were cracked and arcing.

He napped again and then he started talking to

me about Houston, which he pronounced 'Yooston.' I like to keep things straight and his movements had me confused. I had thought at first that he came to Mexico direct from Louisiana. Then it was California. Now it was Houston. Ski was from Houston and it was from that same city that the doctor had departed in haste for Mexico, or 'Old Mexico' as he called it.

'Who is this Ski anyway?'

'He's an old friend of mine. I thought I told you that.'

'Is he a crook?'

'He's a real-estate smarty. He makes money while he's sleeping. He used to be a policeman. He says he made more unassisted arrests than any other officer in the colorful history of Harris County. I can't vouch for that but I know he made plenty. I've known him for years. I used to play poker with him at the Rice Hotel. I gave distemper shots to his puppies. I removed a benign wart from his shoulder that was as big as a Stuart pecan. It looked like a little man's head, or a baby's head, like it might talk, or cry. I never charged him a dime. Ski has forgotten all that.'

'Why did you tell me he was looking for you?'

'He almost caught me at Alvin. It was nip and tuck. Do you know the County Line Lounge between Arcadia and Alvin?'

'No.'

'The Uncle Sam Muffler Shop?'

'No.'

'Shoe City?'

'No.'

'Well, it was right in there where I lost him. That traffic circle is where he tore his britches. I never saw him after that. He has no chin, you know.'

'You told me that.'

'Captain Hughes of the Rangers used to say that if they ever hanged old Ski they would have to put the rope under his nose.'

'Why was he after you?'

'Leon Vurro is the man he really wants.'

The highways of Mexico, I thought, must be teeming with American investigators. The doctor and I, neither of us very sinister, had met by chance and we were both being more or less pursued. What about all the others? I had seen some strange birds down here from the States. Creeps! Nuts! Crooks! Fruits! Liars! California dopers!

I tried not to show much interest in his story after the way he had dozed while I was telling mine. It didn't matter, because he paid no attention to other people anyway. He spoke conversational English to all the Mexicans along the way and never seemed to notice that they couldn't understand a word he said.

The story was hard to follow. He and a man named Leon Vurro had put out a tip sheet in Houston called the *Bayou Blue Sheet*. They booked a few bets too, and they handled a few layoff bets from smaller bookies, with Ski as a silent partner. They worked the national time zones to their advantage in some way that I couldn't understand. Ski had many other interests. He had political connections. No deal was too big or too small for him. He managed to get a contract to publish a directory called *Stouthearted Men*, which was to be a collection of photographs and capsule biographies of all the county supervisors in Texas. Or maybe it was the county clerks. Anyway, Ski and the county officers put up an initial sum of $6,500 for operating expenses. Dr Symes and Leon Vurro gathered the materials for the book and did some work on the dummy makeup. They also sold advertisements for it. Then Leon Vurro disappeared with the money. That, at any rate, was the doctor's account.

'Leon's an ordinary son of a bitch,' he said, 'but I didn't think he was an out-and-out crook. He said he was tired. Tired! He was sleeping sixteen hours a day and going to the picture show every afternoon. I was the one who was tired, and hot too, but we could have finished that thing in another two weeks. Sooner than that if Leon had kept his wife out of it. She had to stick her nose into everything. She got the pictures all mixed up. She claimed she had been a trapeze artist with Sells-Floto. Told fortunes is more like it. Reader and Advisor is more like it. A bullwhip act is more like it. She looked like a gypsy to me. With that fat ass she would have broke the trapeze ropes. Gone through the net like a shot. We had to work fast, you see, because the pictures were turning green and curling up. I don't know how they got wet. There's a lot of mildew in Houston. You can bet I got tired of looking at those things. I wish you could have seen those faces, Speed. Prune Face and BB Eyes are not in it with those boys.'

'You must think I'm a dope,' I said. 'You never intended to publish that book.'

'No, it was a straight deal. Do you know the Moon Publishing Company?'

'No.'

'They have offices in Palestine, Texas, and Muldrow, Oklahoma.'

'I've never heard of it.'

'It's a well-known outfit. They do job printing and they put out calendars and cookbooks and flying-saucer books and children's books, books on boating safety, all kinds of stuff. *A Boy's Life of Lyndon B. Johnson*. That's a Moon book. It was a straight enough deal.'

'How much money did Leon Vurro get?'

'I don't know. Whatever was there, he cleaned it out. It's a shame too. We could have finished that thing in two weeks. We were already through the M's and that was halfway. More, really, because there wouldn't be many X's and Z's. You never know. Maybe Leon was right. You have to know when to lay 'em down. It was a weekend deal, you see. There's a lot of mischief on weekends and not just check-kiting either. Leon cleared out the account on Friday afternoon. I was in San Antonio trying to sell ads for that fool book. The word got out fast on Leon but it didn't get to me. It didn't reach the Alamo City. I got back in my room in Houston on Sunday night. I was staying at Jim's Modern Cabins out on Galveston Road. My cabin was dark and the window was open. You had to leave your windows open. Jim doesn't have air conditioning except in his own office. He's got a big window unit in his office that will rattle the walls. I walked by my front window and I could smell Ski's fruity breath. He has diabetes, you see. These young doctors tell everybody they have diabetes but Ski really has it. I knew he was waiting inside that cabin in the dark and I didn't know why. I left with hardly any delay and then it was nip and tuck in south Houston. I made it on down to Corpus and traded my car for that hippie bus at the first car lot that opened up. I knew I didn't have any business driving a car forty feet long but that was the only unit on the lot the fellow would trade even for. I thought it might make a nice little home on the road. Your top gospel singers all have private buses.'

'Why would Ski be after you if Leon Vurro got the money?'

'Leon's wife was behind all that. Bella set that up. I never said she was dumb.'

'How do you know all that stuff if you left town so fast? That part is not clear to me.'

'You get a feel for these things.'

'I don't see how you could get a feel for all the circumstances.'

'I should never have tied up with Leon. People like that can do nothing but drag you down. He didn't know the first thing about meeting the public and he was never dressed properly. They'll bury that son of a bitch in his zipper jacket.'

'How did you know, for instance, that Leon had cleaned out the bank account?'

'I always tried to help Leon and you see the thanks I got. I hired him to drive for me right after his rat died. He was with Murrell Brothers Shows at that time, exhibiting a fifty-pound rat from the sewers of Paris, France. Of course it didn't really weigh fifty pounds and it wasn't your true rat and it wasn't from Paris, France, either. It was some kind of animal from South America. Anyway, the thing died and I hired Leon to drive for me. I was selling birthstone rings and vibrating jowl straps from door to door and he would let me out at one end of the block and wait on me at the other end. He could handle that all right. That was just about his speed. I made a serious mistake when I promoted Leon to a higher level of responsibility.'

I pressed the doctor with searching questions about the Houston blowout but I couldn't get any straight answers and so I gave it up.

CHAPTER 5

The sun came up out of the sea, or I should say the Bay of Campeche. The warm air seemed heavy and I had the fanciful notion that it was pressing against us and holding us back. I say 'seemed' because I know as well as any professional pilot that warm air is less dense than cool air. I had forgotten about the baloney and cheese in the ice chest. We ate the marshmallows and rolls, and after the rolls got hard I threw them out to goats along the way.

In the town of Coatzacoalcos I double-parked on a narrow street in front of an auto supply store and bought two quarts of transmission fluid and a small can of solvent. This solvent was a patent medicine from the States that was supposed to cure sticking valves and noisy valve lifters. Dr Symes was worried about the clicking noise. He wouldn't shut up about it.

Down the way I found a shady grove of palm trees just off the road. I got out my plastic funnel and red fluid and topped up the transmission. Then I read all the print on the solvent can. There were warnings about breathing the stuff and lengthy instructions as to its use. At the very bottom there was a hedging note in red that had caught my eye too late: 'May take two cans.' I poured half of it through the carburetor at a fast idle and emptied the rest into the crankcase. The clicking went on as before.

Dr Symes said, 'I can still hear it. I think you've made it worse. I think it's louder than it was.'

'It hasn't had time to work yet.'

'How long does it take?'

'It says about five minutes. It says it may take two cans.'

'How many cans did you get?'

'One.'

'Why didn't you get two?'

'I didn't know that at the time.'

He took the empty can from me and studied it. He found the red note and pointed it out to me. 'It says, "May take two cans."'

'I know what it says now.'

'You should have known a car like this would need two cans.'

'How was I to know that? I didn't have time to read all that stuff.'

'We'll never get there!'

'Yes, we will.'

'Never! We'll never make it! Look how little it is!' The size of the can was funny to him. He went into a laughing fit and then a coughing fit, which in turn triggered a sneezing fit.

'Half of the cars on the road are making this

noise,' I said. 'It's not serious. The engine's not going to stop.'

'One can! One can of this shit wouldn't fix a lawn mower and you expect it to fix a Buick! Fifty cans would be more like it! You chump! You said you'd take me to Mama and you don't even know where we are! You don't know your ass from first base! I never can get where I want to go because I'm always stuck with chumps like you! Rolling along! Oh, yes! Rolling along! Rolling on home to Mama!'

He sang these last words to a little tune.

I knew where we were all right. It was the doctor himself who had funny notions about geography. He thought we were driving along the Pacific Ocean, and he had the idea that a momentary lapse at the wheel, one wrong turn, would always lead to monstrous circular error, taking us back where we started. Maybe it had happened to him a lot.

We drove straight through without stopping anywhere to sleep. The road was closed on the direct route across southern Campeche and so we had to take the longer coastal road, which meant waiting for ferries and crossing on them in the night. It also meant that we had to go north up into Yucatán and then south again through Quintana Roo to the border town of Chetumal.

What these ferries crossed were the mouths of rivers along the Gulf, two rivers and a lagoon, I believe, or maybe the other way around, a long stretch of delta at any rate. Dr Symes remained in the car and I strode the decks and took the air, although there was nothing to see in the darkness, nothing but the bow waves, curling and glassy. There was fog too, and once again I was denied the spectacle of the southern heavens.

I had told the doctor that the engine wasn't going to stop and then in the midday heat of Yucatán it did stop. He might have thrown one of his fits if we had not been in a village with people standing around watching us. He sulked instead. I thought the fuel filter was clogged, the little sintered bronze device in the side of the carburetor. I borrowed two pairs of pliers and got it out and rapped it and blew through it. That didn't help. A Mexican truck driver diagnosed the trouble as vapor lock. He draped a wet rag over the fuel pump to cool it down, to condense the vapor in the gas line. I had never seen that trick before but it worked and we were soon off again.

The road was flat and straight in this country and there was very little traffic. Visibility was good too. I decided to let the doctor drive for a bit while I took a short nap. We swapped seats. He was a better driver than I had any reason to expect. I've seen many worse. The steering slack didn't throw him at all. Still he had his own style and there was to be no sleeping with him at the wheel. He would hold the accelerator down for about four seconds and then let up on it. Then he would press it down again and let up on it again. That was the way he drove.

I was rocking back and forth like one of those toy birds that drinks water from a glass.

I tried to read the Dix book. I couldn't seem to penetrate the man's message. The pages were brittle and the type was heavy and black and hard to read. There were tips on how to turn disadvantages into advantages and how to take insults and rebuffs in stride. The good salesman must make *one more call*, Dix said, before stopping for the day. That might be the big one! He said you must save your money but you must not be afraid to spend it either, and at the same time you must give no thought to money. A lot of his stuff was formulated in this way. You must do this and that, two contrary things, and you must also be careful to do neither. Dynamic tension! Avoid excessive blinking and wild eye movement, Dix said, when talking to prospects. Restrain your hands. Watch for openings, for the tiniest breaches. These were good enough tips in their way but I had been led to expect balls of fire. I became impatient with the thing. The doctor had deposited bits of gray snot on every page and these boogers were dried and crystallized.

'This car seems to be going sideways,' he said to me.

The car wasn't going sideways and I didn't bother to answer him.

A little later he said, 'This engine seems to be sucking air.'

I let that go too. He began to talk about his

youth, about his days as a medical student at Wooten Institute in New Orleans. I couldn't follow all that stuff and I tuned him out as best I could. He ended the long account by saying that Dr Wooten 'invented clamps.'

'Medical clamps?' I idly inquired.

'No, just clamps. He invented the clamp.'

'I don't understand that. What kind of clamp are you talking about?'

'Clamps! Clamps! That you hold two things together with! Can't you understand plain English?'

'Are you saying this man made the first clamp?'

'He got a patent on it. He invented the clamp.'

'No, he didn't.'

'Then who did?'

'I don't know.'

'You don't know. And you don't know Smitty Wooten either but you want to tell me he didn't invent the clamp.'

'He may have invented some special kind of clamp but he didn't invent *the clamp*. The principle of the clamp was probably known to the Sumerians. You can't go around saying this fellow from Louisiana invented the clamp.'

'He was the finest diagnostician of our time. I suppose you deny that too.'

'That's something else.'

'No, go ahead. Attack him all you please. He's dead now and can't defend himself. Call him a liar and a bum. It's great sport for people who sit on the sidelines of life. They do the same thing with Dix. People who aren't fit to utter his name.'

I didn't want to provoke another frenzy while he was driving, so I let the matter drop. There was very little traffic, as I say, in that desolate green scrubland, and no rivers and creeks at all, but he managed to find a narrow bridge and meet a cattle truck on it. As soon as the truck hove into view, a good half-mile away, the doctor began to make delicate speed adjustments so as to assure an encounter in the exact center of the bridge. We clipped a mirror off the truck and when we were well clear of the scene I took the wheel again.

Then one of the motor mounts snapped. The decayed rubber finally gave way. Strength of materials! With this support gone the least acceleration would throw the engine over to the right from the torque, and the fan blades would clatter against the shroud. I straightened out two coat hangers and fastened one end of the stiff wires to the exhaust manifold on the left side, and anchored the other ends to the frame member. This steadied the engine somewhat and kept it from jumping over so far. I thought it was a clever piece of work, even though I had burned my fingers on the manifold.

For a little car it had a lot of secrets. Another tire went flat near Chetumal, the left rear, and I almost twisted the lug bolts off before I figured out that they had left-hand threads. Far from being clever, I was slow and stupid! Of all the odd-sized tires on the car this one was the smallest, and when I got it off I saw molded in the rubber these words: 'Property of U-Haul Co. Not to be sold.' A trailer tire!

Dr Symes waited in the shade of some bushes. My blistered fingers hurt and I was angry at myself and I was hot and dirty and thirsty. I asked him to bring me the water jug. He didn't answer and I spoke to him again, sharply. He just stared at me with his mouth open. His face was gray and he was breathing hard. One eye was closed, the red one. The old man was sick! No laughing fits here!

I took the grip and the water jug to him. He drank some chalky-looking medicine and almost gagged on it. He said he was dizzy. He didn't want to move for a few minutes. I drank the last of the tepid water in the jug and lay back in the shade. The sand was coarse and warm. I said I would take him to a doctor in Chetumal. He said, 'No, it's just a spell. It'll pass. I'll be all right in a minute. It's not far to Mama's place, is it?'

'No, it's not far now.'

He took off his long belt and this seemed to give him some relief. Then he took off his bow tie. He unchained the giant wallet from his clothes and handed it to me, along with his flashlight, and told me to see that his mother got these things, a Mrs Nell Symes. I didn't like the sound of that. We sat there for a long time and said nothing.

The booted tire thumped all the way in to Chetumal, and then to the border crossing, which was a river just outside of town. The officer there on the Mexican end of the bridge paid no attention to my faulty papers but he didn't like the doctor, didn't want to touch him or brush up against him, this hollow-eyed old gringo with his mouth open, and he was determined not to let him leave Mexico without his bus. Dr Symes's tourist card was clearly stamped '*Entro con Automóvil*,' as was mine, and if one enters Mexico with an *automóvil* then one must also leave with it.

I explained that the doctor's bus had broken down through no fault of his own and that he intended to return for it after a brief visit with his ailing mother in Belize. The officer said that anyone might tell such a story, which was true enough. The law was the law. Produce the bus. Dr Symes offered the man a hundred pesos and the man studied the brown note for an instant and then shook his head; this was a serious matter and money could not settle it, certainly not a hundred pesos.

I took the doctor aside and suggested that he give the man five hundred pesos. He said, 'No, that's too much.'

'What are you going to do then?'

'I don't know, but I'm not giving that son of a bitch forty dollars.'

I saw a red bus cross the bridge with only a brief inspection at each end. I told the doctor I would take him back to Chetumal. He could wait there until dark and catch a red bus to Belize. Then, very likely, there would be a different officer here at this post. The doctor would probably not be noticed and the bus ride would not be a long one. It was only another eighty miles or so to Belize.

He was wobbly and vague. He had heat staggers. I couldn't get any sense out of him. He had diarrhea too, and he was drinking paregoric from a little bottle. We drove back to Chetumal, the tire bumping.

He said, 'Are you going to dump me, Speed?'

'You won't let me take you to a doctor.'

'I never thought you would just throw me out.'

'I'm not throwing you out. Listen to what I'm saying. You can take a bus across the border tonight. I'll see that you get on it. I'll follow the bus.'

'I thought we had a deal.'

'I don't know what you expect me to do. I can't force these people to let you out of the country.'

'You said you'd take me to Belize. I thought it was a straight deal.'

'I'm doing the best I can. You forget I have my own business to see to.'

'That's hard, Speed. That's strong. I don't know you but I know that's not worthy of you.'

'What you need is a doctor.'

'I'll be all right if I can just get something cool to drink.'

I parked on the waterfront in Chetumal and got him out of the car and walked him over to a dockside refreshment stand. We sat on folding metal

104

chairs under a palm-thatched cabaña rig. He looked like a dead man. When the waitress came over, he rallied a little and tried to smile. He said, 'Little lady, I want the biggest Co'-Cola you are permitted to serve.' She was a pretty Indian girl with sharp black eyes. He tried to wink, and said, 'They're getting these little girls out of Hollywood now.' A man at the next table was eating a whole fresh pineapple with a knife. I ordered a pineapple for myself and a Coca *grande* for the doctor.

There was a rising wind. Small boats were chugging about in the bay. Vultures walked boldly along the dock like domestic turkeys. The doctor drank three Cokes and asked for his wallet back. I gave it to him.

'What happened to my flashlight?'

'It's in the car.'

He saw something shiny and leaned over and scratched at it, trying to pick it up.

I said, 'That's a nailhead.'

'I knew it wasn't a dime. I just wanted to see what it was.'

'I've got to get the spare fixed and I need to see about the bus. I want you to wait right here and don't go wandering off.'

'I'm not riding any bus.'

'What are you going to do then?'

'I'm not going off a cliff in a Mexican bus.'

His old carcass was very dear to him.

We sat in silence for a while. I went to the car and got my Esso map of British Honduras. It was a beautiful blue map with hardly any roads to clutter it up. Just down the bay from here was a coastal village in British Honduras called Corozal. Why couldn't the border be bypassed by water? There were plenty of boats available. It wouldn't be much of a trip – a matter of a few miles.

I proposed this plan to the doctor and showed him how things lay on the map. To keep it from blowing away, I had to anchor the corners with bottles. Over and over again I explained the scheme to him but he couldn't take it in. 'Do what, Speed?' he would say. He was fading again.

Most of the boats were now coming in. I walked along the dock and talked to the owners, trying to explain and sell the plan to them in my feeble Spanish. I got nowhere. They wanted no part of it. There was too much wind and the water was too rough and it would soon be dark. Maybe tomorrow, they said, or the next day. I put the map back in the car and returned to the table. Dr Symes was drinking yet another Coke. The girl wanted her money and he was trying to match her for it, double or nothing. He had a ready line of patter for all cashiers, the idea being to confuse them so that they might make an error in his favor.

'It's no use,' I said. 'The wind is too high. It's too dangerous. It was a bad plan anyway. You'll have to ride the red bus and that's all there is to it.'

'The wind?' he said.

Newspapers were being whipped against our legs and the tablecloth was snapping and donkeys were leaning against buildings and the heavy traffic light that hung over the intersection was standing about thirty degrees off vertical, and into the teeth of this gale he asked me that question.

'A bus. I'm going to put you on a bus. It's the only way.'

'Not a bus, no.'

'Do you want to see your mother or do you want to stay here?'

'Mama?'

'She's waiting for you just down the road. You can be there in no time. The bus is safe, I tell you. This is flat country. There are no mountains between here and Belize, not one. It's a coastal plain. I'll see that you get there. I'll drive right along behind the bus.'

'Send me over the mountains in a bus, is that it? That's your answer for everything. Did you make sure it has no brakes? I don't even know the name of this town. I wanted to go to Belize and you land us in this place instead. Why do we keep hanging around here anyway?'

'You can be in Belize in just a few hours if you'll listen to me and do what I say. Do you understand what I'm telling you?'

In my desperation I had fallen into the doctor's habits of speech. He must have spent half his life shouting that hopeless question. I thought of hiring an ambulance. Surely the border guards would not interfere with a mercy dash. But wouldn't it be very expensive?

Someone pinched me on the fleshy part of my upper arm and I jumped. An Indian boy about seventeen years old was standing behind me. 'Corozal?' he said. He took me over to the slip where his wooden boat was tied up, a slender homemade craft with an old-fashioned four-cycle outboard engine on the stern. It was about a six-horse engine, with a high profile. I asked about life preservers. *No hay*, he said. I indicated that the water was rough and getting rougher all the time. He shrugged it off as inconsequential. We quickly reached an agreement.

The doctor was too weak and confused to resist. I took his wallet again for safekeeping and we loaded him into the boat. I gave the boy a ten-dollar bill and promised him a twenty – a balloon payment to encourage compliance – upon delivery of the old man in Corozal. The boy jerked the rope many times before the engine started. Then he pushed off and I, with great misgivings, watched them leave, the little boat battering sluggishly through the whitecaps. The sun was going down. The doctor had lied to me about his funds. That wallet was packed with twenties and fifties.

I drove back to the border crossing and had no trouble getting out of Mexico. At the other end of the bridge I had to deal with a British Honduras officer. He was a dapper Negro in shorts and high stockings and Sam Browne belt. I had shed my coat long ago but I was still wearing my tie. I was filthy and I needed a shave.

He asked my occupation. I said I was a businessman. He pointed out that my spare tire was flat. I thanked him. Was I a doctor? What was I doing with a doctor's bag? What was the silverware for? I had no very good answers for him. He poked into everything, even the ice chest. The ice had melted days ago and the cheese and baloney were spoiled. The water was brown from the rusting rims of the beer cans. At the bottom of this mess my Colt Cobra was washing about in the plastic bag. I had forgotten all about it. The old man had made me neglect my business! The officer wiped the pistol dry with a handkerchief and stuck it in his hip pocket. He shook his finger at me but said nothing. He was keeping it for himself.

He asked if I planned to sell the Buick and I said no. He wrote his name and address for me on the back of a card advertising the Fair Play Hotel in Belize and said he would be happy to handle the sale. I took the card and told him I would keep it in mind. He said I didn't look like much of a businessman to him. I described my Torino and asked about Norma and Dupree and the dog – and was I knocked for a loop when this bird said he remembered them. He remembered the car and the pretty girl and yes, the red dog, and the fellow with the glasses who was driving; he remembered him very well.

'Played that "Sweet Lorraine" on the mouth harp.'

'No, that wouldn't be him. That wouldn't be Dupree.'

'Yes, and "Twilight Time" too.'

I couldn't believe my ears. Was it possible that some identical people had passed through here with a chow dog in a blue Torino? An antimatter Dupree playing tunes on a mouth organ! A young Meigs! The doctor had told me that I could expect the same old stuff down here but this didn't sound like the same old stuff to me.

I asked about the road to Belize. Was it paved? Should I chance it with no spare tire? He said it was an excellent road, much better than anything I had seen in Mexico. And not only that, but I would now be able to get some good gasoline for a change. The Mexican petrol was inferior stuff, he said, and it smelled funny. Here it had the proper smell.

There was a T-head pier in Corozal and I stood at the end of it and waited anxiously in the dark. The wind had dropped off somewhat. Now it was cool. I supposed there was some colorful local name for it, for this particular kind of wind. I was just fifteen degrees or so above the equator and I was at sea level and yet I was chilly. A cool snap like this on the Louisiana island and the doctor would have a thousand coughing chimps on his hands. I could make out a few stars through the drifting clouds but not the Southern Cross.

I began to worry more and more about that little boat in open water at night. It wasn't the open sea but it was a big bay, big enough for trouble. Why had I suggested this? It would all be my fault, the sea disaster. Criminal folly! The boat would be swamped and the doctor, a nuisance to the end, would flail away in the water and take the Indian boy down with him.

A Spanish-looking man joined me at the edge of the pier. He was barefooted, his trouser legs rolled up, and he was pushing a bicycle. He parked the bike and looked out at the water, his hands in his pockets, a brooding figure. I didn't want to intrude on his thoughts but when the wind blew his bike over I thought it would then be all right to speak, the clatter having broken his reverie. I said, '*Mucho viento.*' He nodded and picked up his bike and left. Much wind. What a remark! No wonder everybody took foreigners for dopes.

I heard the engine popping and then I saw the boat low in the water. Choppy waves were breaking against it. The boy was angry because the doctor had vomited marshmallows and Coke in his boat. The old man was wet and only semiconscious. We laid him out on the pier and let him drain for a minute. It was like trying to lug a wet mattress. I gave the boy an extra ten dollars for his trouble. He helped me get the doctor into the car and then he fearlessly took to the dark water again.

Part of the road to Belize was broken pavement and the rest was washboard gravel. Great flat slabs of concrete had been wrenched out of place as though from an earthquake. What a road! Time after time the Buick's weak coil springs bottomed out, and I mean dead bottom. When we came bounding back up on the return phase, I feared that something would tear loose, some suspension component. I worried about the tires too. The gravel part was only a little better. I tried to find a speed at which we could skim along on the crests of the corrugations but with no luck. We skittered all over the roadbed. The doctor groaned in the back seat. I too was beginning to fade. My head throbbed and I took some more of the bitter orange pills.

CHAPTER 6

It was late when we reached Belize and I didn't feel like asking directions and floundering around in a strange place. It wasn't a big town but the streets were narrow and dark and irregular. I found a taxicab at a Shell station and I asked the Negro driver if he knew a Mrs Nell Symes, who had a church here. It took him a while to puzzle it out. Did I mean 'Meemaw?' Well, I didn't know, but I hired him to go to Meemaw's anyway and I trailed along behind in the Buick.

The church was a converted dwelling house, a white frame structure of two stories. Some of the windows had fixed wooden louvers and some had shutters that folded back. The roof was galvanized sheet iron. It was just the kind of old house that needed the Midgestone treatment.

A wooden sign beside the door said:

Unity Tabernacle
'Whosoever will'

The house was dark and I rapped on the door for a long time before I roused anyone. I heard them coming down the stairs very slowly. The door opened and two old ladies looked out at me. One was in a flannel bathrobe and the other one was wearing a red sweater. The one in the sweater had wisps of pink hair on her scalp. It was a bright chemical pink like that of a dyed Easter chick. I could see at once that the other one was Dr Symes's mother. She had the same raccoon eyes. She used an aluminum walking stick but she didn't appear to be much more decrepit than the doctor himself.

'Mrs Symes?'

'Yes?'

'I have your son out here in the car.'

'What's that you say?'

'Dr Symes. He's out here in the car.'

'Reo. My word.'

'He's sick.'

'Who are you?'

'My name is Ray Midge. He rode down from Mexico with me.'

'Are you with the postal authorities?'

'No, ma'am.'

'We weren't even thinking about Reo, were we, Melba?'

The other lady said, '*I* sure wasn't. I was thinking about a snack.'

Mrs Symes turned back to me. 'Has he got some old floozie with him?'

'No, ma'am, he's by himself.'

'You say he's in the car?'

'Yes.'

'Why is he staying in the car? Why doesn't he get out of the car?'

'He's sick.'

'Go see if it's really him, Melba.'

Melba came out to the car. I opened a door so the dome light would come on. She studied the rumpled figure in the back seat. 'It's Reo all right,' she said. 'He's asleep. He's lost weight. His clothes are smoking. He's wearing those same old white pants he had on last time. I didn't know pants lasted that long.'

Mrs Symes said, 'He may have several pair, all identical. Some men do that with socks.'

'I think these are the same pants.'

'What about his flashlight?'

'I don't see it.'

'It's in there somewhere,' I said.

Neither of the ladies was able to help me unload the doctor. I couldn't carry him but I managed to drag him inside, where I laid him out on a church pew. He was limp and his flesh was cool and his clothes were indeed steaming. Then I went back and got his grip. Mrs Symes was not much concerned about his condition. She seemed to think he was drunk.

'That poison has to be metabolized,' she said. 'You can't hurry it along.'

I said, 'He's not drunk, ma'am, he's sick. I believe he needs a doctor.'

Melba said, 'We don't use doctors.'

'You're lucky to have good health.'

'Our health is not particularly good. We just don't go to doctors.'

The downstairs part was a chapel and they lived upstairs. Mrs Symes asked if I would like some supper. I don't like to eat or sleep or go to the bathroom in other people's homes but this was an emergency. I needed food and I kept hanging about in hopes of just such an invitation. I followed them up the stairs.

The electric lights flickered on and off and then failed altogether. I sat at the kitchen table in the soft yellow glow of a kerosene lamp. Mrs Symes gave me some cold chicken and some warmed-over rice and gravy and biscuits. There was a bowl of stewed tomatoes too. What a meal! I was so hungry I was trembling and I made a pig of myself. Melba joined me and fell to on a second supper. She ate heartily for a crone, sighing and cooing between bites and jiggling one leg up and down, making the floor shake. She ate fast and her eyes bulged from inner pressures and delight. This remarkable lady had psychic gifts and she had not slept for three years, or so they told me. She sat up in a chair every night in the dark drinking coffee.

Mrs Symes asked me a lot of personal questions. She and Melba, unlike the doctor, found my mission romantic, and they pressed for details. I was dizzy and tired and not at all in the mood for a truth session but I didn't see how I could leave abruptly after eating their food. Melba asked to see a picture of Norma. I didn't have one. Some detective! Some husband! They could tell me nothing about Mr Dupree's farm. They had never heard the name. Their church work was concerned entirely with Negro children, they said, and I gathered that they had little to do with the other white people in the country. They did know some Mennonite farmers, from whom they bought milk, and they seemed to have an uneasy professional acquaintance with an Episcopal missionary whom they called 'Father Jackie.' Mrs Symes was suspicious of the doctor's unexpected arrival.

She said, 'Do you know the purpose of his visit?'

'He said he was worried about your health.'

'What else did he say?'

'He said you had a church here.'

'What else?'

'That's about all.'

'How would you characterize his mood? Generally speaking.'

'I would say it varied according to circumstances. He was not in one mood the whole time.'

'I mean his feeling about coming here. Was it one of apprehension? Resignation?'

'I can't say it was either one of those. I don't really know him well enough to answer your question, Mrs Symes. To say whether his mood departed from normal in any way.'

'Is that his automobile out there?'

'No, ma'am. He has a bus but it broke down on him in Mexico.'

'A bus?'

'It's an old school bus. It's fixed up so you can sleep in it and cook in it.'

'Did you hear that, Melba? Reo has been living in a school bus.'

'A school bus?'

'That's what Mr Midge here says.'

'I didn't know you could do that.'

'I didn't either. I wonder how he gets his mail.'

'He doesn't live in the bus all the time,' I said. 'It's the kind of thing you take trips in, like a trailer.'

'I'll bet Reo talked your head off.'

'Well, he didn't talk so much tonight. He's been feeling bad.'

'He didn't talk at all until he was six years old. He was a strange child. Otho thought he was simple. What did he tell you about Jean's Island?'

'He said he had some plans for developing it.'

'Did he say he owned it?'

'No, he didn't say that. He said you owned it.'

'That island was dedicated as a bird sanctuary years ago.'

'I see.'

'How can you *develop* a place, as you put it, if it's already been dedicated?'

'Well, I don't know. I guess you can't.'

'If I turned it over to Reo, the bulldozers would be there tomorrow morning. It would be the biggest mess you ever saw. Some people just love to cut trees and the poor whites are the worst about it.

118

I don't know where Reo gets that streak. Man is the most destructive creature there is, Mr Midge.'

Melba said, 'Except for goats. Look at Greece.'

'I wouldn't mind letting Reo have the place if he would live on it and farm it and behave himself, but he won't do that. I know him too well. The first thing you know. Marvel Clark or some other floozie would get her hands on it. I know Marvel too well and she's got enough of my stuff as it is. But she will never get her hands on that land as long as I have anything to say about it.'

I said, 'Do you think I should go downstairs and check on him?'

'He'll be all right. That poison has to be worked out through the breath. What did he tell you about his arthritis clinic in Ferriday?'

'I don't believe he mentioned that.'

'Did he tell you about his Gifts for Grads?'

'Gifts for Dads?'

'Gifts for *Grads*. It was a mail-order scheme. He was advertising expensive watches at bargain prices in all kinds of sleazy magazines. People would send him money but he wouldn't send them any watches. A postal inspector came all the way down here from Washington, D.C., looking for him. He said Reo was going all over the country making fraudulent representations and calling himself Ralph Moore and Newton Wilcox.'

'Dr Symes didn't say anything about Gifts for Grads.'

'Is that woman Sybil still living with him?'

'I just don't know about that. He was by himself when I met him in Mexico.'

'Good riddance then. He brought an old hussy named Sybil with him the last time. She had great big bushy eyebrows like a man. She and Reo were trying to open up a restaurant somewhere in California and they wanted me to put up the money for it. As if I had any money. Reo tells everybody I have money.'

Melba said, 'No, it was a singing school. Reo wanted to open a singing school.'

'The singing school was an entirely different thing, Melba. This was a restaurant they were talking about. Little Bit of Austria. Sybil was going to sing some kind of foreign songs to the customers while they were eating. She said she was a night-club singer, and a dancer too. She planned to dance all around people's tables while they were trying to eat. I thought these night clubs had beautiful young girls to do that kind of thing but Sybil was almost as old as Reo.'

'Older,' said Melba. 'Don't you remember her arms?'

'They left in the middle of the night. I remember that. Just picked up and left without a word.'

'Sybil didn't know one end of a piano keyboard from the other.'

'She wore white shiny boots and backless dresses.'

'But she didn't wear a girdle.'

'She wore hardly anything when she was sunning herself back there in the yard.'

120

'Her shameful parts were covered.'

'That goes without saying, Melba. It wasn't necessary for you to say that and make us all think about it.'

'Dr Symes didn't say anything about Sybil to me.'

'No, I don't suppose he did. Did he tell you about the hearing-aid frauds of 1949?'

'No, ma'am.'

'No, I don't suppose he did. The shame and scandal killed Otho just as sure as we're sitting here. Reo lost his medical license and he's been a sharper and a tramp ever since. My own son, who took an oath to do no harm.'

I didn't know who Otho was but it was hard to believe that any person in Louisiana had ever keeled over from fraud shock. I tried to think about that dramatic scene and then Melba put her face in mine and started talking to me. Both ladies were talking to me at the same time.

Melba said that her first husband had abandoned her in Ferriday and that her second husband, a handsome barber who didn't believe in life insurance, had dropped dead in New Orleans at the age of forty-four. After that, she made her own way, giving piano lessons and selling foundation garments. She now received a tiny green Social Security check and that was her entire income. Five dollars of it went each month to Gamma chapter of some music teachers' sorority. She didn't remember much about the first husband but she thought often of the opinionated barber husband, idle in his shop in the quiet 1940 New Orleans sunlight, watching the door for customers and searching through the *Times-Picayune* over and over again for unread morsels.

Mrs Symes raised her voice. 'I wish you would hush for a minute, Melba. I've heard all that stuff a thousand times. I'm trying to ask a question. It looks like I could ask one question in my own home.'

Melba didn't stop talking but I turned my head a bit toward Mrs Symes.

She said, 'What I'm trying to find out is this. When you are at your home in Arkansas, Mr Midge, do you get much mail?'

'I don't follow.'

'Cards, letters. First-class matter.'

'Not much, no, ma'am.'

'Same here. I'm not counting all those absurd letters from Reo. Are you a witnessing Christian?'

'I attend church when I can.'

'Do you pray every night for all the little babies in Little Rock?'

'No, ma'am, I don't.'

'What kind of Christian do you call yourself?'

'I attend church when I can.'

'Cards on the table, Mr Midge.'

'Well, I think I have a religious nature. I sometimes find it hard to determine God's will.'

'Inconvenient, you mean.'

'That too, yes.'

'What does it take to keep you from attending church?'

'I go when I can.'

'A light rain?'

'I go when I can.'

'This 'religious nature' business reminds me of Reo, your man of science. He'll try to tell you that God is out there in the trees and grass somewhere. Some kind of *force*. That's pretty thin stuff if you ask me. And Father Jackie is not much better. He says God is a perfect sphere. A ball, if you will.'

'There are many different opinions on the subject.'

'Did you suppose I didn't know that?'

'No, ma'am.'

'What about Heaven and Hell. Do you believe those places exist?'

'That's a hard one.'

'Not for me. How about you, Melba?'

'I would call it an easy one.'

'Well, I don't know. I wouldn't be surprised either way. I try not to think about it. It's just so odd to think that people are walking around in Heaven and Hell.'

'Yes, but it's odd to find ourselves walking around here too, isn't it?'

'That's true, Mrs Symes.'

'All the children call me Meemaw. Why don't you do like they do and call me Meemaw?'

'Well. All right.'

'Have you read the Bible?'

'I've read some of it.'

'Do you go through your Bible looking for discrepancies?'

'No, ma'am.'

'That's not the way to read it. I have a little test I like to give to people like you who claim to be Bible scholars. Do you mind taking a little test for me?'

'Is it a written test?'

'No, it's just one question.'

'I don't mind taking your test, Meemaw, but there is a misunderstanding here. You asked me if I had read the Bible and I said I had read some of it. I did not say I was a Bible scholar.'

'We'll soon know, one way or the other. All right, the wedding feast at Cana. John 2. Jesus turned six pots of water into six pots of so-called wine. His first miracle. His mother was there. Now do you believe that was alcoholic wine in those pots or unfermented grape juice?'

'What does the Bible say?'

Melba said, 'The Bible just says wine. It says good wine.'

'Then that's what I say. I say wine.'

Mrs Symes said, 'It's your notion then that Jesus was a bootlegger?'

'No, it's not.'

'He was no more a bootlegger than I am. That so-called wine was nothing more than fresh and wholesome grape juice. The word is translated wrong.'

'I didn't know that.'

'Do you claim to know the meaning of every word in the Greek language?'

'No, I don't. I don't know one word of the Greek language.'

'Then why should your opinion be worth anything in a matter like this? Father Jackie is bad enough and you don't even know as much as he does.'

Melba said, 'Let's see what he knows about Swedenborg.'

'He won't know anything about Swedenborg.'

'It won't hurt to see, will it?'

'Go ahead and ask him then.'

'What do you know about a man named Emanuel Swedenborg, Mr Midge?'

'I don't know anything about him.'

'He personally *visited* Heaven and Hell and returned to write an astonishing book about his experiences. Now what do you think of that?'

'I don't know what to think.'

Mrs Symes said, 'Have you read Mrs Eddy's books?'

'No, ma'am.'

'What is your work in this world?'

'I don't know what it is yet. I'm back in school now.'

'It's getting pretty late in the day for you to have so few interests and convictions. How old are you, Mr Midge?'

'I'm twenty-six.'

'Later than I thought. Think about this. All the little animals of your youth are long dead.'

Melba said, 'Except for turtles.'

Something small and hard, possibly a nut, dropped on the tin roof and we waited in silence for another one but it didn't come. I asked directions to the Fair Play Hotel, and Meemaw, as I now addressed her, told me I would be more comfortable at the Fort George or the Bellevue. I was agreeable and didn't pursue the matter, but the man at the border had given me a card for the Fair Play and it was there I meant to stay. The lights came back on and in a very few minutes Melba's electric coffeepot began to bubble and make respiratory noises like some infernal hospital machine. Mrs Symes looked me over closely in the light.

'I know you'll excuse a personal reference, Mr Midge. Are you handicapped?'

'I don't follow.'

She lifted one of my trouser legs an inch or so with the tip of her aluminum cane. 'Your feet, I mean. They look odd the way you have them splayed out. They look like artificial feet.'

'My feet are all right. These are new shoes. Perhaps that accounts for their unnatural fullness.'

'No, it's not that, it's the way you have them turned out. Now there, that's better. You remind me a whole lot of Otho. He never could get the hang of things.'

'I've heard you mention Otho two or three times but I don't know who he is.'

126

'Otho Symes, of course. He was my husband. He never could get the hang of things but he was just as good as gold.'

Melba said, 'He was a nervous little man. I was afraid to say boo to him.'

'He wasn't nervous until he had his operation.'

'He was nervous before his operation and after his operation both.'

'He wasn't nervous until they put that thing in his neck, Melba. I ought to know.'

'You ought to but you don't. This boy doesn't want to hear any more about Otho and I don't either. I want to find out something about his wife and why she left him. He hasn't told us that.'

'I don't know why she left.'

'You must have some idea.'

'No, I was very much surprised.'

Mrs Symes said, 'Are you trying to tell us that you and your wife were on cordial terms?'

'We got along all right.'

'Never a harsh word?'

'She called me a pill sometimes.'

'A pill, eh.'

'That was her mother's word but Norma took it up.'

'They were both calling you a pill to your face?'

'Yes. Not, you know, day and night.'

'Did she open your mail and read it?'

'No, ma'am. That is, I don't think she did.'

Melba put her rouged face in mine again and said, 'One moment, Mr Midge. You told us just a while ago that you didn't get any mail. Now you're talking about people intercepting your mail. Which is it? Do you get any mail or not?'

'I said I didn't get much mail. I get some.'

Mrs Symes said, 'I'll bet the little girl's kitchen was just filthy all the time.'

'No, it wasn't either.'

'Can she cook anything that's fit to eat?'

'She's a pretty good cook.'

'Can she make her own little skirts and jumpers?'

'I don't think so. I've never seen her sewing anything.'

'What about raisins? Does she like raisins?'

'I've never seen her eating any raisins.'

'I'll bet she likes yellow cake with hot lemon sauce poured over it.'

'I believe she does, yes. I do too.'

'What about chocolate cake?'

'She likes all kinds of cake.'

'All right then, tell me this. When she's eating chocolate cake late at night, does she also drink sweet milk from a quart bottle till it runs from the corners of her mouth?'

'I've never seen her do that.'

'That's a picture I have of gluttony.'

'I don't know how you got the idea that Norma is a glutton, Meemaw. The fact is, she eats very little. She's very particular about what she eats and how she eats it.'

'A clean feeder then, according to you.'

'Very clean.'

'Melba used to do that very thing late at night. That cake thing with the milk.'

'No, I didn't.'

'Yes, you did.'

'There never was a bigger lie. I don't know why you keep telling people that.'

'I know what I know, Melba.'

The lights went off again. I thanked them for the supper and the hospitality and got up to leave. Melba asked me to wait a minute. She had the burning lamp in her hand and she had turned the wick up a notch or two for a bright flame. Then she went to a dark corner and struck a pose there with the lamp, holding it above her head. She said, 'Now I just wonder if you two can guess who I am.'

Mrs Symes said, 'I know. The Statue of Liberty. That's easy.'

'No.'

'Florence Nightingale then.'

'No.'

'You're changing it every time I guess it.'

'I'm the Light of the World.'

'No, you're not, you're just silly. You're so silly, Melba, it's pitiful. It's downright embarrassing to me when we have guests.'

This time I did leave but before I got all the way down the stairs Mrs Symes called after me. She asked if I thought there was any chance that Reo was going about doing good by stealth. It wouldn't have hurt me to say yes, there was an excellent

129

chance of that, but I said I just didn't know. She asked if I had any Lipton's dried soups in the car, or a fall and winter Sears catalogue. Of course I didn't and I felt bad because I had nothing like that to give them, even though they had roughed me up a little with their hard questions.

CHAPTER 7

I left Dr Symes steaming in the dark chapel and made my way back to the arched bridge over the little river that ran through Belize. I had guessed, correctly, that this bridge was the center of town. Two or three blocks upstream I found the Fair Play Hotel, which was a white frame house like the tabernacle. I parked the car in front and again went through the unpleasant business of waking people up.

A thin Negro woman was the manager of the place. She was surly, as anyone might have been in the circumstances, but I could sense too a general ill-feeling for me and my kind. She woke a small Negro boy named Webster Spooner, who slept in a box in the foyer. It was a pretty good wooden box with bedding in it. I knew his name because he had written it on a piece of paper and taped it to his box. At the foot of his makeshift bed there was a tomato plant growing in an old Texaco grease bucket.

I wrote and addressed a brief message to my father asking him to wire me $250. The woman said she would have Webster Spooner attend to it when the cable office opened in the morning. I gave her a five-dollar bill and a few ten-peso notes – all the money in my pocket – and she pinned it to the message and put it away in a shoe box.

Would my car be safe on the street? It might be or it might not be, she said, but in any case there was no enclosed parking. I thought of removing the cable from the coil to the distributor so as to foil thieves but I was too weary to fool with that car anymore. The woman, whose name was Ruth, went back to bed. Webster Spooner carried my bag upstairs and showed me to my room. He said he would keep an eye on the car. I didn't see how he was going to do that from his box. I knew he was a sound sleeper. The woman Ruth had almost had to kill him to get him awake.

My room overlooked the black water of the little river or creek. I opened a window and I could smell it. One drop of that stinking water would mean instant death! As soon as I arrive at any destination, my first thoughts are always of departure and how it may be most quickly arranged, but it was not so in this case. Fatigue perhaps. I settled in. I went to bed and stayed there for two days.

Twice a day Webster Spooner came by and took my order for a bowl of sliced bananas and a small can of Pet milk. I had the same thing each time and he carefully wrote it down each time in his notebook.

Webster said he had other jobs. He washed police

132

cars and he sold newspapers and greeting cards. The tomato plant was one of his projects. He sometimes referred to the woman Ruth as his 'ahntee,' which is to say his aunt, but I got the impression that they were not actually related. He said she took half his earnings.

He always had a fresh question for me when he caught me awake. Could a Dodge Coronet outrun a Mercury Montego? How did you keep score in the game of bowling? They got very few American guests here at the Fair Play, he said, and the ones they did get drove sorry-looking cars like mine or else they were hippies with dirty feet and no cars at all. Ruth didn't like the Americans but he, Webster, rather liked them, even if they did keep him hopping with their endless demands for ice and light bulbs and towels and flyswatters. Even the wretched hippies expected service. It was in the blood.

I discovered later that Ruth called me 'Turco' and 'the Turk' because of my small pointed teeth and my small owl beak and my small gray eyes, mere slits but prodigies of light-gathering and resolving power. What put it into her head that these were distinctive Turkish features, I had no way of knowing, nor did I know why she should be down on the Turks too, but there it was. 'See what the Turk wants now,' she would say to Webster, and, 'Is Turco still in bed?'

I had him get me some envelopes and an assortment of colorful stamps and I addressed some

British Honduras covers to myself in Little Rock. I slept off and on and I had a recurring dream. I read the Dix book, or tried to. My mind wandered, even on the strong passages that the doctor had underlined. I read a guidebook. The writer said the people of this country were 'proud,' which usually means 'barely human' in the special lingo of those things. But wasn't Ruth proud? The very word for her. I calculated the trip expenses. In the bathroom down the hall I found a paperback book with no covers and took it back to bed with me. I read almost two pages before I realized it was fiction, and worse, a story set in the future. Some bird was calling up for a 'helicab.' I dropped it on the floor, which is to say I didn't fling it across the room, although I could tell it had been flung many times. I listened to the radio that was always playing in the next room. That is, I listened to the English portions. There were alternate hours of broadcasting in English and Spanish.

I paid particular attention to a California evangelist who came on each morning at nine. I looked forward to this program. Was the man a fraud? He was very persuasive and yet there was a Satanic note in his cleverness. I couldn't work it out.

The headboard of the bed was covered with some cheap white synthetic material – in this land of mahogany – and the name KARL was carved into it in block letters. Each time I woke up, I was confused and then I would see that KARL and get my bearings. I would think about Karl for a few minutes. He had thought it a good thing to leave his name here but, ever wary, not his full name. I wondered if he might be in the next room. With his knife and radio he might be on the move constantly, like J. S. Dix.

The recurring dream made me sweat and writhe in the damp bedclothes. I couldn't trace it back to any event in my waking life, so to speak. I relate this dream, knowing it is ill-mannered to do so, because of its anomalous character. Most of my dreams were paltry, lifeless things. They had to do with geometric figures or levitation. My body would seem to float up from the bed, but not far, a foot or so. There was no question of flying. In this Belize dream there were other people. I was sitting at a low coffee table across from an intelligent, well-dressed woman who wanted to 'have it out.' She had a fat son named Travis who was about seven years old. This boy was encouraged by his mom to have opinions and make pert remarks. The three of us were always seated around the coffee table on the stylish woman's pneumatic furniture. She drove home telling points in some dim quarrel while the boy Travis chirped out show-business quips.

'Be my guest!' he would chirp, and, 'Oh boy, that's the story of my life!' and, 'Yeah, but what do you do for an encore!' and, 'Hey, don't knock it if you ain't tried it!' and, 'How's that for openers?' and, 'You bragging or complaining!' and, 'Welcome to the club, Ray! Ha ha ha ha ha ha ha ha.' I had to sit there and take it on the chin from both the woman and Travis.

Ruth sent for me early on the third day. I took a bath and shaved and put on some clean clothes. My legs were shaky as I went down the stairs. Ruth wanted her room money and her Pet milk money. I had heard nothing from Little Rock. Norma had abandoned me, and now, it seemed, my father as well. I tried to figure out how many days I had been gone. It was just possible that he had not yet returned from the Alabama bass rodeo. Flinging his plastic worm all over the lake! His Lucky 13! His long-tailed jigs! He caught fish that weighed three pounds and he talked about them 'fighting.' Killer bass! It was possible too that he was tired of fooling with me, as with Mr Dupree and Guy. Weaned at twenty-six! Places like Idaho had governors my age. The great Humboldt was exploring the Orinoco at my age instead of sniveling about a money order.

Ruth was hard to deal with. Her Creole speech was hard to understand. She wouldn't look at me when I spoke to her and she wouldn't answer me or give any sign of acknowledgment. I was thus forced to repeat myself and then she would say, 'I heard you the first time.' But if I didn't repeat myself we would just stand there in a silent and uneasy impasse.

I offered to let her hold some bonds until my money arrived. She wanted cash and she wanted it at that moment. I didn't know what to say to

136

her, how to keep talking in the assertive Dix manner. She glowered and looked past me. A crackpot like Karl had the run of the place but my E bonds were no good. That was her idea of fair play. Webster Spooner was listening to all this. He was reclining in his box and working in his notebook but he was listening too.

'He have money in that long notecase,' he said. 'Big money.'

It was true. I still had the doctor's wallet and I had forgotten about it. I went back to the room and got it from the suitcase. I paid Ruth twenty American dollars and I thought this would put me on a new footing with her, but it seemed to make her even more disagreeable. I asked her where the government agriculture office was and she ignored me. I asked her where the police station was and she turned her back to me and went through the curtain to her living quarters. I rang the bell but she wouldn't come back.

I was annoyed with Webster for poking around my room while I was asleep but I didn't mention it. I asked if he could run an errand for me. He said nothing and kept working in his notebook. He and Ruth both had decided that I was the sort of person they didn't have to listen to. There were certain white people that they might have to listen to but I was not one of them. I spoke to him again.

'I'm busy,' he said.

'What are you doing?'

'I'm drawing the car of tomorrow.'

'Yes, I see now. It looks fast. That's nice work. Everything will have to wait until you're finished with it.'

I went out into the soft tropic morning. Roosters were crowing all over Belize. My two-day torpor was gone and I was ready for business. Webster had put his tomato plant out on the sidewalk for the sunlight hours. There were two green tomatoes on it.

The little Buick was filthy but it appeared to be intact. There was a leaflet under the windshield wiper. The letters at the top of the sheet were so big and they were marching across the paper in such a way that I had to move my head back a little from normal reading range to make out the words.

LEET WANTS THIS CAR

Hullo, my name is Leet and I pay cash for select motor cars such as yours. I pay promptly in American ($) Dollars. I pay the duty too so as to spare you bother on that Score. Please see me at once on the Franklin Road just beyond the abandoned Ink factory and get an immediate price quotation. Before you deal with a nother person ask yourself these important questions. Who is this Person? Where was he yesterday and where will he be tomorrow? Leet has been in business at the same location for Six

Years and he is not going any where. Here's hoping we may get together soon. I am a White Man from Great Yarmouth, England, with previous service in the Royal Navy. With every good wish, I am, yours for Mutual Satisfaction,

Wm. Leet
Leet's Motor Ranch
Franklin Road
Belize, B.H.

I threw it away and got my Esso map from the glove compartment and retrieved the doctor's flashlight from under the seat.

Where were the government buildings? I set out toward the arched bridge to find them. No one was about on the streets. I stopped to read signs and posters. A band called the Blues Busters was appearing at an all-night dance. The movie house was featuring a film of a Muhammad Ali fight. I made a plan for breakfast. I would stop at the second restaurant that I came to on my left.

It was a Chinese place and not a restaurant as such but rather a grocery store with a coffee machine and an ice-cream machine and a few tables. An old Chinese man was wiping off the stainless-steel ice-cream machine. Maintenance! The firemen of Belize were gathered there at two tables for coffee and rolls. A piece of luck, I thought, my hitting on the very place that the firemen liked. They looked at me and lowered their voices. I didn't want to interfere with their morning chat so I bought a cone of soft ice cream and left.

Across the way on the bank of the river there was a public market, a long open shed with a low tin roof, where bananas and pigs and melons were sold, though not this early in the morning. Outside the shed on the dock there were three men skinning a giant brown snake that hung from a hook. There, I said to myself, is something worth watching. I went over and took up a close viewing position and ate my ice cream. The job was soon done, but not with any great skill. The long belly cut was ragged and uncertain. It might have been their first snake. They kept the skin with its reticulated pattern and dropped the heavy carcass into the river where it hung for a moment just beneath the surface, white and sinuous, and then sank.

As I thought over what I had seen, very much puzzled as to how the specific gravity of snake flesh could be greater than that of water, someone came up behind me and pinched my upper arm and made me jump, as before, in Chetumal. I had come to fear this salute. It was Webster Spooner this time. He had his newspapers and greeting cards. He seemed to be embarrassed.

'Are you vexed with me, sor, for going through your things?'

'I am a little, yes.'

'I was looking for a President Kennedy dollar.'

'I don't have one.'

'I know you don't.'

'You missed the big snake. There was a monster snake hanging up there just a minute ago. Some sort of constrictor.'

'I see him last night.'

'How would you like to tangle with that big fellow?'

Webster twisted about and gasped as though in the clutches of the snake. 'He be badder than any shark.'

'I saw your tomatoes. They looked pretty good.'

'A bug done eat one of 'em up.'

One bug! A whole tomato! I asked again about the government offices and this time Webster was helpful and agreeable. But it was Sunday, I was surprised to learn, and the offices wouldn't be open. I unfolded the blue map and spread it out on one of the market tables.

'All right, Webster, look here. You will recognize this as a map of your country. An American named Dupree owns a farm here somewhere. I need to find that farm. I want you to go to your police connections and get them to mark the location of that farm on this map. I'm going to give you five dollars now and that's for the policeman. When you bring the map back to me, I'll have five dollars for you. How do you like that?'

He took pains to get Dupree spelled right in his notebook and he didn't whine or raise difficulties, as might have been expected from the corrupt Travis. I described my Torino and told him to be on the lookout for it. He asked me if I could get him a Kennedy dollar. He had that coin on the brain. Every time he got his hands on one, he said, Ruth took it away from him.

'I'll see if I can find you one,' I said. 'It's a half dollar and I should tell you that it probably won't be silver. All our coins now are cupronickel tokens of no real value. I want that Dupree information just as soon as you can get it. I'll be walking around town for a while and then I'll be at the Unity Tabernacle. I'll wait for you there. Do you know that church?'

Webster not only knew it, he was a sort of lapsed member. The tomato plant in the Texaco bucket had started as a church project. He didn't go much anymore, he said, because he had seen all the movies. He liked the singing and the Christmas program and the Easter egg hunt and he didn't mind seeing the Heckle and Jeckle cartoons over and over again. But the rest of it was too hard. And Mrs Symes. no fool, had rearranged the schedule so that the Bible quiz was now held *before* the movie – and no one was admitted late.

He showed me his selection of greeting cards. I bought one, and a newspaper too, the first one I had ever seen that was actually called the *Daily Bugle*. It was made up entirely of political abuse, mean little paragraphs, and I threw it away.

For the next two hours or so I made figure-eight walking circuits of all the downtown blocks. I saw a good many Ford Galaxies, the big favorite here, but no sleek Torino of any model. Some of the dwelling houses had cozy English names . . . Rose Lodge, The Haven. I stopped at the Fort George Hotel for coffee. Some British soldiers were there, still a little drunk from the Blues Busters dance, and they were talking to an American woman who was at the next table with a small boy. They asked her why Americans said 'budder' and 'wadder' instead of 'butter' and 'water' and she said she didn't know. I asked them about their regiment and they said it was the Coldstream Guards. Were they lying? I couldn't tell. The Coldstream Guards! The hotel desk clerk was a woman and she said she vaguely remembered a Mr Dupree, remembered his renting a car, and she thought his farm was south of town somewhere but she wasn't sure.

The door of Unity Tabernacle was bolted against quiz-dodgers. I hammered away on it until I was admitted by a boy monitor wearing a safety-patrol belt. The chapel was dark. Mrs Symes was showing a George Sanders movie to a dozen or so Negro children who were scuffling on the pews. She herself was running the projector and I stood beside her and watched the show for a while. It was a Falcon picture. A wild-eyed man with a tiny mustache was trying desperately to buy a ticket in an enormous marble train station. Mrs Symes said to me, 'He's not going anywhere. The Falcon is laying a trap for that joker.' Then she gave me a pledge card, a card promising an annual gift of $5 ( ), $10 ( ), or $25 ( ) toward the support of the Unity mission. I filled it out under the hot inner light of the projector. The name and address spaces were much too short, unless you wrote a very fine hand or unless your name was Ed Poe and you lived at I Elm St., and I had to put this information on the back. I pledged ten dollars. It was just a pledge and I didn't have to pay the money at that moment.

The doctor had been removed to a bed upstairs. I found him awake but he was still gray in the face and his eye looked bad. He was sitting up, shapeless as a manatee in a woman's pink gown. He was going through a big pasteboard box that was filled with letters and photographs and other odds and ends. His hair had been cut, the jaybird crest was gone. He needed a shave. Melba gave me some coffee and a piece of cinnamon toast. She said that the three of us presented an interesting tableau, what with one person in bed, one in a chair, and one standing. Dr Symes was fretful. He wouldn't talk until Melba had left us.

'What happened to your hair?' I said.

'Mama cut it with some shears.'

'Do you need anything?'

'Yes, I do. They won't let me have any medication, Speed. They've put my bag away. They don't even keep a thermometer. I've lost my money and I've lost my book. I can't find my grooming aids. Some Mexican has got my flashlight.'

I gave him his wallet and his flashlight and told him that the Dix book was safe in my room. This

144

brought him around a little. He fingered through the money but he didn't count it.

'I appreciate this, Speed. You could have put the blocks to me but you didn't do it.'

'I forgot all about it.'

'Where in the world have you been?'

'Asleep.'

'Is that asthma acting up on you?'

'No.'

'Where are you staying?'

'At a hotel down there on the creek.'

'A nice place?'

'It's all right.'

'Do they have roof-garden dancing and a nice orchestra?'

'It's not that kind of hotel. How's your diarrhea?'

'I've got that gentleman turned all the way around. I'm excreting rocks now when I can do my job at all. Did you get your sweetie back?'

'I'm not trying to get her back. I'm trying to get my car back.'

'Well, did you get it?'

'Not yet. I'm working on it.'

'Taking to your bed won't get it. You need to get after it.'

'I know that.'

'You need to read Dix. You need to read Dix on how to close.'

'I didn't get very far in that book.'

'He tells you how to close a sale. Of course it

145

has a wider application. The art of closing, of consummation. Master that and you have the key to the golden door of success. You need to let Dix take you by the hand.'

'I read the part about not imposing on people but I never did that anyway.'

'You read it wrong. It is *necessary* to impose on them. How else can you help a sap? Did you read the chapter on generating enthusiasm?'

'I read part of it.'

'Read it all. Then read it again. It's pure nitro. The Three T's. The Five Don'ts. The Seven Elements. Stoking the fires of the U.S.S. *Reality*. Making the Pep Squad and staying on it.'

'I read the part about the fellow named Floyd who wouldn't work.'

'Marvin, not Floyd. Where do you get Floyd? There's no Floyd in any book Dix ever wrote. No, this was Marvin. It's a beautiful story and so true to life too. Old sorry Marvin! Pouting in his hotel room and listening to dance music on the radio and smoking one cigarette after the other and reading detective magazines and racing sheets. Sitting on the bed trying to dope out his six-dollar combinations. That guy! Wheeling his sap bets for the daily double! Dix knew Marv so well. Do you recall how he summed him up – "Hawking and spitting, we lay waste our powers." I was once a Marvin myself if you can believe that. I had the blues so bad I was paralyzed. Then I read Dix and got off my ass.'

'My money hasn't come in from Little Rock yet.'

'What's the holdup?'

'I don't know.'

'How long do you expect me to carry you?'

'It should come in today. I'm looking for it today. Anyway, you've still got my bonds.'

'I don't want any more of your bonds. I'm caught up on bonds.'

'It should come in today. I figure I owe you about thirty dollars.'

'How do you figure that?'

'It's about fourteen hundred miles from San Miguel. I figure sixty dollars for the gas and oil and other stuff.'

'How much for the motorized canoe ride?'

'Do you think I'm going to pay half of that?'

'People are careless when they're spending other people's money. That stuff is hard to come by.'

'It wasn't a canoe. It was a boat.'

'I have to work for my money. I'm not like you.'

He had sorted the memorabilia from the box into three piles on the bed and took a long brown envelope from one of the piles and waved it at me. 'Come here a minute, Speed. I want to show you something.'

It was a new plan for Jean's Island. On the back of the envelope he had sketched an outline of the island, which was shaped like a tadpole. On the bulbous end he had drawn a dock and some rectangles that represented barracks. This was to be a nursing-home complex for old people called

The City of Life. He and his mother would live on the island in a long yellow house, he at one end and she at the other, her bathtub fitted with a grab-bar. Together they would run the nursing home. He would supervise the medical care and she would minister to the spiritual needs. He anticipated a licensing problem because of his record but he thought he could get around that by registering the thing in his mother's name. And in Louisiana there was always some official you could pay to expedite such matters. He had also drawn in a nine-hole golf course. I didn't get the connection between the nursing home and the golf links and I asked him about this but he wasn't listening.

'A lot of bedpans and bitching, you think, but I'm talking about a seventeen-percent bottom-line profit,' he said. 'I don't mind fooling with these old people. Never have. Put a half-grain of pheno-barbital in their soup every night and they won't give you much trouble. They've all got money these days. They all get regular checks from the government.'

'You've got quite a few buildings there. What about your construction money?'

'No problem at all. Tap the Feds for some Hill-Burton funds. Maybe float some Act 9 industrial bonds. Hell, mortgage the island. Roll over some short notes. I figure about eight thousand five hundred square feet under roof for the long house, with about six thousand feet of that heated and cooled. The rest in storage rooms and breezeways. Put your cooling tower down at this end, with about forty-five tons of air conditioning. I don't say it's a sure thing. If it was a sure thing, everybody would be in it. But you have to go with the odds and you have two high cards right off in me and Mama.'

'Your mother said that island was dedicated as a wildlife refuge.'

'Have you been discussing my business with her?'

'She was the one who brought it up.'

'Jean's Island has never been dedicated in any legal sense.'

'I'm just telling you what she said.'

'She meant it was posted, that's all. No hunters and no trespassers. She doesn't know the difference. Why would she be paying taxes on it if it was dedicated?'

'I don't know.'

'You're mighty right you don't. Did you get the impression that she might be willing to come to terms on the island?'

'I didn't get that impression.'

'Not favorably disposed then.'

'She's afraid some woman will get her hands on the property.'

'Some woman?'

'She talked about a woman named Sybil.'

'What has Sybil got to do with it?'

'I don't know.'

'Sybil's all right.'

'Your mother doesn't approve of her.'

'Sybil's all right but she came down here and showed her ass is what she did. She ran her mouth all the time. I was disappointed. It was a misplaced confidence on my part. I should never have brought her down here, but it was Sybil's car, you see.'

'There was another woman. Your mother mentioned another woman named Marvel Clark.'

'Marvel!'

'Marvel Clark. Do you know her?'

'Do I know Marvel. My old valentine. Mama must be losing her mind. What has Marvel got to do with anything?'

'Is she one of your sweethearts?'

'She's a rattlesnake. I didn't see it at first. Mama told me not to marry her. She knew those Clarks. I didn't see it until we were married and then I saw it with great clarity. Even so, I miss her sometimes. Some little thing will remind me of her. Can you imagine that? Missing a coiled rattler.'

'I didn't realize you had a wife.'

'I don't have a wife. Marvel gave me the gate thirty-five years ago, Speed. She said she'd had enough. She said she would shave her head and become a nun in the Catholic church before she would ever get married again. She cleaned me out good. She got my house and she got a lot of Mama's furniture and she even had my medical equipment attached.'

'Well, there you are. Your mother is afraid she will get the island too.'

150

'Get it how? Not through me.'

He searched through the box and brought out an old photograph showing a thin girl in a dotted dress. She was sitting in a playground swing and she was holding a squinting child on her knees. This was the doctor's former wife, Marvel Clark Symes, and their infant son Ivo. Dr Symes with a wife! I couldn't believe it. She was a pretty girl too, and not a floozie at all. And baby Ivo! Of course the boy was grown now; that picture must have been forty years old.

Ivo was a roofing contractor in Alexandria, Louisiana, the doctor told me, where Marvel Clark now made her home as well. He said he had not communicated in any way with her for more than twenty years. I gathered that he was also estranged from his son, calling him as he did, 'a roofing thug,' and saying that he hoped God would let him, the doctor, live long enough to see Ivo in the penitentiary at Angola.

'I don't know what Mama can be thinking about,' he said. 'There is no possible way Marvel could get the land through me. She has no more legal claim on me than does any strange woman passing by on the street.'

'I'm just telling you what she said.'

'The divorce was final. That bond has been severed and forever set at naught. Those are the very words on the decree. That's as final as you can get. How much more do you want?'

'I don't know anything about it.'

'You're mighty right you don't. Go look it up at the courthouse in Vidalia and then you might know something about it.'

I went to the window and watched the street below for Webster Spooner. I looked across the rusty tin roofs of Belize. I couldn't see the ocean but I knew it was out there where the roofs stopped. Dr Symes asked if I would get him some medicine and some shaving gear. I said I would and he began to write prescriptions on scraps of paper. Downstairs I could hear some bouncy 1937 clarinet tootling.

'What is that?'

'What?'

'That music.'

'That's Felix the Cat. Mama loves a picture show. I brought her some cartoons and shorts when I was down here with Sybil. Felix the Cat and Edgar Kennedy and Ted Fiorito with his dance band. I brought Melba a thousand-piece puzzle. Mama loves a picture show better than anybody I know except for Leon Vurro. Listen to this, Speed. Here's what I had to put up with. I would be in that hot cabin in south Houston trying to flatten out those photographs with brickbats and Leon would be off downtown in some cool picture show watching *Honky-Tonk Women* or *Women in Prison*. A grown man. Can you beat it? I've never wasted my time on shows. Don't you know they've got those stories all figured out before you even get to the show? Leon would sit there in the dark like a sap for two or three hours watching those stories and then he would come out on the street just as wild as a crib rat, blinking his eyes and looking around for women to squeeze. Not Bella but strange women. Oh, yes, I used to do it myself. There is very little folly I have missed out on in my life. I never wasted my time on shows but I was a bigger hog for women than Leon ever was. Talk about your prisoners of love. Talk about your boar minks. There was a time when I was out almost every night squeezing women but I stopped that foolishness years ago. A big waste of time and money if you want my opinion, not to mention the toll on your health.'

Melba was sitting in her chair in the next room, the central room, and when the cartoon was over she went downstairs to play the piano. The children sang, their devotions passing up through this bedroom and on through the tin roof to the skies. Dr Symes hummed along with them and sang bits of the hymn.

'This is not a feasible program,' he said, indicating the business downstairs. 'I think the world of Mama but this is just not a feasible setup. Fooling around with a handful of kids. Don't take my word for it. Check it out with your top educators and your top communicators. What you want is a broad base. This is a narrow base. What you want is a healing service under a tent, and then when things go slack you can knock the poles down and fold that booger up and move on. Or a radio ministry. A telephone ministry would beat this. You'll never prosper on a deal like this. It doesn't make any sense. This is like old man Becker in Ferriday. Let me tell you what he would do. He would be in the back of his hardware store weighing out turnip seed at eight cents a pound, just busting his ass with that little metal scoop, the sweat just rolling off him, while people were standing in line up front trying to buy five-thousand-dollar tractors.'

He gave me some money and I left to get the medicine. There were amber nose deposits on the prescriptions. The old man left a mucous track behind him like a snail. I bought a razor at Mr Wu's grocery but I couldn't find a drugstore that was open so I walked across town to the hospital, another white building. The nurse who ran the dispensary was an Englishwoman. She didn't believe those prescriptions for a minute but she sold me the stuff anyway, some heart medicine called Lanoxin, and some Demerol, which I knew to be dope, and some other things in evil little bottles that I suspected of being dope. It was all for a 'Mr Ralph Moore' and the doctor had signed his own name as the prescribing physician. I explained that he was the son of Mrs Symes at the Unity church. He had also asked me to get him a dozen syringes but the woman wouldn't sell me any. I didn't press the matter. Babies were crying and I wanted to get out of that place.

Near the hospital there was a city park, a long

green field with a statue at one end that looked new and not very important. There was a steel flagpole with no flag. The brass swivel snaps on the rope were jingling against the pole. A woman was sitting tailor-fashion on the grass with a sketch pad. I recognized her as the American girl who had been in the Fort George dining room. The small boy was asleep on a beach towel beside her. I waved. She didn't want to raise her busy hand from the pad but she did nod.

The service was over when I got back to the tabernacle. Mrs Symes and Melba and a chubby Negro girl in a green dress were in the doctor's room drinking iced tea. The girl was helping Mrs Symes stick paper stars in an attendance ledger. There was a Scrabble board on the bed and the doctor and Melba were playing this word game. He said, 'The millionaires in Palm Beach, Florida, are not having any more fun than we are, Melba.' I gave him the sack of drugs and shaving supplies and he left at once for the bathroom. Mrs Symes asked where I had attended church.

'Actually I haven't been yet.'

'Did you sleep late?'

'I've been pretty busy.'

'Our lesson here today was on effectual calling.'

'I see.'

'Do you indeed? Do you even know what effectual calling is?'

'I can't say I do, no, ma'am. I suppose it must

155

be some special religious term. I'm not familiar with it.'

'Elizabeth, can you tell Mr Midge about effectual calling?'

The plump girl said, 'Effectual calling. Effectual calling is the work of God's spirit, whereby, convincing us of our sin and misery, enlightening our minds in the knowledge of Christ, and renewing our wills, He doth persuade and enable us to embrace Jesus Christ freely offered to us in the gospel.'

'That's very good, but what about the benefits? That's what we want to know. What benefits do they that are effectually called partake of in this life?'

The girl had a ready answer for that too. 'They that are effectually called,' she said, 'do in this life partake of justification, adoption, sanctification, and the several benefits which, in this life, do either accompany or flow from them. We gain assurance of God's love, peace of conscience, joy in the Holy Ghost, increase of Grace, and perseverance therein to the end.'

'That's very good, Elizabeth. There are not twenty-five Americans who could answer that question, and we call ourselves a Christian people. Or don't you agree, Mr Midge?'

'It was a hard question.'

'Mr Midge here goes to college and he has a good opinion of himself but he may not be quite as clever as he thinks. It may even be, Elizabeth, that we can teach him a thing or two.'

The girl was pleased with her performance. She had finished her tea and now had her hands arranged in a prim manner on her knees, her small pink fingernails glowing against the green dress.

There was no sign of Webster Spooner. Mrs Symes had not seen him. She said Webster was a good reader and a good speller and a good singer but he wouldn't stay in his seat. The girl Elizabeth said he was a bad boy who always answered '*Yo*' instead of 'Present' when the roll was called.

'I don't think we can call Webster a bad boy, can we?' said Mrs Symes. 'He's not a bad boy like Dwight.'

The girl said, 'No, but Dwight is a very bad boy.'

Mrs Symes asked me what the doctor had been talking about and I said very honestly that we had been discussing her missionary work. I felt like a spy or a talebearer, reporting back and forth on these conversations. She said she knew what Reo thought of her program but what did I think? I said I thought it was a good program.

She said one couldn't judge these things by the conventional standards of worldly success. Noah preached for six hundred years and converted no one outside his immediate household. And Jeremiah, the weeping prophet, he too was widely regarded as a failure. All you could do was your best, according to your lights. She told me that there was no one named Raymond in the Bible and that drunkenness was the big social problem in this country.

Then she talked to me at length about Father Jackie, the Episcopal missionary. He had the only Tarzan film in the country, she said, and he had finally agreed to let her have it for one showing. Father Jackie had a prankish nature that was very tiresome, and the negotiations for the film had been maddening and exhausting – but well worth the effort. The word on Tarzan would spread fast! Father Jackie was busy these days drafting a new catechism for the modern world, and he was composing some new Christmas carols too, and so he had decided to cut back on his movies and his preaching and teaching duties in order to complete these tasks. He was an odd bird, she said, but he had a good heart. His mother was now visiting him here in Belize.

Melba said, 'His mother? I didn't know that. His mother is here?'

'I told you about meeting her in the swap shop.'

'No, you didn't.'

'Yes, I did.'

'You didn't tell me any such thing.'

'You never listen to me when I have some piece of news like that.'

'What does she look like?'

'I don't know what she looks like, Melba. She just looks like all the rest of us.'

'The reason I ask is that I had a vision of an older woman with a white parasol. She was holding it on her shoulder and buying something at the market. Eggs, I think. I saw her just as clearly as I see you now.'

'This woman didn't have a parasol. She wasn't even wearing a hat.'

'Was she a kind of yellowish woman?'

'She *was yellow*, yes.'

'Yellow eyes?'

'I didn't notice her eyes so much but her face was certainly yellow.'

'A yellow face.'

'That's what I said.'

'That's what I said too.'

'You said yellow eyes.'

'At first I just said yellow.'

That ended that. I played Scrabble with Melba. Mrs Symes hugged and kissed the girl Elizabeth, calling her 'baby,' or rather, 'bebby,' and the girl went away. I could hear Dr Symes in the bathroom singing a song called 'My Carolina Sunshine Girl.' He was shaving too, among other things, and he looked much better when he came back. He stood beside his mother for a moment and put his arm around her shoulder.

'How are you feeling this morning, Mama?'

'I never felt better in my life, Reo. Stop asking me that.'

A small framed picture on the wall caught his attention and he went over to examine it. It was a picture of something brown.

'What is this?' he said. 'Is this the Mount of Olives?'

'I don't know what that is,' she said. 'It's been up there for years. We never use this room any more since Melba has been staying in her chair.'

'Who painted this picture? Where did you get it, Mama? I'd like to know how I could get a copy of it.'

'You can have that one if you want it.'

He crawled back into bed and resumed the Scrabble game. 'Where is your puzzle, Melba?' he said. 'Where is that jumbo puzzle I brought you the last time? Did you ever finish it?'

'No, I never did start it, Reo. It looked so hard. I gave it to one of the children.'

'It was a funny picture of dogs wearing suits.'

'Yes, dogs of different breeds smoking pipes and playing some card game.'

'Mama, why don't you show Speed here your hurricane poem. He's a college professor and he knows all about poetry.'

'No, I don't want to get that stuff out right now. I've got it all locked up.'

'What about your stories, Melba? Why don't you show Speed some of your stories?'

'He doesn't want to see those things.'

'Yes, he does too. Don't you, Speed?'

I explained that I was very far from being a college professor and that I never read poems or fictional stories and knew nothing about them. But the doctor kept on with this and Melba brought me her stories. They were in airmail tablets, written in a round script on both sides of the thin paper.

One was about a red-haired beauty from New Orleans who went to New York and got a job as a secretary on the second floor of the Empire State Building. There were mysterious petty thefts in the office and the red-haired girl solved the mystery with her psychic powers. The thief turned out to be the boss himself and the girl lost her job and went back to New Orleans where she got another job that she liked better, although it didn't pay as well.

Melba had broken the transition problem wide open by starting almost every paragraph with 'Moreover.' She freely used 'the former' and 'the latter' and every time I ran into one of them I had to backtrack to see whom she was talking about. She was also fond of 'inasmuch' and 'crestfallen.'

I read another story, an unfinished shocker about a father-and-son rape team who prowled the Laundromats of New Orleans. The leading character was a widow, a mature red-haired woman with nice skin. She had visions of the particular alleys and parts where the rapes were to occur but the police detectives wouldn't listen to her. 'Bunk!' they said. She called them 'the local gendarmes,' and they in turn called all the girls 'tomatoes.'

A pretty good story, I thought, and I told Melba I would like to see the psychic widow show up the detectives and get them all fired or at least reduced in rank. The doctor was going back and forth to the bathroom, taking dope, I knew, and talking all the time. He wouldn't read the stories but he wanted to discuss them with us. He advised Melba to get them copyrighted at once.

'What if some sapsucker broke in here and snatched one of your stories, Melba, and then put his own name on it and sold it to some story magazine for ten thousand dollars? Where would you be then?'

Melba was upset. She asked me how one went about this copyright business and I couldn't tell her because I didn't know. Dr Symes said she would be wiser to keep the stories locked in her drawer instead of showing them to every strange person who came in off the street. He gave no thought to the distress he had caused the old lady and he went on to something else, telling of the many red-haired people he had known in his life. Mrs Symes had known some of the ruddy folk herself and she spoke of their hot tempers and their sensitive skin, but the doctor wasn't interested in her experiences.

'You'll never find a red-headed person in a nuthouse,' he said to me. 'Did you know that?'

'I've never heard that.'

'Go to the biggest nuthouse you want to and if you can find a red-headed nut I'll give you fifty dollars. Wooten told me that years ago and he was right. Wooten was a doctor's doctor. He was the greatest diagnostician of our time, bar none. Surgery was only his hobby. Diagnosis, that's the high art of medicine. It's a genetic thing, you see, with these redheads. They never go crazy. You and I may go crazy tomorrow morning, Speed, but Melba here will never go crazy.'

Melba had been stirring her iced tea violently for about four minutes. She put her face in mine and winked and said, 'I'll bet I know what you like.' From her leering expression I thought she was going to say, 'Nooky,' but she said, 'I'll bet you like cowboy stories.'

The morning wore on and still there was no Webster. I thought of calling the hotel and the cable office but Mrs Symes had no telephone. I kept hanging around, thinking she would surely ask me to stay for lunch. I was weak from my dairy diet. The doctor said he would like some jello and I wondered at his craving for gelatinous food. Mrs Symes said jello was a good idea. I could smell the sea and what I wanted was a plate of fried shrimp and fried potatoes.

But jello it was and by that time the doctor was so full of dope and so addled from the heat that I had to help him to the table. His eyelids were going up and down independently of one another and his red eye was glowing and pulsing. He talked about Louisiana, certain childhood scenes, and how he longed to go back. He said, 'Mama, you're just going to fall in love all over again with Ferriday.' Mrs Symes didn't argue with him, this return to the homeland being clearly out of the question. Then he wanted to move the dining table over by the window where there was more light. She said, 'This table is right where I want it to be, Reo.'

Melba and I filled up on lime jello – transparent,

no bits of fruit in suspension – and peanut-butter cookies with corrugations on top where a fork had been lightly pressed into them. That was our lunch. The doctor talked on and on. He held a spoonful of jello above his bowl but thoughts kept racing into his head and he could never quite get it to his mouth.

'Speed, I want you to do me a favor.'

'All right.'

'I want you to tell Mama and Melba about my bus. They'll get a big kick out of that. Can you describe it for them?'

'It's an old Ford school bus painted white.'

'All white?'

'Totally white.'

'Are you sure about that?'

'Everything was painted white. The windows and the bumpers and the wheels. The grille and all the brightwork too. The propane bottle. It looked like house paint and it was brushed on instead of sprayed.'

'Wasn't there something painted in black on the sides?'

'I forgot about that. "The Dog of the South."'

'The Dog of the South? Do you mean to say that was the name of the bus?'

'Yes.'

'All right then, ladies, there you are. Very fitting, wouldn't you say? No, I take that back. A dog, any dog with a responsible master, is well off compared to me.'

Melba said, 'You shouldn't call yourself a dog, Reo.'

'It's time for plain speaking, Melba. Let's face it, I'm a beggar. I'm old and sick. I have no friends, not one. Rod Garza was the last friend I had on this earth. I have no home. I own no real property. That bus you have just heard described is my entire estate. I haven't been sued in four years – look it up: City of Los Angeles versus Symes, it's still pending for all I know – but if anyone was foolish enough to sue me today, that old bus would be the only thing he could levy against.'

Mrs Symes said, 'Whose fault is it, Reo? Tell me that.'

'It's all mine, Mama, and nobody knows it better than I do. Listen. If I did have a home and in that home one room was set aside as a trophy room – listen to this – the walls of that room would be completely barren of citations and awards and scrolls and citizenship plaques. Can you imagine that? Can you imagine the terrible reproach of those blank walls to a professional man like me? You could hardly blame me if I kept that shameful room closed off and locked. That's what a lifetime of cutting corners has done for me.'

'You had some good friends in Ferriday,' Mrs Symes said. 'Don't tell me you didn't.'

'Not real friends.'

'You went to their barbecues all the time.'

'The kind of people I know now don't have barbecues, Mama. They stand up alone at nights in small rooms and eat cold weenies. My so-called friends are bums. Many of them are nothing but rats. They spread T.B. and use dirty language. Some of them can even move their ears. They're wife-beaters and window peepers and night crawlers and dope fiends. They have running sores on the backs of their hands that never heal. They peer up from cracks in the floor with their small red eyes and watch for chances.'

Melba said, 'That was the road of life you chose, Reo. It was you who sought out those low companions.'

'You're absolutely right, Melba. You've done it again. You've put your finger on it. A fondness for low company. I wasn't born a rat or raised a rat. I don't even have that excuse. I wasn't raised a heathern. My mother and father gave me a loving home. They provided me with a fine medical education at Wooten Institute. I wore good clothes, clean clothes, nice suits from Benny's. I had a massive executive head and million-dollar personality. I was wide awake. I was just as keen as a brier. Mama can tell you how frisky I was.'

She said, 'I was always afraid you would be burned up in a night-club fire, baby.'

The doctor turned on me. 'Listen to me, Speed. A young man should start out in life trying to do the right thing. It's better for your health. It's better in every way. There'll be plenty of time later for you to cut these corners, and better occasions. I wish I had had some older man to grab my shoulder and talk turkey to me when I was your age. I needed a good shaking when my foot slipped that first time, and I didn't get it. Oh, yes. My face is now turned toward that better land, but much too late.'

Mrs Symes said, 'You had a good friend in Natchez named Eddie Carlotti. He had such good manners. He never forgot himself in the presence of ladies like so many of your friends would do. He drove a Packard automobile. It was an open car.'

'A human rat,' said the doctor. 'The world's largest rodent. He's four times the size of that rat Leon used to show. That wop is probably in the Black Hand Society now, shaking down grocery stores. I could tell you a few things about Mr Eddie Carlotti but I won't. It would turn your stomach.'

'What about the Estes boy who was so funny? He always had some new joke or some comical story to tell.'

'Chemical story?' said Melba.

'*Comical* story! He and Reo were inseparable chums at one time.'

'Another rat,' said the doctor. 'And I'm not talking now about brown *norvegicus*, your common rat, I'm talking about *Rattus rattus* himself, all black and spitting. Walker Estes would trip a blind man. The last time I saw him he was stealing Christmas presents out of people's cars and trucks. Working people too. I can tell you who didn't think he was funny. It was that sharecropper's little daughter who cried on Christmas morning because there was no baby doll for her, and no candy or sparklers either.'

Melba said, 'It's amazing what people will do.'

'Listen, Melba. Listen to this. I'd like to share this with you. There used to be a wonderful singer on the radio called T. Texas Tyler. Did you ever hear him?'

'When was he on the radio?'

'He was on late at night and he was just a fine fellow, a tremendous entertainer. He had a wonderful way with a song. He sang some lovely Western ballads. They always introduced him as 'T. Texas Tyler, the man with a million friends.' I used to envy that man, and not just for his beautiful voice. I would think, Now how in the world would they introduce me if I had a singing program on the radio? They couldn't say, 'The singing doctor,' because I was no longer a licensed physician. They wouldn't want to say, 'The man with a few rat friends,' and yet anything else would have been a lie. They wouldn't know what to do. They would just have to point to me and let me start singing when that red light came on. Don't ask me what happened to Tyler, because I don't know. I don't have that information. He may be living in a single-wide trailer somewhere, a forgotten old man. Where are those million friends now? It's a shame how we neglect our poets. It's the shame of our nation. Tyler could sing like a bird and you see what it got him in the end. John Selmer Dix died broke in a railroad hotel in Tulsa. It wasn't a mattress fire either. I don't know who started that talk. Dix had his enemies like anybody else. The lies that have been told about that man! They said his eyes were real close together. A woman in Fort Worth claims she saw him flick cigarette ashes on a sleeping baby in a stroller cart. And Dix didn't even smoke! He published two thin books in forty years and they called him a chatter-box. He had the heart of a lion and yet there are people who believe, even to this day, that he was found cowering in the toilet when they had that big Christmas fight at the Legion hut in Del Rio. Anything to smear his memory! Well, it doesn't matter, his work was done. The New York jumping rats have already begun to tamper with it.'

Mrs Symes said, 'Reo, you were speaking of rats and that made me think of the river rat named Cornell something who used to take you duck hunting. A famous duck-caller. Cornell something-or-other. His last name escapes me.'

'Cornell Tubb, but it's no use going on with this, Mama.'

'I remember his full name now. It was Cornell Tubb. Am I wrong, Melba, in thinking that you have some Tubb connections?'

'My mother was a Tubb.'

'It's no use going on with this, Mama. I tell you I have no friends. Cornell Tubb was never my friend by any stretch of the imagination. The last friend I had on this earth was Rod Garza, and

169

he was completely dismembered in his Pontiac. They put a bum in his car and blew him up.'

'You're not eating. You asked for this jello and now you're just playing with it.'

'I wonder if you would do me a favor, Mama.'

'I will if I can, Reo.'

'I want you to tell Speed here the name of my favorite hymn. He would never guess it in a hundred years.'

'I don't remember what it was.'

'Yes, you do too.'

'No, I don't remember.'

'"Just as I am, without one plea." How I love that old song. And I'll tell you a secret. It means more to me now than it ever did. The theme of that hymn, Speed, is redemption. "Just as I am, though tossed about, with many a conflict, many a doubt." Can you understand the appeal it has for me? Can you see why I always request it, no matter where I am in my travels? I never go to these churches where all their hymns were written in 1956, where they write their own songs, you know. Don't look for me there. I'm not interested in hearing any nine-year-old preachers either.'

Mrs Symes said, 'I'll tell you what I do remember, Reo. I remember you standing up there in the choir in Ferriday in your robe, just baying out, "I'd rather have Jesus than silver or gold!" and all the time you were taking advantage of the deaf people of Concordia Parish. You were taking their money and putting those enormous Filipino

170

hearing aids in their ears that squealed and buzzed when they worked at all, and in some cases, I believe, caused painful electric shock.'

Melba said, 'It's amazing what people will do. Look at the ancient Egyptians. They were the smartest people the world has ever known – we still don't know all their secrets – and yet they worshiped a tumblebug.'

The doctor was still holding the green jello in his spoon, quivering and undelivered. This annoyed Mrs Symes and she took the spoon from him and began to feed him, thus shutting him up.

She and Melba conferred on their plans for the Tarzan showing. Folding chairs would have to be borrowed to accommodate the crowd. Perhaps Father Jackie would lend them his self-threading and noiseless and yet powerful new projector, in which case standby fuses would be needed.

I asked questions about this Father Jackie and learned that he had been a maverick priest in New Orleans. There he had ministered to the waifs who gather about Jackson Square. One night these young drifters surrounded his small Japanese car, shook it for a while, and then turned it over. They dragged him out into the street and beat him and left him bleeding and unconscious. When he had recovered from the assault, his bishop pondered over the problem and then decided that Belize would be a good place for Father Jackie. Mrs Symes objected to his breezy manner and his preposterous doctrines and his theatrical attire, but, deep down, she said, he was a genuine Christian. She was well pleased with her Tarzan deal.

I said, 'Wait a minute. I've heard of this fellow. I've handled news accounts about this man. This is the well-known "Vicar of Basin Street."'

'No, no,' she said. 'This is another one. Father Jackie has a steel plate in his head. He plays the cornet. He's an amateur magician. He claims he has no fear of the Judgment. I don't know anything about the other fellow.'

Dense heat was building up in the house. I helped the doctor back to his bed. Mrs Symes went to her own room to nap. There was a box fan in the central room, where we had eaten, and I lay down on the floor in front of it to rest for a minute or two. I was heavy and sodden with jello.

Watch out for the florr! When I woke up, it was almost 3:30 in the afternoon. What a piddler! Melba was in her chair looking at me. No slumber for Melba. That is, I thought she was looking at me but when I stood up, her dreamy gaze did not move from some point in the void where it was fixed. The temperature was about 97 degrees in that room and she was still wearing her red sweater. It wasn't for me to instruct Melba in her Christian duties but surely she was wrong to be trafficking with these spirits.

CHAPTER 8

The post office itself wasn't open but there was a man on duty in the cable office. He leafed through the incoming messages and found nothing for me. I walked back to the hotel. The young men of Belize were shadowboxing on the streets and throwing mock punches at one another. Webster Spooner was in front of the hotel dancing around the tomato plant and jabbing the air with his tiny fists. He too had attended the matinée showing of the Muhammad Ali fight.

'I'm one bad-ass nigger,' he said to me.

'No, you're not.'

'I'm one bad-ass nigger.'

'No, you're not.'

He was laughing and laying about with his fists. Biff Spooner! Scipio Africanus! I had to wait until his comic frenzy was spent. He had taken care of the map business all right, but instead of bringing the map to me he had fooled around town all morning and then gone to the movie.

I saw that I could count on Webster to do one thing but not two things in immediate succession. On the other hand I didn't have his five dollars,

173

or his Kennedy coin. I did have a little money that I had diverted into my own pocket from the doctor's wad, though not as much as five dollars. Webster shrugged and made no fuss, being accustomed to small daily betrayals.

In the white margin at the top of the map the policeman had written, 'Dupree & Co. Ltd. Bishop Lane. Mile 16.4.' This Bishop Lane was not printed on the map and the policeman had sketched it in, running west and slightly south from Belize. He had marked the Dupree place with a box. Nearby was a Mayan ruin, as I could see from the pyramid symbol. He had marked another place in the south – 'Dupere Livestock' – but the spelling was different and this was clearly an afterthought. In the bottom margin he had signed his name: Sgt. Melchoir Wattli.

So at long last I had found them and now I was ready to make my move. Leet had left another leaflet on the windshield of the Buick and I threw it away. I inspected the hood for cat tracks and I had a look underneath. Then I remembered the roll of quarters and I got it from the glove compartment and gave it to Webster, showing him how to conceal it in his fist. It stuck out from one end and made his fingers bulge in a dead giveaway.

The quarter was not a very interesting coin, I conceded, and I said it was true that Washington, whose stern profile was stamped on it, had a frosty manner, and that he was not a glamorous person. But, I went on, warming to this theme, he was a much greater man than Kennedy. *Gravitas!* The stuffed shirt, the pill – this sort of person had not always been regarded as a comic figure. I had enormous respect for General Washington, as who doesn't, but I also liked the man, believing as I did that we shared many of the same qualities. Perhaps I should say 'some of the same qualities' because in many ways we were not at all alike. He, after all, had read only two books on warfare, Bland's *Exercises* and Sim's *Military Guide*, and I had read a thousand. And of course he was a big man while I am compact of build.

Webster pointed out that Sergeant Wattli had used a pencil instead of a pen so as not to permanently mar the beautiful blue map. I decided that I would make a gift of the map to the officer when I was done with it, though I said nothing to Webster at the time. That was my way. These flashy people who make a show of snatching off a new necktie and presenting it to someone on the spot, to someone who has admired it – that was never my way.

The filthy Buick started on the first shot. Detroit iron! You can't beat it! Bishop Lane began as a city street and then at the edge of town it changed abruptly into two sandy ruts, which comfortably absorbed the tire thump. There were no suburbs, not even a string of shanties. I drove across pine flats and I was much surprised at finding this conifer in the tropics. I had heard or read somewhere that the taproot of a pine tree plunges as deep into the earth as the tree grows tall, the identical length, and I didn't see how this was possible. I thought about the happy and decent life of a forest ranger. A fresh tan uniform every morning and a hearty breakfast and a goodbye peck from Norma at the door of our brown cottage in the woods. It was a field well worth looking into.

The sand changed to black dirt and mud. I drove through shallow creeks and the water splashed up on my feet. I was entering a different kind of forest, dark woods that pressed in and made a leafy tunnel of the road. There were scrub trees and giant trees, nothing in between. The big ones had smooth gray trunks and few branches except at the very top where they spread into canopies. Roots flared out at the base for buttressing support. I watched for parrots and saw none.

I met no traffic and saw no people either until I came to the Mayan ruin. Two Indian men were there working with machetes. They were hacking away at brush and swatting at mosquitoes. Here and there on the ground they had placed buckets of smoldering woody husks that gave off white smoke – homemade mosquito bombs.

It wasn't a spectacular ruin, nothing to gape at, just a small clearing and two grassy mounds that were the eroded remains of pyramids. They were about twenty feet high. On one of them a stone stairway had been exposed, which led up to a small square temple on the top. Farther back in the woods I could see another mound, a higher one, with trees still growing from it. I stopped to inquire about the Dupree place.

The Indians spoke no English and they couldn't seem to understand my scraps of Spanish either but they were delighted to see me. They welcomed the break from their hopeless task. They seemed to think I had come to tour the ruin and so I followed them about. I tried to stand in the white smoke and it kept shifting around, away from me. The Indians laughed at this perverse joke of nature, so often on them but this time on me. We looked into a dark stone chamber. There were shiny crystals on the walls where water had been dripping for centuries. The chamber next to it had a canvas curtain across the doorway and there were bedrolls and a radio inside. These birds lived here!

We climbed the stone steps and looked into the temple. I ran my hand over the carvings. The stone was coarse-grained and badly weathered and I couldn't make out the design but I knew it must be a representation of some toothy demon or some vile lizard god. I had read about these Mayans and their impenetrable glyphs and their corbeled arches and their madness for calculating the passage of time. But no wheel! I won't discuss their permutation calendar, though I could. I gave the Indians a dollar apiece. They asked me for cigarettes and I had none. But that was all right too, I was still a good fellow. They laughed and laughed over their hard luck.

I left with no information about the Dupree place. About two miles farther along I came to a pasture airstrip with a limp windsock, and then a house, an unpainted structure made of broad reddish planks. It stood well off the wet ground so that Webster or Travis might have walked upright beneath it. I would have had to crouch. There was a sorry fence around the house, a sagging wire affair, and a sign, 'KEEP OUT THIS MEANS YOU,' on the makeshift gate. There was a porch with a rope hammock hanging at one end. In a shed next to the house there was a green tractor.

I parked in a turnout across the road from the house. It was a turning-around place and a garbage dump too, with bottles and cans and eggshells and swollen magazines scattered about. I had no way of measuring 16.4 miles but I thought I must be getting close. These people here would surely know something about the Dupree farm, unless Sergeant Wattli had put me altogether wrong. There was a terrible stink in the air and I thought at first it came from the garbage. Then I saw two dead and bloated cows with their legs flung out stiff.

I got out of the car and started across the road and then stopped when a red dog came from beneath the house. Was this Dupree's chow dog? He yawned and stretched one front leg and then the other one. He looked deformed with his coat trimmed, his big square head now out of proportion to his diminished body. A clear plastic bag was tied around each of his feet.

He walked to the gate and looked at me without recognition. After a while he registered me in his dog brain as a negligible presence and then he sat back on his haunches and snapped at mosquitoes. I couldn't believe this was the same dog I had known in Little Rock, the same red beast I had seen springing from cover to nip the ankles of motorcyclists and to send small children into screaming flight down the sidewalk. He had been unmanned perhaps by the long journey and the shearing and the plastic bags on his paws.

The screen door opened and Dupree came out on the porch. He was shirtless, his skin glistening with oil, and he was wearing a tall gray cowboy hat. He had grown a beard. His cowboy boots had pointed toes that curled up like elf shoes. This was a new, Western Dupree. He had a new walk too, a rolling, tough-guy walk. He wasn't wearing his glasses and he squinted at me with one eye. The other one was black and almost closed. His lips were broken and swollen. They had already been at him with their fists here. People's justice! He was holding my .410 shotgun by the barrel in the position that is called 'trail arms' in the drill manuals.

'Popo?' he said.

The weak-eyed monkey couldn't even make out who I was. He didn't even recognize his own car.

I said, 'Well, Dupree, I see you have some little boots on the dog.'

'He doesn't like to get his feet wet. Is that you, Waymon?'

He sometimes called me by this countrified version of 'Raymond,' not in an affectionate way but with malice.

'You have a lot to answer for, Dupree.'

'You'll get your money back. Don't worry about it. Who's with you?'

'Nobody.'

'Who told you where I was?'

'Tell Norma to come on out.'

'She's not here.'

'Then where is she?'

'Gone. Sick. How did you get here anyway?'

'I don't see my Torino.'

'I sold it.'

'Where?'

'Everybody will get their money as soon as I can get a crop out. Don't push me. The best thing you can do is leave me alone.'

'I'm coming into that house.'

'No, you better hold it right there.' He raised the shotgun. I didn't think he would shoot but you never know. Here was an unstable person who had threatened the President. It was a pump gun, an old Model 42, and I wasn't sure he even knew how to work it but I certainly didn't want to be killed with a .410.

'This is not much of a place,' I said. 'I was expecting a big plantation. Where are the people who do the work?'

'They're gone too. The head bozo quit and they all went with him. They tore up the generator and

180

the water pump before they left. They shot some of the cows and ran the others off. About what you could expect. I'm through with those creeps.'

'Tell Norma to come out on the porch for a minute.'

'She's not here.'

'Is she afraid to face me?'

'She's gone, vamoosed.'

'I think she's in there looking out at me from somewhere.'

'There's no one here but me.'

'Does your father know you're here?'

'I'm through with him. His day is over. I'm through with you too. You don't have a clue to what's going on. You never did. Are you driving my Buick Special?'

'Yes.'

'How did it do?'

'It did all right but I'm not here to discuss that.'

'I thought clods like you were always ready to discuss cars.'

'Not this time.'

He went over to the hammock and sat down in it with the gun across his knees. I was standing in the road trying to think of what to do and say. I had started with a great moral advantage but it seemed to be slipping away. Was Norma in that house? I couldn't tell. Dupree was a liar but you couldn't even count on him to lie.

I said, 'What about the woman who lives behind the Game and Fish Building?'

'What about her?'

'Why didn't you bring her with you?'

'Because I didn't want to.'

'Did Norma rub that oil on you?'

'These are my natural body oils. We're short of water. Now leave me alone. Everybody will be paid.'

'I'm not leaving until I talk to Norma.'

'She doesn't want to talk to you. She said she was tired of living with a little old man.'

'She never said that.'

'She said she was tired of looking at your freckled shoulders and your dead hair.'

'Norma never told you that. She doesn't talk that way.'

'She doesn't like your name either.'

I knew this was a lie too. From Edge to Midge was at worst a lateral move – no hybrid vigor to be expected from our union – and Norma was never one to make hateful remarks. Leave him alone! Next to me he was the least importuned person in Little Rock – people fled from rooms at the sound of his voice – and he kept saying leave him alone. I took a couple of steps toward the gate. He raised the shotgun.

'Better hold it right there.'

'Why can't I come in if Norma is not there?'

'Because all my papers and my graphics are on the table. Does that answer your question?'

'What kind of papers? I didn't know you had any papers.'

'There's a lot you don't know.'

'Where did you sell my car? How much did you get for it?'

'Everybody will be paid in time. That's if they stop bothering me.'

'Did you think I would come all the way down here just to listen to a few of your lies and then go home?'

'You'll get your money. And then you'll be happy. It doesn't take much for people like you.'

'What will you do, mail it to me? Should I go home and watch the mail?'

'You'll get it.'

'When?'

'As soon as I can get a crop out.'

'Get a crop out. I'd like to see that. What kind of crop? You don't know the first thing about farming, Dupree. You don't know how to do anything. Look at that fence.'

'You don't have to know much. What you have to know is how to make niggers work. That's the hard part.'

'You say that from your hammock. Do you know Webster Spooner?'

'No.'

'He's the bellboy at my hotel. He has three jobs, if not four. I'll bet you haven't made one friend in this country.'

'You goofball.'

'Put that shotgun down, you coward, and meet me out here in this road like a man and we'll see who the goofball is.'

Instead of making his blood boil, my straight-forward challenge only made him toss his head.

'I'm coming into that house, Dupree.'

'Better not try it.'

'Then I'll have to come back.'

'Better not come at night.'

'I have a .44 magnum out here in the glove compartment. It's as big as a flare pistol. You can fire just four more rounds from it and the next day the arch of your hand is so sore and numb you can't pick up a dime. That may give you some idea of its power and range. I'd rather not have to use it.'

'What crap.'

'I'm going now but I'll be back. Tell Norma I'm staying at the Fair Play Hotel in Belize.'

'She's not interested in your accommodations. And I'm through passing along information from lower-middle-class creeps like you. I never did like doing it. Your time is coming, pal, soon. You better just leave me alone. If you people would leave me alone, maybe I could get some work done on my book.'

'Your book?'

'My book on horde control.'

'I didn't know about this.'

'Shaping up the skraelings. Getting them organized. I'll tell them about rights and grievances they haven't even thought of yet in New York City. It's a breakthrough. Nobody has ever been able to get their attention and hold it for any appreciable length of time. I've hit on a way to do it with low-voltage strobe lights and certain audio-visual techniques that I'm not going into at this time. I couldn't expect you to understand it. My outline is almost complete but now I've lost another day's work, thanks to you.'

Letters weren't enough for him. This monkey was writing a book! I said, 'We are weaker than our fathers, Dupree.'

'What did you say?'

'We don't even look like them. Here we are, almost thirty years old, and neither one of us even has a job. We're worse than the hippies.'

'Leave it to you to come up with some heavy thinking like that. You find me trapped here in this land of niggers with your water-waster wife and you say we are weaker than our fathers. That's just the kind of crap I'm through passing along.'

'I'll be back, Dupree.'

'Why do you keep calling me by my name?'

'How do you wish to be addressed now?'

'You're saying my name too much.'

'I'll be back.'

'Better not come at night.'

'I'm leaving this bottle right here in the road. It's Norma's lower-back medicine. Make sure she gets it before a car runs over it.'

He went into the house. After a moment I saw the weak glow of a candle or an oil lamp from an inner room. I called out for Norma. There was no answer. I knew it was my duty to walk into that

185

yard and up those steps and into that house but I was afraid to do it. I thought of ramming the two front pilings of the house with the Buick, thereby causing the house to topple forward and spilling forth Dupree through a door or window. Nothing to disconcert a proud man like a sudden tumble from his home. But might not Norma be injured too, flung perhaps from a bathtub? The hammock was still moving and I stood there and counted the diminishing oscillations until the thing came to rest at bottom dead center. I would lay Dupree out in that hammock when I had killed him. I would take a stick and pry his teeth apart – they would be clenched in a rictus – and I would place the candle between them. I would leave him in the hammock with the candle burning in his mouth and let the Belize detectives make of it what they would. I poked idly about in the garbage dump with my foot and turned up nothing of any real interest except for a one-gallon pickle jar. I put it in the car and left.

When I drove by the Mayan ruin, the two brush-cutters were taking another break and this time they had cigarettes. They were talking to a third man who was sitting astride a three-wheel motor-cycle rig. Little crosses were painted all over the wooden cargo box and the name 'Popo' was spelled out in red plastic reflectors on the back. There were brownpaper sacks in the cargo box. I waved. Then it came to me. Those were probably Dupree's supplies. I turned around and went back.

The Indians thought I wanted to tour the ruin again and so I did. Popo joined us. He was Spanish. We looked into the stone chambers again. Mosquitoes swarmed in our faces. Popo sat on a scooped-out block of stone that must have been a kind of altar. He smirked and crossed his arms and legs and asked me to take his picture. I didn't think he should behave that way on someone's altar but the Indians themselves found his antics funny and in any case I had no camera. Some gringo. No smokes and no camera and no money!

Popo spoke a little English. He said he had seen no woman at the Dupree place, no other person at all since the workers had left, but he had made only one previous delivery and he had not been inside the house. Dupree would not let him go past the gate. I looked through the paper sacks. I found no Pall Mall cigarettes, Norma's brand, or any other kind, and no single item that might have been for her exclusive use, except possibly for a bottle of hand lotion. But maybe Dupree had now taken up the use of Jergen's lotion. It was hard to say what he might or might not be doing in that house, in his strange new life.

I gave Popo a savings bond and told him that Dupree was flying back to the States in a few hours. An emergency at home. He would no longer need this service. Popo was to keep the food and the beer and the kerosene and the change too, if any. Dupree wanted Popo and his family to have these things.

187

Popo was baffled. What about his glasses? What about the *remedios*, the *drogas*? He showed me Dupree's eyeglasses, wrapped in a repair order, and a big bottle of St Joseph aspirins and a smaller bottle of yellow Valium tablets. I hadn't known that Dupree was a pillhead on top of everything else but I can't say I was surprised.

I said yes, Dupree did want the glasses and the drugs and I would see that he got them. Popo was reluctant to go along with all this and I gave him another E bond. The Indians pressed me again for cigarettes and I gave them each a bond too. I asked Popo about these birds. He said they were brothers. They worked for the government and they had been here for years fighting the brush. They could make the clearing no bigger because the stuff grew up behind them so fast. There was a third brother somewhere around, Popo told me, but he was always hiding in the woods and was seldom seen by outsiders.

I made sure that Popo followed me back to town and I drove slow on the sandy part so as not to dust him up.

CHAPTER 9

The Chinaman's store was still open and I bought some crackers and a thick oval can of Mexican sardines and took them to my room. Karl's radio was playing at moderate volume. I don't think I had even noticed it until I heard the announcer say, 'No more calls, please, we have a winner.' Then Karl switched it off for the first time since my arrival.

Or maybe tube collapse or power failure or a political coup at the station itself. They always went for the radio station in these places. I wondered if they had ever had a really first-class slaughter of students here. Better watch my step. Dupree had better watch his smart mouth too. Name your cat or dog after the Prime Minister in a place like this and you would be in the jug but pronto.

And there would be no fool here to go his bail, if they had bail. His papers! His book! His social program! It was some sort of nasty Communist claptrap, no doubt, with people who sounded a lot like Dupree as the bosses. He would tell us what to do and when to do it. The chairman! He would reward us and punish us. What a fate! Give me Mr Dupree any day. The book would never be finished of course. The great outline of history! His slide shows! His skraelings! Pinch their arms and he could get their attention. But was Norma in that house or not? That was the important thing.

I ate my sardine supper and took a bath. I washed the big pickle jar, along with the top, and put them on the windowsill to dry. Then I called down the stairs for Webster Spooner. He appeared with his notebook, ready for any assignment. I showed him the jar.

'A little surprise for you, Webster.'

'Sor?'

'I thought you might have some use for it. It's clean. You can save pennies in it. Keep a pet fish maybe. You would have to change the water. If you decide on the fish.'

He looked it over but I could see he wasn't interested in it and I suggested he give it to Ruth, who could make some household use of it. He took the jar away and a few minutes later I heard Ruth slam it against something and break it.

I went to bed and reviewed the day's events, a depressing exercise. I had not handled myself so badly, I thought, and yet there were no results. I must do better. Tomorrow I would enter the Dupree house, come what may. I would watch for an opening and then make a dash across the road. What I needed was a timetable of things to do. An orderly schedule. I sat up in bed and ruled off a sheet of paper with evenly spaced lines and corresponding numbers down to sixteen. It was a neat piece of work, the form itself.

But I suddenly despaired of trying to think of that many things to do and of getting them in the proper order. I didn't want to leave any blank spaces and I didn't want to pad it out with dishonest filler items either, like 'tie shoes.' What was wrong with me? I had once been very good at this kind of thing. I crumpled the paper and dropped it on the floor.

The sardine stink filled the room and overwhelmed the river stink. Outside on the street I heard the slow grinding whine of a Mopar starter – a Plymouth or a Dodge or a Chrysler. The engine caught and idled smoothly and after a minute or so the car drove away.

Jack Wilkie, perhaps, in his Imperial. He had finally arrived. He had been outside watching my window. But no, Jack would never lurk. He might break down the door but he wouldn't lurk. That was more in my line. I felt queasy. I took two of the orange pills. I can't say I was really sick, unless you count narcolepsy and mild xenophobia, but I was a little queasy. If there had been a gang of reporters outside clamoring to know my condition, Webster would have had to announce to them that it was satisfactory.

I slept and dreamed fitfully. In one dream I was looking through a Sears catalogue and I came across Mrs Symes and Melba and the doctor modeling lawn furniture. They were wearing their ordinary clothes, unlike the other models, who were in bright summer togs. The other dream took place in a dark bar. The boy Travis was sitting on a stool with his legs dangling. That is, he looked like Travis, only his name seemed to be Chet this time. He was drinking from a tall frosted glass and he was waiting for five o'clock and victims to chirp at. I took a seat at the other end of the bar. He didn't see me for a while and then when he did see me he shifted around and said, 'So how you been, Ray? You never come around anymore.' I said I was all right and I asked about his mother. Chet said she was fine. He offered to buy me a drink and I said I had to go to Texarkana.

I woke early and saw that I had been drooling on the pillow. The ear hair couldn't be far behind now. I washed and dressed and ate the rest of the sardines and drove back to the Dupree place.

The hairy monkey was up early too. I had no sooner parked in the turnout than he came to the door with the .410. He said nothing. I opened all the car doors to catch any breeze that might come up and sat in the driver's seat with my feet outside on the garbage. Dupree went back inside. The medicine bottle full of four-dollar capsules was still standing in the road where I had left it.

Now and then I would get out as though to start across the road and he would instantly appear at the door. He must have been sitting just behind it in the shadow. I called out for Norma. I told her that I had her medicine and her silver and that if she would just come to the fence for a minute I would give it to her. There was no answer.

After the engine had cooled off, I sat on the hood with my heels hooked on the bumper. At the end of each hour, just as the second hand hit twelve, I called out for her. Late in the morning Dupree came out and sat in the hammock with the gun on his lap. He read a magazine, holding it about five inches from his eyes.

He wouldn't answer me when I spoke. His plan, I could see, was to keep silent and not acknowledge my presence, except for the countering moves with the shotgun. When he looked about, he pretended not to see me, in the way of a movie actor whose eyes go professionally blank when tracking across the gaze of the camera. The dog picked up on his mood and he too ignored me. Dupree sat there with his magazine, feigning solitude and peace. He fondled his belly and chest with his fingertips the way some people do when they find themselves in swimming trunks. I got one of the rusty cans of warm beer from the trunk and made a show of opening it and drinking it.

Around noon he stood up and stretched. He strolled out into the yard and peered down the road with his watery eyes. I had been waiting for some such move.

'Popo is not coming today,' I said. 'He's not coming tomorrow either.' I held up his eyeglasses but he wouldn't look at me. 'I have your glasses

193

here, Dupree. They're right here. I have your aspirins and your dope too. Look. Here's what I think of your dope.' I poured the yellow pills out and crushed them into the garbage with my foot. He couldn't see what I was doing and the effect was thus lost.

He made no reply and went over to the green tractor and climbed up on it and tried to start it. It was a diesel and by nature hard to start. Dupree lacked patience. His contempt for machinery was unpleasant to watch. He slammed and wrenched things about. A gentler touch and maybe a shot of ether into the breather and it probably would have cranked right up, but Dupree, the farmer's son, knew little of these matters. When he might have been learning how to start a tractor, he was away at various schools, demonstrating in the streets and acquiring his curious manners and his curious notions. The student prince! He even had a place to run to when things got hot.

He went back to the porch and sat on the hammock. I drank another can of warm beer. He suddenly made up his mind to speak, saying, 'I suppose you've told everybody where I am, Burke.'

'Not yet, no.'

He was calling me Burke! There followed a silent interval of about an hour before he spoke again. He said, 'Those aspirins are for my dog.' I had been quietly thinking over the Burke business and now I had to think about the aspirins and the dog. I should explain that Burke worked on the copy

194

desk with us. It is true that Burke and I were only dimly perceived by the world and that a new acquaintance might have easily gotten us confused, might have hailed Burke on the street as 'Midge,' or introduced me to another person as 'Burke,' but Dupree knew us well from long association, knew the thousand differences between us, and I could only conclude that he was now so far advanced in his political thinking that he could no longer tell one person from another. I should say too that Burke was by far the best copy editor on the desk. Even Dupree was better at the work than I, who have never had a firm grasp of English grammar, as may be seen. The flow of civic events that made up the news in our paper was incomprehensible to me too, but Burke shone in both these areas. He was always fretting over improper usage, over people saying 'hopefully' and 'finalized,' and he talked knowledgeably about things that went on in the world. That's enough on Burke.

I got the St Joseph bottle from my pocket and threw it across to the porch. Dupree picked it up and took it back to the hammock and ate four or five aspirins, making a show of relishing them, as I had done with the beer. He said, 'My dog never took an aspirin in his life.' You couldn't believe a word he said.

That afternoon he tried the tractor again. He got it to chug a few times but the black smoke and the noise of the cold idle knock startled him and he shut it down at once. I stayed there all day. It was a blockade. I was ready to intercept any delivery or visitor, but no one came. There was nothing, it seemed, beyond this place. I watched the windows for Norma, for flitting shadows. I was always good at catching roach movement or mouse movement from the corner of my eye. Small or large, any object in my presence had only to change its position slightly, by no more than a centimeter, and my head would snap about and the thing would be instantly trapped by my gaze. But I saw no sign of life in that house. All this time, of course, I was also watching and waiting for the chance to dash across the road. The circumstances were never quite right and, to put it plainly, I funked it again.

It was still daylight when I got back to Belize and I drove aimlessly about town. Sweat stung my eyes. The heat was such that I couldn't focus my mind. The doctor and Webster Spooner and I had all contrived to get ourselves into the power of women and I could see no clear move for any one of us. It was hard to order my thoughts.

I stopped at the Fort George Hotel for something to drink. The bar was on the second floor and it overlooked a kind of estuary. The water was still and brown and not at all inviting. Out there somewhere, I knew, was a coral reef with clear water and fish of strange shapes and dazzling colors. The bar itself was nice enough. I was up to my old trick of rooming in a cheap place and drinking in a better place. I saw the American woman and the boy sitting on a couch by the windows.

Low tumbling clouds approached from the Caribbean. I drank a bottle of Falcon beer. It had a plain label. There were no boasts about choice hops and the stuff had won no medals at any international exposition but it was cold and tasted like every other beer. Exercise, that was what I needed. That always cleared the brain. I could jog around the entire city and look for my car at the same time. But wouldn't children jeer at me all along such a circuit? Pelting me, perhaps, with bits of filth. And what about the town dogs, all at my heels? It would be much more sensible to install some muscle-building spring devices in the privacy of my room. A stationary bicycle. But Webster would have the devil of a time getting that stuff up the stairs. No, a brisk swim. That would be just the thing. An isolated beach and some vigorous strokes in foamy salt water.

The clouds drew closer and gusts of wind ruffled the surface of the brown water. Drops of rain struck the windows. I left my stool and moved across the room for a better look at things, taking a table next to the American woman. Four pelicans in a column were gliding over the water, almost touching it. Behind them came two more. These two were flapping their heavy wings and they were climbing up to the misty edges of the cloud. A shaft of lightning struck the second bird and he contracted into a ball and fell like a rock. The other one took no notice, missing not a beat with his wings.

I was astonished. I knew I would tell this pelican

story over and over again and that it would be met with widespread disbelief but I thought I might as well get started and so I turned to the woman and the boy and told them what I had seen. I pointed out the floating brown lump.

She said, 'It looks like a piece of wood.'

'That's a dead pelican.'

'I heard the thunder but I didn't see anything.'

'I saw the whole thing.'

'I love storms.'

'I think this is just a convective shower. Afternoon heat.'

This woman or girl was about thirty years old and she was wearing blue jeans and one of those grain-sack shirts from Mexico with the faded printing on it. Her sunglasses were parked high on her head. I asked if I might join her. She was indifferent. She had a hoarse voice and both she and the boy had sunburned faces. Her name, I learned, was Christine Walls. She was an artist from Arizona. She had a load of Arizona art in her van and she and the boy had been wandering about in Mexico and Central America. She extended an index finger across the table, for shaking, it finally dawned on me, and I took it and gave it a tentative shake.

I told her that I had recently dreamed of just such a tableau as this – a woman and a small boy and I seated before a low table. She didn't know what to make of me. First the pelican and now this. The details, I should say, didn't correspond exactly. Christine didn't have nice clothes like those of the woman in the dream and Victor didn't appear to be a little smart-ass like Travis, although he was clunking his heels against the seat in a rhythmic way that I found irritating. Still, the overall picture was close enough. Too close!

She asked my date of birth. We exchanged views on the heat. I remarked on her many sparkling rings and said that my wife Norma was also fond of silver and turquoise. She asked me what the prevailing colors were in Little Rock and I couldn't remember, I who am so good on colors. She said her former husband was a Mama's boy. His name was Dean Walls and he wouldn't make a move without first consulting his mother. He was a creepy spider, she said, who repaired watches in a well-lighted cubicle on the first floor of a large department store. We talked about the many different vocations in life and I had to confess that I had none. The boy Victor was being left out of our conversation and so I asked him if he was enjoying his travels. He didn't answer. I asked him how many states he had been in and he said, 'More than you.' Christine said she planned to return to college one day and study psychology, and that she would eventually make her home in Colorado or San Francisco or maybe Vermont. An earlier plan to marry again had collapsed when her fiancé was killed in a motorcycle accident. His name was Don and he had taught oriental methods of self-defense in a martial arts academy.

'They called it an accident,' she said, 'but I think the government had him killed because he knew too much about flying saucers.'

'What did he know?'

'He knew a lot. He had seen several landings. He was a witness to those landings outside Flagstaff when they were kidnapping dogs.'

'What kind of dogs?'

'What kind of dogs were they, Victor?'

'Collies and other work dogs. The aliens stunned them first with electric sticks.'

'Yes, and Don had seen all that and so the government had to silence him.'

I asked if she and the boy would like to join me in a swim before dark.

'In the pool?'

'No, I'm not a guest here. I was thinking about the beach.'

'I love to walk the beach but I can't swim.'

'How does it happen that you can't swim, Christine?'

'I don't know. Have you been here long?'

'Just a few days.'

'How was your trip down?'

'It was a nightmare.'

'A nightmare. I love that. Have you had much trouble with the money?'

'No, I haven't exchanged any yet.'

The boy Victor clapped one hand to his forehead and fell back against the seat and said, 'Oh brother, is he in for it!'

Christine said, 'You're not just a-woofin', buddy boy. This money is really something else. They call it a dollar but it's not the same value as ours. It's worth some odd fraction like sixty-eight cents. Even Victor can't get it straight. Hey, Ray, I want to ask you a question before I forget it. Why are there so darned many hardware stores in Belize?'

'Are there a lot? I hadn't noticed that.'

'I've seen two already.' She touched my arm and lowered her voice. 'Don't stare but wait a second and then look at that fantastic girl.'

'Where?'

'That black waitress. The way she holds her head. See. Her regal bearing.'

Two hardware stores didn't seem like a lot to me. This was Staci talk. Nerve gas. I would have to stay on my toes to follow this stuff. She suddenly went into a contortion, trying to scratch a place on her back that was hard to reach. She laughed and twisted and said, 'What I need is a back scratcher.'

I thought she meant just that, a long bronze rod with little claws at one end, and maybe she did, but then I saw what a good chance I had missed for an initial intimacy, always so awkward. The moment had passed, needless to say, the itching abated, by the time I had worked it all out.

Christine wasn't a guest at the Fort George either. She was looking for a place to take a bath. She had tried to rent a room with bath for an hour or so instead of an entire day but the Fort

George didn't offer that plan and neither did it accept works of art in payment. I volunteered the use of the communal bath at the Fair Play. She quickly accepted and began to get her things together.

Then I thought about trying to get her past Ruth without paying. I wasn't in the mood for any hotel comedy. I had spoken too soon. The towels were never quite dry at the Fair Play. The bathroom was a foul chamber too, and the door wouldn't lock, the knobs and the brass mechanism being completely gone, the wood all splintered around the hole, where some raging guest had forced an entry or an exit. I knew what would happen. This boy Vic would say, 'P.U., Mom!' and make me look bad. So I took them instead to the Unity Tabernacle. They followed me in the van. It was a Volkswagen and it made a four-cylinder micro-clatter. There were decals of leaping green fish and bounding brown deer on both sides of the vehicle, a sporting touch I would not have associated with Christine and Victor – or with Dean, for that matter.

CHAPTER 10

Mrs Symes was in front of the church. She was wearing a man's felt hat and she was talking to a gang of boys who were milling about, waiting to see Tarzan. She was upset because Father Jackie had not yet delivered the film for the big showing.

This Christine distraction annoyed her further but she told me to take the girl in and show her the bath. I expected no less, even though I knew that Mrs Symes's tangled creed must be based more or less on faith rather than works. The doctor himself had told me that she had fed more tramps during the Depression than any other person in Louisiana.

Christine decided to do her laundry too, and I helped her carry it up the stairs, sacks of the stuff. There is always more to these pickup deals than first meets the eye. She proceeded to steam up the place. First she scrubbed Victor down and then she washed her Arizona clothes in the bathtub and hung them about inside on tables and lamps and other fixtures.

Melba didn't like this intrusion. She sat in her

chair sulking and chewing on something brittle, or munching rather. Dr Symes, hearing the stir, peered out from his bedroom. He saw me and he waved a sheet of paper and he came over to join me on the couch.

'Good news, Speed,' he said. 'Hold on to your hat. Mama has agreed to write a letter for me.'

'What kind of letter has she agreed to write?'

'A wonderful letter of authorization. It's a new day.'

She still refused to lease him the island but he had persuaded her to let him use the island in some ill-defined way. Or so he said. In fact, Mrs Symes had written nothing. The doctor had written a legal-sounding statement on a sheet of Melba's crinkly airmail paper that gave him the right 'to dig holes and erect fences and make such other improvements on Jean's Island as he may deem necessary or desirable.' It only remained, he said, to get the old lady's signature, and a notary public to witness it and to squeeze the paper with his pliers-like seal.

Notarized or not, the letter didn't impress me much. 'What about your financing?' I said. 'The banks will want more than this.'

'What do you know about it?'

'My father is in the construction business.'

He read through the statement. 'This would be enough for me. What more could they want?'

'They want to see a lease or a land contract.

204

They want something that will hold up. Your letter doesn't even describe the property.'

'It says Jean's Island plain enough.'

'Maybe there's another Jean's Island. They want metes and bounds.'

'I don't believe you know what you're talking about.'

'Maybe not.'

'I've never believed it. I don't believe you know your ass from first base. I was closing deals before you were born. Mama owns the land outright and that makes her the principal. This letter makes me her agent. Will you sit there and tell me that the law of agency has been repealed?'

What he was groping for, I thought, was a letter giving him power of attorney but I didn't want to go on with this and antagonize him further. For all my big talk of finance, it was I who needed a loan, and a quick one. The doctor went to his bedroom and brought back the big pasteboard box. He pawed angrily through the stuff. 'I'll give you metes and bounds,' he said. 'I'll give you section, township, and range.'

The plan I had hatched while reclining on the couch was to take Christine to the Fort George for a seafood supper, leaving Victor here at the movie. It was an improper sort of business for a married man who was not legally separated but the idea wouldn't go away. An alternative plan was to get supper here at the church and then take Christine out for drinks alone, which would be much cheaper, unless she went in for expensive novelty drinks. I couldn't tell from the feel of things whether they had eaten supper here yet or not.

I asked the doctor cold if he could let me have another twenty dollars.

Instead of answering my question, he showed me a photograph of his father, the squeamish Otho. It was a brown print on crumbling cardboard. Then he showed me a picture of an intense yokel with a thick shock of hair parted in the middle. The boy was wearing a white medical smock and he was sitting behind a microscope, one hand holding a glass slide and the other poised to make a focal adjustment. It was Dr Symes himself as a student at Wooten Institute. Young microbe hunter! The microscope had no solid look of machined steel about it, no heaviness, and my guess was that it was a dummy, a photographer's prop.

There were more photographs, of Marvel Clark with Ivo and without Ivo, of an adult Ivo standing by his roofing truck and his hot-tar trailer, of houses, cars, fish, of people on porches, in uniform, of a grim blockhouse medical clinic, of people at a restaurant table, their eyes dazzled by a flash bulb like movie stars caught at play. He showed me a pic-ture of the Wooten Panthers, a scraggly six-man football team. A medical school with a football team! Who did they play?

The coach was Dr Wooten himself, and Dr Symes, with his bulk, played center. But there seemed to be no picture of the island, the only thing I was curious about.

Suddenly the doctor gave a start and a little yelp of discovery. 'Another one! I missed this booger!' It was a window envelope that had not been opened. He wasted no time in ripping the end off and shaking out a check. It was a monthly insurance check for $215 made out to Mrs Symes. It was almost a year old. 'Some of them go back eight and nine years,' he said, folding it and sticking it in his shirt pocket. 'This makes thirty some-odd I've found so far.'

'Why doesn't she cash them?'

'She cashes some and she forgets some. People like Mama, they don't care whether an insurance company can balance its books or not. They never think about things like that. The Aetna books mean less than nothing to her.'

'What will you do with them?'

'What do you think?'

'Your mother will have to endorse them.'

'They'll be well endorsed, don't worry about it. That's no step for a stepper. And Mama will get it all back a thousand-fold. This is just seed money for the first drilling rig. This is just peanuts. I'm talking big bucks.' He looked about for eavesdroppers and then lowered his voice. 'There's a billion cubic feet of natural gas under that island, Speed. I plan to have two producing wells down by the first of the year. Do you think that's an unrealistic goal?'

'I don't know. What about The City of Life?'

'The what?'

'The nursing home. The long yellow house.'

Waves of confusion passed across his face. 'Nursing home?'

'On Jean's Island. The City of Life.'

Then he was able to remember, but just barely, and he dismissed it out of hand as though it had been an idea of mine. He resumed his search through the big box and he sang softly the words of 'Mockingbird Hill.' He passed along odd items of interest to me. I looked at an old diary that Mrs Symes had kept. It wasn't a very satisfactory one, in that there were only a dozen or so brief entries in it covering a period of five years. The last one had been made on a September day in 1958. 'Dry summer,' she had written. 'Mangoes bitter this year. God's plan unfolding very slowly.' I repeated my request to the doctor for a loan and got no answer.

He was studying a brittle newspaper clipping. 'I wish you would look at this,' he said. 'I don't know why in the world Mama keeps all this stuff.'

It was an editorial cartoon of a fat man with buttons popping from his shirt. With one hand the chubby figure was clutching a wedge of pie and with the other he was holding out a Band-Aid and saying, 'Here, apply this!' to an injured man with his tongue lolling and tire tracks across his head and x's for eyes. The caption underneath said, 'Our own Doc Symes.'

'What's that about the pie?'

'Newspaper humor. Those boys love to dish it out but did you ever see one who could take it like a man? I weighed about two hundred and ninety-five then. I had to special-order all my suits from Benny's in New Orleans. Fifty-four shorts. I'm just a shadow of that man. The Shreveport *Times* put dark glasses and a fez on me and called me Farouk. This was the original frame-up. I was suspended for six months. They accused me of practicing homeopathy, of all things. Can you imagine that?'

'I've heard of homeopathy but I don't know what it is.'

'The hair of the dog. There's a little something to it but not much. There's a little truth in everything. I never practiced it but any stick was good enough to beat a dog like me. Can you see what I'm driving at?'

'Was this the hearing-aid deal?'

'No connection whatsoever. This was my arthritis clinic. The Brewster Method. Massive doses of gold salts and nuxated zinc followed by thirty push-ups and a twelve-minute nap. None of your thermo tubs or hydro baloney. You don't hear much about it anymore but for my money it's never been discredited. I saw marked improvement in those who could actually raise themselves from the floor. The older people found it painful, naturally, but that was the humidity as much as anything. I was to blame for the atmospheric conditions too, you see. Granted, the humidity is around a hundred percent in Ferriday, but everybody can't go to Tucson, can they?

'I worked day and night trying to help those people, trying to give them some relief. I never made so much money in my life and the doctors' gang couldn't stand it. My prosperity just stuck in their craw. 'Get Symes!' they cried, and 'Bust Symes!' and 'Kick him where it hurts!' That was all they could think about for two years. Well, here I am. You will judge of their success. I haven't been a newsmaker for years.'

'I don't see how the homeopathy ties in.'

'It doesn't tie in. Brewster had once been a homeopath, that's all. He later became a naturo-path. So what? He had one or two good ideas. I'll look you square in the eye, Speed, and tell you that I have never practiced anything but orthodox medicine. This was a setup, pure and simple. They were lying in wait. It wasn't my medicine that stirred those boys up, it was my accounts receivable. You can bank on it, that's the only reason any doctor ever turns another one in.'

Christine was bustling about in white shorts and a pale blue work shirt that was knotted in front so as to expose her red abdomen. I could tell she was older than Norma from the fatty dimpling on the backs of her thighs. It was like the patterns

210

you sometimes see in blown sand. She had washed her hair, and her ears stuck through the wet brown strands. I found her very attractive with her sunburn and her hoarse voice and her brisk manner. She was making friends with Melba and I liked that too, a young person deferring and giving her time to an older person. She was showing Melba something, a book or a purse or a stamp album. The old lady had been out of sorts and now she was jiggling her leg up and down, making the floor shake again. Christine was charming Melba!

'A patient named J. D. Brimlett developed osteo-myelitis,' said the doctor. 'That was the claim anyway. I'm convinced he already had it. He had everything else. Emphysema, glaucoma, no adrenal function, you name it. Two little hard dark lungs like a pair of desiccated prunes. He belonged in a carnival instead of an arthritis clinic. The world's sickest living man. No blood pressure to speak of and you couldn't find a vein to save your ass. Renal failure on top of everything else. The Mayo brothers couldn't have pulled that chump through, but no, it was my zinc that killed him. A Class B irritant poison, they said. I should have screened him out. I should have closed my eyes and ears to his suffering and sent him on his way. I didn't do it and I've been paying for that mistake ever since. There's always a son of a bitch like Brimlett hanging around, doing anything to get attention, dying even, and just ruining things for everybody else. Do you want it in a nutshell? I was weak. I was soft.'

He raised a hand to repel shouts of protest and then went on, 'It wasn't the zinc and they knew it. I took a five-pound bag of the stuff to my hearing and offered to eat it all right there with a spoon but they wouldn't let me do it. Brewster himself admitted that it would give the skin a greenish tint. There was never any secret about that. You get a trivial cosmetic problem in exchange for relief from agonizing pain. Many people considered it a bargain. Talcum powder is cheap enough. It's true, in a very few cases the eyebrows fell out but I've seen cortisone do far worse things. Can you see it now? Do you see what I'm driving at? It was all a smoke screen. The point is, you can't cross the doctors' union. Cross those boys and they'll hand you your lunch. Forget the merits of your case. They kicked Pasteur in the ass. Lister too, and Smitty Wooten. They know everything and Symes is an old clap doctor.'

Outside it was dark. I excused myself and went downstairs to get the chest of silverware from the car. When I opened the church door, the milling boys fell back and looked at me in silent terror, fearing another announcement about the movie being delayed. I made my way through them and I saw that Leet or one of his tireless runners had put another leaflet under a windshield wiper.

The silver chest had been knocked around in the trunk. It was greasy and scuffed and the leatheroid skin was peeling and bubbling up in places from glue breakdown. I put the chest under my arm and slammed the trunk lid. I thought I heard someone call my name. I couldn't place the voice, though it was familiar in some way.

I said, 'What?'

'This way.'

'Where?'

'Over here, Ray.'

'Where? Who wants to see me?'

One of the older boys with a cigar said, 'Nobody want to see you, mon. The peoples want to see Tarzan.' A good laugh all around at my expense.

The forks and spoons and knives were jumbled about in the chest and I stopped on the stairs to sort them out and stack them in their proper notches and hollows before making my presentation to the doctor. He said nothing when I set it on his lap and opened it, Mrs Edge's shining array of cutlery under his red eye. I told him that I needed some more money at once and that if I had not settled the entire debt by noon tomorrow the silver service was his to keep. It was all too fast for him, my proposition and the heavy thing on his knees. I said nothing more and waited for him to take it in.

Victor had settled in at my old spot in front of the fan. His mother had spread out the beach towel for him. One side of the towel was a Confederate flag and on the other side there was a kneeling cowgirl in a bikini. Her body was sectioned off and labeled 'Round,' 'Chuck,' 'Rump,' and so on, like a side of beef, and the Western cutie was winking and saying, 'What's your cut?' Victor was belly down on the towel reading a Little Lulu comic book. The book was in Spanish but he was still getting a few chuckles from it. 'Hoo,' he would say, and, 'Hoo hoo.' There might have been a dove in the room. Dr Symes looked about for the source of these murmurs.

I said, 'That's sterling silver. It's a complete set. All I want is fifty dollars on it until tomorrow.'

'Certainly not. Why would I want to tie up my money in spoons? You'd do better to take this to a pawnbroker or a chili joint.'

'It's just until noon tomorrow.'

'Bill me later. That's your answer for everything. It's no good, Speed. You'll never get anywhere living on short-term credit like this. It's a bad game and I just can't keep carrying you. Who is that little chap on the floor?'

'He's the son of that girl in the bathroom.'

'The one who's washing all the clothes?'

'Yes.'

'Now who is she?'

I tried to tell him but as he was swinging his big head around Melba swam into his ken and he forgot Christine. He called out, 'Melba, can you hear me?'

'I heard that,' she said. 'I haven't been listening to you, if that's what you mean.'

'I want you to get up out of that chair this very minute.'

'What for?'

'I want you to get up out of that chair and start walking two miles every day.'

'No, Reo.'

'Now isn't this a fine thing. She says no to her doctor.'

He closed the chest and moved it to one side, away from me, in a proprietary way. I didn't think we had made a deal and I knew I had no money. Mrs Symes had just made the painful trip up the stairs and she was standing at the top gasping for breath, trying to remember something, what the trip was for. She gave it up as a bad job and went back down the stairs.

The doctor handed me another envelope from the box. 'Take a gander at that one, will you? Never opened. I wrote that letter to Mama from San Diego almost three years ago. How in the world can you do business with someone like that?'

'This letter was postmarked in Mexico.'

'Old Mexico? Let me see. Yes, it sure was. Tijuana. I was going back and forth to the Caliente track. Notice the thick enclosure. Rod Garza had drawn up a prospectus for me. I wanted Mama to look it over and see if she wouldn't co-sign a note. I wrote this very letter in Rod's law office.'

I pointed out that my previous loans were already secured by the bonds, that I had returned his wallet when he thought it was lost, and that this silver set was worth several hundred dollars. He appeared to consider the points and I thought he might even be wavering, but his thoughts were many miles to the northwest.

'Rod had been reprimanded twice by the Ethics Committee of the Tijuana Bar Association,' he said, 'but he could always work himself out of a corner. All except for that last one. You can't talk your way out of an exploding car, there's not enough time. And they knew he was no leaper. Oh, they had cased him, all right. They knew just how quick he was off the mark. He's gone now and I miss him more every day. Strawberries! Can you imagine that? We were trying to raise straw-berries on government land. Rod got some boys out of prison to do the work, if you could call it work. As fast as you got one of those pickpockets on his feet, the one behind you would be squat-ting down again. And hot? You think this is hot? Those pimps were dropping in their tracks. Rodrigo would park his black Pontiac out there in the desert and then roll the windows up to keep the dust out. When we got back to it, the seat covers would be melting. Open the door and the heat blast would make you faint. An inferno. You could have roasted a duck in the trunk. Precious memo-ries, how they linger. Listen to me, Speed. If your time is worth more than twenty cents an hour, don't ever fool with strawberries. I helped Rod every way I knew how. We were just like David and Jonathan. When he was trying to get his patent, I took him up to Long Beach and introduced him to a good lawyer name of Welch. Rod had an interest in a denture factory in Tijuana and he was trying to get a U.S. patent on their El Tigre model. They were wonderful teeth. They had two extra canines and two extra incisors of tungsten steel. Slap a set of those Tiger plates in your mouth and you can throw your oatmeal out the window. You could shred an elk steak with those boogers. Did I say Everett Welch? I meant Billy. Billy is the lawyer. He's the young one. I had known his father, Everett, you see, back in Texas when he was a scout there for the Cubs or the White Sox, one of the Chicago teams. He was a great big fine-looking man. He later went to Nevada and became minister of music at the Las Vegas Church of God, introduced tight harmony to those saps out there. He sold water to Jews. Jews are smart but you can put water in a bottle and they'll buy it. He had a high clear voice and when he sang ''Tis so sweet to be remembered on a bright or cloudy day,' you could close your eyes and swear you were listening to Bill Monroe himself. And get this. He's the only man I ever knew who saw Dix in the flesh. He met him once in the public library in Odessa, Texas. Listen to this. Dix was sitting at a table reading a newspaper on a stick and Welch recognized him from a magazine picture. It was right after that big article on Dix, right around the time of that famous June 1952 issue of *Motel Life* with the big spread on Dix, pictures of his trunk and his slippers and his mechanical pencil and some of his favorite motel rooms. The whole issue was devoted to Dix.

There was a wide red band across the cover that said, 'John Selmer Dix: Genius or Madman?' I didn't have enough sense to stash away a copy of that magazine. I could name my own price for it today. That's the only place where Dix's Fort Worth address was ever published in full.'

This was not, as I first thought, a speech or a proclamation that Dix had made in Fort Worth, but rather a post office box number and a zip code.

Dr Symes continued, 'This was during the period, you may remember, when Dix was on strike. He had repudiated all his early stuff, said *Wings* was nothing but trash, and didn't write another line, they say, for twelve years. Nobody really knows why. Oh, there were plenty of theories – that he was drunk, that he was crazy, that he was sick, that he was struck dumb before the immensity of his task, that he was just pissed off about something – but nobody really knows. Do you want my thinking on it? I believe he was actually writing all that time, that he was filling up thousands of sheets of paper with his thoughts and then just squirreling the stuff away in his tin trunk. But for some reason that we can't understand yet he wanted to hold it all back from the reading public, let them squeal how they may. Here's my opinion. Find the missing trunk and you've found the key to his so-called silent years. You've found a gold mine is what you've found.

'Anyway, Welch tried to talk to him there in the Odessa library, whisper to him, you know, across the table, but Dix wouldn't say anything. He wouldn't even admit he was Dix. He wanted to read his paper and every time Welch asked him a question Dix would just drum his feet under the table real fast, to show he was annoyed. Welch handled it all wrong. He got mad and grabbed the man by the throat and made him confess he was John Selmer Dix. Then Welch cooled off and apologized and Dix said that was all right but not to ever disturb him again while he was reading the *Star-Telegram*, that his private life was his own and all that. Now the question is, was that stranger really Dix? If it *was* Dix, answer me this. *Where were all his keys?* Everett Welch admitted to me that he saw no jumbo key ring on the man's belt and that he heard no clinking of keys when he was shaking him. Even so, Welch swears it was Dix he talked to that day. Welch is an honest man but I wasn't there and I can't say. I just don't know. The man may have been a very clever faker. There were plenty of fakers going around then, and they're still going around. You've probably heard of the fellow out in Barstow who claims to this day that he is Dix. I've never believed it. He lives out there in the desert in a caboose with his daughter and sells rocks. Can you beat it? Dix in the desert with his delicate skin. Selling ornamental quartz out of an old Southern Pacific caboose. If you believe that, you'll believe anything.

219

Do you know what he says? He says the man who died in Tulsa was just some old retired fart from the oil fields who was trading off a similar name. He makes a lot of the closed coffin and the hasty funeral in Ardmore. He makes a lot of the missing trunk. Good points, you might think, but I've got a trump for him. *Dix never had a daughter*! There's another faker, in Florida, who claims he is Dix's half brother. Go see him out there on the edge of Jacksonville and he'll let you look at the trunk for a fee. A trunk is more like it. He won't dare to open it and you have to stand back about four or five feet behind a rope to even look at it. That little room is dark too, they say. Let me save you a trip to Florida, Speed. I've seen that crook's picture. They ran a picture of him and his little Dix museum in *Trailer Review* and I can tell you he bears no resemblance whatsoever to Dix and is in no way related to him. You can look at a man's ears and tell.'

Here the doctor paused, having found the title abstract. He thumbed quickly through the pages until he came to the legal description of the island property. He showed me the authoritative figures, taking delight in the fractions and the 'SW' and 'NE,' and then he left for his room to draft another letter.

I was desperate and shameless and I asked Melba if she could lend me ten dollars. She was willing enough but she couldn't help me because she had cashed a check for Christine and had only a dollar or two left in her purse. She showed me the yellow check. It had been folded so long the creases were fuzzy. It was a two-party check on a bank in Mesa, Arizona. There was nothing left to do but go and see Leet.

CHAPTER 11

All that was left of the old ink factory was a tall brick chimney, round and tapering, of the kind that often marks the site of a small college or government hospital. Leet's Motor Ranch, a lesser dream, was a field of weeds that adjoined the factory grounds. It appeared to be more of a salvage yard than a used-car lot, more of a cemetery than a ranch. Two old industrial boilers from the ink factory were standing upright at the entrance to Leet's drive, forming a kind of grand portal. I say 'from the ink factory' but that is only a guess because I know next to nothing about the manufacture of ink, whether it is ever boiled or subjected to bursts of steam at any stage, and these boilers may have had an entirely different origin.

I passed between them and drove down the lane and parked in front of Leet's headquarters shed, which was also his dwelling place. It was lighted in front by a yellow bulb. Behind the shed there were three columns of derelict cars, their hoods and trunk lids raised as though for a military inspection. I could hear the steady hum of insects or of advancing rust in the damp field. The only operable

222

vehicle I could see, the only one on wheels, was a Dodge Power Wagon with a winch and a wrecker boom on the back.

Leet was sitting under the yellow light on a disembodied car seat. He had put his picture book aside and he was listening to organ music that came from two disembodied car speakers. They were connected to a disembodied cassette player which was in turn hooked up to a disembodied car battery with two alligator clips. He was pink instead of white and he had the fat pink hands of a child, little star-shaped hands, remarkably clean for his trade. They were clasped across his belly and he was stretched out with his ankles crossed.

I knew he had just polished off a big bowl of porridge or parsnips or some such dish, I having spotted him at once for a house pig like me who cherished his room and his kitchen treats and other solo and in-house indulgences. Beside him on top of a wooden ammunition box I saw a giant English chocolate bar, about ten inches by four inches by one inch, a stack of car magazines, and a three-gallon water cooler with a tin cup chained to it. Everything was within easy reach of the pink hands.

He didn't rise to greet me. He put on a pair of round glasses and said, 'That looks like an old V-6 Buick.'

'That's what it is.'

'Dual-path transmission?'

'It's air-cooled. I don't know the name of it.'

223

'Noisy timing chain?'

'It's a good car.'

'No doubt, but it has a very rum transmission. Once it goes, that's it. You can't find spares.'

'That should make it all the more valuable.'

'In what way?'

'This car could be a ready source of those hard-to-get spares, as you call them.'

'There's no market, my friend. The demand is zero. Do please give me credit for knowing my own business.'

'I may sell the car if I can get my price.'

'Not to me you won't.'

I confronted him with one of his leaflets. 'You said you wanted this car.'

'No, I don't want that one. What's the true mileage?'

'I don't know. It's a good car. I made it down here all right. That's something, isn't it?'

'Yes, I'll give you that.'

He took a flashlight and raised the hood. 'What's all that wire around the manifold?'

'Coat-hanger wire. Engine restraint. Broken motor mount.'

'Roadside repair?'

'Yes.'

'That's interesting.' He pulled the dipstick from the transmission and smelled the end of it. Then he started the engine and listened to it through a wooden yardstick, his ear at one end of the stick and the engine block at the other. Then he took a rubber mallet and went around tapping on the body panels. I drank a cup of his cold water.

'Mind the bees,' he said. 'They can smell fear.'

There were white beehives in the shadows beside the shed. Striped bees that looked heavy were going about their deliberate business. I had never known they worked at night. Behind the hives I saw a Ford hulk. It was a longhooded Torino covered with dried gray mud. The wheels were gone and it was resting flat on the ground amid some coarse flowers.

Leet completed the inspection and returned to his seat, slapping his palm with the yardstick. 'You've got bad rust, my friend. I happen to know something about oxidation and what you've got is out of control.'

'Where did you get that Torino? That's the first one I've seen down here.'

'You don't see many. These niggers like the full-size models. Galaxies and Impalas.'

'I have one like that, only mine is blue.'

'That one's blue. Fellow burnt up the engine idling it. I hauled it in for a hundred dollars American and sold the air conditioner the same day for two hundred. I got another hundred for the radio and tape deck, and I got eighty for the tires and the baby moon hubcaps. Everything went but the sheet metal, and went fast too. I wish I had another one.'

'How did he burn it up idling it?'

'He was idling it at about fifty-two hundred

rpm's. Fell asleep with his foot on the accelerator. Drunk, I suppose, or a nut case. Just sat there dozing away with the engine screaming until the pistons seized. Beautiful 351 Windsor engine. Clean carburetor, clean battery terminals. Clean valve covers until the paint was cooked. No mess or oil seepage. No corrosion. The car had been well cared for.'

'That's a shame.'

'Yes, it's a great pity. Nice windfall for me, of course.'

I already knew the truth but I moved in for a closer look and I saw my Arkansas inspection sticker in the corner of the windshield. This muddy shell was my Torino. I wiped off some of the mud with my hand.

Leet said, 'I can give you two hundred for the little Buick. I pay the duty. It's an orphan, as I say, and you won't do any better than that.'

'You've already bought my car, Leet. This Torino is my car. I have the title to it.'

'Really?'

'Yes.'

'It's a bit late to be speaking up.'

'Dupree had no right to sell it.'

'He had the car.'

'Are you going to make it good?'

'Say again?'

'I say, are you going to make it good?'

'Do you mean am I going to reconstruct that car for you? Nothing of the kind. What a hope.'

'I mean compensation.'

'It's not on, my friend. I bought it in good faith.'

'I don't believe you did. You said yourself it was a wind-fall. You spoke of Dupree as a nut case.'

Leet flexed his shrimplike fingers. 'I would hardly make those admissions again, would I? To a third party.'

'Dupree had no papers. You bought it without a title.'

'Listen to our little lawyer.'

'I'll have to see about this in town.'

'See about it all you please. Your word against his. It's nothing to do with me.'

'It's more than my word. I have the papers.'

'All right, here's some law for you, chum. The car was licensed in Arkansas and the boy had an Arkansas driving license. He had possession of the car. It was not for me to assume he was a thief. I would have been wrong to do so. That's nothing more nor less than good English law.'

'Is it English equity?'

'Say again?'

'Equity. Fair play, like the hotel.'

'Equity's grandmother. You can't put it all on me. You have a duty to look after your own stuff.'

'That's just what I'm doing, I'll have to see about this.'

'I thought the car was his to sell. I bought it. That's it. Bob's your uncle. Now you come along and say it's your car. Very well, I pay you too. Now tomorrow a third man comes to the Motor Ranch and makes a similar claim. Do I pay him, and the fourth and fifth man as well? How long could I stay in business, paying for the same car day after day? Not six years.'

'Your third man wouldn't have the papers.'

'You and your bleeding papers.'

As a sign that our business was concluded, he picked up his book, *Flags of the World*, and found his place, Morocco and Mozambique, and fell into a deep study of these banners. It was an English or European book from the looks of the murky colors, or maybe it was the yellow light that made them appear so. I had a fellow-pig feeling for him, and I had the feeling too that he was the last of the Leets, that the House of Leet was winding up here in this tropical junkyard.

I said, 'To tell the truth, Leet, I don't care about that car. It's not even mine. My father paid for it like everything else I have. I hate to find it here like this but my quarrel is not with you. I see that now.'

These friendly words dispelled the chill somewhat.

He said, 'The boy was odd and I suspected something. I'll give you that.'

'He has a lot to answer for.'

'I knew it was a funny business, I can't say I didn't. But then you get a lot of funny business in this place.'

'It wasn't the car at all. I see that now.'

'I knew he was a lunatic when I played this. Give

a listen. I found this tape under the seat. You'll think it's a comedy recording like I did. I don't know what it is, a dramatic reading or some loony recitation.'

He put the cassette into the tape player and the voice of Dr Buddy Casey rang out across the dark field.

'"Can you help us, Captain Donahue?" he cried. "Yes, Major," came the stout reply, "my men are fresh and they are just the fellows for that work!"'

Leet laughed. I snatched the tape from the machine. 'That's mine too, Leet.' The sudden noise had made the insects stop their racket for a moment but they were soon at it again.

I drove away in the Buick, not deigning to sell it, and I put the whole thing out of my mind, as though Leet had never been cast upon this shore with his fat fingers. I thought instead of Christine and her wet hair. I speculated on squeezing her, and more, being married to her, our life together in Vermont. She was a very good-natured girl. Resourceful too. Would she have to go to the doctor a lot? They all seemed to collapse right after the vows, even the robust ones like Christine. Female disorders. There are one or two points on female plumbing that I have never been clear on. And yet there was Mrs Symes, in the pink for her age, and Otho in his grave these many years. But what would Christine and I talk about on long drives, or even on short ones? And what about Victor? Turn him over to Dean maybe. Pack all his little shirts and trousers and socks – doll socks! – in a box and send him to Dean. Tag him for Phoenix and put him on an express bus. Then Christine and I could have our own son, little Terry, a polite child, very nimble and fast on his feet.

I passed a sandy turnoff with a sign that said 'TO THE BEACH' or something like that, and I fixed the location in my mind. I would take Christine there, to that very spot, for a night swim. It was just the kind of thing that would appeal to her, a moonlight swim. Perhaps Melba would make us some sandwiches. We would go in the van. If that van could talk! I would teach her how to swim in the luminous sea. She probably thought she would die if she put her face under water. water.

When I drove up to the church, a jeep was pulling away and Christine was in it. She shouted something back to me. The driver was a bearded man in a monk's robe and a planter's straw hat. One of his sandaled feet was cocked up on the floor sill of the jeep in swaggering G.I. Joe fashion. I waved and called after them but they didn't stop, my voice never having arrested anything in flight.

The movie had started. The chapel was packed with excited boys and I could hardly get in the door. I had always liked Tarzan well enough but I didn't see why this white lord of the jungle should be such a favorite with Negroes. Their own people were shown in these films as jabbering and rolling their eyes and dropping their packages and running away at the first sign of trouble. For solid action give me a submarine picture or a picture that opens with a DC-3 having engine trouble over a desert. I pushed my way through to the projector table where Mrs Symes was leaning on her aluminum cane. The boy Victor was sitting there on her stool, hunched forward and looking like Jack Dempsey. He had been into Mrs Symes's paper stars and he had stuck one on each of his fingernails.

Sweat was trickling down the poor old lady's powdered cheeks. She was trembling from the heat and intensity in the room. She was wearing a long black dress for the occasion and some pearl devices on her earlobes. The old projector clattered away, Father Jackie not having seen fit to bring along his deluxe machine. The lip movements on the screen were just a beat or so behind the voices.

I told Victor to get up and let Mrs Symes have the seat. He made a move but she said no, she would rather stand. There was a bright green fly on her veined hand and she didn't seem to feel it. The fly was so still and so cleanly articulated that it didn't look quite real; it looked like something from a jewelry shop or a joke shop.

'Christine wants you to look after Victor,' she said to me.

'Look after Victor?'

'She's gone with Father Jackie.'

'I don't follow.'

'Father Jackie wanted to show her the coconut dolls at the folk art center.'

'At night? How long will that take?'

'She wants you to look after Victor till she gets back.'

'I can't look after Victor.'

'I'm busy, Mr Midge. It's too hot to talk. I'm trying to watch this, if you don't mind.'

'What about Father Jackie's mother? You said she was here. Why can't she look after him?'

'I'm trying to watch this.'

It was an old Tarzan picture I had somehow missed on television. He seemed to be in the Coast Guard this time. He was patrolling the bayous of Louisiana in his cutter and he was having trouble with Buster Crabbe, who was some sort of Cajun poacher or crook. They were squabbling over the same sweetheart too, and the girl didn't know what to do. She had the foolish notion that she might be able to reform Buster Crabbe. Everyone was addressing Johnny Weissmuller as 'Dave' or 'Skipper' instead of Tarzan. A clever wrinkle, this undercover business, but we were all impatient for him to shed his uniform and go into some Tarzan action with vines and big cats and crocodiles. It seemed to me they were putting it off too long.

The boys had settled down by the time Mrs Symes changed the reel. Some were asleep. I saw Webster Spooner standing against the wall, rocking slowly like a small bank guard, his hands behind his back. It was hot and close in that room and I had no place to sit. I was hungry too. I wanted to flee but I was stuck with Victor. Look after Victor! If the kid broke his arm or got sick or run over by a truck, it would all be my fault! Maybe I could get Webster to act as a companion and relieve me of some of the burden.

The show droned on and the boys began to stir and mutter. Before the second reel was done, one of them stood up in the life-giving radiance from the projector and said, 'This don't be Tarzan, Meemaw.'

'It is too,' she said. 'Sit down.'

But it wasn't. It was just Johnny Weissmuller in the Coast Guard and not even at war. We could watch this thing all night and he wasn't going to stop being Dave. Father Jackie had a full bag of tricks!

The boys began to drift out in twos and threes and the door monitor made no effort to stop them. I asked Victor if he didn't want to leave too. He seemed to be drugged, stupefied. I caught Webster as he was making his way to the door.

'How are you tonight, Webster?'

'Meemaw is vexed.'

'I know. Here, I want you to meet Victor Walls. Victor, give me your attention for a minute. This is Webster Spooner, a friend of mine. He's the bell captain at my hotel. I have a job to do and I want you boys to help me.'

'What kind of job?'

'An important job. We're going for a drive.'

Both of them rode in the front seat. I stopped at the Fair Play and told them to wait in the car while I went to my room and put on my boots. Ruth was gone. I went behind the desk and poked around to see if anything had come in for me. I opened the shoebox and found the message to my father, with the money still pinned to it. Ruth had never sent it to the cable office. All my letters were there too, the British Honduras covers I had addressed to myself in Little Rock. What a hotel!

I unpinned the money and took it with me upstairs and searched my room for boots. They were not in the suitcase and they were not under the bed. Where could they be? There was no other place in this bare cube of a room where black engineer's boots might be concealed. A dog, I said to myself. Some town dog has nosed open the door here and carried off my boots in his mouth. But both boots? Could a dog manage that? Two trips maybe. Or two dogs. But had I in fact ever seen a dog in the hotel? No. Not counting the foyer where they sometimes gamboled and fought around Webster's box. I had never seen a dog on the stairs or in the hallway. Then it came to me with a swelling rush that I didn't own a pair of black engineer's boots either, or any other kind of boots.

Next door I could hear a heavy person walking back and forth on the creaking boards. Karl, perhaps, pondering his next move, whetting his knife and pacing, trying to decide whether to buy

234

a new radio or get the old one repaired, the old tube set that had served him so well in so many different rooms. I felt a visceral twinge of pain, lungs maybe, and I sat down on the bed to wait for it to pass. The pain was concentrated in one burning spot about the size of a dime. I wondered if I might have been hit by a small stray bullet sometime during the afternoon. I had handled news accounts of men who had been shot and then walked about for hours, days, a lifetime, unaware of such wounds. Maybe the heart itself. I took the last of the orange pills, first blowing off the pocket lint. Downstairs the boys were honking the horn.

CHAPTER 12

I drove with care on Bishop Lane. The shadows were deceptive under the headlights and it was hard to tell the big holes from the little holes. I soon became fatigued from making so many judgments, half of them wrong, and so I gave up making them, or rather, acting on them, and I hit the holes as they came, without regard to width or depth.

Victor had shaken off his grogginess in the night air. After each violent jolt he would shout, 'Good deal, Lucille!' and Webster would laugh. Victor fiddled with all the knobs too, and he wanted to know why things didn't work, the dash lights and the radio.

He said, 'How much will this thing do, hey? What kind of old car is this anyway? I hate it. You need to get you a Volkswagen where you can sit up high. My mom says Volkswagens are the most powerful cars in the world.' There was a sharp edge to his voice. The little Yankee had never been taught to say 'sir.'

'It'll do plenty,' I said, and I stepped on the gas and we hit the creeks at high speed. Water shot up through the floor and the boys began to squeal and jump about. Now I was driving recklessly.

A catlike animal sprang into the road and then stopped. I saw his face in the glare and it looked almost human in that brief moment of indecision. He decided against chancing it, the full crossing, and scrambled back to his starting place.

'A fox!' said Victor.

'No,' I said. 'That was a coati, or coatimundi. He's related to another animal that we know well. A very clever fellow who washes his food. He has a ringed tail and a black burglar's mask. Can anyone tell me the name of that animal?'

They weren't listening to me. We came up out of a creek bottom and topped a low rise and there in the middle of the road was a dead cow. I swung the car to the left, catching the bloated corpse with the right headlights. It was only a glancing blow and I didn't stop. Both headlights on the right side were smashed and the steering was further affected so that there was now almost a half-turn of slack in the steering wheel. The position of the crossbar on the wheel was altered too, from horizontal to vertical, and with this new alignment I couldn't seem to get my hands placed right.

'Webster?'

'Sor?'

'Who is responsible for removing dead animals from your roads?'

'I don't know.'

'One of those rib bones could go right through a tire at today's high speeds.'

It was more than I could do to keep the car in the narrow lane, what with the steering and the lighting problems. We swung from one side to the other, our progress describing a sine curve. Bushes slapped against the undercarriage each time we left the road. It didn't occur to me to slow down. On one of these swoops we hurtled through the Mayan clearing where the Indian brothers had retired for the night to their stone chamber. That is, I could see the glow of a candle behind the doorway curtain as we passed within inches of it, but we were in and out of the place before they could do much more than exchange apprehensive glances.

The end came a few minutes later. Webster and Victor were wrestling and crawling back and forth over the seat and one of them kicked the shift lever down into reverse, which, on this singular car, was on the far right side of the shifting arc. The transmission shuddered and screeched and quit before I could make a move, my hands being occupied with the wheel. The car coasted to a stop in a marshy place.

'Now see what you've done!'

We got out and stood around in the mud. The boys were quiet for a change. I would have cut a limb and gladly beaten them both but you always have to weigh one thing against another and I didn't want to listen to their bawling. They might have run too, the second one anyway. I could hear transmission fluid dripping and I could smell the odor of burnt sugar. There was another sound that I couldn't place immediately. Something unpleasant was disturbing the air. Then I figured out that it was rock-and-roll music and that it must be coming from the Indians' transistor radio.

I said, 'All right then, we'll walk. It's not far now. There better not be any more monkeyshines, I can tell you that.'

'Where are we going?'

'We're going to see Guy Dupree.'

'You don't have no electric torch?'

'We don't need one. I can see at night. I can see stars down to the seventh magnitude. Just stay behind me and step where I step.'

Above the trees in the narrow cut of the road there was a dazzling band of stars. My eye went directly to the Clouds of Magellan, although I had never seen them before. I knew then that I would not be able to see the Southern Cross, not at this time of year. I had only a rough picture in my mind of the southern celestial sphere but I did know that the Southern Cross was very far away from those clouds, perhaps as much as 180 degrees. I pointed out the two galaxies to Webster and Victor, or tried to. They found the large cloud easily enough but I couldn't make them see the pattern, the luminous smudge of the small cloud, low in the south.

I said, 'Can anyone tell me what a galaxy is?

A little knowledge about these things can greatly increase our enjoyment of them.'

There was no answer, as before, with the much easier raccoon question. Webster asked me about a red star, not Betelgeuse or Antares, directly overhead. I couldn't identify it. 'These are poor horizons,' I said, 'and I'm not really familiar with these skies. Now here's something interesting. Victor and I can't see all those stars where we live. We have different stars, you see, depending on how far north or south we live.'

Victor spoke up. 'My mom says this is the age of Aquarius.'

I set off down the road at a brisk marching pace. Victor continually disobeyed my orders. He ran ahead and stirred up some small hopping birds, shooing them before him with his hands.

'Stop chasing those birds, Victor. You can't catch a bird. I want you both to stay behind me. I'm supposed to be in front at all times.'

'What kind of birds are they?'

'They're just road birds.'

'Can they talk?'

'No.'

'Do they lay their tiny eggs in the road?'

'I don't know. Get behind me and stay there. I won't tell you again.'

'I hate this road and I hate all these trees.'

'You boys must do just as I say. I want us to stay together. If you mind me and don't give me any more trouble, I'm going to buy you each a nice gift when we get back to town. But you must do just what I say.'

Webster said, 'I already know what I want. I want a tack hammer and a rubber stamp with my name on it and a walkie-talkie radio.'

'The tack hammer and the rubber stamp are all right. I'm not buying any walkie-talkie.'

Victor said, 'I don't get this. What are we doing out here anyway?'

'I told you we're going to see Guy Dupree. He has my wife in his house out here and I mean to go in there after her. I'm through fooling around with him. It's a long story and I don't want to go into it any further than that.'

'What was his name again?'

'Guy Dupree.'

'You mean you're going to fight this Guy Dupree?'

'Yes.'

'Oh boy, this will be good. I'm glad I came now. Will you have to kill him?'

'No more chatter.'

'Oh boy, this will really be good. What we ought to do is cut off Guy Dupree's head with a knife and see what his eyes look like then.'

'What I want you to do is hush.'

'If somebody got my mom, I'd cut off his head and see if it could talk and then I would watch his eyes to see if they moved any.'

'Webster is minding me and you're not. Do you know what that means, Victor? That means he'll get a nice gift and you'll get nothing.'

No sooner had I commended Webster for his silence and put him forward as an example than he pinched my arm and asked a question. 'Does Guy Dupree be in the hands of the devil?'

'Guy Dupree is sorry. We'll leave it at that. I can't answer any of your questions about the devil. That's out of my field.'

'Meemaw say the devil he have a scaly body and a long tongue that run in and out of his mouf like a snake.'

'That's a traditional representation, yes. And goat feet.'

'She say he have a gold pocket watch a million years old that don't never run down.'

'I've never heard anything about the watch.'

'He always know what time it is.'

'My mom says there's no such thing as the devil.'

'Your mom is misinformed about many things, Victor. She may well be wrong about that too.'

'How do the devil be everywhere at one time?'

'I don't know, Webster. I tell you I can't answer questions like that. You see me as a can-do guy from the States, but I don't have all the answers. I'm white and I don't dance but that doesn't mean I have all the answers. Now I want you both to listen up. From here on in we're playing the quiet game. I don't want to hear another peep out of anybody until I give the all-clear signal, which will be my open hand rotating rapidly above my head, like this.'

Victor said, 'I want a pellet gun for my present. I want one you can pump up about thirty times.'

'I'm not buying any pellet gun. Forget it. That's out.'

'Why can't we have what we want?'

'I'm not buying any expensive junk. The pellet gun and the walkie-talkie are both out.'

'I hate these mosquitoes.'

As for the gifts, I had already given some thought to setting Webster up in the snow-cone business. No one seemed to be selling snow cones in this steaming land. A small cart and an ice scraper and some flavored syrups and conical paper cups and he would be ready to roll. Mr Wu knew a good thing when he saw it. He was making a fortune off soft ice cream and spending it on God knows what Oriental cravings, or more likely, stashing it away in a white Chinese sock with a toe pouch. Webster would have the advantage of being mobile. He could take his refreshing ices directly to the chicken fights and harvest festivals. One thousand grape snow cones at the summer corn dance! I had not yet mentioned the idea because I didn't want it to get out. Something cheap would do for Victor. I had seen a little book called *Fun with Magnets* in the window of a variety store in Belize. The book was faded and shopworn and I could probably get it for less than a dollar.

He was walking along behind me chanting, 'Guy Dupree, Guy Dupree, Guy Dupree,' and Webster picked it up, this chant. I made them stop it. Victor asked me if they could walk backward.

'You can walk any way you please as long as you keep up and don't make a lot of noise.'

'Can we hold our knees together and just take little short steps?'

'No, I don't want you to do that.'

'You said—'

'I don't want you to walk like that. And if you don't shut up I'm going to put a rubber stopper in your mouth.'

'A stopper? I don't get that.'

'One of those things that babies suck on. With a flange and a ring on the outside. If you behave like a baby, I'll have to treat you like a baby.'

He was quiet for a while and then he began to pester me with questions about the Buick. How would we get back to town? What if a crook stole it? What would I do if it was full of animals when we got back?

'I may just leave it there,' I said. 'A man told me today that there are no spare parts here for that particular transmission. I'm no longer interested in that car and I'm not answering any more questions about it. Do you hear me?'

'You can't just leave your car out in the woods.'

'The subject is closed. I don't want to hear another word. I haven't had anything to eat since this morning and I can't answer any more questions.'

'If you leave it there, how will you get back to Texas?'

'I'm not *from* Texas.'

'You can't ride in our van.'

'Have you heard me say at any time that I wanted to ride in your van?'

'We just have two bucket seats. One is mine and one is my mom's.'

'For your information, Victor, I plan to fly home with my wife.'

'Yeah, but what if the plane goes into a tailspin and you don't have a parachute to bail out in?'

'The plane is not going into a tailspin for the very simple reason that these commercial pilots know what they're doing. All those planes get regular maintenance too. So many flying hours and that's it, they're back in the shop.'

There was no light in the Dupree house and I wondered if he had heard us coming. All this chatter. He was very likely posted at one of the darkened windows and cooking up a plan. I felt sure he couldn't see us in any detail with his feeble eyes. He wouldn't be able to make out that Webster and Victor were children. For all he knew, they could be short hired thugs or two boy detectives. I had a plan of my own. I didn't intend to expose the boys to any real danger but I thought they could serve well enough and safely enough as a base of fire. I knew that the attacking force should always be at least three times the size of the defending force.

I marked off a place beside the garbage dump and told the boys, whispering, to gather rocks and place them in a pile there.

'What kind of rocks?'

'Rocks like this, for throwing. Not too big and not too little.'

We set about our task without speaking. The quality of the rocks was poor, running mostly to thin limestone shards, and even these were hard to find. Victor appeared to be doing a fine job. He scurried about and made two and sometimes three trips to the pile for every one that Webster and I made. Then I saw that he was just picking up whatever came to hand, sticks and cans and clods of dirt, and was making the rock pile ridiculous with these things. He soon stopped work altogether and said he was tired.

'All right,' I said. 'We'll rest for a minute.'

Webster said, 'What do these rocks be for?'

'We're going to throw them at that house.'

'At Guy Dupree's house?'

'Yes.'

'I don't like to do that, sor.'

'Dupree has my wife in that house and she may be sick. People get sick down here.'

Webster was shamed into silence.

'How would you like it if a gang of howling raiders came over here from Guatemala and stole your women? You would strike back, wouldn't you? And very properly so. We'll make Dupree keep his head down with these rocks and then I'll dash across the road. I'll be in the house before he knows it.'

We lined up three abreast and flung a volley

across the road. I was disappointed by the puny effect, by the soft thunks of the rocks striking wood. I had the boys lie down, against the possibility of a shotgun blast, but there was no answer of any kind, not even a bark.

I stepped up the attack. With each salvo our aim improved and before long we were breaking windows. Webster and Victor quickly got into the spirit of the thing, so much so that I had to restrain them. Still there was no response. I mixed things up so that Dupree could not count on a recurring pattern. One volley might follow another instantly, or there might be an interval of several minutes. Once, instead of loosing the expected flurry of small rocks, I heaved one big rock the size of a cantaloupe onto the porch. Watch out for the florr! Dupree would soon be whimpering for his pills.

But he was clever and after a while I could see that his plan was to sit out the barrage. He hoped to discourage us and wear us down. Two could play that game. I stopped all activity.

'We'll wait one hour exactly,' I said. 'If we keep perfectly quiet, he'll think we've left and then we'll let him have it again harder than ever. That's the thing that will break him.'

'When will you make your dash, sor?'

'I'll make my dash when I'm ready. Put that in your notebook.'

The minutes dragged. I anticipated a problem keeping the boys still and I wished I had brought something with which they could pass the time, perhaps a little ball they could roll back and forth. But they were exhausted and they fell asleep at once despite the mosquitoes.

I lay down too, behind a low rock parapet. It was very quiet out there for a jungle, or more accurately, a marginal rain forest with a few deciduous trees. I strained to see and hear things, always a mistake, the reconnaissance manuals say, leading one to see animated bushes. Once I thought I could make out two small, dim, ratlike figures walking upright, holding hands and prancing in the road. I even imagined I could hear rat coughs. Curious illusion. I checked the time again and again. My watch crystal was fogged on the inside. I lost interest in the wheeling stars. It occurred to me that if I had brought along the doctor's flashlight I could move about giving fake signals.

I crawled forward a few feet and fashioned myself a new watching place, recalling that Pancho Villa had been a great night mover. The troops would be sitting around the campfire and he would yawn and say, 'Well, boys, I think I'll turn in,' or something to that effect in Spanish, and then he would lie down and roll up in a blanket in full view of everyone. But he wouldn't stay in that place! He would move three or four times during the night and not even the most trusted of his Dorados could say where General Villa might finally turn up the next morning. I crawled forward again. And perhaps once more.

I dozed and woke. I thought I could see the

Southern Cross, the broken cross pattern of stars, just brushing the southeast horizon. But was that possible? I dozed and woke again. Baby frogs with a golden sheen were capering about at my feet. They were identical in size and appearance, brothers and sisters hatched from the same jellied mass, and they all moved as one like a school of fish when I wiggled a foot. I looked at them and they looked at me and I wondered how it was that I could see them so clearly, their placid frog faces. Then I realized it was dawn. The frogs only looked golden. I was lying in the middle of the road and I had slept for hours. The world's number one piddler had taken to his bed again.

Webster and Victor slept on. There was an odd stillness as though some familiar background machinery had stopped. I could see on the porch scattered evidence of the rock storm. I got up and entered the yard through the flimsy gate. The dog was nowhere about.

At the foot of the steps I called out for Norma, although I knew there was no one in the place. I could sense this was an empty house. I went about inside from room to squalid room. There were containers of water everywhere, buckets and cans and jugs. On the back porch there was a washtub filled with water. A drowned gray bat was floating in it, his fine wet fur slightly darker than the galvanized tub. There were no Dupree papers to be seen on the kitchen table, only some orange peelings and a slender bottle of red sauce and a small photograph. It was a picture of Dupree and his dog that had been taken in one of those coin-operated photo booths. There they were, their heads together, Gog and Magog, looking dully at me. I came across nothing of Norma's, no golden hair on a pillow, but I didn't look closely at things and I didn't stay long.

CHAPTER 13

The Buick was sunk to the bumpers in black mud. A D-9 Caterpillar couldn't have pulled it out of that muck, von Guericke's vacuum principle being what it is, implacable, and in another day or so the car would be swallowed whole by the earth. Leet's scouts had not yet found it and the windshield was clear of leaflets. I could see inside that a disgusting mound of living mud had forced its way up through the floor hole.

We walked on to the Mayan ruin, our trouser legs wet with dew and picking up grass seeds along the way. We were sore from sleeping on the ground and our faces and hands were blotchy with mosquito bites. I led the way. We kept our early-morning thoughts to ourselves. Victor carried a rock that was coated with dark green moss on one side. He wouldn't answer any questions about it, wouldn't say what his plans were for the rock. He just kept shifting it from hand to hand as his clenching fingers grew tired.

Our approach to the ruin was in no way noisy or alarming but neither was it stealthy enough to permit us a glimpse of the third brother. He had already flown to his hiding place. The other two were as merry as ever at the prospect of another full day in the brush. They greeted us with shouts of laughter and they gave us some coffee and tortillas and canned white lard from their meager stores. We spread the lard on the tortillas.

After breakfast we toured the ruin. They pulled a stone from the pyramid and showed me their hidden cache of figurines and other artifacts, but they wouldn't let me handle the objects. Then they pointed to the tire ruts in the soft earth and they acted out a car blasting through the clearing, each in his own way, in a kind of motor dance. A drunken Popo, I suggested, but they indicated that Popo's rig was much smaller and slower than the phantom machine. They asked me for cigarettes again and I gave them some of the money I had taken from Ruth's shoe box. They got out their E bonds and I thought at first they were trying to give them back to me. They went to the cache and brought back an incised monkey skull to add to the bonds. Finally I got the drift. They wanted to exchange these things for a little nine-volt radio battery. Of course I had no battery and I gave them the rest of my money and accepted the skull. We shook hands all around.

Victor and Webster were dozing in the grass. I got them on their feet and we walked another two miles or so before we caught a ride in a pickup truck. The driver was an American, a hippie-looking fellow but rugged too at the same time, a pioneer. We rode in the back with the milk cans, our rigid limbs splayed out in all directions to provide support.

We got out at the market in Belize. The air was moist and very still. Webster treated us to some Pepsi-Colas at the Chinaman's store and I was a little surprised at this because most children are close with their money. Mr Wu himself was indisposed, or maybe around the corner making a deposit at Barclays Bank, under that heraldic black eagle sign, or maybe he was just sleeping in. His mother or wife or sister was running the store. The firemen were at their table and I said to myself. Things are happening all over and they go on drinking their coffee. As long as it isn't a fire, they don't care.

Webster left for his hotel duties. Victor and I walked on to the tabernacle. Christine's van was parked in front of the place and so was Father Jackie's jeep. I knew Christine would have some sharp words for me when she saw her son's swollen face.

The door was open but no one seemed to be about. The chapel was in disarray. Some of the borrowed chairs were overturned and the floor was littered with flat scraps of paper that would be hard to sweep up. The movie projector was still on the table uncased, the lenses unprotected from drifting bits of lint that would take on a hairy, jerky life when magnified and illuminated.

We went upstairs. Christine had moved her bags

in and there by the door to the doctor's room was his pebbly grip, all packed. More suitcase facts. The breakfast or supper dishes were still on the table. I couldn't understand the sudden house-keeping decline. I stood there and thoughtfully ate some cold black beans from a bowl. I was eating at every opportunity. Victor curled up in Melba's chair. His chin glistened with lard. Christine prob-ably wasn't much of a cook. The lard tortillas had been perfectly acceptable to him.

I roused him and we went back downstairs and then we heard voices from behind the movie screen. There was a door in the rear wall that opened into a yard and it was there we found them – Dr Symes and Melba and Christine and Father Jackie. But where was Mrs Symes?

This back yard was a nook I had not known about, a small fenced area with crushed white shells on the ground. Roses grew along the board fence and there were chairs made from rough sticks and leather straps, although there was none for me. Under the roof drain there was a rain barrel, to catch soft water for hair-washing. The place was no doubt intended as a meditation spot, a private retreat, but on this occasion everyone was eating watermelon. Dr Symes used salt. He couldn't see the fine white grains as they dribbled from the shaker and he bounced them off the back of his hand so as to gain some idea of the rate of flow. The flesh of the watermelon was orange instead of red.

Victor went at once to Christine's lap. The rock was a gift for her. She said, 'Hey, a super mossy!' and she looked it over and then put it aside and began to pick bits of dirt and gravel from Victor's hair. She had no words at all for me and no one was curious about our adventures because of a grave development that overshadowed such things. Far from being a luau, this was a wake!

Mrs Symes had suffered a stroke and, I gathered, had died during the night. Dr Symes and Christine had taken her to the hospital in the van, and had stayed there with her until they were told there was no hope. I couldn't believe it. A person I knew. Here one day and gone the next. An old enough story but it never fails to knock me for a loop. Then I get over it about as fast as anyone else and very soon I am able to carry on again. Melba cut me a section of watermelon and I sat on the rough shells and ate it with my fingers.

Father Jackie, who had a strong nasal voice, was doing most of the talking. He said, 'She drank far too much ice wanter but you couldn't tell her anything.'

Dr Symes shifted his weight about on the sagging leather straps. He was fully dressed, even to the hat and bow tie and flashlight. On the ground beside his chair there was an old-fashioned steel lockbox, of a dark green color. He wiped his sticky hands on his white trousers. I could see he was impatient with Father Jackie's lay opinion, with the notion that cold water could cause death or even serious illness. He had been holding his mother's aluminum cane between his knees and now he began to rotate it rapidly back and forth between his open hands, like a scout trying to make fire. All this in preparation for an important statement.

Before he could get it out, Father Jackie said, 'I know one thing. There was nothing on this earth that Meemaw was afraid of.'

'She was afraid of hurricanes,' said Melba. 'Waterspouts. Any strong wind or black rain from the south. That little cloud right up there would make her uneasy. She was afraid that bits of flying glass would cut her neck.'

Father Jackie told a story about a trip he had taken with Mrs Symes to a place called Orange Walk. They had gone in his jeep to attend a sale or an auction of some kind at a bankrupt ranch. Throughout that day he had played various good-natured tricks on her, some of which she turned back on him to good effect. It was an interesting story, if a little long, full of lively incident illustrating different aspects of the old lady's character.

What part of the U.S.A. did Father Jackie hail from? I wrestled with this problem and couldn't work it out. He talked on and on. A theory formed in my head on the origin of his nasal tones. It was this. When he was a small child, his prankster father – a bitter man, jealous of the boy's promise – had taught him to speak in this fashion, taught him to honk, to recite, 'The three lintle kintons they lost their mintons and they began to cry,' thus fixing the habit early and assuring his failure in the world, the boot from every job, even street attacks. But was that really probable? Wasn't it more likely that this was just a kind of pulpit whine that was taught in his particular seminary?

The Orange Walk story was a pretty good one, as I say, and when it was over, Christine laughed and squeezed his knee in an intimate way and said, 'You stinker you!' One of his knees showed through the parting of the brown robe. He reached over and plucked a shiny coin from Victor's ear and said, 'My goonness, what's this?' But the boy was in a stupor again, his mouth ajar, and the illusion did not delight him.

Dr Symes saw his chance and got his statement out. He said, 'I don't know what the poets of Belize are doing this morning but I can tell you what they should be doing. They should all be in their little rooms composing memorials to that grand lady.'

A large speckled insect flew slowly about before our faces, going in turn from one speaker to the next as though listening. Melba slapped at it ineffectually. She asked me if I had a camera. I said no and then she asked Dr Symes. 'I sure don't,' he said. 'Marvel used to have a little box camera but I myself have never owned one. I have never personally photographed anything in my life. Why do you ask such a question?'

'I thought it would be nice to have our picture taken out here with the roses and then later we could look at it and say, Yes, I remember that day.'

Dr Symes said the last time he had his picture made was in California. It was for his driver's license and they wouldn't let him wear his hat. 'Don't ask me why. It's just some rule they have. No hats and no caps. They've got a million rules in California and that just happens to be one of them.' He shook his head and laughed at the memory of the bizarre place.

Melba said, 'If it's your own hat, I don't see why you couldn't wear it if you wanted to.'

'I don't either, Melba, but you can't. I've seen plenty of good pictures of people wearing hats. Some of the finest pictures I've ever seen have been of people with their hats on. All I'm saying is that it's forbidden in California.'

Father Jackie said he had a 35-millimeter camera at his cottage. But this was just by way of information and he made no move to go and get it. Christine said that her former husband, Dean, had a number of expensive cameras and that his favorite subject was his watch-repair tools. He would arrange the tiny instruments on a green cloth and photograph them from atop a stepladder, the challenge being to capture all the tools with a minimum of distortion. She was not allowed in the room while he was doing this but afterward he would show her the finished prints and ask her which one she liked best. After she had left Dean

258

and moved to Mesa, she said, he annoyed her by prowling outside her apartment at night and shining different kinds of lights through her windows. I don't know whether she meant lights of different intensities or lights of different colors because all she said was 'different kinds of lights.'

Father Jackie asked Melba if she wanted him to arrange for death notices in the local papers and the New Orleans papers.

'Let's hold up on that,' said the doctor. 'We don't want to rush into this thing.'

'I'll be glad to type up a full obituary if you'll give me the information. I'll tell you right now, these newspapers will just throw your stuff in the wastebasket if it's not wrinten up on a typewriner. I found that out from wrining lenners to the ennitor.'

The doctor said, 'Just hold up on that, if you will, my friend. You can do what you please at this end, but I have already told Melba that I will handle the Louisiana end. I will make all the notifications that need to be made. Do you understand what I'm telling you?'

'It's no trouble, I assure you.'

'I appreciate that and I appreciate your concern but I want you to leave that part of it alone.'

'Whatever you say.'

'Fine, fine. That's what I say.'

Dr Symes then told Melba that he didn't like the idea of his mother being buried here in this Honduras mud, so far from her real home in

Louisiana where Otho lay. Melba said it was a question of a person's wishes. Mrs Symes had insisted on burial in the Belize cemetery with the pirates and drowned children and nameless wanderers, and a person's last wishes, when reasonable, had to be respected. She had not insisted on one of those simple funerals that cause everybody so much trouble, but there were one or two special requests. Her age, for instance. She was sensitive about her age and didn't want a date of birth inscribed on her tombstone. So be it. Melba intended to see that all of Nell's reasonable wishes were carried out.

The doctor made no strong protest. 'Very well,' he said. 'I leave it in your hands, Melba. I know you'll do the right thing. Whatever you decide to do will just tickle me to death.'

'I don't see why you can't stay for the funeral.'

'You know I would if I could. We can't always do what we'd like to do, Melba. I'm needed in Ferriday now and it's a trip I can't put off. It's imperative that I be on the ground there personally. I won't be missed here anyway. There'll be so many mourners at the service that you'll have to put up loudspeakers outside the chapel. And all around the altar, just beaucooz of beautiful flowers. I'd give anything if I could see that lovely floral display, or just one glistening tear in the eye of some small child whose heart Mama had touched.'

They had already been over this ground, I could tell. Melba sent me to the market for a second watermelon and when I came back they were discussing very frankly the disposal of Mrs Symes's property. Melba had been a witness to the will and she knew the terms. It was clear that she and the doctor had already chewed over this matter too, and were returning to it now for mere secondary comment. Even so, I was able to get the picture and it was a bleak one for Dr Symes. His mother had left him nothing. Nothing, that is, except for the green lockbox, which contained a poem she had written about a hurricane, of some three hundred-odd verses. The tabernacle went to Melba, and certain sums of money to the girl Elizabeth and to a cabdriver and handyman named Rex. The rest of the estate went to Mrs Symes's great-granddaughter, Rae Lynn Symes, who was Ivo's daughter. It was a handsome settlement and was to be used to further the girl's music education.

Wasn't this a sensational disclosure? A bombshell? The doctor's hopes all dashed? And yet he showed little concern. He was subdued, all right, but there was also a kind of monstrous jauntiness in his manner.

I said, 'What about Jean's Island?'

'She gets the island too,' he said. 'There's not a thin dime for me but there's hundreds of thousands of dollars for Rae Lynn and her piano lessons. You can see where that puts Marvel. Right in the driver's seat. Mama has now brought about the very situation she so hoped to avoid.'

'Then there's nothing to be done.'

'I wouldn't say nothing.'

'What then?'

'Let me tell you how it is, Speed. I need to be on the ground in Louisiana. All right? Nuff said?'

It wasn't quite enough but it was all I was ever going to get.

Victor was asleep. Christine held him with one arm and she was sketching something with her free hand. She said, 'How old was Meemaw anyhow?'

I said, 'Melba just got through saying that her age was a secret, Christine. Didn't you hear that about the tombstone?'

'I didn't hear that. What was it?'

It wasn't that Christine's question was improper in itself but I thought she should have been paying closer attention to what people were saying. I had been thinking about the tombstone business all along, even during the more important will discussion, wondering at this posthumous vanity. What were Mrs Symes's fears? That cemetery strollers would pause before her stone and compute the age? *Here, look at this one. No wonder she's dead.*

Christine tore the sketch from her pad and passed it around. It was a portrait of Melba with her hands clasped together on her lap in resignation. Christine may have been an artist, who can say, but she was no draftsman. The only thing she got right was Melba's hair, the wisps. The face was misshapen and dead, a flat, identikit likeness with one Mongoloid eye lower than the other. But Melba herself was pleased, if not with the portrait, at least with the attention. She said, 'You're a fine girl, Christine.'

Dr Symes came to his feet and stretched. He asked Melba if he could keep the aluminum cane and she said he could take what he pleased from his mother's personal things.

'No, no, the stick is all. I have my lockbox and I'll just take this stick along for support and protection. It will also serve as a memento, what is it, mori.'

'We ought to be ashamed of ourselves, talking like this, and poor Nell down there in the hospital struggling for her life.'

'She's beyond the struggle, Melba. You can take my word for it as a physician.'

'I don't know, Reo. You remember way back there when she had the incurable bone disease. The doctors just gave up on her. You remember they said she had to die. They said she would never rise from her bed. Five doctors said she had to die in three days. They wanted to give her a shot and just put her to sleep like an animal. And that was thirty-six years ago. I expect every one of those doctors is dead today.'

'Pneumonia, Melba. Aspiration. Pulmonary fluids. The infection is setting in at this moment and she'll never be able to throw it off. I've seen way too much of it with these old people. You can take my word for it, church is out this time.'

He gathered up his lockbox and said, 'And now if you good people will excuse me I'm going to the hospital and kiss my old mother goodbye.' He tapped my shoe with the cane and said, 'Speed, behave yourself,' and he went away.

I had rebuked Christine for not listening and all the time it was I who had been asleep at the switch. Mrs Symes had not yet expired!

A few drops of rain fell on us, big ones. Melba said the big drops meant that we could expect a downpour, along with violent electrical discharges from the sky. She caught a silver drop in her hand and closed her fingers on it and said it reminded her of something we might find interesting. It was a recent vision. She had seen Dr Symes being struck down by a big truck on a busy American highway. It was night and sleet was falling on the expressway and she could only see him off and on by the headlights of the giant trucks as they hit him over and over again, tossing him about like a bullfighter.

As she spoke, the speckled insect hovered in front of her eyes in an annoying way. She slapped at it again and said, 'Get out of here, you naughty bug!' She asked us not to divulge the grim vision to Dr Symes if we saw him again, and she went inside.

There followed an awkward silence, as with strangers being suddenly thrown together. Then Father Jackie leaned toward me and said that Mrs Symes was a good woman but she had no business baptizing little children, or anyone else. She had no authority. And she had no business filling their heads with a lot of Calvinist nonsense. As for Melba, he said, tapping one finger to the steel plate in his own reconstructed skull, she was a little cracked. She laughed at inappropriate times. She had once given a little girl a toasted mouse for her cat. I didn't say anything because I didn't want to invite further confidences from this fellow.

Christine asked me who John Selmer Dix was and I told her he was a famous writer. Father Jackie said he had read a number of Dix's books and had found them excellent. He said he had always been fond of English detective stories, though he objected to the English practice of naming all the American characters Hiram or Phineas or Homer, and of making them talk in an odd way. I couldn't follow that, and then I saw that he must have Dix mixed up with some other bird, with the vain grunts of some other writer. He asked Christine if she would like to join him for lunch at his cottage.

'Some of the guys and chicks from the Peace Corps are dropping in for a rap session,' he said. 'I know you'll like them. They're really neat dudes. It's a regular thing we have. Nothing fancy, I assure you. We just have red wine and cheese and crackers and other munchies and we kick around a few ideas. But don't say I didn't warn you! It can get pretty heated at times!'

Christine said she thought she would stay at the tabernacle and relax and visit with Melba and listen to the rain on the tin roof.

He said, 'How about you, Brad?'

He thought my name was Brad! I recognized the polite afterthought for what it was and I suspected too that those Peace Corps people might have guitars and so I too declined.

CHAPTER 14

Melba was right about the downpour. There wasn't a great deal of lightning but the rain fell and the wind blew. Wooden shutters were battened down all across town. Broken palm fronds and power lines had fallen to the streets. The electricity was knocked out early and all the stores were dark inside, though it wasn't yet noon. I sloshed through the foyer of the Fair Play Hotel where an inch or so of water had already accumulated. Ruth was gone. Webster's sleeping box had begun to float and I put it up on the counter.

I ran up the stairs and found a skinny stranger sitting on my bed. He was wearing heavy boots of a European design, with laces running from one end to the other. He was sitting there in the gloom writing in a spiral notebook. He jumped when I opened the door and he closed the notebook and shoved it under a pillow. This bird has been composing something! I had caught him in the very act of putting pen to paper and his shame was painful to see.

'What do you want?' he said.

'This is my room.'

'This is the one they gave me.'

'Where's my suitcase?'

'I don't know. This is the room they showed me. There was nothing in here. Are you checking out?'

'I didn't think so, no.'

He was tall and yellow and fleshy around the middle, an ectomorph with a paunch. He looked to be an intelligent person. His stuff was packed in a rubberized cloth bag that was choked off tight at the top with a drawstring. He pulled it closer to him and rested one hand on it in a protective way. He saw me as a threat not only to his notebook but to his bag too.

I questioned him. He said he was booked on a Nicaraguan Airlines flight to New Orleans but it had been canceled because of the weather. For the past few months he had been back in the hills prospecting for immaculite and jade and tail feathers from the rare quetzal bird. He was now going home to see his brother ride in a prison rodeo, and, if it could be worked out, he also wanted to attend the state fair. Then he would return here to his immaculite diggings and to certain jade-bearing stream beds.

'What is immaculite?' I said. 'And why is it mined?'

'It's a fine crystal that is used in precision optical instruments.'

'Is that it?'

'That's it. That's the story of immaculite.'

'It's funny I've never heard of it. I wouldn't mind seeing some of that stuff.'

'I don't have any with me. I don't have any jadeite or quetzal feathers either.'

The way he said it made me think he was lying. My clothes were soaked and I was dripping water on the floor. We had to speak with raised voices because of the rain drumming on the tin roof. The din was terrible and I thought of Christine, who was not often treated to a tattoo like this in Phoenix.

'I'm wondering about my things,' I said. 'Did the boy or the woman take my suitcase out of here?'

'I don't know anything about it. This is the room they gave me. I've already paid for it but if there's been a mistake I'll be glad to move to another room.'

'Look here, why should there be a problem about going to the state fair?'

'There's not any problem that I know of.'

'I got the idea that there was some problem. It's no great trick to go to the fair, is it?'

'The rodeo is in Huntsville and the fair is in Dallas.'

'Two widely separated towns then. That's all you meant to say.'

'Yes.'

He was still uncomfortable from having been caught red-handed at his vice – writing songs or what? – and I could see too that our loud, expository conversation was distasteful to him, he just having come in from the solitude of the bush. The wind peeled back a sheet of tin above his head. The thing flapped up and down a few times and then blew away. It will be understood when I say 'tin' that I am using the popular term for galvanized and corrugated sheet iron. A cascade of water came down on the bed and we pushed it to an inside corner of the room. Now we had to talk even louder because of the wind shrieking through the hole in the roof. But that hole, I told myself, will act as a safety vent and will keep the house from exploding or imploding under a sudden pressure differential. The floor heaved and the walls creaked. The frame structure was ill-suited for withstanding these violent stresses.

'I think this is a hurricane,' he said. 'What do you think?'

'It's certainly a severe depression of some kind.'

'Maybe we should go to another place.'

'All the other houses are just like this one.'

'The Fort George Hotel is fairly solid.'

'But don't they say stay inside? Where you are?'

'I think we should try for the Fort George.'

'You may be right.'

He took his own sweet time in opening the bag and packing the notebook and tying it up again, in a special way. It was all something of an act, this cool manner we were at such pains to display to one another, but in fairness I must say that I was not unnerved by this convulsion of nature.

The storm made a change from the enervating heat and it is not going too far to say I found it bracing – or much too far. I should say too that it provided a welcome distraction from my personal problems.

The Texas fellow carried his bag under one arm. His running gait was badly coordinated and funny, mine deliberate. He ran like a duck. Water was running in the streets, which made it hard to lift our feet. We moved in a darting fashion from the lee of one house to that of another. The black creek was backed up and out of its banks, whether from the heavy rains upstream or from the driven sea blocking its discharge, I couldn't say, perhaps both. There seemed to be no pattern in the way the wind was blowing. It came from all points of the compass. The velocity was irregular too, and it was the gusts that did most of the damage. My concern was for the twisted sheets of tin that were banging about. One of those things could take your head off. Some of the roofs had been completely stripped, leaving only exposed beams and stringers. I saw a gum tree with its limbs more or less intact but every leaf blown away. It had a wintry look.

We didn't make it to the Fort George. A policeman hustled us off the street into a fenced compound and put us to work in a sandbag brigade. The wire fence enclosed a motor-pool area behind the police station, and this was a scene of wild activity. Men were running about and Bedford trucks and Land-Rovers were coming and going through the gate. Most of the workers seemed to be prisoners. They had been turned out of jail to fill small sisal bags with sand and broken oyster shells. The stuff was piled up in mounds at a construction site near the garage bays.

There weren't nearly enough shovels. The Texas fellow and I were assigned to the loading detail. We carried sandbags, one in each hand, and slung them up into the truck beds. They were then hauled away to build dikes and to weigh down the flimsy roofs – much too late, it seemed. A big black officer with a riding crop and a bullhorn was directing things. I couldn't understand a word he said. They called him Captain Grace. He had a Webley revolver in a canvas holster on his hip. As befitted his rank, he was the calmest man in the yard.

Everyone had his job. Webster was there and he and some other boys held the bags open while the prisoners filled them. A third gang tied the tops with string and the rest of us were loaders. The rain swept across us in blinding sheets, and the sand, wet though it was, swirled about in eddies, stinging our arms and faces. We were working in the open but the chainlike fence provided some protection from flying objects. I had no opportunity to ask Webster about my things.

There were two white Americans among the

jailbirds – a young doper and an older, heavier man. He was barefooted, this older fellow, as were all the prisoners, and he wore a knit shirt that was split on both sides from his exertions. He appeared to be the boss of the shovelers. They were hard put to keep up, there being so few of them, and he was trying to prod them on to heroic efforts with a lot of infield chatter. His team! He was digging like a madman and yelling at the boys for being slow and for not holding the bags fully open. I had noticed him early but he was little more than a noisy wet blur to me.

I soon made a pickup at his station and he said, 'Wrong way! Wrong way! Get your bags on this side and go out the other way!' I had been holding my head down to protect my eyes against all the blowing stuff and when I raised it to get a look at this loud person I was knocked for a loop. It was Jack Wilkie! I spoke to him. He recognized me and waved me off. We were meeting under strange circumstances in a faraway place and there were many questions to be answered – but this was no time for a visit! That was what I understood him to be saying with his urgent gestures. He hadn't shaved for several days and there were clumps of sand stuck to his copper-wire whiskers. He had to keep hitching up his trousers because he had no belt.

I went back to work and considered the new development. Someone called out to me. It was the skinny fellow from Texas, hanging on the back of a truck and holding to one end of a long wooden ladder. He had been shanghaied into a new gang, a ladder gang. His bag was stowed in one of the garage bays and he wanted me to keep an eye on it while he was gone. I nodded and waved, indicating that I would do so, message understood. The truck pulled away and that was the last time I saw that mysterious bird alive. His name was Spann or Spang, more likely Spann.

Three army trucks came through the gate and wheeled about together in a nice maneuver. British soldiers jumped to the ground with new shovels at the ready. Now we had plenty of shovels but there was no more sand. The army officer and Captain Grace conferred. A decision was quickly reached. All the small boys were left behind and the rest of us were herded into the trucks and taken to some grassy beach dunes north of town. The captain led the convoy in his blue Land-Rover. Jack and I were together and there were about twenty other men in the back of our truck. We had to stand. The tarpaulin top was gone and we clung to the bentwood frame members. I could see that I was taller than at least one of these Coldstream Guards, if indeed that's who they were. We were flung from side to side. Jack punched out angrily at people when they stepped on his bare toes.

Captain Grace had made an excellent choice. This new place was the Comstock Lode of sand

and I could hardly wait to get at it. The dunes were thirty feet high in places and were situated about three hundred yards from the normal shore-line, so we were fairly well protected from the sea. Even so, an occasional monster wave swept all the way across the beach and broke over the top of the dunes, spraying us and leaving behind long green garlands of aquatic vegetation. The sand had drifted up here between an out-cropping of rock and a grove of palm trees. The slender trunks of the palms were all bent in picturesque curves and the fronds at the top stood hysterically on end like sprung umbrellas. None of the trees, however, had been uprooted, and I decided then that this blow, already falling off somewhat, was probably not a major hurricane.

It was a good place for sand, as I say. The only catch was that the trucks had to cross a strip of backwater on the inland side of the dunes. The water wasn't very deep but the ground underneath was soft and the trucks wallowed and strained to get through it with a full load of sandbags. We were now filling them and loading them at a much faster rate. Jack took charge once again and whipped us up into frenzies of production. No one seemed to mind. The prisoners and the soldiers thought he was funny and the officers stood back and let him do his stuff.

The truck drivers followed one another, taking the same route across the water each time, such was their training or their instincts or their orders, and they soon churned the fording place into a quagmire. As might have been foreseen, one of the trucks bogged down and we, the loaders, had to stand in the water and remove every last bag from the bed. Thus lightened, the truck moved forward about eight inches before settling down again.

The officious Jack stepped in and began to direct this operation too. He took the wheel from a soldier. It was a matter of feel, he said. The trick was to go to a higher gear and start off gently and then shift down one notch and pour on the steam at the precise moment you felt the tires take hold. Jack did this. The truck made a lurch, and then another one, and things looked good for a moment, before all ten wheels burrowed down another foot or so, beyond hope. Jack said the gear ratios were too widely spaced in that truck. The young British officer, none too sure of himself before, pulled Jack bodily from the cab and told him to stay away from his vehicles 'in future' – rather than 'in *the* future.'

The second truck went down trying to pull the first one out and the third one made a run to town and never came back, for a reason that was not made known to us. We had a mountain of undelivered bags and no more empties to fill. Shovels were downed and we lay back against the bags, our first rest break in four or five hours. By that time there was very little fury left in the storm, though the rain still came. An army sergeant walked back and forth in front of us to show that he himself wasn't tired.

'Good way to get piles,' he said to us. 'Best way I know. Sitting on wet earth like that.' But no one got up, just as no one heeded him when he warned us against drinking a lot of water in our exhausted state.

Jack was breathing noisily through his mouth. He was the oldest and he had worked the hardest. The palms of his hands were a ragged mess of broken blisters. I watched my own fingers, curled in repose, as they gave little involuntary twitches.

It was our first chance for a talk. Jack said he had had his Chrysler towed into Monterrey, where he arranged to have the drive shaft straightened and two new universal joints installed. There had been no difficulty in tracking me from San Miguel. The juiceheads at the Cucaracha bar had put him on to the farm in British Honduras. He couldn't locate me immediately in Belize. He went to the American consul and learned of the two Dupree farms in the country. I had missed a bet there, going to the consul, but Jack missed one too. He went to the wrong place, the Dupere farm, the one south of town.

The ranch manager there was an old man, he said, a Dutchman, who claimed he knew nothing of any Guy Dupree from Arkansas. Jack wasn't satisfied with his answers and he insisted on searching the premises. The old man reluctantly allowed him to do so and before it was over they had an altercation, something about an ape. It must have been a pet monkey, only Jack called it an ape.

'That nasty ape followed me around everywhere I went,' he said. 'He stayed about two steps behind me. The old man told him to do that. I had seen him talking to the ape. Whenever I opened a door or looked into a building, that nasty beast would stick his head in and look around too. Then he would bare his nasty teeth at me, the way they do. The old man had told him to follow me around and mock me and spit on me. I told that old Dutchman he better call him off but he wouldn't do it. I said all right then, I'll have to shoot him, and then he called him off. That was all. It didn't amount to anything. I wouldn't have shot the ape even if I had had a gun. But when I got back to town they arrested me. That old guy had radioed ahead to the police and said I pulled a gun on him. I didn't even have a gun but they took my belt and shoes and locked me up.'

The black prisoners had begun to stir. They had come to their feet and were muttering angrily among themselves. The young American doper said they wanted cigarettes. Their tobacco and their papers were wet and they wanted something to smoke. It was a cigarette mutiny! Captain Grace whacked the ringleader across the neck with his leather crop and that broke it up. He ordered everyone to be seated and he addressed us through his bullhorn.

I couldn't make out what he was saying. Jack couldn't make it out. I asked a red-faced corporal and I couldn't understand him either. The young doper had acquired an ear for this speech and he explained it all to us. The emergency was now over. The prisoners and the soldiers were to wait here for transport. Those of us who had been roped in off the streets were free to go, to walk back to town if we liked, or we too could wait for the trucks.

Captain Grace got into his Land-Rover and signaled the driver to be off. Then he counter-manded the order with a raised hand and the driver stopped so short that the tires made a little chirp in the wet sand. The captain got out and came over to Jack and said, 'You. You can go too.'

'Thanks,' said Jack. 'Are you going to town now in that jeep?'

'Yes, I am.'

'How about a lift?'

'Lift?'

'A ride. I need a ride to town.'

'With me? Certainly not.'

'You've got my shoes at the station. I can't walk all the way in like this.'

Captain Grace was caught up short for a moment by Jack's impudence. He said, 'Then you can wait for the lorries like everyone else.'

We walked all the way back to Belize, my second

long hike of the day. Since Jack was handicapped, I let him set the pace. We soon pulled ahead of the others. Jack was barefooted but he was not one to dawdle or step gingerly on that account. He stopped once to rest, hands on knees, head low, in the dramatic posture of the exhausted athlete. The sun came out. We rounded a bend in the road and a cloud of pale blue butterflies appeared before us, blown in perhaps from another part of the world. I say that because they hovered in one place as though confused. We walked through them.

Jack talked about how good the fried eggs were in Mexico and how he couldn't get enough of them. They were always fresh, with stand-up yolks, unlike the watery cold-storage eggs in our own country. He talked about eggs and he talked about life. There was altogether too much meanness in the world, he said, and the source of it all was negative thinking. He said I must avoid negative thoughts and all negative things if I wanted my brief stay on earth to be a happy one. Guy Dupree's head was full of negative things, and so to a lesser extent was mine. That was our central problem. We must purge our heads, and our rancorous hearts too.

For all I knew he was right, about Dupree anyway, but this stuff didn't sound like Jack. This didn't sound like the Jack Wilkie I knew in Little Rock who had a prism-shaped thing on his desk that said, 'Money Talks and Bullshit Walks.'

It was my guess that he had been reading something in his cell. Two or three days in jail and he was a big thinker! The ideas that are hatched in those places! I told him that Dupree's malaise, whatever it might be, was his own, and that to lump the two of us together was to do me a disservice.

'Food for thought,' he said. 'That's all. I won't say any more.'

The waters had receded from town. We were greeted by a spectacular rainbow that arched from one end of the estuary to the other. I watched for it to shift about or partially disappear as our angle of approach changed but it remained fixed. The color bands were bright and distinct – blue, yellow, and pink – with no fuzzy shimmering. It was the most substantial rainbow I've ever seen. There were mud deposits in the streets and a jumble of grounded boats along the creek banks. They lay awkwardly on their sides. Their white hulls had fouled bottoms of a corrupt brown hue not meant to be seen. Everyone seemed to be outside. Women and children were salvaging soggy objects from the debris. The men were drunk.

Jack went into the police station to claim his things. I stayed outside in the motor pool and looked around for Spann's bag. It was gone. I had told him I would keep an eye on his bag and then I didn't do it. Someone had made off with it. Someone was at this very moment pawing over his songs and his jade and his feathers, which, I suppose, Spann himself must have stolen, in a manner of speaking. I found out later about his death. He was hanging sandbags over the crest of a tin roof – one bag tied to each end of a length of rope – when he slipped and fell and was impaled on a rusty pipe that was waiting for him below in the grass.

Jack came out on the porch fully shod in his U.S. Navy surplus black oxfords. His socks, I guessed, had been mislaid by the property clerk, or perhaps burned. He stood there chatting in a friendly way with a black officer, Sergeant Wattli maybe, two comrades now in law enforcement. All was forgiven. Jack saw me and waved his car keys.

The yellow Chrysler was parked in one of the garage bays. We looked it over and Jack pointed to some blood spatters on the license plate and the rear bumper. He laughed over the success of his trap, which was a razor blade taped to the top of the gas-filler cap. An unauthorized person had grabbed it and sliced his fingers. For a person whose own hands were bloody, Jack showed amazing lack of sympathy. No such security measures had been taken at the front of the car. The battery was gone. The two cable heads hung stiffly in space above the empty battery pan. Jack was angry. He said he was going to demand restitution. He was going to demand of Captain Grace that the city of Belize buy him a new battery.

'I'll be right back and then we'll go get us some bacon and eggs.'

He went into the station again but this time he didn't come out. I grew tired of waiting and left a note in the car saying I would be at the Fair Play Hotel taking a nap.

CHAPTER 15

I made my way through a sea of boisterous drunks. It was sundown. There would be no twilight at this latitude. The air was sultry and vapors were rising from the ground. The drunks were good-natured for the most part but I didn't like being jostled, and there was this too, the ancient fear of being overwhelmed and devoured by a tide of dark people. Their ancient dream! Floating trees and steel drums were piled up beneath the arched bridge. Through a tangle of branches I saw a dead mule.

A man pinched my arm and offered me a drink from a bottle – clear rum, I think. A few translucent fish scales were stuck to the bottle. He watched me closely for signs of gratitude. I took a drink and sighed and thanked him and wiped my mouth with the back of my hand in an exaggerated gesture. At the edge of the stream some children were taunting a coiled black snake with an inflated inner tube. They were trying to make him strike at it. He would bump it with his snout but he had already sensed that the fat red thing wasn't living flesh, only a simulacrum,

284

and he refused to bring his hinged fangs into play.

I asked about Webster. The children hadn't seen him. I wondered how he and other people had fared during the storm, thinking of them one by one, even to Father Jackie's mother, on whose yellow flesh I had never laid eyes. Had Dr Symes made it safely out of town? And if so, how? He wouldn't ride a bus and he wouldn't fly and he was certainly no sailor. What did that leave?

Cars and trucks were moving once again in the streets. There was a lot of honking, at drunks who blocked the way, and in celebration too of life spared for another day. I picked out the distinctive beep of a Volkswagen and almost at the same instant I saw Christine in her van. She was caught in the traffic jam. She was beeping away and slapping her left hand against the door. Victor was in his seat blowing a plastic whistle.

I went to her and said, 'You shouldn't be out in this.'

'I'm all right. It's Melba.'

The glass louvers on the driver's side were open and I saw Melba lying down in the back, nestled in amid all the art and green coconuts.

'What's wrong with her?'

'I don't know. I'm trying to get her to the hospital.'

'This is an emergency then.'

'You bet your boots it is.'

I walked point, flapping my arms in front of the

van and clearing the way like a locomotive fireman shooing cattle from the tracks. 'Gangway!' I shouted. 'Make a hole! *Andale*! Coming through! *!Cuidado*! Stand back, please! Hospital run!' I can put up a fairly bold show when representing some larger cause than myself.

All the rolling tables were in use at the hospital and I had to carry Melba inside the place and down a long corridor jammed with beds. She weighed hardly anything. She was all clothes. Her eyes were open but she wasn't speaking. There was standing room only in the emergency room and not much of that. Victor found a folded wheelchair in a closet and Christine pulled it open and I set Melba down into it. We couldn't find anything in the way of restraining straps and so I put a big Clorox carton on her lap to keep her from pitching forward.

Christine waylaid a nurse or a female doctor and this person looked into Melba's eyes with the aid of a penlight and then went away, doctor-fashion, without telling us anything. I rested Melba's chin on top of the empty brown box to make her more comfortable. A male doctor, an older man, began to shout. He brandished a stainless-steel vessel and ordered everyone out of the room who wasn't a bona-fide patient. He had to repeat the order several times before anyone made a move. Others took up the cry, various underlings. Christine told me that proper identification was very important in a hospital. We looked about for admittance forms and name tags. But now the crazed physician was shouting directly at us. He wouldn't allow us to explain things and we had to go. I wrote 'MELBA' on top of the box in front of her chin and we left her there. I couldn't remember her last name, if I had ever known it.

Scarcely was I out of the room when I was pressed into service again. This time it was helping orderlies push bed-ridden patients back to their rooms. These people, beds and all, had been moved into the central hallways during the storm, away from the windows.

Christine went off on her own to look for Mrs Symes and to buck up sick people. She made a cheery progress from bed to bed, in the confident manner of a draft-dodger athlete signing autographs for mutilated soldiers. Some were noticeably brightened by her visits. Others responded not at all and still others were baffled. Those capable of craning their necks stole second and third glances as she and Victor passed along.

I worked with a fellow named Cecil, who knew little more about the layout of the hospital than I did. He was out of sorts because it was his supper hour. He looked sick himself and I took him at first for an ambulatory patient, but he said he had worked there almost two years. Once he led us blundering into a room where seven or eight dead people were laid out on the floor, the tops of their heads all lined up flush as though by a string. Spann must have been among them but I didn't see him that time, having quickly averted my gaze from their faces.

Our job was not as easy as it might seem. The displaced beds were not always immediately outside the rooms whence they came, and there were complicated crossovers to be worked out. The patients were a nuisance too. They clamored for fruit juice and dope and they wanted their dressings seen to and they complained when we left them in the wrong rooms or when we failed to position their beds in precisely the same spots as before. Cecil, old hand at this, feigned deafness to their pleas.

I was dead on my feet, a zombie, and not at all prepared for the second great surprise of that day. I found Norma. It was there in that place of concentrated misery that I found her at last, and my senses were so dull that I took it as a matter of course. Cecil and I were pushing her into an empty room, a thin girl, half asleep and very pale, when I recognized her from the pulsing vein on her forehead. Her hair was cut short and there was a red scarf or handkerchief tied around her neck, just long enough to tie and leave two little pointed ends. Some thoughtful nurse has provided this spot of color, I said to myself, though it was no part of her job to do so. My heart went out to those dedicated ladies in white.

I spoke to Norma and she looked at me. There were dainty globules of sweat on her upper lip. She had trouble focusing. I had a weak impulse to take her in my arms, and then I caught myself, realizing how unseemly that would be, with Cecil standing there. I drew closer but not rudely close. I didn't want to thrust my bird face directly into hers as Melba had done so often to me.

'Midge?' she said.

'Yes, it's me. I'm right here. Did you think it was a dream?'

'No.'

She couldn't believe her eyes! I explained things to Cecil, babbling a little, and I searched my pockets for money or some valuable object to give him, to mark the occasion, but I had nothing and I just kept patting him on the back, longer than is usually done. I told him that I would now take charge of her and that he could go on about his business. Cecil was turning all this over in his brain and I could see he didn't believe she was my wife, even though she had called my name. I could see in his eyes that he thought I was a perverted swine who would bear watching. And it is to his credit, I suppose, that he refused to leave me alone with her. He stood in the doorway and watched for his supper and kept an eye on me.

I questioned Norma at some length. Her answers were slow in coming and not always to the point. I was patient with her and made every allowance for her condition. She said she had been in the hospital about a week or ten days. Her appendix had been removed. A week ago? Yes, or maybe longer. Then why was she not yet on her feet? She didn't know. How had she happened to get appendicitis? She couldn't say. Had she been in a private room all along, or a ward? She couldn't remember. Couldn't remember whether there was anyone else in her room or not? No. Did she not know there was a great difference in the cost of the two arrangements? No.

She turned away from me to face the wall. The maneuver made her wince. She stopped answering my questions. I had been careful to avoid mention of Dupree and other indelicate matters but I had somehow managed to give offense. I smoothed out her sheet and pulled it tight here and there. She didn't shrink from my touch. She had turned away from me but my touch wasn't loathsome to her.

'I have a little surprise for you,' I said. 'I brought your back pills all the way from Little Rock.'

She extended a cupped hand behind her.

'I don't have them now but I did have them. What is your doctor's name?'

No reply.

'I want to have a talk with that bird. What is he giving you? Do you know?'

No reply.

'Do you realize you're just skin and bones?'

'I don't feel like talking, Midge. I'm trying to be polite but I don't feel good.'

'Do you want to go home?'

'Yes.'

'With me?'

'I guess so.'

'What's wrong with me?'

'You just want to stay in the house all the time.'

'I'm not in the house now. I could hardly be further out of the house.'

'You don't want me back.'

'Yes, I do. I'm hard to please too. You know that.'

'I don't feel like talking right now.'

'We don't have to talk. I'll get a chair and just sit here.'

'Yes, but I'll know you're there.'

I found a folding chair and settled in for a vigil. An elderly fat woman passed by in the hall and Cecil grunted and directed her into the room. It was his mother. She had his supper in a plastic bucket. He glared at her for being late, a hurricane was no excuse, and he picked over the food and rejected outright some of the things in the bucket. I was surprised she didn't know what he liked after all these years. Maybe it was impossible to antici-pate his whims. They exchanged not a word. Cecil had no thanks for her and she was content to stand there and hold the bucket in silence and watch him eat, a slow, grinding business.

An unconscious old man was wheeled into the room and then a girl came by with trays of food on a cart. Norma drank some tea but I couldn't get her to eat anything. The sick man in the other bed was snoring. I ate his supper. A nurse stopped in to take temperatures. She ordered Cecil to the nursery, where he was needed to clean up a mess.

He said he was off duty now and was going home, addressing the nurse as 'Sister,' though she wasn't a nun. He and his mother left.

The nurse told me that Norma was slow in recovering because she would eat nothing but ice. She was dehydrated too, from a long siege of diarrhea. But there was no fever to speak of and no other signs of peritonitis. Weren't intravenous fluids indicated, I asked, in cases of dehydration? At this implied reproach the nurse became snippy. As for the current plan of treatment, she said, I would have to take that up 'with doctor' – not 'with *the* doctor.'

I crumbled some bread into a glass of milk and every half-hour I woke Norma and forced her to swallow a spoonful or two. Later, another nurse came around with some candles and asked that the lights and the fan be turned off so as to allow more electricity for areas of greater need. It didn't matter to me about the light because the emergency generator was producing just enough wattage to heat the bulb filament a dull red. I missed the fan for its companionable hum. After the first candle burned out, I didn't light another one. A small gray coil of anti-mosquito incense smoldered on the windowsill. The smoke curled about the room in a long tendril that kept its integrity for quite some time. I fanned Norma with a magazine when I thought about it. She asked me to stop waking her. I told her it wouldn't be necessary if she would only finish eating the bread and milk and the little cup of yellow custard with the nutmeg on top. She grudgingly did so and then we both slept, I in my chair.

She woke me before daylight and asked for a glass of crushed ice. Ice at five in the morning! I got some ice cubes at the nursing station and chopped them up with a pair of scissors. Now she was fully awake and ready to talk. I suppose it came more easily to her in the dark. She crunched on the ice and told me about her travels with Dupree. I was fascinated. Her voice was little more than a whisper but I hung on every word. She could have been one of Melba's psychic heroines, with eyes 'preternaturally bright.'

What a story! What a trip! They had first gone to Dallas, where Dupree was to meet with the well-known radical photographers, Hilda Monod and Jay Bomarr. I say 'well known,' although Norma had never heard of these people. Dupree had been in touch with them through a third party in Massachusetts, a fellow who had vouched for him, telling Hilda and Jay that Dupree had threatened to kill the President and was okay. He also told them, or maybe it was Dupree himself, that Dupree owned a shopping center in Memphis which produced a vast income that was now available to the radical movement. Hilda and Jay were eager to confer with him, or so they said.

But they didn't show in Dallas, telephoning instead from Florida to say they would be delayed, that they were conducting a workshop at a home for old radicals in Coral Gables. Dupree was to continue on to San Angelo and wait. There was another hitch and he was told to proceed to Wormington and see a fellow named Bates. Bates was to put them up in his house. But Bates had not been informed about the arrangement and he refused to talk to Dupree. Bates owned a cave near Wormington in which the temperature remained constant at 59 degrees Fahrenheit. How this grotto figured in the overall plans of the radicals, or if it figured at all, Norma couldn't say, and it must remain a matter for speculation. She and Dupree checked in at the motel. He paced the room and became impatient and called Hilda and Jay with an ultimatum. Either they stopped giving him the runaround or he would take his money and ideas elsewhere.

A meeting in Mexico was agreed upon, at San Miguel de Allende. Hilda and Jay were to take part in a seminar there with a visiting radical from Denmark. It would be a safe and quiet place to talk business. But they needed a car. Could Dupree furnish them with a car? Not at that time, he said, but once in San Miguel, on completion of a satisfactory personal interview, he would give them the keys to a Ford Torino.

So off they went to Mexico. Norma drove most of the way because Dupree wanted to polish up the presentation he was preparing for the two infamous radicals. He shuffled his papers and muttered to himself and ate candy bars and drank pink Pepto-Bismol from a bottle. He was very excited, she said, but he wouldn't discuss his ideas on the new social order with her, saying she was too dumb to understand his work.

Why, at that point, did she not slap his face and come home?

'I don't know,' she said.

She didn't know! She knew he had threatened the President of the United States and that he was now involved in some other devilish political enterprise and on top of that he was making rude personal remarks, and still she hung around for more! Then I saw the answer. I'm slow but sure. I had read things and heard many songs about people being poleaxed by love and brought quivering to their knees and I thought it was just something people said. And now here it was, true love. She was in love with that monkey! I was amazed but I couldn't really hold it against her. I knew she was puzzled by life and marriage, thinking the entire range of men ran only from Dupree to me and back again, and I couldn't really be angry with her, in her pitiable condition. She told me later that Dupree had promised her they would be remarried 'in a forest,' where they would exchange heart-shaped rings and some sort of on-the-spot vows. He had no shame.

Jay and Hilda limped into San Miguel a week late. They had been held up for a few days in Beaumont, Texas, after a tailgater had rammed their Saab sedan from behind, and there had been many subsequent breakdowns along the way. Neither of them drove, of course, and they traveled with three flunkies who handled all such chores. Five stinking radicals in a three-cylinder Saab! Norma couldn't remember the names of the flunkies. She said they wore small caps and moved about quickly like squirrels and smiled in a knowing way when they looked a person in the face. Jay and Hilda were polite to her but the flunkies made fun of her accent.

The conference was a failure. Jay and Hilda were upset to learn that Dupree owned no shopping center and had no money of his own and no intention whatever of giving them a car. Not only that, but he talked to them in a familiar way, as an equal or a superior, as one having authority, saying he wanted them to revise their entire program from top to bottom, incorporating, among other things, a new racial doctrine. He showed them some provocative slogans he had written, for shouting. He even lectured them on photography. They couldn't believe their ears! Norma said Jay Bomarr was particularly indignant. Since the Beaumont crash he had been wearing a rigid and uncomfortable plastic collar around his neck and he couldn't easily turn aside as Dupree ticked off important points on his fingertips.

The meeting ended with recriminations and with Dupree's papers scattered on the floor of the Bugambilia Café. There followed several empty days. Dupree walked about town with his dog.

Norma had already begun to suffer from internal disorders and she didn't range far from the hotel. I forced her to describe every bite she had eaten since leaving Little Rock, so far as she could remember. She became peeved and irritable as I hammered away at her but it was worth it in the end because in this way I was able to put my finger on the rancid peanuts that had started her trouble. Once the point was cleared up, I permitted her to go on with her story.

She said the radicals passed most of their time in a snack bar just off the square. Long-distance calls could be made there and Jay was a great one for the telephone. There they sat at a table all day, holding court before young admirers and taking their skimpy meals and conspiring lazily and placing and receiving numerous phone calls. One flunky was posted in the crumpled Saab at all times to watch the camera gear. The other two called themselves the Ground Observer Corps, and they moved around town and eavesdropped on conversations and then reported back to Hilda and Jay on what people were saying, the topics of the day in that particular place. Hilda, who had little to say, appeared to be the real boss of the gang.

Dupree stopped in once and tried to stare them down from the doorway of the snack bar. They turned their chairs around. He came back the next day and walked slowly through the place with his dog. He went out the back door and reappeared almost instantly at the front door again. The chow dog was now in on the trick! If the radicals were knocked for a loop, they didn't let on and they continued to regard Dupree with a contemptuous silence.

The Dane never showed up but they had the 'seminar' anyway, under some shade trees in a place called the French Park. Jay Bomarr opened it with his famous speech, 'Come Dream Along with Me.' I had heard it myself, at Ole Miss of all places, back in the days when Jay was drawing big crowds. It was a dream of blood and smashed faces, with a lot of talk about 'the people,' whose historic duty it was to become a nameless herd and submit their lives to the absolute control of a small pack of wily and vicious intellectuals. Norma said it went over fairly well with the young Americans and Canadians, judging from the applause. No Mexicans came except for the professor who was chairman of the thing. Dupree was there, standing at the front, and he heckled Jay for a while. He had a New Year's Eve noisemaker, a ratchet device that he swung around. The flunkies took it away from him and carried him off in the woods and beat him up.

Hilda followed Jay at the speaker's stand, to discuss her prize-winning photographs of 'hermits.' That is the word Norma understood Hilda to say, though it may have been something else. Varmints? Linnets? Spinets? Harlots? Norma couldn't be sure because Hilda was interrupted early by Jay, who had a disturbing announcement. Their thermos jug had been stolen. He said no questions would be asked if the person who had taken the jug would return same without delay. The appeal failed. Hilda tried threats. She said she was going to stop talking if the jug was not returned at once. There were groans of consternation from the crowd of young shutterbugs. The three flunkies made a lightning search through the park and turned up various objects but nothing in the way of a thermos jug. Someone offered Hilda a replacement jug of comparable size and quality. She said that wouldn't do at all and she put away her lecture materials and declared the seminar suspended until further notice. Jay and the professor tried to persuade her to continue, promising a full investigation. She said it was out of the question. The radicals packed their visual aids and returned to the snack bar, there to await the collapse of the conscience-stricken thief.

All that is fairly clear. Norma told it to me in a straightforward way and I have made it even clearer in my summary. But she could give me no satisfactory account of the rest of the journey, nothing but tantalizing scraps. She couldn't even remember when the idea first came up of going on to British Honduras. Dupree had told her it was an idyllic spot. She looked forward to her forest wedding there.

Then, she said, he began to behave 'strangely,' and for her to make such an acknowledgment I expected to hear next that Dupree had been seized by nothing short of barking fits. But it wasn't quite that. After leaving San Miguel he spoke to her through a small megaphone. She had asked him to repeat some remark – on just one occasion – and after that he pretended to believe she was deaf. He rolled a piece of cardboard into a cone and taped the ends, and he pretended to believe she couldn't hear him unless he spoke through it, directly into her ear from a foot or so away. The memory of the farmhouse made her shudder. She was there for about four days and sick the whole time. Terrible things went on outside. The workers shot the cows and beat up Dupree and destroyed the water pump. From that point on he was impossible. He went into a rage when he caught her bathing in the washtub, using scarce water. He accused her, through the megaphone, of malingering, and he accused her of introducing worm pills into his food. He had some deworming medicine for his dog and he couldn't find it. By that time the pain in Norma's side was hardly bearable and even Dupree could see that she was seriously ill. He drove her into town at night and left her at the hospital, and that must have been the night he got drunk and burned up my Torino.

What a story! Denmark! Coral Gables! But I was beginning to fade and I could no longer follow the details. Norma asked me to get her some more ice and I told her what we both needed now was not ice but a little more shut-eye.

The old man in the other bed woke at dawn. He woke suddenly and raised his head about an inch, gravity overtaking him there, and said, 'What the devil is going on anyway?'

'I don't know,' I truthfully replied.

He had one boggling, red-rimmed eye like Mr Proctor. He wanted coffee and I went to see if I could find some.

CHAPTER 16

Ruth had bounced me from the Fair Play without a hearing and Webster had taken my bag to a cheaper hotel called the Delgado, and told the manager there, another woman, that I was a model roomer in every way except for that of payment. She took a chance on me. There was no difficulty. I went personally to the cable office and wired my father for money and got it the next morning. The Delgado wasn't as conveniently located as the Fair Play and had fewer amenities. The rates, however, were very reasonable.

I took Norma from the hospital in a taxicab and put her to bed in my room. The woman boss at the Delgado made a kind of fish soup or stew that was pretty good and I fed this to Norma, along with boiled rice. The English doctor had told me she could eat whatever she liked but I thought it best to be on the safe side and I allowed her no fried foods. I had to turn down her request for fresh pineapple too, it being so coarse and fibrous. After two days of forcing soup down her gullet I had her on her feet again, taking little compulsory hikes about the room. She tottered and complained. I bought her a shark's-tooth bracelet. I read to her from old magazines until she asked me to stop doing it.

Mrs Symes had slept through the hurricane. She herself was released from the hospital that same week, though she continued to be more or less bedridden. Christine and the girl Elizabeth attended to her. The stroke had left a slight paralysis in her left arm and a slight speech impediment. Still, she didn't appear to be severely disabled.

'Another blast from Almighty God,' she said to me. I nodded, not knowing whether she meant the storm or the stroke. Christine was flexing the old lady's arm and fingers so that the muscles would not become atrophied.

'Do you know why these things are sent?'

I said, 'No, ma'am, I don't.'

'They are sent to try us. Tell me this. Are the doors sticking too?'

'Yes, they are.'

'I thought as much. It makes it hard for us when the doors stick.'

'I was wondering if you would do me a favor, Meemaw.'

'I will if I can, hon. You see the sorry shape I'm in.'

'I was wondering if you would write a note to Captain Grace on behalf of a friend of mine. He's in jail and needs some help.'

She had forgotten my first name and she asked

me what it was. I told her and she told me once again that there was no one named Ray in the Bible. But that was all right, she said, Ray would do as well as any other name here on earth. Only God knew our true names.

Everyone was either sick or in jail. Melba was laid up in the bedroom with the brown picture on the wall. There had been nothing really wrong with her at the hospital but when she came out of her trance in the emergency room she got up and walked home and it was this unaccustomed trek across town that had put her under. So she was in bed too, for the first time in years, and Christine had her hands full, what with all the cooking and nursing. Brave Christine! The girl Elizabeth was a good worker too, and Victor was a useless whiner. I asked him why he didn't go outside and play and get out of Christine's hair and he said a chicken had pecked him on the street.

I did what I could, at the urging of Mrs Symes, to find out what had happened to the doctor. I inquired at the bus station and the airport and the consular office. I took another look at the dead bodies in the hospital, where I saw poor Spann, his busy pen stilled forever. I inquired at the Shell station and the Texaco station. I talked to fishermen. When I visited Jack in jail, I looked over all the prisoners. Of course I had my eye out for Dupree too. I thought there was an excellent chance he might have been arrested again, for one thing or another. I found no trace of either of

304

them. Mrs Symes said she had a strong feeling that Reo was dead, cut off abruptly in his sins. Melba said no, he was still very much alive and she knew it in her bones. I found Melba's hunch the more convincing of the two.

I had dropped in at the tabernacle to report my investigation a failure, and to pick up the silver set, having in mind a nice surprise. I was going to take one of those round spoons from the silver chest and feed Norma her soup with it, and then, with a flourish and a roguish smile, reveal to her the familiar floral pattern on the handle. This, I thought, an unexpected touch of home, would trigger happy domestic memories, by way of the well-known principle of association.

But first I had to go by the newspaper office. Mrs Symes wanted me to call there and have the doctor's name added to the published list of missing persons. Webster and some other boys were in front of the place dividing up a stack of *Bugles*. On an impulse, and this was very unlike me, I gave him Mrs Edge's silver. I called him over and said, 'Here, do you want this? I'm tired of fooling with it.' The chest was wrapped in an old towel and he was suspicious. 'It's not a jar this time,' I said. 'That's sterling silver.' I advised him to take it to Father Jackie or some other trustworthy adult for safekeeping or for sale.

'My point is this. I don't want you to let Ruth take it away from you.' I told him to cultivate good study habits and I left him there holding the heavy chest and went to the Delgado and told Norma what I had done, apologizing for my rash action. She said she didn't care. She wanted to go home.

Finally I was able to get Jack released from jail, no thanks to the American consul. That bird said it was none of his business and he wouldn't interfere even if he could. The testimonial note from Mrs Symes did the trick, combined with an irregular payment and a promise that Jack would leave the country immediately. He was glad to be free again. We got a used battery at the Texaco station and I suggested a quick run out on Bishop Lane. I would show him the Dupree place and he could look around and maybe pick up some leads, see some things that had escaped my untrained eye. But Jack was no longer concerned with Dupree. He said, 'You can do what you want to, Ray. I'm going home.'

Norma and I rode home with him in the Chrysler. He drove all the way with his sore hands, not trusting other people at the wheel. What a trip! What a glum crew! Norma snapped at me, and Jack, who had been reading things in his cell again, talked about economic cycles and the fall of the Roman Empire and the many striking parallels that might be drawn between that society and our own. Norma called me 'Guy' a couple of times. My own wife couldn't even remember my name.

I told them about the pelican that was struck by lightning. They didn't believe it. I tried to tell them about Dr Symes and Webster and Spann and Karl and their attention wandered. I saw then that I would have to write it down, present it all in an orderly fashion, and this I have done. But I can see that I have given far too much preliminary matter and that I have considerably overshot the mark. So be it. It's done now. I have left out a few things, not least my own laundry problems, but I haven't left out much, and in the further interests of truth I have spared no one, not even myself.

Our journey home was a leisurely one. Jack drove only during daylight hours. We stayed in nice motels. Norma perked up a little after I began to let her order her own meals. We stopped at a beach south of Tampico for a swim in the Gulf. Norma wore her dress in the water like an old woman because she'd didn't want Jack to see the raw scar on her abdomen. A man came along with a brazier made from a bucket and he broiled some shrimp for us right there on the beach. The food and beer made us sleepy and we stayed the night. Jack slept in the car.

Norma and I lay on the warm sand all night under a piece of stiff canvas that Jack carried in his trunk. We listened to the surf and watched the incandescent streaks of meteors. I pointed out to her the very faint earthshine on the darker, gibbous part of the new moon. She admitted that her escapade with Dupree had been very foolish and I said we must now consider the matter closed. We reaffirmed our affection for one another.

The next day we were all in good spirits and we

sang 'Goodnight, Irene' and other old songs as we approached the border at Matamoros. The euphoria in turn passed as we drew closer to home and when we reached Texarkana we were pretty much ourselves again. Jack became solemn and he began to pose rhetorical questions. 'What is everybody looking for?' he said. Norma didn't hesitate; she said everybody was looking for love. I gave the question some thought and then declared that everybody was looking for a good job of work to do. Jack said no, that many people were looking for those things, but that everybody was looking for a place where he could get food cheap – on a regular basis. The qualification was important because when I mentioned the cheap and tasty shrimps we had eaten on the beach, Jack said yes, but you couldn't count on that Mexican bird coming by every afternoon with his cooking can and his bulging wet sack.

Much later we learned that Dupree had gone overland – walked! in cowboy boots! bumping into trees! – down into Honduras, the genuine Honduras. He went first to a place on the coast called La Ceiba and then caught a ride on an oilsurvey plane to the capital city of Tegucigalpa. I looked for him to come dragging in after a few months. A lot of people leave Arkansas and most of them come back sooner or later. They can't quite achieve escape velocity. I expect it's much the same everywhere. But that monkey is still down there, as far as I know.

I never said anything to Mr Dupree about my Torino. I do know he paid off the bail forfeiture and I suspect he used his political influence to have the charge against Guy shelved, if not dropped altogether. Dupree's whereabouts are certainly no secret but nothing has been done toward having him picked up and extradited.

His mother has flown down there twice to see him, the second time to take him a pit bulldog. That was the kind of dog he wanted and he couldn't find one in Honduras. She must have had no end of trouble introducing that dog into another country by air, particularly a grotesque animal like the pit bull, but she managed to do it. I don't know what happened to the chow dog. She tells everyone Guy is 'thinking and writing' and is doing fine. I have heard from other people that he walks around Tegucigalpa all day in a narcotic haze, nodding at Hondurans and taking long strides in his runover boots. He keeps his left hand in his pocket, they say, with the right hand swinging free in an enormous military arc. I assume she sends him money. You can cadge drinks but I think you have to have money for dope.

At Christmas I mailed Mrs Symes a Sears catalogue and I enclosed my own copy of Southey's *Life of Nelson* for Webster. I heard nothing from Belize and I suspect the parcel was lost or stolen.

Norma regained her health and we got on better than ever before. We went to football games and parties. We had a fine Christmas. We went to the

Cancer Ball with Mrs Edge and one of her florid escorts and I even danced a little, which isn't to say I became overheated. In January I got my B.A. degree and I decided to stay in school and try engineering again, with an eye toward graduate work in geology and eventual entry into the very exciting and challenging field of plate tectonics. Then in April, after the last frost, Norma became restless again. She went to Memphis to visit a friend named Marge. 'Goodbye, goodbye,' she said to me, and the next thing I knew she had her own apartment over there, and a job doing something at a television station. She said she might come back but she didn't do it and I let her go that time. It's only about 130 miles to Memphis but I didn't go after her again.

TF175300

DEAD INNOCENT

Hearing that a fifteen-year-old girl is missing from Totterdown, Kate Creech is filled with alarm, for her niece Maisie is fifteen and lives in that area of Bristol. Then a girl's corpse is found in a local park and Maisie's dad is the prime suspect. Even though Bristol is out of his jurisdiction, Detective Inspector John Bright adores Maisie as though she were his own and, frustrated by the local force, he resorts to his own unofficial methods of investigation. There are many people with secrets to keep but Bright is sure he is getting close to the solution.

DEAD INNOCENT

DEAD INNOCENT

by

Maureen O'Brien

Magna Large Print Books
Long Preston, North Yorkshire,
BD23 4ND, England.

British Library Cataloguing in Publication Data.

O Brien, Maureen
    Dead innocent.

    A catalogue record of this book is
    available from the British Library

    ISBN   0-7505-1543-0

First published in Great Britain by Constable & Company Limited, 1999

Published in Large Print 2000 by arrangement with Constable & Co., Ltd.

Magna Large Print is an imprint of Library Magna Books Ltd.

Printed and bound in Great Britain by
T.J. (International) Ltd., Cornwall, PL28 8RW

For Michael, without whom...

ACKNOWLEDGEMENTS

Thanks to Sergeant Martin Thompson of Avon and Somerset Constabulary. He put me in touch with Inspector Pinnock at Broadbury Road Police Station, who gave generously of his time and patience. If I have taken poetic licence with some of Inspector Pinnock's invaluable information, the distortions are mine, not his. Again, I'm deeply grateful to Imogen Olsen, my perfect copy editor, for sorting out my *im*perfect hold on the time factor. To Tara, my editor, for her patience and support. And to Peter James, a great theatre director, whose unforgettable production of *As You Like It* (Designer, Roger Glossop) at the Crucible Theatre Sheffield I have shamelessly drawn upon.

1

AN OPENING

The gun was still in her hand. Her head was turned away but you could see from the faces of the others that hers was a horrifying sight. Neither her husband nor her friends could speak. They stared down at her in appalled silence. Then the judge said with a shudder of distaste, 'People just don't do things like that.' A nervous gasp whispered through the air. The shocked silence returned. The room slowly went dark. The silence continued. Then the applause broke out. The actors came back into light and took five calls.

Jostled out into the buzz of the foyer Bright felt shaken. 'Come round afterwards,' she'd said. But how did you do that? He fought his way through the crowd to the bar. Managed to attract the attention of a bar girl who spoke into the security phone. She gave him a sweet smile: 'Kate says that's fine. Just wait there. Someone will come to take you through.'

He waited, uneasy. The atmosphere seemed hysterical to him. The level of noise

11

in the bar now was like a football crowd only higher pitched. And how did you face a person you'd just seen do what Kate had done? On stage she was a tiger. Beautiful, fine, clever, ruthless, vulnerable. All that she was in real life only magnified. Transformed. He was off his pitch. Out of his depth. He'd never even been backstage before. What was he doing here? What was expected of him? This was not a new question in connection with Kate. It was just more acute here, now, on the opening night of a play.

'Ankate, you're alive!'
'Just about, Maisie.'
'I really thought you were dead.' All wisps and wafts of white silky stuff, in her new frock, Maisie threw her arms round Kate. 'Oh Ankate, it was fantastic, it was the best. We're bringing all our mates, aren't we, Allie?' She dragged forward a tall shy dark-skinned girl. 'This is my friend Alison.'

Dressed in black, sophisticated for fourteen and of devastating beauty, Alison had a deep voice: 'Yurr, it was rully brullian'.' The Bristol accent came as a surprise. Some more exotic sound might better have suited her appearance.

Kate was already out of the corset and the rest of the gear. She sat to take off the make-up. The dressing-room phone rang. 'Can

12

you get that, Maize?'

'Hello? Oh, I'll ask her.' A hoarse whisper: 'It's John Bright. Is it okay if he comes up?'

'Yes!'

'Kate says yes.' Maisie hung the phone back on the wall. 'Someone's showing him the way.'

Kate felt a sudden sand-blast of apprehension, glad her face was hidden by the mask of cleansing cream.

Maisie said to Alison, 'He's Ankate's policeman.'

'Maisie!'

Maisie laughed. She whispered to Alison, 'Detective Inspector John Bright.'

The girls watched mesmerised as Kate wiped the make-up off her face. And Kate watched them in the mirror. Maisie, tall now, with pale translucent skin, narrow limbs, and an aureole of reddish fair hair, an Arthur Rackham girl. Alison, even taller, a Nefertiti head and an easy athletic grace. The puma and the butterfly. Lovely together. Alison awed being backstage. Maisie impressed too, but acting cool. Kate said, 'What do you think of my dressing room then?'

Maisie shrugged. 'It's okay, I suppose.'

Alison said, 'I thought it would be more – posh, like.'

'Posh is for the punters.' Kate dragged a brush through her hair. 'They get the red

13

plush. We get the breeze blocks.'

'Shall I put these in water for you?' Maisie picked up a cellophane-wrapped Interflora bouquet.

'Sure. Thanks.'

'Oh, they're from him,' Maisie said. 'Your policeman.'

A knock at the door. Kate said, 'Let him in. And don't call him that to his face.'

Bright sidled in. He nodded at the girls, then at Kate in the mirror, but didn't speak.

She nodded back. 'You came then.'

'A-ha.' He looked round, awkward in these surroundings, as lost for words as she was. 'So this is where you hang out.'

'Not luxurious, is it?'

'Bit like Kentish Town HQ.'

Kate introduced the girls. Maisie said, 'I've never met a detective inspector before.'

Alison said, 'Neither have I.'

'He saved Ankate's life, you know.'

'Yurr?'

'We've got all the newspaper cuttings. We kept them.' Maisie adopted a ghoulish tone. '"The Body in the Bath".'

Alison shuddered in a snaky movement from heel to head. Both girls laughed. They were flirting in that shy bold way that young girls do, not quite in control but trying to look it. Bright caught Kate's eye in the mirror and gave her a smile. He did this without moving a muscle of his face. It

14

always gave her a shock. She still didn't know how he did it.

Alison got serious. She asked him, 'Did you like the play?'

Kate cringed.

Bright said, 'I don't know if *like* is the word.'

Kate drooped. This was the reason you never asked: you might get the truth.

Alison agreed with Bright. 'The people in it aren't very nice, are they?'

'Tesman and Mrs Elvsted are.' Maisie was drinking Bright with her eyes.

'Yurr, but they're boring. The nasty people are quite interesting though.'

Maisie made a swooning face. 'Yeah. I loved Eilert Lovborg.'

'Oh yurr, he's gorgeous.' Alison's deep Bristol voice gave the word a rolling relish.

'Will he be in the restaurant, Ankate?'

'See? They're not interested in art. Just sex.'

'Ankate!'

'Come on. Let's go.'

Renato's was heaving. Smoke hung in veils. No point shouting over the din. Kate mouthed, 'Red wine?' Bright muscled into a space at the bar. Waiting to be served he watched her disappear into a scrum of congratulating bodies: *Kate, you were wonderful, amazing, marvellous, fantastic.*

15

Embraces, kisses, hugs.

The girls were gazing rapt at Eilert Lovborg, an ascetic-looking man, almost imperceptibly gay. He bathed in their adoration like asses' milk. Bright handed them their Cokes. They now barely glanced his way, more exotic fish to fry.

Kate fought through the pack and grabbed her red wine, gasping thanks. He lifted his glass and clinked it on hers. 'Get a lot of rewards in your job, don't you? They don't tell me marvellous wonderful when I get a villain to cough.'

'Trouble is believing it. I never can.'

'Well, you should.'

'You mean that?'

'A-ha.'

'Oh.' She kissed him. The kiss became more than a kiss of congratulation given and received.

'Hey! Put this woman down!' Another rampant acquaintance. Kate pulled away but kept his eyes with a kind of astonishment.

They ate one of Renato's lasagnes in the bar and downed another glass or three. The pace had quietened. Most of the punters had gone, leaving only the hard core of elated actors with their closest mates. Eilert Lovborg was seriously explaining his interpretation of the role to his two fans, whose avid eyes roamed his face as he

16

talked. Kate and Bright sat side by side, their first chance to exchange a quiet word.

'You liked it then?' she said.

'A-ha. I liked it.'

'That's all right then.'

'You care what I think?' His voice held real surprise.

Her hair, crunched into a tight little knot to look meagre for Hedda, had sprung out on its release into a wild thicket round her head. As she turned to give him a *don't act innocent* look it swung across his face. He got a piercing shock: the palpable presence of Millie Hale. For a second he was lost. Confused. Somewhere else.

Kate was worse than a cat for picking things up. She backed off, like a cat that bucks an alien scent, the merest flicker in the eyes. He gave an inward groan. He'd screwed it up again.

'Ankate? Can we go on to dad's place?'

Kate looked at the time. 'Okay, Maisie. Sure. It's not that late.' She looked at Bright. 'Fancy going on to Dave's place?' She was distant with him now. Matey, no more.

They walked to Dave's, the air a cool surprise after the fug of the bar. The girls danced ahead, whispering, laughing. They crossed the road and went down the steps to the quay. Boats rose and fell on the breathing water. Lights were on in some. You could see the people in their tiny rooms, drinking, talking, washing up.

The boat house rose up over to their left, a tall black wooden structure, still with its loading doors and hoists. Maisie started to run, Allie after her, both with a touching extreme of grace.

Maisie pulled on a rope and a ship's bell clanged. A window opened at the top of the boat house. A head appeared. Bright saw long ringlets hanging over the sill. 'That's Maisie's dad?'

Kate laughed at the package of misgivings crammed into Bright's tone. 'He's quite nice when you get to know him.'

They followed the girls up the dark stone staircase. On the landing the stone stairs ran out. Open-tread wooden steps took over, creaking and shifting slightly as they climbed. On the second landing they could see Dave above. Maisie ran up the last three stairs. 'Dad?'

'Maisie. Hello, hon.' He threw wide his arms and crushed Maisie to him. He was dressed in white. Thick linen tunic and loose trousers, a poetic figure. Maisie, wispy, slight and pale, was lifted off her feet. The candle and the moth, Kate thought.

Shadows flickered across the trembling light in the doorway. Music pounded from inside the loft: 'A white-er – shade of – pa-

18

ale...' Bright said, 'Bloke likes Procol Harum can't be all bad, I suppose.'

'Dad? This is Allie. Allie, this is my dad.'

Dave took Alison's hand and gazed seriously into her eyes. 'Dave,' he said.

Abashed, Alison said, 'Is it a party, then?'

'Well, there's food and there's people and there's music. If that makes a party it's a party, I guess. Go on in.'

The girls disappeared inside.

'Hi, Dave.'

'Kate!'

Kate avoided being crushed by the thin powerful arms. 'This is John Bright.'

'Hi, nice to meet you. What are you doing here, Kate?'

'I opened in a play tonight, Dave, at the Old Vic.'

'Ah. I see. How was that?'

'It was pretty fucking phenomenal,' Bright said. He rarely used the Anglo-Saxon, except to make a point.

Dave got the point. He grimaced at Kate, shamefaced charm. 'Sorry, Kate, I should have known.'

'Yes, you should. I'll forgive you this once.'

'I'll catch it later in the run.'

'I bet.'

The shadows, made huge by candle-light, moved in slow frenzy in the vast wood-walled space. Twenty-odd young people

19

danced, or lay around on cushions. Dave asked Bright, 'Would you like a drink?'

'I could use a scotch, mate. No water, just ice.'

'Sorry, I don't have alcohol. There's all kinds of juice, though, and of course, water.'

Bright was shocked into silence. He gave Kate a look that made her laugh. 'Dance?' she said.

'*Dance?*' he said.

Kate had never danced with him before. She was amazed. He danced the way he drove: with an effortless rhythmic invention that made her feel high.

'No booze?' he said. 'He a Muslim or something?'

Kate smiled but did not reply.

'Guess he finds it cool to get stoned on other substances,' Bright said.

Kate stopped smiling. She looked at Bright with a touch of alarm. He gazed back, his squint impenetrable. Was he joking or not? She sensed a shift in the room, a general movement. She stood on tiptoe to see what was going on. In a space on the wide floorboards Maisie and Allie were dancing. The whole roomful of young people one by one stopped to watch Allie and Maisie dance.

Allie's movements were strong and graceful, like a powerful black cat. Maisie, ethereal and white, the wisps of her frock

20

sprayed round her like shreds of torn wings. They circled each other swaying, their arms turning and twisting to the intricacies of some music Kate didn't know, the ethnic drumbeat slow, the melody a subdued and undulating howl.

Nobody moved. Even breathing seemed to stop. The light trembled about the two beautiful girls, who seemed unconscious of the awe they induced. Kate knew from her own girlhood they surely were aware of the admiration, though not of the subtle and fierce longings in some of the admirers. They'd discover those later. Much later, she hoped.

Bright, leaning against the rough wooden planks that divided the kitchen area from the main room, was acutely aware of these longings, not least in himself. He felt a sudden tingle of alarm. Not sure what had caused it, he unlocked his gaze from its intense absorption in the girls and turned it on the faces around him, lit reddish by candle flames.

A young man stood a few feet away, arms folded across his chest. No awe there. No admiration. Anger gripped the mouth and lasered out of the eyes. Bright watched awhile then moved closer. He spoke in his softest catlike purr: 'What's up?'

The young man's head did not turn. 'It's hideous.'

'Two lovely kids dancing?'

'The way they're all watching.'

Bright recalled his own twinge of guilt. 'The blokes, you mean?'

'The *adults*.' The boy spat the word out like a foul taste. 'Look at them. Hungry. Predatory. Those girls won't escape. It'll get them. It'll suck them in.'

'What will?'

'What will? The corruption will. And it will get them soon. They're on the brink.'

'Innocence isn't always all it's cracked up to be, you know.'

The rage blow-torched into Bright's face. 'Innocence is real. It doesn't necessarily belong to youth. Not many possess it. But those two girls do.'

'Sometimes it's not innocence, it's just ignorance, and it gets them into trouble.'

'You work for the police, I believe.'

Bright was rocked back on his heels. 'Er... Yeah.'

'So you would think that, wouldn't you? Excuse me.' The young man disappeared out of the candle-light into the shadowy gloom. The music stopped. The beautiful dancing came to an end. Conversation murmured once more in corners. Bright didn't see the boy again.

'You're late.' Lizzie looked immensely tall at the top of the steps.

'Our fault, Lizzie. We went on to Dave's.'

'How are you getting home, Alison?'

'We're taking her. We're just dropping Maisie off first. This is John Bright, by the way.'

Lizzie barely gave him a glance. 'Hello.' Her tone was cold.

He had a nose for petty tyranny. Never warmed to it. He gave Lizzie a brief nod, no more. ''Night then, Maisie,' he said. She fluttered down the steps and hugged him, then threw her arms round Kate. She whispered 'It was a great night, Ankate, I'll never forget it as long as I live.'

'Just how I feel, Maize.'

Alison lived down the street, past the little mosque, and up a sloping crescent. Outside a house with sunflowers in the garden, heads drooping in the night air, she took a key from her pocket. Bright and Kate looked surprised. 'They trust me.' Alison gave a proud lift of her chin.

'A-ha?' Bright's expression was dubious. 'That right?'

Alison grinned. 'Dad'll be waiting up actually, he just pretends not to worry. He wants me to be independent. You know.'

And indeed a tall black man opened the door before she had got her key in the lock. She reached up and put her arms round his neck. Over her head he smiled. 'Thanks for bringing her home safe.'

'He's a bit of a contrast to your sister,' Bright said, walking back down the hill.

'Take no notice of Lizzie. She can't help her manner. It's not personal.'

'You could fool me.'

Outside his awful hotel Bright said, 'I've probably sobered up enough to give you a lift?' A silence fell. He didn't look at Kate; he looked at his shoes.

'That would be nice?' Her questioning inflection precisely echoed his own. He grinned.

She brought the mugs of coffee and led the way to her living room: angled ceilings, white walls, striped rug in shades of Etruscan red. 'Mmm,' he said.

'Nice, isn't it?'

He prowled, learning the territory, listening for rustles in the undergrowth, sniffing the air. He stopped to look out of the window. 'Great view.'

'Where do you sleep?'

'Here.' She sat on the sofa. 'It becomes a bed. With a flick of the wrist.'

'A-ha.' Non-committal. They exchanged a glance. He drank some coffee, walked about again, stopped to study a painting. 'That's nice.'

'Caroline. My landlady. She's a painter.'

'The people you know.'

'Only the best.' She looked at him.

He looked back, under his eyebrows. 'That so?' he said. He sat down, on the edge of the chair, thoughtful. 'You're good at friends.'

'I am?'

'I don't have any,' he said.

'No friends?' She was shocked. 'Are you sure?'

'I'm sure.'

'But why?'

'The job. The unsocial hours.'

'No more unsocial than mine.'

'The life then.'

'What, no one wants to be friends with a cop?'

'I dunno. Acquaintances, I've got. Plenty. Blokes that I've enjoyed working with. Women that I've ... well. You know. But not what I'd call friends.'

'There's your ma.'

'Lily? A friend?' He rubbed a hand over his hair. 'Yeah.' He sounded doubtful.

'She welcomes your people in.'

'Yeah, but they all become *her* friends.'

'Like me.'

'Like you.'

'But I was your friend first.' She sounded seven years old, heard herself and laughed. She said, 'I'm your friend.'

He didn't laugh. He said, 'You want to keep it that way?'

25

'Well... Of course I do.' She couldn't say all the things she felt about him. How highly she valued him. It would sound daft.

'See...' He was struggling to speak to her in a way that was hard for him. 'What happens with me' – at last he'd managed to get to the point – 'When things look like getting serious I – slide out,' he said.

'So do I!'

'See, with Millie...'

Her heart sank. Would every conversation with him always forever come back to Millie Hale?

'See...' He struggled on. 'We were alone, me and Millie. I didn't know any of her people. She didn't know any of mine. We were a secret. It was like we were on an island. I mean we were on a boat, for Christsake. A boat is a kind of island, right? We were in this – secret world. We were hiding where no one could get at us. We both wanted that. Me as much as her.'

'What are you trying to say?'

'I dunno.' He shook his head. 'I used to be good at – you know – casual encounters. Coppers are good at that. We're opportunists.'

'That right?'

'You bet that's right.'

'But you've changed?'

'I seem to have, yeah.'

'Since Millie? Because of Millie?'

26

'Seems like that, yep.'

'You telling me I'm flogging a dead horse here?' She spoke in an airy tone, light as a feather.

'Well, I hope not dead exactly.' A hint of his old humour.

'Just resting?' she said.

He laughed. Then got serious again. 'The thing is...' He grimaced, squinted ferociously, scratched an ear. 'I don't want to – let you down.'

She corrected him. 'You don't want to let yourself down.'

He ignored her emendation, deep in his subject. 'I've only been – emotionally involved like that just the once. It was – like I went through a barrier. It was amazing. It was the best thing that ever happened to me. But it stopped. You see? It was yanked from under me. She...' His fury, his desperation, his passion, silenced Kate. 'See, since then, I can't...' He made a hopeless gesture, drank down his coffee and handed her the cup. 'I shouldn't have come up here.' He stood up and scraped a hand through his hair. 'Ah shit. Sorry, Kate. I thought it was going to work out.'

She was close to tears. 'Well, never mind.'

'You should mind.'

'I do mind.'

'You do mind?' Intense surprise.

'I mind.'

27

'You always sound like you don't.'

'I'm good at casual,' she said. 'I'm good at sounding it.'

'Oh.' He folded his arms, listening.

'But, you know,' she said, 'it's possible just to – pretend.'

'Pretend what?'

'Pretend it's casual.'

'Pretend to who?'

'To yourself.'

'What for?'

'To make it possible to – begin.'

'Oh. A-ha. I see.'

'I always do that. Find out as you go along.'

'I used to do that too.' He shook his head. 'Can't, these days.'

Her tone changed. 'You look dead tired,' she said.

'Yeah, I got an early start tomorrow.'

'And I'll be dead to the world till afternoon.' She took him to the door and kissed him lightly goodnight, letting him off the hook. 'Thanks for coming tonight.'

'Ha.' He gave her a look: anger with himself, tenderness for her, despair and affection mixed. He gave her a wave from the first-floor landing. She heard his footsteps continue down the stairs. She heard the front door closed with care. She listened a moment then closed her door with equal care. She looked at her empty flat. She'd done it again. She sure was good at getting rid of people. He'd never even taken his scruffy leather jacket off.

flat. She'd done it again. She sure was good
at getting rid of people. She'd never even
taken his scruffy leather jacket off.

2

NEXT YEAR

'You've not seen much of Kate lately, John.'
'Mmm?'
'I said—'
'She's away filming, ma.'
'Till the middle of June, she said. She should be back by now.'
'A-ha?' He was deep in the newspaper pretending not to hear.
'Anything interesting in the *Standard?*' Lily was in one of her *talk to me talk to me* moods.
He put the paper down. 'All right, ma. What's on your mind?'
'There was a thing on the news this morning,' she said. 'A girl's body under someone's shed.' He didn't respond. 'Round your way,' she said.
He used his occasional squint to pretend he wasn't looking in her direction. He'd been doing that since he was two. It didn't take her in. Nothing he did deceived her. 'Is it your case?' she said.
'It's my case.'
'I see.'

30

'You see what, ma?'

'I see why you're in such a bad mood.'

'Yeah.' He sighed.

'Do you know who did it?'

'I've got a good idea.'

'Can you get him?'

'Not yet.'

'Why not?'

'Evidence, ma. It's always evidence.'

'You'll get it, John.'

'Not necessarily.'

'You always do.'

He gave a dry laugh. 'There's always a first time.'

She'd got him talking. She cheered up. 'I think I'll have another scotch.'

'Two? You're going it a bit. What's up?'

She wriggled in her chair, wagged her head this way then that way. 'I don't know. Everyone's away. On their holidays. Even Mary next door's gone off on a coach trip and you know her, she never goes anywhere. It's the weather. It affects people. It's too hot outside. There's nothing to do in the garden even.'

He handed her her scotch. 'That's because you've got it so nice.'

'Flattery'll get you anywhere.'

He grinned. She knew he never flattered. 'Cheers.'

'And you know me,' she said. 'I can't sit doing nothing.'

She hardly ever told him she needed him. When she did, it was serious. He was on duty tomorrow and South Norwood wasn't convenient for Kentish Town police HQ, but what the hell: he'd stay the whole weekend, not go back to his dog kennel in Crouch End. 'Well, I'm not working Sunday,' he said. 'We can go somewhere.'

She turned on him her most glorious smile. It had always been worth it, pleasing her.

Saturday he came in later than late, and looked tireder than yesterday. 'Hi, ma.'

'There's a fish pie in the oven.' She wheeled her chair in the direction of the kitchen.

'I'll get it.' He poured himself a scotch first. He'd already had a few, she could tell.

He stretched – 'Aagh' – standing at the french windows.

She wheeled over to join him. They gazed at her feast of a garden, creamy roses cascading over the walls. 'How's the case?' she said.

'Ma, you don't want to know.'

'Yes, I do, or I wouldn't ask. What's happened? Can't you get the bloke?'

'Yeah, we got him. The neighbour.'

'You got him? So why aren't you pleased?'

'We found some stuff. Under the floorboards in his bedroom.'

'Oh no.' She didn't want to imagine.

'And now he's talking. He's been telling me about it all afternoon. Can't shut him up.' He turned away from the window. 'That's all they want in the end. They just want to tell. And the confession won't stand up on its own. The CPS will want their pound of – yeah, well.'

'You'd better eat, my lad.'

'A-ha.' He downed the scotch and went off to the kitchen.

Lily followed. She manoeuvred her wheelchair through the doorway and watched him ladle out the steaming pie. It was one of her classics. She'd been making it since he was nine years old. Normally he'd be delighted. Tonight he ate it like it was cardboard. Casually she said, 'I rang Kate.'

'She's back then?' No interest at all. And he wasn't pretending tonight. He was in a bad way.

Lily persevered. 'She's found a flat.'

'Oh, has she?'

'Moving in next Saturday, she says.'

He put down his fork, folded his arms and gave her his most piercing inquisitorial squint. 'Okay, ma. What's your point?'

Lily said with bland innocence, 'Maybe she could do with a hand.'

3

MAKING A MOVE

A big 1860s house at the end of Lady Margaret Road. Nice, even viewed through pouring rain. Paved front garden with a spiky yucca plant. Iron balcony still intact over the bay window. Mass was letting out, hordes of people running from the Catholic church, piling into their cars. Suddenly the street was empty. He parked then ran up the path to the green front door and rang the bottom bell before he chickened out.

She was smaller, standing there in her doorway, more vulnerable than the Kate he carried in his mind. She didn't say anything, or smile, just waited. It was her honest eyes that daunted him. 'How are you?' he said.

'Okay,' she said. 'You?'

'Better for seeing you.' He meant it. She gave him a wide smile.

Inside, she opened a door into a spacious entrance hall, even in this weather full of light. An arch led to a huge square room, its right side a galley kitchen with a glass roof. Kate opened the french windows.

It was all gardens at the back. All round.

Trees and birdsong. The garden had grown rampant, roses and clematis and lavender bushes gone wild. The rain had slowed to a peaceful drizzle, sunshine shimmering through the drops. They strolled across an old brick terrace oozing weeds and moss.

He lifted a long whip of thorny rose so she could duck under the trellis arch and down a paved path that curved between small vegetable beds.

Standing down there at the bottom of the garden, water dripping off the trees on to the shed roof, Bright looked quizzical. 'You haven't moved far, have you?'

'Oh yes I have.'

'Your old place is just over there.'

'Yes, but I can't see it. Gardens in between, and the trees.' Changing the subject, she opened the door of the shed. 'Look, isn't this great? I've never had a garden shed before.'

He shivered.

'What's up?'

He turned away from the shed and she remembered his horrible case. 'I'm sorry, I forgot.' He seemed this tough cockney mongrel nothing could touch. But was full of surprises.

'We're all sick round the station,' he said. 'Sick.'

'The bloke who killed the neighbour's daughter?'

'Not just *this* neighbour's daughter.'

'Oh.'

'No.'

'I'm sorry.'

'You wouldn't believe the stuff we found. Assembling the evidence they call it. And are we ever.'

'You caught him. There must be satisfaction in that.'

'Nah. The stuff wasn't hard to find.'

'But you did find it.'

'Just routine.'

'But you had to suspect him, didn't you? In order to search in the first place?'

Bright shrugged. He never saw what he did as anything great. 'He couldn't wait to tell me. Got an audience at last. Sometimes I think that's all they want. All the gory details. Weeping and wailing how evil he is.'

'And is he? Evil.'

'He's sick. The psychiatric reports will say he's sick. And he is. He is sick. He'll go to Rampton with all the other sick evil bastards and they'll pass round the smuggled pictures and entertain each other with their juicy stories. Why are they alive? There's three little girls dead and that craphead alive and thriving. Why?'

She'd never heard him talk so much. Or talk like this. He heard himself and stopped. He sniffed a yellow azalea that spilled over the terrace. Kate sniffed the air:

36

'Amazing smell.'

'A-ha. Been bred out of the others, I guess.'

'Think things ought to be bred out of humans?' she said.

'I'd be out of a job.'

'So would I.'

'How come?'

'Well, if everyone were nice and good, there wouldn't be anything to write plays about.'

'What, evil's more interesting? That what you think? Not in real life it's not. It's boring. Boring. Boring.'

'But, it's the *problem* of evil we're obsessed by. The *existence* of evil. What's it for? Evil, pain, suffering, death?'

He shook his head. 'You're the only person I know talks like this.'

'Oh. Sorry.'

'So you should be.'

She grinned. He looked more cheerful too. They went back in.

He'd never seen her like this, simple delight in simple domestic arrangements. It hit him now: her little house in Leverton Street, what its contamination had meant to her, what her enforced homelessness had meant ever since. 'Does it have a bathroom?' He squinted with wicked intent.

'Just here as a matter of fact.' A biggish

room. A stained-glass panel letting in jewels of light. Stark white tiles. Nice fittings. A state of the art shower enclosed in glass. 'No bath?' he said. 'That's funny.'

'Yeah,' she said darkly, 'it's a scream.' She shut the door, on this bathroom and on memories of another. She said, 'I think I really am over it. At last.'

He nodded. They both wished he could say the same about his obsession with Millie Hale. They exchanged a look on this subject but no words. God, she was easy to get on with, was Kate, he thought. 'Show me the rest then,' he said.

She opened the tall double doors to the front room. Stripped pine floor, stripped pine fireplace, tall bay window. She opened the wooden Venetian blind. Sunlight sparkled through the rain and patterned the room with stripes of light. The tiles of the fireplace deep blue. 'Bedroom,' she said.

'A-ha.'

Silence. They both contemplated that other bedroom, in her other little house round the corner. Bedding all over the place. Someone else's stains on her sheets. At least this bedroom was empty. It had the empty smell of newly sanded pine.

'Where did you store your furniture?' he said.

She paused. 'I sold it.'

'Everything?'

'Sent it to auction.'

'Don't do things by halves, do you?'

'It stayed in store for months before I decided.'

'What decided you?'

'Earning enough to buy some more.'

He gave a short laugh. Shook his head. 'You're crazy.'

'I went to Habitat and said I'll have that and that and that. It was amazing. I felt like a millionaire.'

'You won't feel like one now, then.'

'No, I'm broke again now.'

'A-ha.'

'I just got the necessities. Bed, sofa, table, chairs. Like those apartments you see in the house and garden magazines. All white walls and wood floors and no mess. I'll be so stylish.'

They picnicked at her nice long table under the glass roof. She put on Radio Three while he opened the wine. It was the Bach second orchestral suite. Very joyful music. She laid out a warm French loaf and cheese. He poured the wine into her greenish glasses. She loved watching him do things, deft, spare, not a movement wasted, practical, neat, fast.

'What you looking at?' he said.

'Nothing.'

'A-ha. Cheers.'

It was going to be all right. This time, at last, it was going to work out. He broke the bread, he cut the cheese. He speared the cheese on his knife the way peasant men did, the knife a part of him. She watched his hands. He said, 'Don't do that.'

'What?'

'Watching my hands.'

'Does it make you feel shy?'

'It makes me feel randy.'

The first real honest look of the day passed between them.

'Oh, heck.' She laughed, shaky.

'Eat,' he said.

The bread was like bread, the cheese was like cheese. Both were the best she'd ever tasted. Flavours sharp, coarse, raw, on lips, palate and tongue. And the wine, chosen by him: you could get drunk just sniffing it. The music ended and the news came on. She turned the wine bottle to read the label. The news reader said, 'Police in Bristol are searching today for a fifteen-year-old schoolgirl who disappeared two days ago from her home in the Totterdown area of the city...'

They stared at each other frozen in attitudes: she turning the bottle, he sipping the wine. The news reader moved on to the next headline. They didn't move. They didn't hear it. They heard nothing. There was no sound in the world. Kate placed both fists between her breasts in the position of her heart. Her chest would not move to admit breath. Her lungs hurt. Focusing again on Bright's face she discovered him also transfixed. He let out his held breath in a sort of silent laugh. He swallowed. He said, 'Bristol's a big place.'

'Totterdown's not such a big place.'

'A few thousand schoolgirls though.'

'Of fifteen?'

'I thought Maisie was fourteen.'

'That was last summer. She was fifteen three weeks ago.'

'Lizzie would have phoned you if Maisie had gone missing.'

'Oh! Yes!'

'She'd have expected her to come here to you.'

'Yes?'

'Wouldn't she?'

'Yes?'

'You're not convinced?'

'No.'

'Phone her.' He took his mobile out of his pocket. 'Phone Lizzie.'

'No.'

'Go on.'

'No. She'd think I was daft.'

Kate's phone rang. For a second they both again turned to stone. Then Kate picked it up. 'Hello?' Her voice wary.

'Kate?'

'Lizzie!'

'You heard.'

'No, Lizzie, oh God, not Maisie?'

'Not Maisie, no.'

'Oh, thank Christ. Oh, Lizzie–'

'It's Alison,' Lizzie said.

A long silence. Bright stared at Kate. She stared at him but did not see him. 'Alison?' she said.

Bright got up and stood by her.

'Yes.'

'Maisie's best friend Alison?'

'Yes.'

Kate closed her eyes. 'Alison's missing,' she said.

'They were round at Dave's two nights ago.' Lizzie's voice had no expression, flat with fear. 'Alison left about an hour after Maisie. She wasn't on her own – even Dave wouldn't let a fifteen-year-old walk home on her own – she was with two friends, students of Dave's. They say they left her outside her house. But she never went into her house. She had a key. Her parents had gone to bed. They weren't worried. They trusted her. She'd promised to be in by eleven. And she would have been if – if she'd actually gone in.' Lizzie's voice broke off.

'When did they realise–?'

'They found her bed empty in the morning.'

'What do they think, Lizzie?'

42

'Well, you know Alison. She's not the type to run off without leaving a note. Or to run off at all. Or even to stay the night somewhere and not let them know. They rang me to see if she was here with Maisie. Then some other school friends. Then they rang Dave. Then they rang the police.'

'And she didn't have any plans to–?'

'Maisie says not. And Maisie would have known.'

'Would she? I mean–'

'Oh Kate, for heaven's sake. Don't give me that stuff about how secretive teenagers are. She and Maisie tell each other everything.'

Kate remembered how selective best-friend confidences had been, from her own adolescence, but this wasn't the time to argue with Lizzie. 'So what do they think has happened?'

'Well, they're questioning everyone. Especially Dave, as that was the last place she went. And the students she walked home with. No one's seen her. No one has a clue. She just seems to have vanished off the face of the earth.'

4

JUST MISSING

She stayed at Lily's that night. Bright insisted on taking her there. 'Can't leave you alone here tonight, girl.'

Their unspoken plans for the afternoon had been spiked. Kate wondered if every place she ever lived in would be contaminated by some terrible event. Was she condemned never to have a home she could feel good about? She went with him in his car. 'I'll drive you back in the morning if you want to come.'

The familiar sense of safety at Lily's place. The room, at the back, overlooking the long and lovely garden and the railway beyond, a small square box done in a restful parchment colour with a pretty border. An old hand-operated Singer sewing machine on a table under the window. Lying between the cool cotton sheets Kate looked at the ceiling. Where was Alison tonight? Somewhere she wanted to be, or somewhere she didn't? Alone? Alive?

She rang Lizzie in the morning. No news. 'The police have been round again, asking

Maisie things. Maisie's distraught. She's spending a lot of time down with Allie's parents. We're all just waiting, here.'

Bright made a call to a detective inspector he knew in Bristol. 'A-ha,' he said, 'a-ha,' in varying tones of voice. Then, 'Thanks, mate, let me know? 'Preciate it. Thanks.' He turned to her and Lily. 'They don't know anything. Nothing from boyfriends. No sightings at stations, airports. No known reason for doing a runner.' He looked depressed. His recent case had prepared him for the worst. A lot of his cases prepared him for the worst. But he was a policeman, a certain pessimism about the human race endemic to his profession.

'Girls do do things like this,' Kate said with a bleak expression.

'That's true.' Lily's face was stiff with pretended hope.

Kate didn't go back to town with Bright. He was too haunted by his recent case, his thoughts too dark. She stayed in the comfort of Lily's Scottish common sense. 'All this despair.' Lily shook her head. 'That won't help find the girl. Come on. Help me dead-head my roses, or they won't be the envy of the neighbourhood any more.'

Out in the sunshine, birdsong and scents, it was hard to believe in the wickedness Bright encountered every day. Kate began to hope. Surely their fears would be magicked away in the course of the day. Alison was bound to turn up. Rueful, defeated, or just bleary from some weird druggy experience. But safe, and, within reason, well.

On the news that night, however, the police showed her picture and appealed to the public for help. 'If you have seen this girl...'

'Ohh.' Lily caught her breath. 'She's beautiful, Kate.'

Yes. There was no mistaking Alison. If you had seen her you wouldn't forget. No news from Lizzie and when Kate rang there was no reply.

The next morning the item was missing from the news on Radio Four. If Alison had turned up she would have been news. Still missing she was news no longer. She would only become news again if – Kate rang Lizzie. Lizzie, dashing out to work, late as always, only had time to gasp into the phone, 'No news, got to go.'

Kate got a vision of her lovely spare clean new flat and the things she needed to do there. She kissed the top of Lily's head. 'Thanks, Lily. Give John my love. I'll be in touch.'

'I hope you mean that.'

'I mean it.'

She bought her copy of the *Big Issue* at the

46

station. The seller was a boy of maybe eighteen, shaven head, ear-ring, scruffy small dog curled up on an old coat. The boy was thin with blemished skin. She thought about the homeless on the streets, gave him a fiver and scoffed at her prodigality: she wasn't going to give him a home, was she? Share her nice new flat with him? Would she encounter Alison one day, outside a tube station or hunched in a doorway? Would she give her a quid and walk on feeling good about herself?

She read the *Big Issue* on the train. It had changed since its early days. Not so much the news from the streets percolating up, as the news of the trendy trickling down. Still, it had a different perspective here and there, made a better read than the newspapers all round her, the same headlines on all of them, the same point of view.

Her flat looked so beautiful she almost cried. She walked through the spacious rooms. She opened the french windows and smelled roses, lavender, rosemary. She discovered you couldn't feel desperate all the time. If you were this lucky you had to rejoice in your luck, had to have a bit of gratitude at least. Even the guilt of having what other people were not lucky enough to have, shouldn't spoil the joy. Surely she was allowed to feel a little bit good?

But next morning the *Big Issue* lay open at

the Missing Persons page, four blurred black and white snaps with a column of description underneath, most of them young, most lost for ever, and for no reason ever known, some depressed, some mad, some in search of adventure, and some... Her mind stopped there. Not Alison?

She slowly got dressed, couldn't face breakfast yet, wandered out on to the terrace, pulled up some weeds from between the uneven bricks. Gazed into the pond. A frog appeared on the surface gulping and gazing with his cheerful unblinking little eyes. 'Hello, frog,' she said sadly. Sunshine sliced across the end of the garden. She joined it there, accepting the warmth on her back while she absently dead-headed the crimson rose, letting the petals fall between her fingers. Dead-heading suddenly seemed a sinister term. Lily had used it yesterday. John Bright. It was early but he might already be at work.

'John?'

'Kate?'

'Have you got a minute?'

'Taking statements in the psycho case all day. No news?'

'No new news.'

'I'll see what I can do. Meet me lunch-time.'

'I talked to the bloke in Bristol.'

48

Her face turned to him full of dread. She didn't speak.

'Nothing much,' he said. 'They've questioned the two students who dropped her off. Their story seems to hold up. They didn't see her go into the house. But she went up the path to her front door. They were on something. Natch. When are the kids not on something these days? They're not saying so, but...'

'On what?'

'Oh, just been smoking a bit of dope, I expect.' He shrugged. 'So I don't expect they're that clear about how they left her. They don't seem to be hiding anything, except the fact they were on something. But you never know. They didn't think anything could happen to her outside her own front door.'

'No.'

'And maybe it didn't.'

'What?'

'They're questioning her father.'

Kate was shocked. 'Desmond Holt? But he's a really nice man, solid, reliable–'

'They always do that. They got to. They don't suspect foul play yet. No reason to.' He gulped some beer. 'They're questioning Maisie's dad too.'

Kate winced. 'Dave?'

'Yeah. No special reason, don't get in a state. They're questioning the whole crowd

49

of those layabout kids who were at Dave's place. And they're working through the kids in her class. Alison's a clever girl, the bloke in charge says to me, as though clever girls don't get into trouble.'

'And?' she said.

'Nothing. Nothing odd in her behaviour, nothing new in her life – that anyone knows about or is saying they know about – nothing she mentioned or did. So far. It's early days yet, the guy said.'

'Early days.' Kate shivered.

'She's probably crashed out somewhere, some bloke's place probably, lucky sod. Too much Ecstasy. Or whatever. Too much booze? Too little experience to handle it.'

'She's not the type.'

Bright gave her one of his sideways squinting looks. 'Come on, Kate.'

'Yes, I know that's what they always say, but–'

'Look. We only dropped in on that Dave's place for a minute after your first night party last year, but there was everything going down there. Wasn't there? Come on, don't be innocent. You can drop a kid almost anything. She could be out of it for days on a bad trip. Or even on a good one. Don't assume the worst. That's all I'm saying. Bad experience, teach her a lesson, might not even be all bad.'

Kate looked at him levelly. Knew he was

right in general. Knew he was wrong in this case. She shook her head.

'A-ha,' he said. 'Yeah, I agree. She's not the type. Something about her. I'll keep in touch with the bloke in charge. If there's any inside gen I'll get to know.'

'Thanks.'

Kate's face was sad. He pushed her hair away from her temple.

She felt the peculiar dry warmth of his hand and leaned the weight of her head there for a moment. Only a moment. She put her arms round him quickly, kissed his cheek. ''Bye then. Thanks.'

'See you soon?' He lifted an eyebrow.

She grinned sideways, then got serious. 'I'm actually off to Bristol again in two weeks' time.'

5

FAMILY MATTERS

Kate heard the announcement while she was packing the car. 'The body found today in the Bedminster area of Bristol has been identified as that of missing schoolgirl Alison Holt who disappeared from home three weeks ago. Police say they are treating it as a murder enquiry.'

She shut the boot of her yellow Beetle. She came inside. She closed the front door and sat on the bottom stair. Put her head in her hands, shaking. A feeling like bottomless hunger in the gut, bottomless space under the feet. She pulled herself up by the newel post. Walked down the hall feeling her way as though in the last few minutes the world had gone dark. Opening the door to her flat, she was surprised to see daylight through the back window.

She stood at the phone table, a fist either side of the phone. Tears fell off her face. A kid, fifteen years old. One of the most beautiful girls she'd ever seen. And someone had to kill her. Kill all that promise, all that potential, all that beauty. Why? She punched the wrong number. Her brain hadn't forgotten it; her fingers did. Like they didn't want to make the call. The third try she got it right. 'Lizzie?'

'Yes.'

'I just heard.'

'Yes.'

'How's Maisie?'

'You can imagine.'

'Is she there?'

'She's at the school. That's where all the kids have gathered. They didn't know where else to go. Even the delinquent ones are there. And some of the teachers have come back off holiday specially. They just want to be together. All these kids carrying flowers. There's a mountain of flowers in the playground and all the teachers and the kids clinging together and crying. I had to come away and leave her there. I couldn't stand it.'

Kate said, 'I'm just about to set off.'

'Where to?'

'To Bristol!'

'Oh, you don't need to come.'

'Lizzie, I'm working at the Old Vic again. We start rehearsing next week.'

'Oh, yes, I forgot, with all this.'

'So I'll see you in a few hours.'

'Take care.'

'Yes, Lizzie.'

'I know how you drive. It's time you got rid of that car.'

Lizzie. Even in this extremity she couldn't resist.

In London people would be changing lanes, cutting up, taking side roads, chancing it, keeping it moving. But here... Everyone obediently in slow procession, at speeds between dead slow and stop. Miles of it. Visible uphill miles.

At last she reached the roundabout. Some of the cars branched to the right towards Bedminster. She was moving now at least, only ten miles an hour but getting there. She shot across the Wells Road on to St John's Lane, hills in the distance, did the sharp right into steep Oxford Street, past the small gaggle of shops with young people hanging around on corners, downhill again past the sweet little terraced houses, to the Glasnost Restaurant, Totterdown's one claim to being upmarket, up again to the brow of William Street, and she was there.

She jumped out without unloading and ran up the steps. Lizzie opened the door, she must have been watching out. She looked fine, perfectly groomed, but for the slight hysteria in the eyes and the tight lines round the mouth. You could never hug Lizzie, she had a force field round her, particularly when terrified and in need of help. No hello, no greeting; just 'I'll help you with your bags.' And there she was down the steps, dragging stuff out of the old yellow Beetle, nagging: 'Scrap metal's all it's good for. It'll blow up on you one of these days. On the motorway probably.'

'Beetles last for ever, Lizzie.'

'Out to prove that, are you?'

Lizzie was still jealous of Liam after all this time. Jealous of their dead teenage brother who'd bequeathed Kate the car.

'Anyway I can't afford a new one,' Kate said, clinching the argument.

Lizzie turned her attention to the pile of gear in the boot. 'You've brought enough for a year.'

'I'm here for eight weeks.'

'Oh yes, I keep forgetting.'

'Lizzie! I only need one bag for now. Please let's get inside?'

'Oh.' Lizzie came to a stop. 'All right.' She hoisted Kate's big holdall on to her shoulder and trudged up the steps.

The house had been newly painted outside. Sky blue and white. 'House looks nice,' Kate said.

'Just had it done. Cost the earth.'

They went in. Kate shut the door. 'Where's Maisie?'

Lizzie leaned her head against the wall in the hallway and howled. Kate put out a tentative hand but she flinched away. All

55

you could do was stand and wait. At last she calmed down and Kate led the way to the kitchen.

Pretty kitchen, red and white, cheerful as hell. Lizzie sat down on a shiny red chair and blew her nose; Kate put the kettle on. Familiar positions; comforting in a way. Lizzie sniffing and patting her eyes and catching the drips from her nose. Kate making tea. Lizzie sipped from the jolly clown mug and put it down. 'Maisie–' She stopped and waited for the emotion-stricture to leave her throat. '–won't come home.'

'Come home from where?'

'Dave's.'

'She's staying at *Dave's?*'

'She says she feels safer there.'

'Safer! With Dave?'

'It's what she says.'

'Oh, Lizzie!' Kate was full of sympathy. This wasn't just Lizzie, turning everyone's problem into *Lizzie's Problem* as she usually did; this was really bad.

'I'm the one who's supported her, nurtured her, done everything for her. He abandoned her. That's all he's ever done, leave people in the lurch. And who makes her feel safe? Who's the one she wants now? I can't bear it, Kate, I can't.'

'I'll go over there,' Kate said.

'Kate!' Dave flung his arms wide and held her in a vice. They nearly overbalanced on the rickety stairs.

'Okay, Dave, okay.'

He let her go. 'Come in.'

Light of candles, smell of incense. Young people in hippie gear lounging on cushions. It looked like a movie about the sixties, but Dave had been an infant in the sixties, his acolytes not even born. New Age music gurgled out of the rough wooden walls. Everything was wood in here, rough planks crudely nailed. And a small iron stove. It was nice. It *was* romantic. Kate felt its spell, but did not forget what she'd come for. 'Where's Maisie?' She peered into the flickering candle-gloom.

'I'm here, Ankate.' She sounded kind of – stoned. Kate felt alarm.

She found Maisie half lying in the laps of three nouveau hippies. A New Age *pietà*. She looked dazed, woozy, half asleep. Kate came closer. 'You okay, Maisie?'

Maisie gave a groan, didn't get up to greet her, didn't leave the cradle of arms.

Dave had separated a small cooking area off from the main room with a screen of upright planks. Kate followed him in there. Here there was electric light.

His hair was still long, ringlets down past his shoulder blades, but now it was grey in parts. He was still thin, his body hard and

57

strong. But his face was starting to look gaunt. He stretched out his arms to take hold of her again, Dave the Great Protector. She backed to the wall and leaned there, folding her arms. He shrugged and half smiled. They knew each other well. This was his charming quality, that he accepted what you were. But his detachment from other people was the other side of that. Frightening.

'How is she?' Kate kept her voice low.

'She's safe here.'

'Safe from what?'

'Safe from what she fears.'

'What is that?'

'That whoever killed Allie will come after her next.'

'Christ.'

'Or after another one of her friends.'

6

EXCERPT FROM A DIARY

i

2 a.m. A moonless night. I crouched in the car listening. My legs had grown numb. I lifted my head for a second. Nothing. No one. I sat up. The school building loomed blacker than the night. But you never know. Someone could be lurking in the dark behind those windows. I opened the car door. Quietly. And got out.

I have good circulation but crouching so long in the cramped space on the floor of the car had turned my legs to jelly. I walked weakly a few steps. How can you suffer numbness and pain at the same time? It seemed this sensation, or lack of it, would never stop but it did. It took two minutes. Two minutes I hadn't planned for. Two minutes is a long time.

In that time I hobbled to the barrier gate that divided the road from the hill and shuffled a little way along the path. I stopped to listen. Nothing. Nobody. I turned and started back, the school a big black shadow on my left. I had to believe there was no one behind the windows. If someone saw me the game was up. I had to take that chance. I had no choice. This was the optimum place, the nearest I could park the car to the spot I had chosen. Normal feeling had returned to my feet. I sprinted softly back to the car. I listened. Nobody. Nothing. I opened the hatch-back.

The tightly wrapped bundle filled the boot space. I rolled it towards me using both hands and all my strength. Then I bent at the knees stooping to receive the weight on my right shoulder. I took the head end, hoisted it over my shoulder, held the bundle round its waist, let my thighs take the strain and rose to a standing position, pulling the legs up with me as I stood. My own legs shook with the weight. But I had practised this manoeuvre many times. I knew it could be done. And the carrying. Only a short distance. It could be done.

But I had not taken account of the fear. Nerves make you weaker. I panted. My legs shook, and not just with the weight. But I managed to lower the hatch-back without banging it shut. Then I bent at the knees and went with small swift steps through the barrier gate again, along the path a few yards to my chosen spot. Not the first opening in the bushes, but the second. Of course the first would be easier but the second was perfect for my purposes, worth the extra three yards along the path. The first opening was low, too far to bend, and the slope down was immediate and steep. The second opening was higher, the initial slope more gradual, down to a plateau, lower than the path and deep in the shadows between trees.

This was the most delicate part of the operation. To duck in under the thick bushes, without tripping, falling, or dropping my weighty burden. I tottered (I laugh now at my choice of word, so close to Totterdown, just the other side of the hill) down the slope a few steps, but somehow righted myself, trying to be silent but grunting with the strain. Branches scratched my hood but all hair was well taken care of. They'd find no traces at this scene to satisfy their craving for forensic evidence. No skin visible. No hair. Only my eyes to see with. And I *could* see now in the dark. The human eye is adaptable beyond belief.

I struggled down to my small plateau. I knelt, lowering the shoulder over which the head lolled. A thump as the head hit the earth. And a subdued thud as the rest of the bundle came to rest. (As it were.) I pressed my hands round my thighs just above the knees as though this pressure would help me to breathe more freely. My arms now trembled with the strain they had been under. A heavier burden would have been too much for me. I had to admit this now. Alive she had been light as a feather. Dead she was a weightier problem.

My lungs cleared. The drums ceased pounding in my ears. I lay down. This I had not rehearsed but my exhaustion was immense. Inexhaustible. Inexhaustible exhaustion. Many a paradox I was discovering tonight. I lay down by her side. The black sky up there through the leaves and the cool breath of the night. Imagine lying with her like this, alive, side by side on the hill. I did imagine it. For a moment. Not an altogether pleasurable moment. Then I got up. On to my knees. I took the knife out of my pocket and opened out a blade.

I quickly cut through the clothes line holding the bundle together. I cut it in six places. At the neck. The chest. The waist. The top of the thighs. The knees. The ankles. I opened up the plastic sheet. I rolled her away from me off the sheet and bundled up five of the lengths of clothes line in the plastic, squeezing the air out as I wrapped. With the sixth length I tied the whole lot together. It made an untidy parcel but heavy enough to throw. I scrambled down the slope from my plateau, between bushes and trees, to the railings that border the railway. I threw the bundle hard over the railings on to the rails.

I'm a strong thrower. Good at ball games at school. The night was too black to see how far it spun. I didn't care. The plastic and rope could be bought in any super-market – I'd checked – and had never been touched by human flesh. Hand in glove.

Everything is a question of time. It would take them time to find the parcel. When they did the plastic and rope would be ragged, snagged on bushes, blown by wind, soaked by rain, shat on by birds, run over by trains. Traces of me and mine weathered away. Withered away. Whither away?

Now I could return to her. I composed myself. I crawled back slowly up the slope through the thicket to my plateau, where she lay and where I could stand upright. I looked down at her. She was on her front, face pressed into the grass and weeds. I knelt by her and rolled her on to her back. A blade of grass and a torn leaf adhered to her right cheek. I removed them gently. Stroked them away.

Her eyes were shut. I had shut them myself. I feared at the time that they might open again. But they had not. And they did not now. It was unlikely they would at this stage, but the fear persisted. Rigor mortis had not yet set in but I did not have much time. I had got down a book from the medical section of the library at work. I found that though rigor mortis occurs quite quickly, it can go off again in as little as twenty-four hours, especially in the summer months. No one had ever told me this. I had wanted to keep her by me longer but knew now I must not. Rigor had always seemed to me a necessary concomitant of death. Just as no one tells you the facts of life, so no one tells you the facts of death. Her eyelids stayed closed down over her eyes.

The fine gold chain round her neck had got twisted. I worked it round so that the cross hung dead centre (dead centre, that's good) resting in the soft declivity of her throat between the delicate branches of her collar bone. I had left on her bra and pants for modesty. The white shapes hovered, it seemed, over the darkness which was her brown flesh. I took her right hand and bent her arm so that her hand rested on her left breast. Then I did the same with her left hand, placing it on her right breast. I straightened her legs, running my hands from knee to ankle, bringing her feet together. Her feet were bare. Shoes weigh a lot, would have made her heavier to carry. Also, her feet were beautiful. Long, narrow, smooth, strong. Amazon's feet. With long straight toes.

I was kneeling on the damp grass. The night was barely cooler than the day. I wanted to stay there by her side, stretch out again, even sleep a while. But I must not linger. I touched her hands briefly but could feel nothing. I longed to peel off the gloves and feel her flesh with my hands. I stood. I turned my back on her. I squeezed my eyes shut and said a quick prayer. For her. For me. A prayer. That's a joke. The things we do.

I stooped to make my way out of the bushes. Cool leaves stroked my face. I heard the noise of a train, distant, approaching, the heavy clatter of goods wagons, getting closer, its noise splitting my skull. I put my gloved hands over my ears until the noise faded. Noise is bad for me. Something happens in my head. I held on until the noise had completely gone then took my fists away. And heard a closer noise. A smaller, more sinister noise. I stayed still, not breathing at all, for minutes, while the pressure mounted in my skull, in my chest, in my throat.

The footsteps came from the same direction I had come ten minutes before. This person had passed my car. Had been watching my activities in the dark? You can hear footsteps clearly there on the tarmac path, at night. Only one set of footsteps, in this case, but a voice went along with them. A voice, whispering, intensely sibilant. Did this mean there were two people, one in shoes, the other in trainers? (Trainers are silent, I wear them myself for that reason.)

Or one person, talking to itself, hurrying along in the night earnestly settling a score?

This whispering was real, as the footsteps were. It was not in my head. Schizophrenics hear voices in their heads. It has recently been discovered that where most of us can distinguish between our own thoughts and the voices of others, schizophrenics cannot. Their own thoughts come to them as outside voices. This does not happen to me. But of course I talk to myself. I believe others do. Most others perhaps?

I could not creep out to see how many shadowy figures were passing by outside the bushes. For a moment there seemed to be many, a multitude, gliding silent and swift, fiercely whispering. I just had to wait.

I crouched, waiting, a long time, determined not to give in to the temptation to move, to creep up the slope and peep. So I shall never know how many people passed. I shall always see a shadowy three-legged racer. A person with his shadow strapped to his side. Whispering.

All the time I was listening I forgot her behind me there. Which is strange because she after all was the reason I was listening so hard, hiding there, and waiting. But now that I was about to leave her I received the most terrible stab of pain. A physical jolt of longing, to turn and go back to her and lay my face on her body. I had to go, however. I knew the time had come.

I turned just once to look upon her, unsullied, uncorrupt, perfect, fixed. I held my breath. Then I ducked out of the bushes. I did it fast. Anyone could have heard me. But my shadowy passer-by had long gone. And at two thirty in the morning surely not that many people would be crossing Windmill Hill. Night after night I'd been out there and hardly seen a soul.

I jogged in my silent trainers down the path back through the barrier gate. These days it's less suspicious to run than to walk. Joggers are out at all hours now. Keeping fit. Keeping trim. Keeping in shape. Anoraks on the move. And it was better, running. More in time with my heartbeat, jerky, uneven, but fast.

There are still five cars parked along there. I jog past mine. I can barely believe my will-power. In this supreme testing moment of my life, I have the supreme strength not to get into my car and drive off. A kind of rejoicing floods me. Freedom, pride, excitement. A joyous exhilaration buzzes my head. I nearly lift my arms with clenched fists to punch the night air.

But I go on running in a steady earnest way like the serious types you see every day, timing themselves. What are they keeping fit *for?* To carry on running? I nearly laugh out loud but I don't because I'm now down by the awful tunnel and it's only this lucky euphoria that impels me in there.

Shiny slime in the dark running down the brown brick soot-encrusted walls. The hollow drip, arhythmic, magnified, like my heartbeat. The pale horseshoe at the far end of the tunnel doesn't get any bigger, like I'm running on the spot. My feet squelch in a sudden silver puddle and when I look up the pale horseshoe of hope is bigger than me and within seconds I'm out. Through hope and out the other side?

I cross the road. Nobody. Jog down past the city farm. Nobody. Even the rare-breed sheep asleep. Past the printing works. Lights and the faint sound of machinery but nobody. Nobody. I come to the Philip Street Chapel. *We have peace with God,* the poster tells me, *through Our Lord Jesus Christ.* Yeah.

A step or two from Bedminster Parade I hear a car engine. I can tell the car is going slowly but I can't see it from here. Its lights waver towards me. I'm across the street from *Motaman. Car Parts And Accessories.* I'd like to flatten myself into a doorway but there is no doorway deep enough. So I scuttle silently back round the chapel corner into Bartley Street. I can keep watch from here on the Parade, if I keep still and out of the light.

A police car comes into my sights, crawling along the Parade in my direction.

So slow. Like they're looking for someone. Like they're looking for me. I guess they do this every night, trawling for thieves. Maybe I should pretend. Pretend what? That I'm merely a thief? For a moment I actually consider this. But quickly regain my senses and stay where I am.

They crawl past. Slow motion. They didn't see me. Unless they're pretending, waiting out of sight for me to emerge into the Parade? I'm gripped now by the urgent need to empty my bladder. And my bowels. I can't stay here any longer, I have to get home. Quick. Now.

I strolled. I did. I strolled, in spite of the fear, in spite of my urgent bodily needs, out into the Parade, past the shiny hub caps and complex tools in the car-parts window, and sauntered round the corner without even peeping round first. Nobody. The squad car gone. Nothing else moving. Litter in the street lights. In spite of the red-brick library and the grey stone police-cum-fire station long disused, this is a mean place. A place for what my mother would call 'the common people'. Not for the uncommon people. Like her. Like me, now, I realise. Like me. An uncommon person like me. I wonder what proportion of the population has done what I've done. Killed. A fellow person. Killed. Not in war or accident. But like me. How many? I must find out.

Statistically interesting. I'll look it up. Add my name to the list. I do let out a laugh now. You don't get on a list till you're found out. The only list worth belonging to is the one that can't be made. I ran again.

I ran all the way home. I ran to jingles to take my mind off my more and more urgent guts. This little piggy went to market, this little piggy stayed at home. This little piggy had roast beef, this little piggy had none. Had none. This little piggy had none. It was a hell of a run – now here's a clue for anyone who might find this and read it – I have not yet found my perfect reader – uphill all the way. And I didn't meet a soul.

Later.

More comfortable now. A complete evacuation. I even vomited. That's curious. Interesting. Purgative. Macbeth uses that imagery, to the doctor, to whom of course it would have relevance: purgatives, rhubarb, senna, talking about tearing out a rooted sorrow from the mind, as evil from a land. Sins are purged. I was purging mine perhaps. Rambling thoughts. I didn't sleep.

Very early in the morning I went down-stairs to the kitchen. I heard the change-over from World Service to Radio Four. Then hours of news while I drank tea, shivering slightly on a stool. I couldn't eat. I took up mother's breakfast. And when I came down again they were making the announcement. It was strange hearing it in bald words like that: 'The body of a girl...' A jogger found her. I could barely suppress a laugh. Just what I had hoped. He must have been out at the crack of dawn. Poor chap.

I hung about for as long as I could. Mustn't be too early. Then I went down to Temple Meads station. I waited for the London train to come in. I watched the people coming through the barrier. The barrier was unmanned. Some passengers dropped their tickets on the ground. One or two placed them in the litter bins. The litter bins were full so it was easy to retrieve a few tickets. The first one I picked out was a return half. Lucky first time. And it gave yesterday's date as the journey time. I could barely believe this smooth silent slotting-in to my plan. Though I know it's nonsense, I felt I was controlling events. My will had willed this.

I pocketed the ticket and slipped out of the station, mingling with the people who *had* been on the train. I had a bag with me, of course, in case police should be watching. Or any observant person. Actually I believe there hardly is such a thing as an observant person. They walk round deaf and blind to the world around them. Their world is a little hard ball of self-interest located in their skull, their stomach, their genitals, their purse. I loathe them, one and all. Well, never mind that.

I wondered if I should draw attention to myself in some way in case of complications later. It might be as well to have been noticed here, now. But I decided against it. Those little tricks can easily misfire. The person who saw me would swear it was a different day or a different time or even a different place. So I strolled over the crossing and up towards the roundabout. Then, turning right, over the muddy river down towards Bedminster, I avoided Windmill Hill. Must not draw too much attention to myself. The police would still be up there, milling about, keeping an eye out for suspicious characters. Like me.

I came down the top end of the Parade, before the pedestrianised section, and turned the corner. My heart, interestingly, took on an insistent rhythm, pounding as though located actually in my ears. And when I crossed the road approaching the tunnel my legs actually began to shake. I noted all these reactions. The reason the legs shake in such circumstances is that all the muscles in the back, the neck, and the legs themselves, go rigid, contracted, tense. The legs do not shake out of weakness but out of a kind of concentrated strength. Too much strength.

I breathed out slow, slow, long breaths as I

have taught myself to do, out and out and out, expelling the last atom of air, thus relaxing stomach, neck, back muscles. Out, out. That was better. My legs shook less. Even in the dank tunnel their function continued to improve. I came out of the tunnel into the lane alongside the school.

The police had stretched blue and white tape all round the parked cars. There were five cars. Mine farthest away at the front. A young policeman stood close to the back car. I approached him. 'Excuse me, officer,' I said.

He looked at me. He felt a spurt of excitement and terror at the sight of me. I might be the murderer! Speaking to him! Imagine! He did not allow any expression of these feelings to appear on his face. 'Yes?' he said.

'I suppose all this is because of that young girl?' I said.

'That's right, sir.'

I assumed an expression of concern. 'Yes, I see. Only I don't quite know what to do. You see, one of these cars is mine.'

Again he managed to stop the thrill showing in his face. Good control. I admire that. 'Yes, sir? Which one would that be?'

'The Renault. The grey one. You see?' Nothing ostentatious for me. Oh no.

'The one parked closest to the barrier, sir?'

'Yes, it is.'

'Can I ask you why it is parked just there?'

'Oh yes. I always park there in the morning if I can and then run over the hill.'

'Why, sir?'

'Well, it's a good place to run. And there are those exercise bars. I use them. Cheaper than a gym. And in the open air too.'

He looked blank this time. Floored. Couldn't think what to ask me next.

I helped him out. 'I visit people over there.'

'Visit?'

'I work for social services.'

'You're a social worker?'

'Of sorts. I assess people with special needs and report back. Yes.'

'So why was you parked there overnight?'

Here we go. 'Well, yesterday I had to go to London. We have a small flat there which we rent out. It's between tenants now and my mother asked me to go and make sure it was okay. So I parked early yesterday, did my run et cetera, then caught my train to London. I've only just got back.'

It was a good story. He didn't know what to think now. 'I see.' He looked round as if for help. None came. He said, 'Wait here a moment, would you, sir?'

'Yes, of course.' I must remember not to talk too much. Not to say too much. Explaining about the flat was quite unnecessary. Round and round the garden like a teddy bear. One step, two step... He's coming back, accompanied by an older man in a suit. A type I hate. Big. Square body, tight belly, beery face. But eyes that weigh you. Cold.

'Hello, sir,' he says. So genial. Baked Alaska.

'Er, hello?'

'James Ryan, CID. I'm in charge here.'

'Oh. Yes.'

'The Renault at the front. That's yours, I hear.'

'Yes.'

'We're going to have to impound it, sir.'

'Yes?'

'Forensic will want to search it thoroughly.'

'Oh. Well, yes, of course.'

'That all right?'

'Yes!'

'You don't mind?'

'No, of course not.'

'It's not just yours, sir. It's all the cars parked here overnight.'

'I understand.'

'Routine, sir. Has to be done.'

'Yes, yes, it's fine.' In spite of all this co-operation with the Law I allow myself to look a little bit scared. Because anyone would be, wouldn't they? The most innocuous person. The innocent.

'Will you give your details to the constable, sir? We'll let you know when we've finished with the car. Sorry for the inconvenience. And we'll need to ask you a few questions later on. I hear you use the hill quite a bit.'

'Yes, I do.'

'Yes, so you might have noticed something. See if you can think of something. Anything. Help us out. Anything at all unusual. Or usual come to that. Yesterday morning. Thank you, sir. Go ahead, constable.' And he strolled off back to the hill. Hard, nasty. Really quite menacing. A worthy opponent, actually.

I gave the young policeman my name, address, phone number et cetera. I said, 'Can I go across the hill now, or is it out of bounds?'

'You have to go the long way round, sir, I'm afraid. Up this way and over through the garden bit.'

'Oh fine, I'll go that way.'

'Just one thing, sir.'

'Yes?'

'Can I have a look in your bag, please?'

'Oh yes. It's just my overnight stuff. And my running gear, of course.'

I opened my bag. Watched his hands touching my things. Feeling around. Looking for clues. I didn't like this at all. I felt invaded, contaminated. Strange. Just things, aren't they? Not me. My self. My flesh. Just things.

'Okay, sir. Thank you. Just routine.'

I wonder if they say that on Death Row as they strap them into the chair: Just routine, sir. Okay?

I zipped the bag up again. 'That's all right,' I said casually. ''Bye.' 'Bye! And off I went up behind the school, where I could have looked down at the police goings-on but didn't. I went through the 'garden bit' to the other side of the hill.

JUSTICE AT WORK

The slow buzzing pace of the court limped on. What kind of nonsense was this where every word the witness said had to be repeated for the recording then read back again at the end of the testimony to make sure it was correct? This was trial by tedium. Bright was fed up. He'd done everything to catch this gook. Not easy. His wife and all his mates off the estate keeping stumm or telling the same story: he's a really nice bloke, loves kids, wouldn't harm a fly.

The prosecution lawyer was Jack Grimley, stocky cock-of-the-walk body in a sharp suit. Natty dresser, big gold signet ring on the little finger. Yellow hair, florid face. But he did the business. He'd done his homework, cross-examined all the cagey relations and the mumbling witnesses.

The defence was crap. Two depressed-looking blokes, brothers, inherited the firm from their dad, looked like they'd been dug up, dandruff on their miserable grey suits, searching vainly through their papers, losing their place, can't find the crucial document, haven't even called the psychiatric expert.

You do the leg work, you want your result, but Christ – the Gook should at least have a chance. Bright could have done a better defence job himself. The prosecution had to prove intent to kill. That was all. A decent defence could have turned it around. Not responsible for his actions, criminally insane.

He felt the rage and misery of the dead girls' families breathing down his neck from the little gallery behind him. And the loathing of the Gook's family farther along. All together in one box, the only place to watch the proceedings. Nice families. All here because one sick bastard couldn't keep his hands off little girls.

The magistrate called recess for lunch. The Gook was led downstairs eyeing his mother with despair. The families filed out of the box, Gook's family glaring at Bright with hate, eyes darting venom as they passed him one by one. You had to get used to that. He was hated by a few families of guys in jug. It was all about families in the end. That was the job.

He told his DC to get him a pint and a sandwich in the pub, found a small room down the corridor and got on his mobile. Got through to Bristol HQ and asked for DI Ryan.

'Ryan here.'

'Oh, yeah. Look, we met at that evidence conference last year. John Bright, Kentish Town CID.'

'Oh yes?'

'I've got a bit of an interest in this case of yours.'

'And what case would that be, then?'

'Come on, mate. The black kid found in the bushes.'

'Oh, that case?'

'Just wondering how you're treating it.'

'We're treating it as murder.'

'Er, yeah, a-ha, I read that in the papers. Are you looking at the serial angle?' Silence. 'Just a thought.'

'It's a possibility.'

'Yeah, I–'

'One of many.'

'A-ha?'

'The case is wide open at the moment.'

'No assault, I gather, no signs of–'

'I remember you now. You're that *little* geezer. Gave a speech, didn't you? At that conference. Scruffy leather jacket. The rest of us in suits, the hoi polloi.'

'Er–'

'Yes, I remember you.'

Bright got the message. 'Okay. Sorry. It's just I'm connected to the case personally. The er – the niece of a – friend of mine –was the victim's best friend, and I just wondered... Yeah. Never mind, mate. I'll

80

wait for the six o'clock news like everyone else. Forget I called.'

'It wasn't a bad speech as I recall.'

'Oh?'

'How the work's being screwed up by PACE. All the f– All the paperwork.'

'Right.'

'You want to come here, I'll talk to you. On the phone, forget it.'

'I'm in court this next day or two. A committal hearing. Looks like the charge'll be murder.'

'Feather in your cap.'

'Hmph.' Bright had never heard himself say hmph before. Thought he must be getting old.

The rich Irish voice at the other end said, 'See you in a few days then, maybe.'

'Thanks, mate. 'Preciate it.'

'Sure.'

8

LOSS AND GAIN

Later in the night Maisie extricated herself from the arms of her sleeping protectors and threw herself on Kate. Kate put her arms round the lacewing-light body. 'Did the doc give you something to calm you down?'

'Yeah, Valium, I think. It's knocked me out. I don't like it.'

'Won't do you any harm, just at the moment.'

'Don't want any more.'

'I'll tell them.'

'Oh Ankate, it's so terrible.'

'I know.'

'Nobody can know.'

'Well, no.'

'It's like I lost my dad. All over again. I lost my dad...' Her voice went up in a glissando scale.

Kate rocked her like a baby. Tears rolled out of Maisie's eyes. Kate gave her a handful of tissues. She knew this: how one loss stands for all losses, brings back old losses, worse losses, adds its pain to the great hollow knowledge of loss. Maisie's burst of crying began to subside.

'My best friend and my dad.' Her voice was small again, diminished.

'Is that why you wanted to stay with your dad?'

Maisie nodded, then said, 'I dunno really. Yes. It must be that.'

'I'll tell Lizzie.'

'I know what mum thinks. I told her it wasn't because I didn't – you know – want to be with her. I asked her to come with me. We could all be here together.'

'I can imagine how she'd react to that.'

Maisie gave a wan smile. 'Yeah. So now I've injured mum as well.'

'Maisie, you haven't injured anyone.'

Maisie wiped more tears away but didn't pursue this subject. She yawned suddenly.

'Where do you sleep round here? Apart from draped around the floor.'

Maisie pointed up. 'That's a sleeping platform up there. But there's people on it.'

'What about your dad's room?'

'That's his private space. He never shares that.'

'Not even tonight?'

Maisie's hopeless eyes looked almost black in the candle-light.

'Stay here.' Kate loosened the girl's arms and stood up groaning – her legs had gone to sleep. She hobbled to the door in the wooden wall at the opposite end to the kitchen.

A big space, nearly as big as the main room, two Velux windows in the pitched roof, the moon dead centre in one of them. In the moonlight she made out a big futon on the floor, on it Dave, on his back, straight out, arms crossed on his chest. Alone. When she opened the door he was up and on his knees in an instant. 'Who's that?'

'Dave?'

'Kate–' He was ready to give her the spiel how this was his private space and he never shared it.

'Dave, you're going to have to share your private space tonight. You have a daughter here in need of a little contact comfort.'

He looked angry a moment, then – was it scared?– Then – maybe knowing how it would look to refuse – he said nothing at all.

'Okay?' Kate stood her ground.

'Sure.' As much welcome in his voice as he could muster.

'Maisie?' Kate brought her in.

He'd got himself together by now and was holding out those protecting arms. Maisie walked into them. Kate wouldn't have liked it but Maisie did. Kate hobbled back to her uncomfortable chair.

9

EXCERPT FROM A DIARY

ii

The stomach clenched like a fist. Bubbles of fear rising now and then to the throat. Sudden production of salt saliva. Sudden loss of voice as something interferes with the flow of breath through the vocal cords. Is this how an actor feels waiting for the curtain to go up? The process is not totally unpleasant. I am enjoying it, in the way that an actor must who knows in spite of his nerves that he is a great actor and that he is going to get them hanging on his every word.

They won't find a thing in the car. The plastic sheet I parcelled up and threw over the railings down on to the railway line. It will be anywhere by now, churned up by trains, soaked in standing water, blown away by winds, too contaminated by extraneous gunge to reveal original traces. And of course she had never been in my car. Except dead. And plastic-wrapped.

They'll go over it with minute precision in

their space suits and plastic gloves. They are plastic-wrapped too. An ironic detail I hadn't anticipated. They'll collect dust particles, wading through all the old gunk that collects in a car like mine. It's a tip. I pride myself on my unsmart car. The detritus that squeezes down between the seats and in the ridges of those awful rubber mats on the floor. And the boot. Ah, the boot. Spills of potting compost, bought at any supermarket garden centre, and a puddle of toilet cleaner – ditto – not very well wiped up. I love to think of them going to work on all that with their tweezers and little plastic bags. The worker ants. The scavenger wasps, eating up the messes others leave behind.

The phone rings at five o'clock. It's not the great Irish wolfhound Inspector Ryan, just one of his minions. 'Just to let you know we're finished with your car. You can collect it at any time between ten and four tomorrow. Sorry for the inconvenience.'

'That's okay. I've managed without it.'

'We'll be in touch regarding a few more questions if that's okay.'

'Yes, sure.' I'd like to keep him chatting, suddenly. About the hill. About police work. I want to know what they found in my car. But there's no question I can formulate at this moment that won't implicate me.

'By the way, sir, you'll be glad to know

your car was clean.'

I laugh. 'Clean? I'm afraid it was shamefully dirty.'

'Well, you know what I mean, sir.'

'Yes. Sorry. Of course I do. Thanks.' My car was 'clean'. I knew that. Of course I did. But there's always that little niggle of doubt. A hair, a fragment of skin, an eyelash. You never know. And maybe they were pretending, to catch me off my guard. How about that for an idea?

10

MISSING AND MATCHING

'How'd it go?'

'One up to us.'

'It's to be a murder charge, you mean?'

'That's it, ma.'

'Is it the right thing?'

'Well, he's in the system now. He'll get life. They'll do worse things to him in jail than he'd get in the loony bin. If he'd had a better defence it coulda been Rampton. Take your pick. At least the neighbours' daughters'll be safe. Till the next sick bastard. Sorry, ma.'

'You look tired, John.'

'Long few days.'

'Are you suited to this work?'

'It's what I know how to do. The due process of law. Want a drink?' He was already mixing her scotch. Half an inch in the big glass she liked, two lumps of ice, a flick of the wrist with the water, just to wet it. Poured one neat for himself, swallowed it in one, poured another over ice and swirled it a bit. 'There you are, ma. Cheers.'

'Cheers. Congratulations, anyway.'

'A-ha.'

They clinked glasses. She sipped and sighed. 'Ah that's good.' She wheeled into the living room and they drank looking out at the garden. Tired August time but she always had it nice. He would cut the grass next weekend.

'Kate rang,' she said.

'What?'

'Before you got back.'

'What she say?'

'She got your message at her sister's. Things are not so good there, she says, everyone upset and scared, but okay apart from that, and will you call her.'

All the time she's talking he's swirling the drink in his glass and watching it closely. Now he took a big mouthful –'Okay' – and put the glass down. He went out into the hall and up the stairs, a bit of the bounce back in him, two at a time.

Kate came down the stairs. 'Who was that on the phone?'

'Your policeman.' Lizzie was crushing the shopping into the fridge.

'I suppose you mean John Bright?'

'I told him you were in the shower. He said he'd phone back.'

'My policeman!' Kate started washing the lettuce for dinner.

Lizzie said, 'Are you sure she's all right round there?'

'Well, *I* wouldn't be, and you wouldn't be. But yes. She's surrounded by all these people. Ever such nice gentle souls. Oozing Lurv. You know. I'd punch their faces in if they laid a hand on me. But they sit there holding her close for hours on end making encouraging noises. And Dave occasionally opens those wide enfolding arms.'

'The human harbour.'

They both laughed, a rare event with Lizzie. Forgiveness. Good terms precariously restored. Kate moved close to her, placed the lettuce leaves in a tea towel. 'She *is* okay, Lizzie. And I think she'll get tired of it quite soon.' Kate did not believe this, but Lizzie needed cheering up. It was no use trying to explain about the complex twining of two losses, father and friend. Lizzie might get the drift but she'd pretend not to, and get mad, and the whole thing would end in tears over the salad. Kate reverted to John Bright: 'He's coming down, by the way.'

'Your policeman?'

'I'm warning you, Lizzie.'

'When?'

'Tomorrow.'

'Where's he staying?' This was not a simple question. Like a lot of Lizzie's questions it carried hidden weight: Do you sleep together? Do you expect him to stay here? Will you be staying with him elsewhere?

'Well, maybe he could have Maisie's room while–'

Lizzie looked mutinous.

'Just while he gets fixed up somewhere else? A couple of days? A day?'

Lizzie's knife sliced into a tomato. 'Is it serious, Kate?'

'Oh for heaven's sake, Lizzie.'

Lizzie piled the scarlet slices into a bowl. 'Because I just don't think he's right for you.'

'Right for me? In what sense precisely? As a lover? As a companion on life's weary way? As a financial adviser? A gardener? *Right* for me? We're *friends!*'

Lizzie looked a little abashed. A little. Not much. 'Well, he doesn't seem...'

'What? Seem what? In the right class? Out of the right drawer? Remember where we came from, Lizzie.'

'He doesn't seem – good enough for you, that's all.' Lizzie was mumbling, a bit unlike her.

'Well, thanks for the advice. You're a fine one to be advising others in their choice of blokes, I must say.'

Lizzie turned away. Kate could tell by the set of her shoulders that she'd gone too far. Not fair, alluding to the fiasco of her relationship with Dave. 'Sorry, Lizzie, but you don't half provoke a person. He is coming here to help.'

'Kate.' Lizzie turned solidly to face her. 'I don't like him.'

Kate groaned. 'Lizzie, nobody likes him. That's the whole point.'

'But you do, for some reason.'

'I got to know him. And there is the small factor that he saved my life.'

Doubt crossed Lizzie's face, the merest passing cloud, but Kate took advantage. 'You have to admit, Lizzie, with a lot of blokes it's the other way round. You like them a lot before you get to know them, and a lot less after.'

Lizzie scowled but didn't give up. She slapped down her strongest card: 'He looks like a crook, Kate.'

'Oh for heaven's sake!' Kate's sudden anger startled both of them. 'Forget it. I'll book him into a hotel. That gruesome place near the station should suit him fine, it's exactly like Wormwood Scrubs.'

'Kate!'

But she'd gone, slamming the door, stomping up the stairs just like all their childhood rows. Nothing changed since Lizzie was twelve and she was seven. Two little figures popping in and out of a clock, controlled by a mechanism they couldn't dismantle, couldn't change.

Standing at the window looking down at the street, Kate calmed down. Just the knowledge that he was coming made her safer. Made them all safer.

11

EXCERPT FROM A DIARY

iii

Well, I got my car back. It looks unnaturally neat. It's the way I'd like it to look all the time, frenziedly clean, the crumbs sucked out of the interstices. But that would not suit my purpose: I'm seen as the easy-going type, relaxed, laid back. I'm so cool! No anal characteristics, no obsessional neuroses. You read all the books, you create for yourself the character you want. It's just the same as what an actor does. Only an actor does it serially, one character after another, grown then discarded like snake skins. I spend my life perfecting just this one character. A supreme creation that takes everyone in. I'm a comedian but I'm the only member of the audience in on the joke, the only one laughing. I can see I could tire of that one day. I can see the temptation to hint, then even to tell ... I wonder. I wonder now...

Later.
  I've been QUESTIONED! At the

94

STATION! Inspector Ryan popped in to look at me. Is that an indication of my status? I'm important? A prime suspect. THE prime suspect even?

I told my story again in a windowless room. They asked if I had proof of my journey to London. 'Well...' I scratched my fetchingly tousled head. 'I might still have my ticket. There was nobody collecting them at the barrier when I got back.'

'Have you got it on you, sir?'

I felt in my pockets. 'I'm afraid not. But it might be somewhere at home. You know the way you empty your pockets. Where would I have... ? Anyway, I'll have a look when I get back.'

'P'raps one of my officers could accompany you home while you look for it, sir?'

I looked startled.

'Not unless it suits you, of course,' says Ryan in his most silkily threatening Irish tone.

'No, no, sure,' said I, like I'm seeing my place in my mind's eye, a little bit uneasy. They don't know if I'm worried because: a. there is no ticket; b. there is a ticket but my place is a bit of a mess for guests to see; c. anyone worries about the police coming to their place; d. I'm nervous because I'm guilty; e. I'm guilty of something but not necessarily this – some minor misdemeanour – porno mags, S&M videos, paedophilia

95

on the Internet. Could be anything.

I can see them guessing, getting intrigued. I really enjoy this. It's scary. That flutter in the throat. They DON'T suspect I'm enjoying it, I'm sure. I let them speculate a bit. Then: 'It's just my mother,' I say. 'She's a bit of an invalid. She'll be a bit worried. You know, the police coming to the house.'

Their metaphorical brows clear. 'Don't worry about that, sir. We'll send a woman officer. We won't alarm her.'

'Well... Okay then.'

'Right, sir. Shall we go?'

'Now?'

'Why not?'

'Oh. Yes. Okay.' I'm still looking perturbed as we leave. They've primed me now. They've given me the idea. This is improvisation. It's titillating. Lives with his mother. Bit of a momma's boy, bit feeble, tied to her apron strings, under her thumb, possibly gay; probably gay. They've got to follow me up, obviously.

So they come with me. Well, after me. Me in my nice 'clean' car, nondescript, ten a penny. To mother's house. Oh! Nice house! I can hear them thinking. I know what they expected: a first floor over a shop in Montpelier; a basement – sorry, garden-flat – in Kingsdown Parade; not this, impressive classic Georgian, up here in Clifton.

They look oddly at me when I await them

on the pavement. For the first time they see me as an anachronism. They nod at me, then look up at the house. Nice shiny paint, navy front door, shiny brass knocker, geraniums in pots. They follow me up the steps and wait patiently while I unlock the front door.

The hall is cool. It smells of flowers and furniture polish. Mother says all houses should smell of those two things. She's right. She calls out, 'Is that you, darling?' as we come in.

'Yes, it's me.'

'Are there people with you?'

'Yes. A couple of people from work. Come to pick up some case notes.'

'Oh.' I hear her taking this in. 'Hello there!' she calls.

The policeman coughs and says 'Hello' in a subdued way. He actually blushes. But the policewoman is tough, in a pretty, blonde, English blue-eyed kind of way. 'Hello there!' she calls back, confident.

I hear mother grow silent. I can't call out don't worry, it's only a colleague, or any other elaboration of my deception; I'd risk sounding quite mad. It will have to wait. Mother calls out peevishly, 'I really need my tea, darling!' And I say, 'I won't be long, truly.'

I show them into the living room. I'm always struck myself by its beauty. There's a bunch of anemones in a blue and white Chinese bowl on the mahogany table in the back window. Light through the garden leaves and reflections in the polished surface. I invite them through to the kitchen: 'Do you mind if I just put the kettle on for my mother's tea? I am a bit late.'

'No, go ahead.'

Their eyes are going everywhere, it's weird. You feel quite vulnerable as these eyes sweep round all the pots and jars, weighing up what could be lurking under the disguise of innocent household substances, self-raising flour or sugar or dried ceps. They weigh it up against the likelihoods. I want to say something clever, daring them to look in the jars, but I don't. I'm much too clever to be clever with them.

'What's wrong with your mother?' That's the policewoman. She's much brighter than her colleague. Knows what to ask.

'Well, giving birth many years ago, something went wrong. It was the epidural. Too much of something, or something. She doesn't talk about the details. Well, not to me. That's all I've been able to glean. Paralysed legs.'

'Giving birth to you?' she asks.

I'm busy with the tea. 'No,' I say. My back is to them. 'To my sister,' I say.

'And where is she now? Your sister.' She makes her questions sound like anyone's,

98

showing interest, making conversation. She's good. But so am I. I'm not taken in by this. 'She lives in Ireland now. West Cork. She runs a B&B. All by herself. It's a lovely place.'

'It's usually the girl who stays and looks after the mother.'

I shrug. 'Oh well. Yes. She escaped and I got sort of – landed. But actually I don't mind.' I meet the policewoman's eyes for the first time and give a slight smile. She nearly smiles back, a real smile, not a professional one. She doesn't let herself go all the way. But she has felt my charm. Not too much; just a pinprick. In her flesh. I can always tell. She looks away.

'Now,' – I've filled the kettle and emptied the old tea-leaves out of the pot, placed the Doulton cup and saucer and the milk jug on the tray. I switch the kettle on – 'I'll just have a look for that ticket.'

I pick up my overnight bag which I've dumped on the kitchen chair next to my briefcase. I go right through both bags, I don't know how I have the nerve. I dump every single thing out on to the kitchen table. 'No. Not here.' I stand, hands on hips, thinking hard. 'Where could I have put it?' They watch me. 'I'm sure I've still got it. I'm sure I didn't throw it away.' I look embarrassed. 'Honestly!' Suddenly I hit my forehead with the flat of my hand. 'I know!'

I race from the room and pound up the stairs. So boyish, so genuine. I shout from up there, 'Got it!'

Mother calls, 'What?'

'Nothing.'

'Not my tea?'

'I'll get it now.'

'What about your friends?'

'Going soon.'

'They don't have to rush away.'

I dance down brandishing the ticket. 'In my other jacket!' I shake my head. 'Of course. How could I have forgotten?' and hand it over.

The constable or whatever he is scrutinises it. The woman says, holding my eyes, 'She seems nice.'

'My mother? She's okay.'

Constable Mastermind has finished his minute perusal of the piece of red and yellow card. 'Well, sir, that seems to be in order.'

'Yes?' I smile, so relieved.

She's still looking at me. She stretches out a hand for the ticket. Gives it a comprehensive glance, nods and hands it back to me. 'Keep it in a safe place,' she says. 'Don't throw it away, okay?'

'Oh. Right. Yes. Thanks.' It's great, this acting lark. I've noticed the closer you stick to your own real feelings the easier it is and the better the effect. I did feel a certain relief, a certain gratitude. The only factor I concealed was my delight, my triumph. I hid behind a becoming modesty. This policewoman was my audience. In the palm of my hand. She was ready to be caught though she did not know it. She's lucky she's not my type. Ten years too old for a start, and too fat. Well, plump, to be charitable. Sturdy policewoman's legs.

She smiled again when I said thanks. I did sound a bit absurd. I meant to. 'Can I say hello to your mother?' she said.

Oh, she wasn't such a pushover after all, playing the same game as I, I discovered.

'Oh.' I got all nervous again. 'Well, the thing is, you're a policewoman and–'

'Woman police officer.'

'Oh yes, sorry–'

'And?'

'Well, actually she's – my mother might be–'

'Give her a shock, you think?'

'Well, yes. I don't think she knows about the awful – I didn't let her read the papers. It could prey on her mind.'

'No, I see.'

They look at each other– What do you think? He on the level? Well, let's leave it for now, get further instructions - and she says, 'Oh well.' She gives me this really inviting smile. 'I can always come back another time. Maybe in plain clothes.'

I laugh, a little uneasily. 'Oh, er, yes, of course.'

'All right, sir. Thanks very much.' He's got the door open on to the sunny street.

She gives me a last conspiratorial smile and follows him out. 'Thanks,' she says. 'I might drop by some time.'

I watch her plump little bottom tremble as her feet hit the steps. Then I go in.

The kettle has boiled. I measure out two teaspoonfuls of Lapsang, reboil the water, pour it into the Chinese teapot and put both my arms round my own body, hugging myself while I wait for the tea to infuse.

PRIVATE LIFE, PRIVATE DEATH

He was never happy outside London. He got this nervous feeling on the M4, the rolling hills flashing by, pretty but worrying. What did people do out here in the sticks? Bristol wasn't bad, it was a city, it had personality. But the country? Fearsome. All this wide green space.

It wasn't the countryside making him nervous, though. It was Kate. Was he right to invite himself? Did she really want him there? Could he be of use or was he just muscling in? And was he walking into another stand-off without the guts to see the thing through? And what did he want anyway? They'd have to talk. And he feared that the most. Talking about this stuff - how did you do it? He'd talked to Millie, no problem, didn't know why that was, no explaining it, no barrier, like talking to yourself.

They'd just walked into it, he and Millie, this conversation, like old mates, old sparring partners, suddenly met in another country, on another plane, something, he couldn't explain it. Trouble was, it had him by the balls. Other women – he liked them, fancied them to hell, like Kate. But when it came to it – he just couldn't – go through with it. And it was Millie's fault. How much longer could she stick around to ruin his life? He tried to get angry at her and couldn't. Just got the usual sick sense of loss in his gut. How could he explain this to Kate, in any way that she could tolerate? And what did he want her to say: *Oh, I understand, darling, and of course I'll wait?*

An articulated truck thirty feet long pulled out in front without signalling, just as he started to overtake it. A flash in the mirror showed a car coming up in the outside lane. If he braked the car on his tail in the middle lane would be up his arse and he'd be under the truck. He had to risk pulling out. He flashed his lights and honked long and hard as he went. The truck swerved back to the inside lane. The car coming up on the outside braked squealing and Bright swept on accelerating like a jumbo jet on the runway, praying as fast as he moved.

It was over. He was okay. All was okay. No one was dead. He felt suddenly cheerful. What the hell. Things change. Living things change. Just like Millie: nearly got him killed for just thinking about another woman. He slowed down to eighty in the middle lane as he overtook a mock-Tudor

Morris, then cruised into the inside lane and tootled along at eighty-five. A glorious day and the sun not round to his windshield yet. He got his mind back to the case. After all, the reason for his trip.

Alison. She's dead. No change possible there. He wished he hadn't met her. He wished she wasn't connected to Maisie who was connected to Kate. It was tough clearing the decks in your head to think hard and straight about the thing.

Alison. Beautiful, bright, fifteen years old. And black. That might be a factor. Leaves Maisie's dad's place – Dave, is he called? – with two other young people round ten thirty at night. Dave and all his guests are agreed on that. This does not make it true.

These two young people leave her at her door.

Correction: They say they leave her at her door.

She never gets into her house.

Correction: The parents say she never gets into her house.

No one sees her again.

Correction: So far no one has been found who saw her again.

Someone sure as hell saw her again because she turns up dead three weeks later and someone was responsible for that. And for the laying out. He's heard of some things but to lay a body out on a hillside to be found, like an effigy on a cathedral tomb, hands crossed on her breast, legs straight out, face to the sky. Kind of reverent. And untouched. No one laid a finger on her.

So where was she those three weeks? Who with? Who did that to her? Did what to her? Was she killed or did she die? Why was she left there? By whom? One or more than one? Did she disappear by choice? Or by abduction? And did she know her abductor? Why would she go with this person? Unless this person was known to her. She was too bright to be tricked. That's what people would say. Only, no matter how bright they are, well-brought-up kids of Alison's age have an innocence the rest of us can barely recall. And the brightest can be the easiest to fool.

Maisie, Kate's niece, a little cracker, thin as a twig, hair like candy floss, eyes like a puppy dog. Full of fireworks, going off in all directions, and clever. Maisie wrecked. What do you do at fifteen when this happens to your best mate? Then the mother, Lizzie. He knew his charm was not of the ingratiating kind, but most women kind of responded, given time. Not the formidable Lizzie. He winced at the memory. 'Hello, Lizzie, I've heard a lot about you. Nice to meet you at last.'

She was polite. Brutally polite. Graciously insulting! 'How do you do? Come in. I won't offer you tea because you'll want to get an early start, I expect. When are you going back to London?'

Maisie whispered to him, 'Take no notice of mum, she's just like that. It's not personal.'

'Oh yes it is.' Kate grinned. 'She hates you, mate.'

He winced.

'I thought you liked to be disliked. I thought that was your stock in trade.'

'Yeah, but in this instance I was actually trying to be nice!'

'Well, there you are, you see. You shouldn't act out of character. Just be horrible like you usually are, and Lizzie will be eating out of your hand.' Mind you, Kate was mad at him that day because— The sign for the A32 to Bristol appeared in the middle of this vaguely disturbing reverie and he sat up and signalled. He got an uneasy feeling as he slid on to the slip road. He was moving off his patch into unmapped territory.

13

VISITATION RIGHTS

The bell clanged. It was a big brass bell like a school bell, three floors down. You rang it by pulling on a rope. Maisie leaned out of the window. She was about to throw down the key, the normal way to let people in when the boat-house door was shut. But she saw it was a policeman down there. With a policewoman. The policewoman called up, 'Could you let us in, love?'

Maisie said, 'It's the police.' In the room there was a hiatus, then a slow silent bustling, people moving around purposefully purposeless. 'Shall I go down, dad?'

'Yes, Maisie, fine.' His face had that concentrated hawkish look, staring like she wasn't there. She thought for a moment he was a bit scared. But he had no reason to be scared. Did he? Except of course all people with radical attitudes, with the courage to live life by their own rules, their own beliefs, and not to go along with convention, maybe they were all a bit scared of the police. And maybe they were right to be scared.

She felt stronger, protective, as she made her way down the dark stone staircase of the lower floors. She unlocked the door with the big key.

The police held out their cards just like on the telly. She didn't dare look closely to see if they were who they said they were. She wondered if anyone ever did.

'Who are you, love?' the policewoman said in quite a friendly way.

'I'm Maisie Creech.'

'We're looking for David Fowler.'

'That's my dad.'

'Your dad?'

'That's right.'

'What you say your name was again?'

Maisie knew what they were implying: *funny, father and daughter, different names, weird set-up here.* Just the usual conventional attitudes. She was used to it. 'I have my mum's name. Yes, he's in.'

'We'd like to have a word with him. Thanks.'

She was shocked. They were already in and on the way upstairs without her permission like they already knew where to go. She wanted to protest but had no idea what to say. Feeling humiliated she shut the big door and locked it again, then ran lightly up behind them.

'Is it about–' She stopped a moment then said, 'Allie?'

'She was your best friend, that right?' The policewoman was quite young, could almost have been a sixth year at Maisie's school. Sounded sympathetic.

Maisie nodded. She dared not speak in case of starting to howl again. The policewoman didn't go on. Seemed to realise.

The policeman said, 'How long's your dad lived here then?' He wasn't sympathetic at all.

'Oh, years.' Maisie had got her voice under control. 'About ten years, I think.' He'd been there ages before it became the thing to live in lofts, he was ahead of his time in so many ways.

'A lot of his students hang out here, that right?'

'Yes.' She tried to find words dignified enough to express the amazing rapport Dave had with the young people he taught, and even with those he didn't. 'They think very highly of him,' she said.

The police people exchanged a glance but didn't say anything.

'Why aren't you at home with your mum?' The woman did not sound unfriendly saying this.

'Well, I just wanted to be with my father for a while, that's all.'

The woman gave her a little smile. She was nice. 'Stay with him quite a lot, do you?'

'Well...' Maisie was torn between the

110

picture she wanted to paint, and the truth. 'Well, no actually. We get on very well but I have so much homework and everything, there usually just isn't time.'

'But you stay with him sometimes?'

'Just once or twice really. When my mum's had to go away somewhere.'

'You stay here on your own with your dad?'

Maisie felt uneasy about this question without quite knowing why, like they were implying something horrible: 'Not really. There's always a lot of people here. Dad's really popular. Lots of people don't get on with their parents, things like that, and dad says it's important that someone is there for them.'

'And he is there for them, right?'

'Yes, he is, always.'

The policeman looked at the police-woman. He had a funny expression but he didn't say anything. The rickety wooden stairs took over from the cold stone ones below. The next floor was Dave's place. The woman said, 'Did Allie come here?'

Maisie felt uneasy, wary, she didn't know why, felt she might have betrayed someone or something, felt it had all moved too fast for her, she'd lost track. 'Yes, she came here with me sometimes.'

'To stay?'

'No, not to stay, no.'

'She ever come here on her own? Without you?'

'She never said she did.'

'Would she have told you?'

Maisie's face showed shock. 'She was my best friend.' Tears filled up her eyes. The policewoman looked abashed.

They were at the top of the stairs. The man banged on the door then pushed it open without waiting. Everyone was lounging about as before but now they looked somehow posed, stagey, deliberately arranged in casual attitudes.

Maisie went straight to Dave. Into his arms. Enfolding her, he faced the Law. 'What have you been saying to her?'

'Just chatting, sir, on the way up.'

'Look at her!'

The policewoman said, 'I think it was just the mention of Alison, wasn't it, Maisie?'

Maisie didn't reply. She knew this to be not quite the truth but it was too complex to explain and anyway she was too upset to speak.

Dave said, 'What about Alison?'

'Just wondering if she ever stayed here, sir.'

Maisie felt Dave's body stiffen and go quite still. Pressed against his chest, she couldn't see his face but his voice came out quite smooth. 'Did she, Maisie? I can't remember.'

'They asked me if she stayed here on her own.'

'Just if she came here on her own, sir.'

'Yes, I believe she did, once or twice.'

Maisie looked up at his face. It had the look she found perplexing. A very truthful helpful look, but under it she sensed – not a lie exactly – but a different truth, a version withheld. She wanted to say, 'Allie never told me,' but she felt Dave willing her not to. So she looked at him and said nothing.

'Why would she come on her own, sir?'

'Well, as you see...' Dave looked round the room. There were at least five people scattered about on cushions in here and someone standing in the kitchen doorway. 'Young people do tend to hang out here.'

'Why is that, sir?'

'I wish you'd stop calling me sir. Sounds very odd. Well, I think you should ask them. Why do you hang out here, Josie?'

A large soft girl with big brown eyes fingered the fat plait over her shoulder and said, 'Oh, Lord, well, I dunno, just because it's nice here, it's a good feeling, and Dave kind of helps, you know? If you've got a problem or anything, Dave's the person you think of to discuss it with. There's love and peace here, you know?' Her cheeks glowed red and, embarrassed, she faded away, sticking the end of her plait in her mouth as if to stop herself saying more.

113

The boy in the kitchen door said, 'Cool, Josie, yeah. It's a place to chill out, man, you know? It's a haven.'

A voice from the floor said, 'Yo.'

Dave gave the police a faint smile. He shrugged. 'I also hold seminars here.'

'Seminars?'

'I lecture in English Literature.'

'At the university, we know.'

'Sometimes this is an atmosphere more conducive to learning. Well, to intelligent discussion anyway.'

The policeman made no comment. 'So, can I ask all of you when you last saw Alison Holt?'

General shifting. People sat up, looked at each other.

'You first, sir.'

Dave loosened his grip on Maisie, held her, lightly against one arm. 'Missing Persons took a statement at the time she was reported missing.'

'Yes, sir.'

Dave said, 'Well, it was three weeks ago. Her parents rang the next day to find out if she was still here.'

'And she wasn't here?'

'No. She'd been here the night before – the Friday. She'd left about ten. This must all be on record.'

'Yes, sir.' The policeman waited.

'She left with two or three other people.

114

You'll have their names on record. Who lived in the same direction.'

'And had she been staying here?'

'No, just visiting. With Maisie.'

Maisie, in tears again, nodded.

'You didn't leave with her, love?' The policewoman was always the one who addressed Maisie, as though the man were not allowed to.

'No. I left first, round nine thirty, with Lennie, a friend of ours. He walked me back home. My mum likes me to be in by ten. Allie gets a special dispensation Friday nights.'

'Alison left about ten, I think,' Dave said.

Josie took the plait out of her mouth, said, 'I was with her,' and put it back in.

The boy in the doorway said, 'So was I.'

'Who are you, sir?'

'Stephen Hudson. Steve.'

'Anyone else with you?'

'Yeah. Martin, wasn't it, Josie?'

'Martin, yeah. I was with them up as far as – as – Windmill Hill, then they went up the steps to Totterdown, you know, Pylle Hill Crescent and Richmond Street and all that, and I went off to my place. Yeah.'

'We went along St Luke's Crescent then up Alison's street. We all chatted outside Alison's place,' Steve said. 'Then she went in, we thought, and Martin and I went off to the Indian chippy, you know, top of Alison's street near the shops. There was a queue so we decided to go down into town. We bumped into a mate of mine down by Temple Meads. Andy. And he got us into this club in King Street. I lost track of the others right away in there. You took statements at the time, you know.'

'Yes, sir. Thank you.'

Dave said, 'Anything I or any of us can do to help, I'm sure...' He looked around and all the people nodded. The boy flat on the floor raised a hand in agreement. '...we will. Anything.'

'Well, we would like a word with you in private, sir, now you mention it. Down at the station, if you don't mind.'

'Down at the station?'

Even the supine boy sat up straight. Josie said, 'Dave?' in a panic-stricken voice. Stephen said, 'Are you arresting him?'

Dave said, 'Well? Are you?'

The policeman said, 'No. But Inspector Ryan would like to ask a few questions. You're not being accused of anything but you might have things to tell us.'

'I think I've told you everything I can remember.' Dave was about to go on but didn't. Maisie knew he stopped speaking out of fear, that dry throat that won't let your voice escape. And she could feel his heart. Dave? Scared? Then she thought, So would I be scared if they wanted to take me

116

to the police station. It is frightening.

'Could you come with us now, sir?'

'Well...' Dave looked round, thinking of things to keep him there. All the young people watched him like dogs losing their master.

Stephen said, 'Listen, man–'

But Dave said, 'It's okay, Steve. I don't mind.' He tossed Stephen the keys. 'Keep an eye on the place, will you, till I get back?'

'Yeah, man.'

'Dad? Shall I come with you?'

'Christ. Listen, I'm going to have to make some arrangements about my daughter here.'

'That's okay, sir, we'll drop her off at her mother's.'

'Will Lizzie be in yet, Maisie?'

'Dad?' She wanted to stay there till he came back at least.

'Better go, Maize.' Dave picked up the phone and punched Lizzie's number.

'Our colleagues are waiting down the street. You can follow them in your own car, sir.'

'I don't own a car,' Dave snapped. 'It's against my principles.' He spoke into the phone: 'Oh, Kate, it's you.'

The young people milled about collecting their belongings while Dave explained the situation to Kate.

The policeman said, 'We'd like you all to

stay here, please.'

They looked at each other, wary.

'Why?' A girl with long blonde hair appeared, looking down from the sleeping platform. Maisie had not seen her before.

'Just a few questions, love.'

'No obligation,' the policewoman said. 'But you don't mind, do you?'

The girl looked as though she had not long been awake. The policewoman grinned. 'Doesn't look like you've got anywhere that urgent to go.'

'Oh.' The girl swept her hair back with a pale hand. 'No. I guess ... not.'

'So?'

'Okay then.'

Dave put the phone down. 'Kate's coming over for you, Maize.'

Maisie nodded, miserable with the dread of her mother's reaction when she arrived home tail between her legs. 'Okay, dad.'

Dave looked round the room: 'And listen, help these guys. We've all got to help as much as we can. We all knew Alison, a little at least. We might be able to throw some light.' He had pulled himself together. The young people straightened up, bathed in the light of his restored confidence.

'Okay, Dave.' The blonde girl gave Dave a special kind of look as she came down the ladder.

'What's your name, love?'

118

The girl swept her hair back again and said shyly, still looking at Dave in that special way, 'Sally. Sally Leventon.'

Maisie felt a particular misery surge up inside her. She'd had this feeling before when girls looked at her father like that. Maybe it wouldn't be such a bad thing to be back at her mother's just now.

'How's mum?'

'Well, Maisie, you're going to have to–'

'–to be careful. I know.'

'She'll be glad to have you back.'

'Yeah but she won't show it, will she?'

'She can't.'

'Why not? Dad does.'

Kate bit her tongue. She did not say Lizzie cares more than he does, she said, 'She cares too much.'

'I know.' Maisie groaned. 'She just makes everything so heavy.'

'Yup.' Kate came to an unexpected halt. The Ford Capri in front waited to make sure the traffic lights were well and truly green to take off his handbrake and put his car in gear. 'Oh, these Bristol drivers.' She had a swift mind-flash – John Bright's capable hands on the steering wheel, his instinctive handling, more like flying than driving – which led her to add, 'By the way, John Bright's coming down.'

'Your policeman!'

'Maisie!'

'It's what mum calls him.'

'Exactly.'

'Is he coming down to solve the case?'

'Hell, no. I mean, he might be able to glean a bit of inside information from the bloke in charge, but that's about it. This is not his patch.'

'So why is he coming then?'

'Well...'

'Is it because he's your bloke?'

Kate glanced into Maisie's pure young eyes. 'Christ, Maisie, the things you say.'

'Well, I thought–'

'No, he's not my bloke.'

'Not yet anyway,' Maisie said.

'Maisie!'

'Well, you haven't given up, have you?'

Kate, speechless for a moment, rallied. 'No. Actually. I haven't.'

'I liked him.' Maisie offered her sturdy support.

'Oh well then, in that case, I'd better not give up.'

Silence for a block while trains of thought took separate tracks. Then Maisie said, 'That's the first time I've stopped thinking about Allie since...'

Kate looked at the tired pale face.

Maisie said, 'I don't want to stop thinking about her. Not for a minute. If I forget her a minute, a little bit of her goes and I'll never

120

get it back.'

'Oh Maisie.'

'I can't stand it, Ankate. I don't know how to stand it.'

Kate took a hand off the wheel and held Maisie's hand.

'And what did they take dad for?' Maisie wailed.

HELPING THE POLICE WITH THEIR ENQUIRIES

Ryan's bulk made him feel flimsy, made of muslin, ghostlike, but he was holding his ground. He sat with his arms folded firmly across his chest and held the gaze of whoever spoke to him.

'Listen, son.' Ryan was only five years older than Dave, if that. 'Listen, son, there's no need to be defensive. We're not accusing you of anything.'

'I should think not.'

'Like my officer said, we just want you to tell us everything you know.'

'You took me away in a squad car in front of my daughter and my students–'

'I know, son, and I'm sorry about that.'

'Oh, are you?'

'I am, and the sooner we get this over with the sooner you can get back to your daughter and your – students.'

'Not all your students, are they, sir?' The hard-faced policeman assisting Ryan.

'Not all, no. Not officially.'

'Quite a number of nubile young females,

I'm told, sir.'

Dave managed to say nothing.

'Wouldn't you say so, sir?'

Dave addressed Ryan: 'This officer seems to be making insinuations which in the tragic circumstances I find offensive. And if this is to be the level of your questioning I want a lawyer. I want to call my solicitor now and I refuse to say another word until you allow me to do that.' He found himself standing up, had no idea how this had come about, but knew he made a daunting figure when roused.

However, these two hard-noses remained undaunted. 'Sit down, please, sir,' Ryan said, bored.

Dave could have said, I won't sit down, and got himself involved in a farcical stand-off, or stand-up, but he knew too well as a teacher not to get into a battle you can't win. He stood irresolute.

'I told you,' Ryan said, 'you're not accused of anything. My officer DC Hughes apologises for getting out of line. Don't you?'

Hughes eyed Dave with contempt. 'Yes, sir. Sure.'

'Obviously heartfelt, DC Hughes.' Dave spoke with the sarcasm he used on the clever clogs student trying to put him down in front of the rest – you got the odd one now and then. He was pleased to see it work on Hughes if only to rile him up. Dave kept his eyes on the guy's face as he lowered himself back into the chair, then he took the initiative. 'Look,' he said. 'I met Allie – Alison – a few times. Three, to the best of my knowledge. Maisie brought her once or twice. And once, I think, she came by herself. And yes, I have young girlfriends, but I am not a child-molester. The girls I have affairs with are well of age and never up to now in my experience, virgins. I'm not saying I haven't been tempted. I doubt if you could meet a male who could state honestly that he hadn't been tempted...' He looked hopefully into the two faces across the table. They remained impassive. 'And Alison was, I have to admit, a little bit smitten. I gave her an avuncular talk and, basically, sent her off to get on with her homework.'

The two cops looked at each other. Ryan said, 'What does avuncular mean, DC Hughes?' Hughes said, 'I don't know, guv, we'll have to look it up.' It had gone wrong. This sort of stuff didn't wash with them. In their eyes everyone was guilty unless proved innocent. The more truthful you managed to sound, the better a liar that proved you to be. They let a long silence elapse.

Then the DC said, 'I imagine if we searched your place we might find the odd illegal substance stashed here and there, sir.

Don't you think so?'

'That right, Mr Fowler?' Ryan said.

Dave felt like a deep sea diver about to get the bends. He could get no grip. He didn't know what to do. Condemned by speech, condemned by silence, condemned simply by their suspicion, he felt paralysed. He actually wanted to weep. Only pride and bloody-mindedness stopped him. He crossed his fingers against his heart and hoped to die. 'I very much doubt it,' he said. He hoped every scrap of dope had been gathered up when Maisie went down to let the bastards in. But you never know. And if they decided to raid the place... Or search the young friends they'd detained there... 'And I hardly see the relevance anyhow.'

'There's things a young girl might do stoned out of her gills that she wouldn't do sober, sir.'

'Is that so?' Dave wished he had not said that. Cheeky, feeble. Their expressions showed they knew they had provoked him. He crossed his arms harder, tighter, across his crossed fingers, across his heart.

Ryan looked through the file on the table in front of him. He looked up. He said, 'I see from your statement when Alison first went missing you didn't mention this crush she had on you.'

NO PLACE LIKE HOME

Bright stood at the window, bouncing slightly on the balls of his feet, jangling the change in his pockets. Lizzie watched him. He'd given up attempts at conversation. He wished she would at least leave the room. She knew this and sat on. Even though she had things to do. She embarrassed him on purpose. At last she said, 'Why would they be questioning Dave again?'

'It's a murder enquiry now. They got to start again. Don't suppose they suspect him in particular. They got to start somewhere.'

'Why with him?'

'Alison went there a few times, you said.'

'Well, so what?' Lizzie had no idea why she was suddenly defending Dave. Except that she disliked Bright more.

'I didn't arrest him.' Bright turned his oh so amused squinting glance on her, those small brown eyes, sharp as broken glass.

Her face went pink. 'No. Of course not. But they questioned him at the time and...'

He relented. 'It'll be the same with every

bloke she had contact with, from the postman to her eight-year-old cousin. They got to turn all the stones.' She wasn't convinced, he could see. He hoped he was speaking the truth. For Maisie's sake, and therefore for Kate's. And speaking of Kate–

The yellow Beetle yakkered to a halt on the steep street outside. She saw him at once and pretended not to. He felt oddly pleased by this. Maisie dawdled up the steps, head down, Kate nudging her to be nice to Lizzie. Lizzie had shot out to the front door.

Bright expected to hear the nagging start as soon as she opened it. But no. Silence. Maisie at last came into the room.

'Hi, Maisie.'

She moved her mouth – you couldn't call it a smile – and gave him a sort of wave.

'Sorry to hear...' He nodded the rest of the sentence and she nodded back.

Kate had gone into the kitchen with Lizzie. Maisie came to stand by the window with him. They looked at the house opposite with its depressing replacement windows and bottle glass front door. After a minute or two she said, 'They took my dad.'

'A-ha, I heard.'

'What will they do to him?'

'They got to question people at the station these days. Get it all down on tape. It's just rules.'

'Will they lock him up?'

'I don't think so.'

'Why not?'

'Well, I don't think they suspect him of doing anything bad. They just think maybe he knows something. Something maybe he forgot last time.'

'Knows something?'

'Or someone.'

'You mean one of his student people?' Maisie turned this white strained face on him that would break your heart. You lose your best friend like this, and then they start accusing your father of untold crimes.

'I'll find out,' he said.

'From the police?'

'A-ha.'

'Will they tell you?'

'They might.'

'Because you're a policeman too?'

'A-ha.' He didn't say because he was a policeman with a certain amount of clout in this field. He said, 'I'm not making any promises, okay?'

She sighed and sat down. 'Even mum doesn't want him arrested,' she said.

'Hello.' Kate stood in the doorway. Hair all over the place, eyes with that challenging look when she wasn't sure of her ground but was giving it a go. 'Came here first then?'

'A-ha.' What did she mean, first? He didn't ask.

'Well, I'd better take you to where you'll be staying.'

'Oh.' This was a surprise. He didn't show it. 'Right.' He picked up his bag. Felt a bit daft assuming he'd be staying here. She raised her eyebrows in conspiratorial amusement. This made him feel marginally less daft. 'Now?' he said.

'Probably a good idea. What do you think, Maisie?'

'What? Oh. Yes.'

Kate laid a hand on her niece's head. 'Go and get a cup of tea in the kitchen. You're starved.'

Maisie got up and moved slowly to the door. She turned and looked at Bright. 'I'm glad you're here anyway,' she said.

Bright, touched, didn't know where to look. His eyes met Kate's and the old thing happened again. Islanded in a dangerous place, no way forward, no way back, no way in, no way out.

She ended it: 'Come on then, let's go.'

The hotel foyer was like a huge airport departure lounge. Insidious noise loosely describable as music filled the air-conditioned infinitely carpeted pinkish space. Employees like cabin staff discreetly handed out forms to be filled, electronic room keys that also turned on the lights, offers to carry baggage too small to be

129

worthy of the name.

'Think I can manage, thanks.' Bright lifted his small overnight bag, hated all this deferential bullshit. Kate grinned.

'And Mrs Bright?' The smooth young man gave her a toothful smile. Kate blushed, felt idiotic. Bright made a muffled groan and Kate laughed. 'I'll help him carry his baggage,' she said. 'I haven't got any.'

The room too was pinkly carpeted and lit. 'I'm sorry about this,' she said. 'Lizzie just–'

'A-ha. Don't explain. I got the picture.' He threw his bag on the bed. 'Well? What now?'

She decided to keep this impersonal. 'I wish I knew.'

'I guess I phone Ryan.'

'Really?' Her face filled with hopes he felt certain to disappoint.

'Not that I expect to find out much.'

'You won't be able to protect Dave?'

'No.'

'No.' She put her hand over her eyes. 'It's Maisie. I just can't bear–'

'No.'

'And nor can Lizzie. It's worse for her.'

'A-ha.'

She sat on the bed while he took his toothbrush out of his pocket and placed it in the glass in the pink-tiled ensuite bathroom. 'Want to meet later on?' he said.

'Oh.' He was telling her he had to be alone to phone Ryan. She felt stupid. Stood up.

Ran through her Bristol haunts and ended up with the one she always chose. 'See you at – eightish – in Renato's. Next to the Old Vic. In King Street.'

'I remember.'

'Italian place. Well, obviously.'

'I remember.'

'Oh yes.' She was flushed, flustered. 'We could eat there too.'

'I remember, okay?' She aroused a tenderness he found hard to withstand. ''Course I remember.'

'When you came to the play.'

'When I saw you're this great actress.'

'Oh, piss off.'

'Which I already knew.'

'Okay, I'm going. You certainly know how to get rid of a girl.'

'I have my methods.'

'I've noticed.' She was at the door. So was he but she didn't hang about. 'See you at eight.' She was gone.

16

EXCERPT FROM A DIARY

iv

I bought the paper today. Pictures of the grieving children at the school. They LOOK like children in the pictures. With their teachers. By the piles of flowers in the playground. But they're not children really. They're women and young men. They are to a certain extent innocent – or should I rather say ignorant? – of the ways of the world. But they are not children. She was a woman. Perfect in every detail. Before the world could touch her. Contaminate her perfection. It was about to begin, the contamination. It was beginning. I saw her smoking spliff with those types who visit Mr Wonderful. In his loft. The lofty types. Next it would be something a little more sophisticated, a little more exciting, a little more dangerous. I'm sure like all of them she took Es like sweeties.

In a few weeks, or even days, her virginity would have gone and she'd be just like all the rest. Spoiled. The spoils of a vile kleptomaniac who would have to have that, just that, for himself. To add to his collection. His stash.

I'm crying again, looking at these pictures. The problem is, I can't explain to them. They think she's lost. I can't explain to them that she's saved. One perfect unspoiled thing saved. I'm sorry to have to hurt them all like this. If only there were some way to tell them WHY.

The picture of her parents is not very good. They're rather blurred. Gazing straight out, sitting at a table. Oh yes, it's when they were on TV making their appeal. That's why it looks odd. Those lines across the picture. They have got what they deserve. They allowed her into these dangerous ways. Freedom they call it. It has got to stop. Oh, for the general run it will do. But there are certain rare creatures of such perfection of form, of grace, of soul, of mind, that the world must not be allowed to corrupt them. If these people do not realise what they have been entrusted with, have not learned to protect it, they must be taught. It is hard. But they must learn. They have other children. Perhaps they'll be more careful of them now. I'm not a cruel person, not at all, I am tortured with tenderness. But in my silent secret way I will teach the world this lesson. They will see. Eventually.

And they'll see I'm not cruel. I didn't

harm her. I preserved her perfection. They'll see that. These people, journalists, police, are used to adding two and two together, it's their job. They'll pick it up, won't they? Surely they will.

I went to a house today. There were two small boys under school age. No trousers, snot running down their faces. They played on a littered floor, sticky with spilt drinks and food. The baby lay in its pram with food all over its face and a nappy soaked and soiled. No father to be seen, of course, and the mother lying back, eyes rolling in her head, the gear lying on the floor by the couch within reach of the children. Everybody happy.

Why not kill *them*, you'll ask. They're already killed, that's why. They're gone. 'Special needs?' You bet. I'll fill in the forms for them. Get them to write their names. If they can. As I was leaving she said, 'Got a fag, love?' She said, 'I got to have a fag, see, just to keep floatin'.' I gave her a cigarette. I don't smoke myself. I loathe it, detest it, but sometimes it's the only way to break the ice. It's currency. They all smoke, these people. All of them. They have skin like wrinkled grey paper. From the age of nine. Earlier, some of them. I've never figured out how they survive at all. Those of us with the money and the nous to eat the right food, stuffing ourselves with the right vitamins and minerals and the ginseng and the royal jelly and the evening primrose oil and the echinacea, from morning till night, can barely survive. While these creatures of the underclass spawn, as profligate with their genes as sycamore and thistle, breeding on waste ground.

17

MUSCLING IN

The Broadbury Road police HQ, a terrible seventies building, stood on a windy corner surrounded by roadworks in a housing estate of red-brick pseudo cottages that would have been nice with their original windows and doors. Bright crossed the tarmac car-park into the public entrance and stated his business through a microphone and bullet-proof glass. He was getting the impression this was a rough area.

Ryan came out of the pass door with Dave. Bright turned his back as best he could in the cramped entrance. He didn't want to embarrass Dave. He also didn't want Ryan to see they knew each other. Not yet.

Dave said to Ryan, 'An Irish detective inspector. It seems odd somehow, incongruous. Not in Ireland of course, but here. Don't you think?' He meant it man to man but it didn't come out like that; it came out big lad cheeking teacher. Bright felt glad he'd turned his back.

Ryan saw Dave off the premises without a

word, came back scowling and saw Bright. 'Oh, it's you,' he snarled.

''Fraid so.'

'Yeah, sorry. That guy gets on my tits: "Incongruous, don't you think"! Doesn't take anyone in, that stuff. Him with the long hair down his back. Not that I'm prejudiced, mind. Ringlets down to your arse doesn't make you a criminal. But it sure as hell gets up my nose.'

'How's it going?'

Ryan got coffee from the machine on the landing outside his office. 'Uniform branch just blew it.'

'Jumping the gun?'

'They march in there when he's surrounded by his so-called students. We were hoping to catch him with something incriminating just to have something to hold him on. They'd have everything flushed down the toilet before those guys were up the stairs.'

'You figure him then?'

Ryan growled. 'Maybe he didn't kill the girl. Maybe. Maybe he didn't abduct her. Maybe. But he's not telling everything, not by a long chalk. He's done something, or he knows something, that he's not telling us. Something has happened that connects him. Something. I've a nose for guilt and Mr Guru Man stinks of it. Clever he may be, and charismatic for these poor kids

137

maybe, but the fear coming off him is a stench to a nostril like mine.'

Bright took his coffee, impressed. 'I'd better state my interest.'

'You already did.'

'I've met the guy socially. I know his daughter.'

'You're screwing her auntie the actress, that's the word round here.'

Bright covered the lower half of his face with his hand, his eyes contorted into one of his fiercer squints. He had to decide fast which way to jump with this guy. On impulse he said, 'Not screwing as it happens. No such luck. We're – friends, that's all. Since–'

'Since the body in the bath case.'

'A-ha.'

'That right, now?' said Ryan. 'She's a great-looking girl. Not many guys round here would say no to a piece of that.'

'Nor would I, believe me, mate. It just hasn't happened. Looks as though it never will.'

Why his frank admission of lack of success with Kate should endear him to Ryan he hadn't a clue. But it did. He'd spoken on instinct. He knew Ryan would assume the refusal was on her part. Well, anyone would. A copper screwing a key person in a case like this was a bad risk. Being turned down by a foxy lady, however, was not a thing a bloke liked admitting. So the admission was likely to be true. Ryan thought so anyway. He sat back in his chair, relaxed. He seemed to grow in size. He regarded Bright, nodding his head several times. 'So what do you want to know that the papers can't tell you?'

'I dunno. The stuff that gives you the feel. The scene, the pictures, the lab reports–'

'Alcohol and barbiturates and no struggle, looks like the old polythene bag.'

'But you're sure it's murder?'

'The way she was laid out. Weird.'

'A ritual killing?'

Ryan shook his head. 'No. Only one set of footprints. Trainers. No distinguishing marks.'

'How are the evidence reports looking?'

Ryan groaned. 'Any idea the sheer number of witnesses? Kids know so many people. The whole feckin' school have got something to tell you, some vital sighting on the day or the day before or the day before that, something she said in the changing room before gym or the school hall during assembly, it drives you mental.'

'Got it on the PNC?'

Ryan nodded. 'And we're setting up HOLMES.'

'Where's your incident room?'

'Bishopsworth. You're not getting in there.'

Bright grinned. 'Nothing to go on? Apart from Dave?'

Ryan sighed and shook his head. 'Nothing you can get hold of. We've got six uniforms knocking on doors.'

'Heard you were talking to her father.'

'Nothing there. Well...'

'A-ha?'

'He's hiding something but I don't think it's anything to do with this.'

'Why?'

'No sign of anything wrong in the house. No abuse. Nothing.'

'Talk to the guy who found her?'

'The jogger? Poor sod. Yeah, shitting himself. Imagine, you go into the bushes for a quiet piss and what do you find? Black Beauty lying dead at your feet.'

'Any history?'

'No. Never seen a corpse in his life before. Nothing there either. Clean as a whistle.'

'So that's it then. No one else been questioned?'

'A few people who had their cars parked close by. You know the Bedminster approach to the hill? Right by the kid's school, where my fellas had been asking questions for days. Five cars had been parked there overnight. All gone over with a fine-tooth comb. All clean. But one of the uniform branch, pretty little mare by the name of Goldilocks. Helen Goldie, that is. Hang on...' He riffled through the files on his desk. 'Here we are: she fancied one of these car-owners for it. Guy who lives up in Clifton. Don't know why him. His car was pure as the driven snow. No evidence whatever. But Goldilocks Had A Feeling.'

'Worth following up?'

'Not on the basis of female intuition. Sorry.'

'No other connection to Alison? Or anyone who might know Alison?'

Ryan looked at Bright. Something had changed in the guy's posture. Or something. His little brown eyes. Sometimes they squinted, sometimes they didn't, weird. Something in him had perked up. His eyes had sharpened like needles. A hard metallic light that hadn't been there before. Ryan said slowly, 'You suffering from female intuition as well?'

'I dunno. Why was his car parked there if he lives in Clifton?'

'He works in the Bedminster/Totterdown area, some kind of social services thing. Home assessment visits, something.'

'Could he have done a home assessment visit to Alison's family?'

'They're not that kind of black. Father works in the DSS. Managerial. The mother's a teacher. They're the respectable type.'

'Why would he leave his car just there?'

'Health-conscious. He jogs over the hill on his way to work and on his way back.'

141

'To work? Jogging makes you sweat. He the type to arrive at work sweaty?'

'Well, his car was a mess. And he's another long-hair. Not like our friend Dave Fowler the guru but aiming for that league. Holes in his sweater, that sort of stuff. And the kind of people he's visiting? Believe me, they wouldn't notice if he smelled like a doss house. But I don't know. I don't know.' Ryan's big fist came up to his mouth. He pondered over the file then handed it suddenly to Bright. 'Have a look at it, I'm busy. Don't tell a soul. And don't remove it from this office.'

18

PARTINGS AND MEETINGS

Maisie insisted on going to the school, so Kate went with her. A river of flowers flowed from the site on the hill where the body had been found, down the path, spilled in a bank along the wall of the school to the gate, through the gate, ending at a kind of altar in the playground where some people knelt and prayed.

Kate thought, This is the new mourning. People of the national disaster generation have invented it for themselves. It's television. It creates national news, and that creates demonstrations. Outward signs of inward grief. Maisie left her, to join two girls who put out their arms. They stood entwined, the Three Graces.

Kate looked at the pictures of Alison, the poems and messages attached to the flowers. A young woman stood next to her. She said, 'Excuse me, but you're Kate Creech, aren't you?'

'Yes. How–?'

'I go to the Old Vic. I saw your Hedda.'

'Oh.' Kate didn't want this conversation

over the grieving flowers.

The young woman saw her discomfort. 'Sorry. Not the place. I just wanted to say –Well, it was remarkable, that's all.'

'Oh. Right. Thanks.' She never knew how to deal with this kind of thing. Gave the girl an awkward smile.

The girl didn't smile back. 'Did you know Alison?' she said.

'Yes. She was a friend of my niece.'

'Oh.' The young woman looked over at Maisie. 'Maisie,' she said.

'You know Maisie?'

She smiled and nodded.

'Are you a teacher here?'

She shook her head.

'A neighbour?'

'I know her father,' she said.

'Dave?' She didn't look Dave's type. She was tall, athletic-looking, with a strong face, long eyes set wide apart, an amused mouth, mid-length mid-brown hair. Dave liked them more ethereal – long blonde hair and long soft frocks, diaphanous and sweet. And younger. This girl wore a flowered cotton dress down to her calves and sensible sandals. She looked capable, practical.

Maisie left her friends and came back wiping her eyes. The young woman said, 'Hello, Maisie.'

Maisie looked blank.

'We met at your dad's place. I'm Margaret.'

'Oh. Yeah. Hi.'

Margaret gazed at Maisie, eyes full of sympathy and sorrow.

Maisie turned to Kate. 'Let's go, Ankate.'

'Okay.'

'No use being here.' She wandered towards the gate.

Kate turned to say goodbye to the young woman, but she had gone. She caught up with Maisie at the gate. 'Who was that?'

'Who? That woman?' Maisie shrugged. 'There's always so many women at dad's place. I can't remember them all.'

'You made a greater impression on her than she did on you, then!'

'Oh well, I'm dad's daughter. They have to keep in with me, don't they?' She gave Kate a wan smile.

They stood at a loss for a while outside the school walls. Where now? What now?

Kate said, 'Fancy seeing my digs?'

Kingsdown Parade was a high point of the city. Not as high up, geographically or socially, as Clifton, but with lovely Georgian houses, and a certain village feel. Kate had stayed up here last summer, an attic flat five floors up, windows looking through breaks in the roof parapet, nothing grand, just a kitchen you could eat in and living room you could sleep in. Nice. She liked it. And she liked the family downstairs. Luke lectured at the university, media studies. Caroline painted, still lifes of flowers, mainly for classy greetings cards.

Kate opened a door in the garden wall and led the way up a brick path overgrown with silvery things, lavender, rosemary, curry plants, all releasing heady aromas as they brushed past. The best of the summer flowers were over but honeysuckle was making a last ditch stand and some late roses swelled on the trellis. Maisie trailed after her and stood passive on the step while Kate rang the bell.

'Kate! How are you? It's great to have you back!' Caroline and the youngest, Thomas, leapt on Kate. The cat, George, more circumspect, kept his watchful distance but didn't run away. Caroline made space on the table, pushing aside her painting things and a bowl of tall spiky flowers of an extraordinary blue. 'The last of my delphiniums,' she said. 'I'm recording them for posterity.'

'They deserve it. They're gorgeous.'

'They are.'

Thomas leaned against Maisie's knees, gazing up into her face. 'This is my train,' he said. He waved the bright painted wooden object under her nose. Tears ran down Maisie's face. 'You're cryin',' he said.

Maisie nodded and cried more.

'I cry,' he stated proudly. 'A lot.'

'That's certainly true.' Caroline poured

tea. 'It's Earl Grey. Is that all right?'

'We were down at the school,' Kate said.

Caroline passed round big mugs of tea. Thomas stared at Maisie. Caroline and Kate stared at each other. The cat George stared at Kate. Even Maisie's crying made no noise. Thomas placed his train in Maisie's lap then clambered up after it. He settled himself back against her. She put her arms round him and rested her cheek on his head. It was the first time Kate had seen her look truly comforted.

'Joe Paxton's got the flat. He leaves tomorrow morning,' Caroline said. 'I'll change the sheets and stuff tomorrow and you can move in the next day. Is that okay?'

'That'll be fine,' Kate said. She turned her head and met the eyes of George, a chunky tabby. He knew her of old but was taking his time, just checking. He made a sudden leap from the window sill and landed in her lap. He turned round a few times, trying out positions, fixed on one curled sideways, his back pressed against her stomach. She too felt oddly comforted.

19

A WAY IN

Bright spent a few hours going through the file. There was nothing you could put your finger on. The parents were beyond suspicion. The neighbours, heartbroken, bewildered, equally easy to eliminate. Ryan was right. Dave, and the atmosphere surrounding Dave, were the nearest anyone could get to something odd. And the fact that Alison had been there last was damning.

The report on the visit to the guy in Clifton with the invalid mother was the last in the file. Bright read it twice then got up and left the office.

The CID room went quiet when he walked in. People got busy. Bright understood: it made them feel wankers, thinking the boss had called him in. They didn't like it and weren't bothering to hide their feelings. He stopped at the first table. A guy staring into a computer screen pretended he didn't see him then got real startled when Bright spoke. 'Oh! Sorry! What did you say?' He didn't do it well. His performance lacked subtlety to say the least.

'I'm looking for WPC Goldie. Helen Goldie.'

A few laughs, and a guy down the room whistled. 'Aren't we all, mate?'

Bright's squint intensified but no amusement showed. Glances were exchanged.

'Canteen, I should think.' The computer guy went back to his screen.

She was easy to recognise. A bit on the plump side for him but pretty, all right. And the blonde looked almost natural. 'WPC Goldie?'

''S right.'

He introduced himself. She looked impressed. 'You're the one who got that garden shed bloke.'

'A-ha.'

'Did Ryan invite you down to help with this?'

'No. I invited myself.'

'We could do with some help. Not getting far.'

'I wanted to ask you about this guy in Clifton.'

'Why?'

'Your report. You thought he should be followed up.'

Her fine blonde skin coloured, pearly pink. 'My guv'nor said–'

'A-ha. I know.'

'And the DC who went with me. He thought the guy was okay.'

'But?'

'Well, I don't know...'

'Yes you do. You say I don't know in that vague way and they'll all go on ignoring you. Come on, give it some elbow, love.'

'Oh.' She coloured again, this time as though he'd goosed her. She looked at his face. He had a slight squint, now she looked close. It gave him a foxy look, kind of amused, only the rest of his face stayed stock still, like a mask, like he was listening behind it, like what she said might be important.

'Take your time,' he said.

She shut her eyes and clasped her hands as though she were praying, and maybe she was. She opened them, hands and eyes. 'Okay,' she said. 'Right. He was – it sounds daft but he was, like crowing.' She looked at him, ready to be mocked, but his face didn't move. Only the squint had gone. Was that possible? And needle points of light had come into the small brown eyes.

'A-ha?' he said.

'Well, it was like he was *glad* we were there, like he wanted to be questioned, like he thought he was okay, we couldn't touch him for some reason. This posh house and everything.'

'Having a posh house doesn't necessarily

150

make you a killer.'

'Oh.' She looked upset. 'No...'

'Though it can help, of course.'

She looked at him closely then laughed. 'No, I don't mean that, only it was like he knew we'd think he was all right because he was posh and lived in Clifton and had this posh invalid mother.'

'I've got an invalid mother.'

'Have you?'

'A-ha. But she's not posh. So I'm all right.'

She knew now he was teasing her. She relaxed. 'He wouldn't let me see his mother. Kept saying how the police would startle her and all that.'

'How'd you rate him in the pulling stakes?'

'What?'

'Don't you call it that out here in the sticks? Did you fancy him?'

'Oh! Oh right!' No superior officer had ever talked to her like this before. 'Oh, well, no, I didn't fancy him, but you could see someone could. He certainly seemed to fancy himself.'

'Pretty boy?'

'Yeah, very, like, boyish, you know? Lovely hair, a little bit long but not too much, and kind of scruffy but, you know? streetwise. Long sweater with holes, and jeans with holes, and these nice boots. This lovely neck.' She stopped for a moment.

'You sure you didn't fancy him?'

She gave him a come-off-it look and a small smile. 'Lovely neck, nice smooth brownish skin, and square shoulders, and no spare flesh.'

'Well, he jogs.'

'Yes. Over Windmill Hill.' She spoke with serious significance.

'Exactly,' Bright said. 'Just like about three hundred other people.'

'Yes, but they don't live up there where he lives.'

'Eh?'

'He lives in Clifton. The Downs are three minutes away. There's miles of Downs to jog over. Up there, looking down on the suspension bridge and the river and all that fresh air and space. I mean if I lived up there I wouldn't go over to Windmill Hill to jog. Would you?'

'There you are,' he said. 'You've done it.'

'What?'

'You have a feeling, you have to go at it. Prod away at it till you come up with the bit of it that isn't just a feeling. Anything will do if it convinces the right people. See what I mean?'

'Oh. Yeah!'

'That's a significant anomaly you've found there.' He squinted at her and waited.

She gave her small smile again. 'I know what anomaly means, thanks.'

He laughed, revealing these surprising

white teeth and at the same time a curious beauty. Talking of fancying, she fancied him all right. She was shocked at this discovery and looked down at the table to hide her eyes.

He saw all this. He felt bad for a moment. She wasn't his type and anyway he ruled colleagues out, no matter how fetching. And this one was nearly young enough to be his daughter. 'Okay,' he said. 'You have discovered the one serious anomaly in his behaviour. That's the significant fact that should go in your report.'

'Yes. Sure. I see that. But I've only just realised that.'

'Because you talked it through.'

'Yes, but I couldn't talk it through with anyone here. They wouldn't listen.'

No, he thought, too busy twinkling into those blue eyes and lusting after that lovely mouth. 'So talk it over with yourself.'

'Okay.'

'And once you've got your big anomaly to convince the guys, then you get back to the serious stuff.'

'Serious stuff?'

'Your funny feeling about the guy.'

'Oh!' *You're wonderful,* her eyes said. *I'm yours for ever.*

He rubbed his face all over. 'Come on then,' he said.

'Right. Okay. Well, he was flirting with me.'

There's a surprise, Bright thought. 'And were you flirting back?' he said.

'Oh yes.'

'I thought you told me—'

'I was putting it on.' She spoke with easy scorn for the gullibility of the male.

'Oh, were you now?'

'Yes, because he wanted me to think he had me in the palm of his hand. Know what I mean? I don't know if he fell for it or not. But—' she got excited here – 'he liked it, whether I was pretending or not! See what I mean? He liked the kind of – sport – of it. You know? The – contest? Well, that's what I thought anyway.'

Bright sat back and really smiled at her. She smiled back into his eyes and he fully appreciated that whether a bloke was sure or not he would certainly enjoy the contest. 'Could you get back in there?' he said.

'Well, I told him I might come back. Out of uniform.' She blushed again, pale pink like a little seashell.

'And what was his reaction?'

'He said he'd like that.'

'A-ha?'

154

20

THE LIVING AND THE DEAD

They came out of the door in the garden wall. It felt like the expulsion from the Garden of Eden. They stood skinless, vulnerable in the blinding afternoon sun.

'What now, Ankate?'

'I don't know, Maisie. Any ideas?'

'It was nice in there.'

'Yes.'

'I wish I had some brothers and sisters.'

'It doesn't always work out so well.'

'No, but at least they're there. When you need them.'

Kate thought of her beloved brother Liam dead at seventeen. 'Well...' she said.

'Oh Ankate, I'm sorry. I always forget.'

'It's okay, Maisie. You've got things on your mind.'

'You've been through the same thing.'

'A long time ago.'

'But you've never got over it.'

'No.'

'Does that mean I'll never get over Alison?'

'Probably.'

'I'm glad. I don't want to get over it.'

'It gets gentler. Most of the time. But every now and then, you can be standing in the queue in Sainsbury's, or just going into your dressing room at lunchtime, or taking your washing out of the machine, and it comes back as though it's only just happened, and you find yourself in tears. But then it goes away for long periods. Only you do think of the person every single day. In that sense they're still alive. And they're still alive as they were. Liam was seventeen. I was only a year older. So he's never older than seventeen. I'll be old enough to be his mother soon.'

'Will you have any babies?'

'God, Maisie.'

'But do you think about it?'

'I seem to think about it continuously these days.'

'I do.'

'Do you?'

'Alison and I used to talk about it a lot. She wanted six children.'

'And you?'

'I just want a baby. I want one so much, Ankate.'

'Don't start getting ideas. I shouldn't have brought you to this house. I shouldn't have introduced you to Thomas. What would Lizzie do to me if you got pregnant? I'd get the blame. She'd even forget there had probably been some male involved.'

Maisie laughed with a note of hysteria. So did Kate.

'He's a lovely baby though, isn't he, Ankate?'

'You can come and visit there when I move in.'

'Would they let me baby-sit?'

'Let you? They'd anoint your feet with oil.'

'Wheee!' Maisie raised her arms in the air and danced a few steps. Then she turned a horrified face to Kate. 'Allie's dead and I'm...'

'And you're alive,' Kate said.

21

EXCERPT FROM A DIARY

v

Well, she said she would come to see me again, and she came. Wasn't that nice? Out of uniform too. Dressed all in summer style, gauzy flowered frock and the blonde hair loose and nice gentle eyeshadow, not too much but just enough to bring out the blue.

The doorbell rang this afternoon. I had just taken mother her tea. She complained of pain and wanted me to rub her back. But the doorbell rang. I looked out of the landing window and there was my little police lady. I got a surge of excitement that shot from my groin to the top of my head like an electric shock. Left my scalp tingling.

'Who is that?' mother called out in that fearful way she has always faced the ring on the doorbell.

'It's all right. One of my colleagues from the other day. She won't be here long. Then I'll rub your back.'

She smiled so shyly when I opened the door. She blushed, even. I thought of actors again. Eleonora Duse was said to blush, literally, when the part required it. But can we really achieve control over our involuntary physical reactions? And could someone like this, an ordinary little English scrubber in the police force of all things, possibly be able to harness her emotions as skilfully as an actor, to blush to order? I think not. I think she is really a little smitten. Oho, this is fun.

I smiled shyly myself. And played it very surprised to see her. 'I hardly recognise you,' I told her, 'looking so – well –ethereal.'

She laughed. 'I don't think ethereal is the word exactly,' she said. 'Not unless I lose a few pounds.'

There was an awkward moment then. She didn't know if I was going to invite her in. And, I have to admit, neither did I. I allowed this moment to lengthen a little.

'Well...' She smiled.

'Well...' I smiled. I flirted into her eyes and she flirted back. Then she looked down as though embarrassed. It was then I decided to invite her in. But I played with her a little longer. 'Is this allowed?' I said. 'A police officer consorting with a suspect?'

Her head came up. 'A suspect? But you're not–' She broke off.

'Is that so?' I said.

'Well, no more than anyone else in this enquiry.' She put a hand over her mouth. 'I shouldn't have told you that.'

I knew of course now that she was attempting to trap me. Why do people who think they are clever always do something blatantly stupid? I hope of course that this does not apply to me! I am aware at any moment that it could. No, dearie, you *shouldn't* have told me that. So why did you? She can't have seen in my eyes what I thought of this ruse. I looked dawning relief disguised by nonchalance. I was very good, I knew it. Again I wished I had an audience to appreciate the conviction and subtlety of my performance. But she startled me.

'I'm sorry.' She spoke in a different tone. Without the flirtation but still with a certain shyness. 'I shouldn't have said that. And it's not true anyway. You are still on the list, because of obvious reasons. No more so than a few other people they're questioning. But I wanted to see you anyway. If my governor got to know, I'd be in trouble.'

No. Not convincing. I know the sort of person that goes into the police. They like rules. They obey orders. They suspect everyone and do nothing without a purpose. On the other hand, nothing said by me in such a situation would be on the record. Even if I admitted everything and she had it all on tape, they'd do her for entrapment. Look at the Wimbledon Common murder. They've got to do it by the book these days.

I suddenly laughed.

'Look,' I said. 'Come in anyway. What on earth does it matter? Come and have a cup of tea.'

Following me through the dim and fragrant hall she said, 'You always seem to be making tea.'

'My mother is an addict, and so am I.'

'Oh. It's coffee with me.'

I could see the conversation was going to be scintillating at this rate. Why is it always the dullards who wield the power? This little miss, not fit to lick my boots (or any other part of me, I hope), has the right to barge into my life, question me, spy on me. Make me a little nervous if the truth were told. She might have considerable native cunning but she is no intellect, that's for sure.

In the kitchen I had my back to her and I suddenly turned. 'You're all the same, aren't you?' I said.

She looked startled so I explained: 'Your eyes.'

She didn't know whether I meant the eyes of pretty young girls or the eyes of police-men. 'Eyes?'

'Always darting about, aren't they? Making sure they don't miss anything. It's all right, you can look in all my jars if you like.' I picked up a charcuterie knife we brought back from France years ago. It's the sharpest thing I've ever seen. I cut myself on

161

it once. An event that gives me the jitters even to think about. I held it quite easily in a way that might or might not be threatening. 'And this,' I said. 'This is a very sharp instrument. It's meant for cutting up meat. But you have to see it as a potential weapon. You have to suspect everyone you see of being up to something criminal. Don't you find that a strain sometimes?'

She watched me quite calmly. That took some nerve. I did admire her. 'Yes,' she simply said. 'But it beats working in an office. Or in a supermarket.'

'Surely it would not have come to that?'

'Well, things are tough these days. Jobs aren't easy to come by. You must be aware of that. Your line of work.'

She had turned the conversation round, with consummate ease and considerable courage. I felt almost in love with her.

'Ah, my job. Yes indeed.'

'We're in the same field in a way,' she said.

'Are we?' I did not relish this idea and almost allowed the coldness I felt to appear in my tone.

'Well, we deal with mostly society's rejects, don't we? We both pick up the pieces.'

'Well, you pick them up to put them in prison. I pick them up to keep them out.'

'A lot of the time we're just called in to put the victims in the body bags.'

I gave a shudder. 'Like Alison Holt,' I said.

I put down the knife.

'Did you know her family?'

'No.' They had omitted to ask me this down at the station. Her effrontery took my breath away. They should make her police superintendent.

'Oh. I thought you might have been called in to them some time, in your job.'

'No.' I had recovered. 'From what I've read they seem to be a rather respectable family. Quite comfortably off.'

'Yes, but they mightn't have always been like that.'

'No, I suppose not.' I was finding it hard to keep up my bantering superior pose with this determined creature.

'I wondered if you'd met her dad.'

'What?' Lucky for me the kettle boiled then. Gave me an excuse to turn my back on her. Gave my hands something to do.

'Well, you both work for the DSS, don't you?'

They had not asked me that either, down at the station. Was she thinking up these piercing questions all by herself? Or had she been told to ask them? 'Yes,' I said. 'But in different departments. It's a pretty big organisation, you know.'

'Yes, but you worked in the same building for a while, didn't you?'

I carefully placed the tea cosy over the pot. 'Did we?'

'Nine months ago, actually.'

'Is that so?'

'Yes. I checked.'

I wondered if I might arrange a little accident with the boiling kettle. That would put paid to the peaches and cream complexion and the smug determination. 'You checked? Why?'

'I didn't want to – you know – get to know a person socially who might have – well, you know...'

'Who might have what? Killed someone? Abducted and killed someone?' I blazed anger at her. Again I discovered that when you are acting it is good to stick close to your real feelings. Use them. 'And did you check whether I had met Alison's father?'

'He said you hadn't met. But with so many employees he mightn't remember.'

'He's quite right. I certainly don't remember him.'

'And one black man is hard to distinguish from another anyway, don't you find?'

'How dare you say a thing like that?'

'Well, I find that.'

'That's because you are a–' I was furious. How dare she imply that I feel racial prejudice. That the killing of Alison was some kind of racial attack. Was this the line they were pursuing? I controlled myself. 'Are you a racist?' I said. 'I know the police tend to be.' I didn't give her time to reply.

164

'Because I would like to state here and now that I am not. On the contrary. Most of my work up to now has been in the St Paul's area of Bristol. I prefer black people as a matter of fact. Most of them have more beauty and more life and more humour and more wit and certainly more grace in their little fingers, as we say, than—'

'Okay, okay!' She was actually smiling. She held up her little plump hands. 'I'm sorry!'

'The police think Alison was killed by a racist?'

'We think it might have been that. Perhaps even a racist group.'

'But surely a racist group would have inflicted damage, harm, defilement. She was undefiled, wasn't she?' Oh dear, I suddenly couldn't remember if this was a fact generally known. I had actually allowed her to goad me into saying too much.

I was standing facing her. Silence fell between us. She looked at me and I looked at her and I knew and she knew that I might as well have said in so many words that I myself was the killer.

She had a serious expression. I don't know how I looked. There have not been many occasions in my life of which I could say the same. I suspect I looked somewhat wild. I felt that my hair stood out round my head like a nest of writhing snakes. I also have no idea how long we stood like that staring. I realised quite slowly that she was afraid now and I wondered why. Then of course it was obvious why: now that she knew almost for certain she was standing in a kitchen with a man who murdered girls and not from racist motives, a man with a super-sharp knife, and no one in the house but a crippled woman upstairs – oho – she was in acute danger.

But – I quickly saw – she was only in danger if I knew that she knew. People always distrust their own first impressions. If I were to behave with utter innocence, I could turn this whole thing around. At least for long enough to do the things I should have to do now.

So I let go of the work surface behind me and blinked. 'Heavens,' I said, laughing. 'That made me angry. I'm so sorry. I frightened you, I think? It's just that I hate racism in all its forms. I see so much of it. I mean the results of it. Systemised racism, the relegation of those with dark skin to the lower class, the joblessness, the discrimination by teachers, employers, psychiatrists, police of course, officials of all sorts. It really horrifies me. I see the end results of it. The drug addiction, the neglected children. All the children who die from neglect and drug abuse.' Suddenly this was my own anger speaking as it had only ever spoken before to myself. No Acting Required. Dangerous.

I stopped and laughed again but actually strangely felt close to tears. Closer than I had felt since the night I laid Alison out on the hill.

'Sorry again,' I said quietly. 'Look, I'll take this tea up to my mother. And then we'll go up on the Downs. How would you like that?'

'Well...' She was a little breathless, hesitant.

'Listen.' I moved just a little closer to her. She didn't flinch, brave little thing. 'I know you think there's some weird reason why I wouldn't introduce you to my mother. But it's really simple. She's terrified of people. Yes! I know she calls out nice messages when she thinks I have friends here. But what she is really saying to me is GET RID OF THEM FAST, GET THEM OUT OF THE HOUSE. She's always been the same. My sister and I always knew that. We were never allowed to have people in.'

'You had no friends, then?'

'It made friendship difficult though not impossible. But my sister and I were very close.'

'You must miss her now.'

'Oh, I visit her every now and then.'

'What does your mother do if you are away?'

'I leave her food for several days. She has a little fridge in her room. And a Teasmade.

167

She can manage certain things for herself.'

I watched the disguised policewoman. She wanted to ask about my mother's bodily functions, but her English upbringing made her hesitate.

'Yes,' I said. 'I know what you are thinking. She can lever herself out of the bed on to her commode chair. And vice versa. Not comfortable or easy. But she can manage. If she could not, I wouldn't be able to work, would I?' I was telling her the utter truth. She felt it.

'Oh...' She almost sighed the word. 'I was wondering about that, yes.'

'You can creep up and peep in her room if you like. Just hope she doesn't spot you. I wouldn't like you to think I was keeping any secrets from you.' I gave her my sexiest, feeliest smile.

She didn't smile back. She was having second thoughts. She was also a bit scared to go upstairs.

'Go on,' I said. 'I dare you.'

'Did you use to do this as kids? Dare your friends to creep up there.'

I smiled. Wouldn't she like to know?

She said, 'I need to use the loo actually anyway.'

I went up the stairs with her. On the landing I spoke to mother. 'Here's your tea, darling.' I pushed mother's door a little and Miss Policewoman peeped in as she tiptoed past. I put mother's tea on her bedside table, sped out of the room, heard the noises of decorous toilet use behind the closed bathroom door, and descended to the ground floor. I opened the door under the stairs, closed it behind me and descended one floor more to the basement. Well, it's more of a cellar really. Just the place to keep a young girl prisoner for three or four weeks, wouldn't you say? I opened the door under the stone steps and left the house by the back way.

22

COVER BLOWN

She peeped in again coming out of the loo. The woman in the bed held a cup to her face. But she bore a resemblance all right. Helen didn't know what she'd expected. A ventriloquist's doll, a full-sized blow-up toy, an embalmed corpse, a tape recorder with recorded messages? To see a real woman shocked her. This level of imagination was not essential for a job in the police force. Mostly it told against her. Not till John Bright–

Helen said, 'Hello?'

The woman in the bed looked frightened. A person on the landing, not her son? Frozen in tea-drinking mode, staring at the doorway, she didn't speak.

Helen pushed the door a little. 'Sorry to disturb you. I just came to see your son about some work. I'm Helen.' She went no closer. The woman sat petrified, the cup shaking on the saucer. 'Sorry, sorry.' Helen backed off. 'It's okay, I'm going now. I'm going, really.'

She closed the door behind her and

170

tripped lightly down the stairs. The stairs were lit from a long window on the landing but the window was draped with lace curtains and the back of the house faced north, so the light was dim. In the hall she called, 'Hello?'

She felt the silence and knew the kitchen would be empty. She knew he'd done a runner. She knew she'd blown it. She wanted to impress John Bright so much it had thrown her way off beam. She ran to the front door and opened it. The blaze of sunshine hit her like a punch in the face.

Bright saw her and sat up. He was out of the car, over the road, and up the path faster than she could blink.

She said, 'Did he come out this way?'

'Think I'd still be sitting there if he had?' Bright whizzed past her, into the house. He darted into the drawing room and out again, into the kitchen and out again. Stood a second in the hallway. Opened the cupboard under the stairs and disappeared. His voice came back thin and muffled: 'Is there a light switch up there?'

She fumbled over the surface of the wall. Hit a switch. The hall lit up, and the lobby down by the kitchen. Hit another and the dark stairs below appeared, in the light of a forty watt bulb that swung on a wire fifty years old. Bright's feet sounded on stone.

'We didn't know there was a basement.'

She sounded feeble, she knew.

'There isn't at the front. It's all these hills.' Bright pushed a door, pushed harder, and it jumped open. They went out into a stone-flagged yard. The stones were black, not the clean honey beige of the house front. High walls, a small stone outhouse, neglected plant pots, two dustbins. The outhouse was locked, its small window opaque with grime. Bright dragged at the door in the far wall and it scraped open on to an alley. Weedy cobbles and high garden walls. The alley was dark in the shade of the tall houses. One end was shut off by a double garage where men were working. Helen ran that way without discussion. Bright ran down the other way towards the street.

Two ten-year-old lads stood astride their bikes on the pavement where he emerged. 'See anyone come out of here, lads?'

'When?'

'Maybe five minutes ago?'

'Are you the cops?'

'A-ha. CID.'

'Wow! Is it a murder?'

'Yes,' he said.

'You're kidding us!'

'A young man, nice-looking, scruffy long sweater, jeans, mid-length brown hair.'

The lads longed to have seen him. But they hadn't. Regretfully they shook their heads, Bright all the time searching the main street with his eyes.

He joined Helen at the garage where the men with spanners and oily rags shook their heads in the same regretful way.

'Do you know the people who live at number seven?'

'No. Only the woman who lives here at the end house. She gets fed up with the noise, comes and bawls us out. Otherwise they come out to get their cars. No one talks to us. We're the lowest of the low round here.'

'Keep your eyes open. It's the murdered girl.'

A tall young black man turned round, sharp. 'Alison?'

'You knew her?'

'No, man. But she a sister, you know?'

'This bloke at number seven done it?'

'We don't know. We'd like to talk to him. Or to anyone who knows him.'

'Believe me, man, we find him, you'll have him. After we finish with him.'

Bright tried every garden door, peered into yards. Tried basement doors, found them locked. They went back round the front. At the house on the left they got no reply. At the one on the right a tall Indian woman in her thirties opened the door. A small boy with round brown eyes clung to her skirt. 'Oh,' she said. 'I know who you mean. He never speaks to us. Nor does his sister.'

'Sister?' Bright stared at Helen.

'He told me she lives in Ireland.'

'Oh, she might do,' the Indian woman said. 'I wouldn't know. I see her now and then.'

'How do you know it's his sister?'

'She told me she was. She's a bit more friendly than him. Just visiting, she said she was. While her brother was away. To look after the mother. The mother's an invalid. I've never seen her.'

'She's bedridden.'

'I offered to look in on her. I thought the young bloke was going to hit me. He was offended, you know? Said he could manage fine by himself. So I never offered again.'

'She doesn't like strangers.'

In the car Bright said, 'Alert social services. The mother is going to need help.'

'You think he's really done a runner?'

'You were too good, Helen. You got your man.'

'I let him go. I lost him.'

'My fault,' Bright said.

'No. I questioned him too hard. I went too far. I could have done a convincing job, you know, that I fancied him et cetera. But I got carried away. I had to go upstairs to see his mother. I couldn't just leave it alone. Impatience, you see.'

'It was my idea, this stupid piece of entrapment. I'm supposed to be your superior,

174

not just in rank but in experience and wisdom, and I've blown this. This is not just your ordinary villain, this is a murderer of young girls. On the run. Ryan is going to have me busted. And it's no more than I deserve.'

She looked terrified.

'Don't worry, I take full responsibility. You did good.'

But when he dropped her at her car even her flimsy dress drooped. He was tempted to take her for a drink, cheer her up.

Cheer himself up.

He drove on, to present himself to Ryan. He couldn't wait.

23

SALLY MAKES A SACRIFICE

Sally was waiting in the big doorway when Dave returned. He was pale. His face was grim. Harsh lines and hollows from eyes to chin. His body shook a little. A tremor that was not precisely visible.

'Oh...' First afraid – he hadn't expected anyone to be there – then dulled. 'Sally.'

'Aren't you pleased I waited?'

'Er, yes, I...' First appalled then polite. 'Yes, of course.'

'Would you rather be alone?'

His eyes looked beyond her. 'No. No.'

She had to take the key from him and put it in the door. His hand shook. Before they entered the cavernous stairwell he looked behind him. A car passed and he watched it down to the end of the street and round the corner before he would go in. She went ahead of him up the stairs. He looked behind him all the time.

Inside the big room she lit candles. He sat on an old basket chair. He put his long hands over his eyes. She moved about the loft in bare feet. Her small noises comforted

176

him. She brought him a mug of steaming tea. 'Thanks, love,' he said. He sat with both hands round the mug. She smiled, grateful for his thanks and glowing that he'd called her love. She sat cross-legged on the floor at his feet. She leaned against his legs.

After he had drunk all the tea he said, 'They've been following me. They've been watching me. All these weeks. They've been watching this place. They know everyone who's been here, when, with whom, and for how long. They know everything I've done, everywhere I've been. They think I killed Alison.' His voice rose and he began to sob. He got up and walked about wiping tears and snot with his hands, his shirt hem, his sleeves.

Sally was frightened. She said, 'What can I do, Dave?'

He said, 'Lizzie. I need Lizzie. I need her so much.' He was in the kitchen doorway holding on to the door-frame with either hand.

Sally knew Lizzie was his former – not wife exactly – the mother of his child, the exquisite daughter Maisie that all the girls wanted to look like. Sally had never thought to be jealous of Lizzie – heavens, she must be the same age as Dave and everyone knew men had no use for women their own age. But now a sharp pain pierced her. 'Lizzie?' she said.

He was crying so bad, these big heaving noises, he didn't seem to hear her. But her devotion knew no bounds. No matter her pain: if he wanted Lizzie, he should have her. She knew Maisie's name was Creech. She pulled the phone book from under the table. There it was: E. Creech and an address in Totterdown. She dialled the number.

Lizzie toiled up the hill from Temple Meads. Painting clowns' faces on mugs all day was not the best therapy for her present state. And panting up the hill afterwards wore her out, but it beat sitting in a bus in ossified traffic. Sarah from next door had stayed on the bus and would still be sitting there, still down by the roundabout, roasting behind glass.

Around lunchtime Lizzie had called home with the certain knowledge that something had happened to Maisie. She felt Maisie's danger in every limb, every pore. Her finger-ends tingled with it. And when she rang there was no reply. She told herself Kate was there and Kate would not leave Maisie alone. Just like the pair of them to go waltzing off without leaving word. *Oh, Lizzie will be all right.* All afternoon her fear fed her anger and her anger her fear. Both fuelled her climb up the hill, pounding in her ears.

When she opened the door the phone was ringing. It was the police to tell her Maisie was missing, she knew this. 'Yes? Who is this?'

'I'm – I'm sorry. I'm – I'm – Sally. I'm a - friend of Dave's.' The breathy little voice nearly gave out in shock at the rage in Lizzie's voice.

'Dave?' Of all the people she did not want to hear from now–

'He – he needs your – he needs – he asked me to call you.'

'What's happened? Is it Maisie? Has he heard something about Maisie?'

'Maisie? No.'

'Yes, Maisie, his daughter Maisie. If he's got news of Maisie I want to know. If he doesn't, I don't.'

'Oh. No. Sorry. I'm sorry to bother you.'

'I should think so.' Lizzie smashed down the phone. And now didn't know where to call, whom to ask. She looked into the living room. Cushions and newspapers everywhere, specks all over the carpet. *Typical. Go out toiling for the daily bread and what do they do? Lounge around chatting. Maisie telling Kate all the secret things she would never tell me.* She pounded up the stairs. Maybe they were both asleep. Or Maisie prone with headphones clamped to her ears.

Maisie was not in her room. Every garment she owned had been thrown in the

179

air, whirled in a vortex and dropped. It looked normal. It looked normal for when Maisie had just gone out. It was oddly reassuring, the typhoon effect.

Some of her fear dissipated but the anger filled the space. She dragged the vacuum cleaner out of the landing cupboard and bumped it downstairs. So when they did come in she didn't hear them.

'Mum!' Maisie hit her between the shoulder blades. 'We're back!' and then backed away at the sight of her face. 'What's the matter?'

Lizzie couldn't speak. She shut off the cleaner, yanked the plug out of the socket, manhandled the thing upstairs and threw it into the cupboard. Kate and Maisie flattened themselves against the wall as she came downstairs and thrust past them to the kitchen.

They stared at each other as cupboard doors slammed and plates clattered, Lizzie's footsteps clomping back and forth on the floor. She didn't need to say what they'd done wrong. They knew. They had no excuse. Kate had more courage than Maisie. She went and stood in the kitchen door. 'I'm sorry, Lizzie. I didn't think.'

More banging. Lizzie's implacable back. A hot volcanic torrent of water spurting into the sink over the neglected breakfast washing-up. No use now to say, *I'll do that,*

I'll do everything, I will not only make the supper, I will be the supper. It was too late. 'I was just thinking of Maisie. How to keep her occupied and try to—'

'Excuse me.' Muttered through clenched teeth as Lizzie pushed past her in the doorway, a bag of garbage clutched in her fist. Sudden street noise and the clash of dustbin lids. Then the bang of the front door as she clomped back in. Kate felt exhausted with guilt.

'Lizzie, listen, don't make supper. Why don't we all go out? I will take us out to eat.'

'Oh yes, that's always your answer, isn't it? Let's go out. Let's escape from whatever we're supposed to be doing. Let's leave it all and go out. Only it's always waiting, Kate. It's always waiting there for you for when you come back. It's frozen vegetarian chilli and you'll have to lump it.'

'Don't do that, Lizzie.'

'Don't do what?'

'Don't pretend you think I want to go out because I don't like your food. You know it's not true and it's not fair.'

'Oh, isn't it?'

They were both yelling.

'Fight about what you're fighting about.'

'And what's that? That nobody cares enough to let me know where they are even though if they did give it a moment's thought they'd know I was worried sick? And right to be?'

'Yes, that's right! Nobody gives a fuck about you. Especially me and Maisie. There. You believe that? You see? You don't really believe that. You just use it as a big stick to beat people with.'

'Out of sight out of mind–'

'This child is grieving. And all you can do is berate her for not putting you at the forefront of her mind every minute of her day and night. You're supposed to take care of her; not she of you! You're the mother, for Christsake; not Maisie!'

Lizzie's face was a picture. Kate followed her eyes. Maisie stood in the doorway appalled. In the silence, she said, 'Phone, Ankate.'

'Lizzie, we all follow your example and spend most of our time thinking about how much we fail you.' Kate said this quietly. She was taking advantage and she knew it. But blood was up and for once she refused to resist temptation. 'Nobody can please you whatever they do.' She made a *my God what have I done* face at Maisie, passing her in the doorway.

Maisie whispered, 'It's John Bright.'

When she came back to the kitchen Lizzie was sitting at the table. Maisie half-leaned against her, the closest you could get to an embrace in Lizzie's behaviour code. The room was quiet. Just the friendly buzz of the fridge.

Kate said, 'He's waiting at Renato's. I totally forgot we had an arrangement.'

Nobody replied.

'We were in such a state about getting back in time for you, Lizzie, you see. Everything else went out of our heads.' She tried a sheepish grin.

Maisie flinched and shut one eye. Lizzie leaned her tired face on one hand and gave Kate a long and silent stare. She sighed heavily.

'I thought we could all go,' Kate risked. 'We could just have a spaghetti in the bar.'

Maisie looked anxiously at Lizzie, but didn't push her luck.

'You wouldn't have to cook,' Kate went bravely on. 'I'll pay. I'm rich at the moment.'

Lizzie was looking at her fingernails with close attention.

'I know you don't like John Bright, Lizzie. But I think Maisie might like the change of scene.'

'Well?' Lizzie turned to Maisie.

'Renato's is nice, mum.'

'I look a mess.'

'You don't.'

'I'll have to change.'

'Okay.'

'I'll be ten minutes.'

183

'We'll wait.'

'Put that chilli back in the fridge, Maisie.' Lizzie marched out of the room. 'We'll just have to eat it tomorrow now.'

24

DROWNING SORROWS

Renato's was quiet. It was Monday night. And it was early. Bright was emptying a large scotch when they walked in. It was clear to Kate this was not his first. He ordered their wine and another large scotch for himself. They took a table near the bar.

Kate introduced her family to Signor and Signora Renato. They remarked on Maisie's loveliness and noticed her resemblance to Lizzie. While they talked, Kate asked John Bright, 'What's the matter?'

'I think I know who killed Alison.'

Kate went white.

'Don't worry. It's not Dave.'

She bent her head, let out a breath.

'I found him and I let him go. He's done a runner.'

'How could you find him in so short a time?'

'I'm a fucking genius, how d'you think?' He swallowed the scotch like it was full of goldfish.

As he so seldom swore, she decided to ask no more questions. 'I think you'd better eat,' she said.

'Whatever.'

She went to the counter and ordered him lasagne. Maisie joined her. 'Lasagne for mum. Napolitana pizza for me.' Maisie looked around her at the black and white ten by eights of actors on the walls. 'I love this place, Ankate. It's really theatrical, isn't it?'

Kate thought of all the bars in all the cities, the refuges of actors away from home, in need of a place to celebrate or commiserate. This was one of the best. 'It truly is, Maize.'

Maisie leaned close and whispered, 'What's up with John Bright?'

'I'll tell you later.'

Bright sat staring into his drink at one end of the table. Lizzie chatted with Signora Renato at the other. Kate and Maisie looked on. The evening did not look like being a social success.

But later a couple of actors turned up. They had just arrived in Bristol to start rehearsing *As You Like It* and come to Renato's first, the one place where they were sure to find comrades. Kate introduced Lizzie. Alan Tate, a man of no mean charm, decided to chat Lizzie up. Lizzie, who seldom went out, and seldom drank, on her second glass of Chianti began to glow.

186

Maisie, on her second glass of Coke, freed from looking after Lizzie, entered into a deep conversation with John Bright to try and cheer him up. They had embarked on the subject of fathers. During a lull, John Bright was heard to say, 'I had no dad because he died. Your dad isn't dead.'

Lizzie suddenly looked stricken and covered her face. She gathered her handbag and left the table.

'Lizzie?' Kate came into the Ladies, concerned.

'Kate, I am such a bitch.'

Kate decided to keep it light. 'Well, I won't argue with you there.'

But Lizzie drove on. 'Dave rang me. Well, he didn't ring me; he got some bloody girl to ring me, that's partly why I got so mad. I told her to piss off, basically, I refused to speak to him. But I just realised: he must have been in an awful state to get her to ring me. They must have just let him go. The police.'

'We could drop by on the way back.'

Lizzie looked horrified. She had never set foot in Dave's Bachelor Pad, as she called it.

'Come on, Lizzie. Why not? There's got to be a first time.'

'Why?'

'He's not a suspect any more, by the way. John Bright has managed to – well – get the enquiry moving in another direction.'

'No?' A Mexican wave of serial emotions ran over Lizzie's face. 'You mean they've caught someone?'

Kate took a breath. She must not knock John Bright off the pedestal Lizzie had just put him on. 'It's not as simple as that, apparently.'

'Why?'

Lizzie drunk asked impossibly simple questions.

'Well, I think it's a question of gathering evidence – or something.'

'I see. But they know who it is. So Dave's off the hook?'

'Looks like it, yes.'

'Oh, Kate.'

'You didn't think it was Dave, did you, Lizzie?'

Lizzie lifted her hair off her brow and gazed into the mirror. 'Frankly, I thought him capable of anything.'

'Oh,' Kate said in wonder.

'But when John Bright said to Maisie her dad wasn't dead. I thought, what have I done? I've made it so hard for her all these years. What you said tonight–' Tears came running out of Lizzie's eyes. Kate was appalled. 'It was all true, I deserve it. Why do I have to be such a bitch?'

Kate watched her big sister sob. She had never in her life before seen Lizzie humbled and contrite. She said, 'It's just unhappiness, Lizzie. You've always had too much responsibility.'

'Oh God, I look a sight.'

'No. You don't.'

'What will Alan Tate think?'

'He'll think he's had more of an effect than usual.'

Lizzie actually laughed. 'Okay then.' She wiped carefully under her eyes where the mascara had run, and blew her nose, smoothed down her white linen blouse and skirt, and turned to face Kate. 'Let's go and visit Dave.'

25

EXCERPT FROM A DIARY

vi

It was extraordinary going out on to the cobbled alley. The sense of escape. Fleeing. Flying. Fleet of foot. The men at the garage didn't see me. It wouldn't have mattered if they had. They've seen me a hundred times and not seen me, why should they care? Out in the street some boys on their bikes jousted and laughed, too absorbed to notice an adult of no interest to them. One of them was the beautiful boy Laurie from next door. I have watched that child from afar, his graceful manners, Swiss milk chocolate brown skin, innocent shining eyes. If his parents knew that my eye was upon him! I, the Preserver of Innocence. They would remove him from my path. Now they will never know because I can never return. I knew this day would come at last. When I would leave this life behind. I embrace my flight.

I sped past, wings on my heels. My bag was not heavy, did not slow me down, but I had to find a place to change my clothes. My absence would be discovered in no time. I must not answer their description. The nearest possible place was Clifton Village. I went round the edge of Victoria Square under the trees. The diagonal path across the middle was too exposed. Briskly under the stone arch, past the pharmacy, the florist. I thought of going into the high-class second-hand clothes shop, a changing room the obvious place, to go in as one thing and come out as another. But the shop was empty apart from the assistant. Again, too exposed. I needed a place crowded with people intent on their own affairs.

I crossed into the village. The bakery café was too empty and too genteel. The Clifton ladies in there would notice an anachronism such as I. Almost next door was the more raffish hippie-type market. Many different stalls, lighting not too bright. I went in. Up the central aisle past the clothes, into the handmade sofas, past the posters and cards. This was a favourite haunt of my youth. I knew it by heart. But I couldn't for the life of me recall a loo. So I zipped to the left through the junk shop and out into quiet little Wellington Street.

Up to my right the Rainbow, the restful café with the secondhand books. Yes! The door was open. I squeezed between the gaggle of customers in the queue and trod lightly down the aisle between the tables. No one gave me a glance. My worst danger would be that someone should already be using the loo. I pushed the door with my fingers actually crossed. Empty. And cool. I bolted the nice pine door, changed in less than a minute, thought about leaving my bag and old clothes there, decided that would be too conspicuous.

Two people looked up as I came back through into the café, but with no interest, intent on cake and conversation. No idea even that I had come from the loo. I could have been leaving after a pleasant lunch. No queue now at the counter, and all the staff had their backs to me, preparing food for their customers.

I walked out into a wall of light and heat. Opposite, the big garage where they sell old clothes and junk was just opening up. What better place for some old clothes than an old clothes shop? The depressing person who presides there was deep in the gloom of the interior. I left the bag with my clothes in it behind a forties tea trolley piled with cracked plates and tarnished cooking implements. So suitable.

I could afford to relax a little now. A little but not too much. I had to think what to do next. Many courses of action were open to me. I had to fix on my next immediate step. The sense of untrammelled flight was going from me now. I could feel the descent to earth. I even suffered a pang about mother. But mother had had the use of me all these years. Oh had she ever! It could not last for always. She must have known that. Now it was someone else's task. Someone else would turn up. People like her always find somebody. They have to.

I had cut off a whole side of me. A whole side of my life. No one, now, in the world, knew who or where I was. There was nowhere I had to be. At this point in my thinking, I also suffered a pang about my job. I had hated almost every moment of that job. I hated the squalor. I hated the people I dealt with. I loathed the hapless emptiness and mess of their miserable lives. I feel disgust for the social order that robs such people of culture and education, of the desire for culture and education. And I loathe myself for being part of that social order, perpetuating it with the hand-outs that enable such vermin to stay just about alive, running like rats, feeding on the leftovers that the rest of us cannot manage to consume. And yet I would miss it.

I found myself already passing the front of the university. Though this was vacation time there were always students. Summer courses. Out on the grass soaking up sunshine and knowledge. I recalled my days there and felt rage choking me. Mr

Wonderful. And Mr Wonderful's favourites. The coterie. The subtle ways they have of making it clear they do not want you around. The little fortresses they make to keep themselves feeling good. They the Insiders. Fortresses with human walls, walls of human flesh. More impregnable than stone. Unscalable. The heat of humiliation spread over me like a strawberry mark spreads over the skin. This heat was hotter than the sun. Altogether too hot.

Distracted by this detritus in my head I took the left fork below the university building. I had meant naturally to go down Park Street past the design centre and George's many bookshops, unnoticeable in the crowds. Instead here I was in the wide dull street inaptly named Park Row. I crossed to the shady side. Cooler at least. In all senses. I had shaken off the torment. The intolerable torment of my thoughts. I only state them here because I believe that somebody should one day understand me. Should understand what has made me, formed me. This attempt at clarification will now fill my days. My diary shall become the centrepiece of my life. It will take the place of my job, and of my mother.

As I reached this precise point in my thought, there appeared across the road, illuminated by the blazing sun, as though my thoughts had conjured them up, two people ... I stood still. I watched them as they got into the little yellow Volkswagen. I watched while the car nosed out into the traffic and disappeared down the hill. And I laughed inside my head. I laughed. The perfection, the smooth rounded beauty of the perfect moment. How was it possible to explain this sublime synchronicity?

The whole thing came together in my mind. Connections, you see. E. M. Forster is not the only one to have made the great discovery. Everything is connection. Connections are mysterious and sometimes almost miraculous. And when a connection clarifies itself to you, at that moment you feel in your body a jolt, of power, an electrical current that seems to have thrust from far out in the universe to hit you like a comet, like you are the focus of all the fates. It is impossible to describe the physical and mental shock, the terror and the ecstasy of these moments, these leaps of under-standing. These sudden apprehensions of connection are not generated by me but revealed to me. That's what you have to understand.

Now I have her. She will be told day by day what I have done, what I do, what I mean to do. She will not know who I am. Or where I am. But she will be my Recipient. My Repository. She will almost in a sense be the cause. The Onlie Begetter. I will become part of her life. She of mine. Our destinies will be intertwined. In a sense this means they have always been intertwined. All time comes together here. I have taken the threads of fate and tied them together. Here. Now. This sense of power intoxicates me. The beauty of the idea intoxicates me. All eternity of these little lives, I have ordered into significance. It has been worth living for this.

26

FAMILIES FUNCTION

'Listen, Lizzie. John looks a bit the worse for wear. I think I'd better take him back to his hotel. I can join you at Dave's afterwards?'

'Don't do this, Kate.'

'What? Do what?'

'You always do this. You get people jumping to your tune and then you leave them in the lurch.'

This accusation left Kate speechless, it seemed so wide of the mark. Maisie stifled a laugh. Maisie too by now had consumed a fair amount of good Italian red wine. Though not of the best Italian grappa, Signor Renato's welcome-back gesture after their meal.

'I cannot go to Dave's on my own,' Lizzie insisted.

'I'll be there, mum.'

Lizzie barely acknowledged Maisie's crumb of comfort. 'After all these years. How can I just walk in there: Hello, Dave, how's things?'

'Sounds like quite a good opening line.'

'Listen.' Bright spoke low and slow. 'You

go. I'll be okay. Just point me in the direction of that barracks they call a hotel. I don't need a chaperone.'

Maisie rolled her eyes. 'You are really drunk,' she said.

'What?' Bright reeled back. 'Who is this child? She is wise beyond her ears.'

Maisie and Kate started to laugh. 'What's so funny?' Lizzie hated to be left out of their laughter.

'Wise beyond her ears.'

Bright smiled. 'And eyes *between* her ears.'

Maisie stopped laughing. She took his arm, stood on tiptoe and kissed him.

'What'd I do to deserve that?'

'Come and see my dad with us. He makes good coffee. Then mum won't have to go on her own. On her own with me.'

Kate said quickly, 'It's the best solution, Lizzie.'

Bright and Maisie, arm in arm, swayed along ten yards ahead.

'It's a big space, Dave's loft. I'll disappear John when we get there. Put him to sleep in some dark corner. You'll never notice him.' Lizzie and Kate were already drawn along in the wake of the two in front.

Lizzie sighed. 'Nothing ever seems to go my way.'

Maisie guided Bright through the traffic. They crossed to the quayside and waited. Lizzie made Kate wait for the lights to change. The cobbles shone like polished metal in the lamplight. The water held a rippling moon. Even this time of night the heat had not left the air. Warm eddies lapped their faces, their arms. The boats hardly moved on the water. A few people strolled like them enjoying the warm night. At the end of the quay on their left the boat house loomed up black. There were no lights even in Dave's windows on the top floor. Or were there? That wavering glow could be candles, could be reflection of sky, moon, lamplight.

Lizzie held Kate back by the arm. 'I can't do this, Kate.'

'Yes you can. Remember what you said at Renato's.'

'That was an impulse. It's gone off me.'

'Well, it was a good impulse. Stick with it.'

'Anyway, look, it's in darkness, he's gone to bed, he's asleep, we don't want to wake him up.'

Dong dong dong. Maisie pulled on the bell. A window was pushed up, on the top floor. Dave's hair came over the sill, like Rapunzel in the fairy tale. 'Dad? It's us.'

Dave stayed quite still a moment then disappeared.

'Oh God,' Lizzie said. 'He's coming down.'

He reappeared in the window. 'Catch!'

Maisie caught the key like an expert and

unlocked the small door cut out of the big boat door. They ducked through the opening in single file. Into a dark lofty space, where the stone stairs rose into deeper darkness.

'It's okay.' Maisie led the way. 'Dad'll bring a candle in a minute.'

Sure enough above them a shaky flame created shadows that jerked and swayed up the stairs.

Dave saw that one of them was Lizzie. He stood quite still with shock.

She eyed him, defiant. 'Hello, Dave.'

He nodded, speechless, and gestured for everyone to go in, shook hands with John Bright, no idea who he was, but did not take his eyes off Lizzie.

There were candles lit in the room but the space swallowed their feeble light. Maisie went round lighting more. The only person there was the young woman who had spoken to Kate in the school yard that morning. 'Hi.' She sat, unusually for Dave's visitors, in a chair, and was still in her practical cotton print frock. She was friendly and relaxed. 'We met this morning,' she said to Kate.

'Yes. Margaret, isn't it?'

'You remember!'

'Well, yes.'

'They let Dave out this afternoon.'

'Are you the only person here?'

'I think the others are a bit scared to come back. After the police raid.'

Kate looked at John Bright. 'Raid?'

'Hoping to find dope – or whatever – something to pin on him.'

'But they didn't?'

Bright shook his head. 'Went off at half cock.'

Kate saw Margaret's puzzled face. 'Oh, sorry. Margaret – this is John Bright. He's a–'

'I'm a copper, love.'

'And a friend of mine.'

'You're here as a friend then,' Margaret said.

'That's it.'

'From London?'

'Yup. Off my patch.'

'Is it very different here?'

'It is for me, love.'

Maisie had been busy in the kitchen. She brought him a coffee. 'It's really strong,' she warned.

'Thanks. I'll be careful.'

Dave and Lizzie had remained on the landing. Now they came in. Lizzie looked uncomfortable but gratified. As though she had leapt a chasm and was surprised to find herself safe on the other side. She looked up at the big sleeping platform, the rafters and lofty roof, the amazing moon through a Velux window; and around at the cushions and lovely drapes, the old basket chairs, the fifties juke box. She looked into Dave's sleeping room: dark wood and white linen, peaceful and calm. She looked into the kitchen: primitive wooden surfaces and minimal mod cons, but attractive, warm. Her head moved from side to side in surprise. Kate wondered what she had imagined. A brothel draped in purple velvet?

'Oh Lizzie, this is Margaret. Margaret, this is my sister Lizzie.'

'Oh.' Margaret stood to shake Lizzie's hand. 'You're Maisie's mother. I've heard a lot about you.'

'How?' Lizzie's brusqueness stopped just this side of rude.

'Well, from Dave.'

'Oh? You must have expected the wicked witch of the west.'

Margaret smiled. She had a beautiful smile. Her face in repose had a slightly lifeless quality. Her smile irradiated it. 'Not at all. I expected a sort of goddess.'

'Oh, I see. Made of stone.'

'Well, marble at least.'

'Ha.' Lizzie looked baffled, pleased, offended, all at once.

Kate and Maisie laughed. Margaret smiled.

Dave said, 'I'm so glad you came.' He addressed all of them but clearly he meant the words for Lizzie.

Maisie curled herself around Dave. Lizzie looked away, whether because the sight gave her pleasure or pain or both, Kate couldn't tell.

'Was it terrible at the police, dad?'

'Yes, it was terrible, Maisie.'

'They gotta do it, mate.'

'What?' Dave gave Bright his most arrogant look, head high, tossing the ringlets back.

'Dad, you met him before. He's John Bright.' Dave looked blank. 'Kate's policeman.'

Kate rolled her eyes at Bright. 'They insist on calling you that.'

'A-ha.' Bright's inscrutable mask, but she suspected a complex reaction behind it. As complex as her own. She was glad of the weak flickering candle-light.

Margaret smiled from him to Kate. 'How did you meet?'

'He saved my life. I was a–'

'She was a suspect in a murder case.' Bright and Kate spoke together.

'A dead body was found in Ankate's bath.'

'They thought Kate had done it.' Lizzie made this sound like a typical act of carelessness on Kate's part.

'John didn't think so.'

'So she has to be grateful now for the rest of her life.' Bright squinted at Kate.

'For my life.' Kate did not smile at all.

Dave said, awed, 'Of course. You've been through this, Kate. I forgot.'

'If you don't want to be around mysterious deaths, you probably shouldn't be around me.' Kate spoke lightly.

'Certainly shouldn't be around me,' Bright said.

'Or any of us, now.' Maisie's little face crumpled. Dave hugged her tighter. Lizzie's expression couldn't be read. Kate suspected a deep joy which Lizzie would refuse to admit.

'It is hard not to be superstitious about these things.' Margaret's voice had a peaceful resonance.

'What things?' Bright liked brass tacks.

'Well, coincidences, patterns.'

'Being around one murder is hardly a pattern.'

'Two now,' Kate murmured.

Margaret said, 'Two is the beginning of a pattern.'

Bright stood up and walked round the room. He didn't like this conversation. He stopped near Margaret. 'What do you do?'

'How do you mean?'

'For a job, love.'

His tone was insulting. She chose to ignore that. 'Well, I've done various things. I got my English degree. Dave was one of my teachers. But then I worked mostly with animals. Things for charities. A donkey sanctuary, for instance, in North Devon. Now I've stopped work for a while. I'm...' She hesitated then plunged. 'Well, I'm trying to write.'

Dave spoke dutifully. 'That's good, Margaret.'

Lizzie did not hide her disdain. 'Write what?'

Margaret squirmed a bit. It was the first time Kate had seen her less than composed. She caught Kate's eye. 'I hesitate to say drama, but...'

'Plays?' Kate tried to sound encouraging.

'Well, I don't think I could write for the theatre. I think that's too difficult. But I've got a number of television ideas and almost-finished scripts and I'm hoping if I give myself enough time to concentrate, I might actually complete something. I know it's a hard world to break into, but – well – you have to try in this life or–'

'I agree.' Kate summoned more enthusiasm into her voice than she felt. 'You have to give it a go.'

Lizzie disapproved: 'What are you going to live on?'

'I've saved a bit. Not much; I'll probably have to get a part-time job soon. But I can last for three months, I think. I'm very frugal.'

'Oh.' Lizzie's expression relented a little.

'I'm hoping to get some advice and criticism from Dave. That's why I came round.'

'Glad of your company,' Dave said.

Kate said, 'This is the first time I've ever seen this place not draped with people. How do you stand that wall-to-wall social life, Dave? I'd go mad.'

'I need it. I'm not self-sufficient like you and Lizzie.'

Lizzie refused to return his look.

'Gotta go.' John Bright made a slightly unsteady route to the door.

'I'll come with you.' Kate stood up.

Margaret also stood. 'Mind if I come along? I live in Totterdown too.'

'Oh.' Kate and Bright looked at each other. He gave her what she had come to recognise as a smile. 'Can you find your way back to the hotel, John?'

'If I can't I'll ask a policeman,' he said.

Down by the water the night had grown cooler. Kate shivered. ''Night then, John. I've hardly seen you.'

'I need sleep. Ryan will be flaying me alive tomorrow.'

'And I've got the read-through in the morning.'

'I'll see you for lunch if Ryan hasn't had me deported.'

'Where?'

'The theatre bar?'

He put his arms round her. She smelt his biscuity smell, felt his warmth, the firm pressure of his hands on her back. His hands made her feel safe. Even the sight of them. She held the back of his neck a moment and thought they ought to get a little drunk more often. 'Take care, John.'

He released his hold. 'I'd see you ladies home but I do not think I'm likely to be a lot of use to you just at this time.' He raised a hand and walked off down the quay, keeping a careful straight line. Kate always hated seeing him go.

Crossing the little foot-bridge Margaret said, 'Mr Bright seems rather unusual.'

'Yes, he is. Seems like your average little cockney wide boy, but actually – well, he has unexpected qualities.'

'I suspect he's good at his job.'

'Oh, he's that all right.'

'So why is he in trouble?'

Kate, embarrassed, suddenly did not know how much she should say. 'Oh, I don't know. He offered to help out because he's recently been involved in a case like this. A chap in London who had killed his neighbour's daughter and buried her under his garden shed.'

'Oh, that case!' Margaret looked impressed. 'But he said he's going to be hauled over the coals?'

'Well, he thought he'd found Alison's killer. But apparently it didn't work out.'

'I'm sorry. I've embarrassed you.'

'No—'

'Yes. Obviously you shouldn't be talking about it. He'd have told you in confidence. I'm so sorry.'

'No.' Kate warmed to the girl's simple straightforward style. 'Only, I don't know how much I'm supposed to know. Things were a bit confused tonight.'

They walked in silence for a while. Just as they were about to enter under the railway bridge Margaret shivered. Kate looked surprised. The girl was so strong-looking, and taller than Kate. 'I don't like tunnels,' she said.

'Well, they're scary in the dark.'

'I think it's the echo.'

Kate listened. 'Yes. You can't be sure there's not someone behind you.'

At last they came out into the open. The houses of Totterdown rose in tiers to their left, the black shape of Windmill Hill sloped gracefully up to their right.

Margaret let out a breath. 'I'm always glad to be out the other side.'

Kate laughed. 'I wouldn't come this way alone. Especially now.'

'No. Especially now. How's Maisie coping?'

'Well, it's hard. I don't know how well

she's doing. In a sense nobody copes well.'

'No, because you're coping with an absence. Not with a thing but with nothing.'

'Yes, that's it!' Kate almost found herself speaking of her brother, a thing she seldom did with friend or stranger. She stopped. 'At least with this there's something to focus the anger on.'

Margaret seemed puzzled. 'What do you mean?'

'Well, somebody did it. Somebody killed Alison. Deliberately. Somebody knew where she was for three weeks and didn't let anybody know and then they killed her.'

'They are sure of that? That she was deliberately killed?'

'They're treating it as murder, yes!'

'You feel mainly anger. Yes.'

'Grief is mostly anger in my experience.' Kate sounded grim. 'Only in most cases there's nowhere to place the anger. No one to blame.'

'I've never lost anyone close to me. So I wouldn't know. My father had already disappeared from my mother's life before my brother and I were born.'

'Orphans.'

'As good as. He seduced my mother when she was fifteen. He was the father of her best friend at school. Awful scandal. Kept quiet, of course. They were rather a prominent family. My mother was their guilty secret.

He put money in a trust for her. So we've never been short – of a bob or two as they say. But after he abandoned us she lost touch with all the people she knew. They were hypocrites.'

They fell silent climbing the steep steps up to Richmond Street. They needed their breath. At the top Kate marvelled at this strange little area, Totterdown. The way the pretty little terraced houses climbed over the hill and round the hill. These on her left backed on to the railway cutting, a ravine rivalling the Avon Gorge in depth. She and Margaret looked back down at Windmill Hill, way below them now.

'That's where she was found,' Margaret said. Even from up here they could see the shimmering mounds of flowers that had been placed at the scene, like a ghostly lake in the moonlight.

'Yes.' Kate sighed. 'Poor child.'

'They shall not grow old...' She had a beautiful voice, this Margaret.

'That's no comfort to me, I'm afraid. They shall not grow up either, or grow anything, or grow at all. And anyway, no one had the right to decide for her.'

Margaret nodded. 'Sorry. There's nothing one can say actually, is there?'

'Well, I'd better get over to William Street.'

'Is that where you live?'

'Where my sister lives. I've got digs up

near Kingsdown Parade. I'll be moving there soon.'

'They'll miss you.'

Kate winced. 'I know. But I'm here to work. That's what I'm being paid for. And I need my own place. I need to concentrate. I'm a bit of an all-or-nothing-er.'

Margaret spoke shyly. 'You can tell by your work. That you're very – dedicated.'

'Oh hell.' Kate laughed, embarrassed.

'Your Hedda really was remarkable. I wasn't exaggerating this morning. The way you played her hatred of the pregnancy? It's usually played as though she's repelled by the physical humiliation, the loathsome marriage. You played it that she *wanted* to give birth – not to a human being – she feels nothing but despair for the human race – she respects only Art. She yearns to be part of the genesis of a work of art. So when she burned the manuscript and said, "I'm burning our child," one felt the real sacrilege of what she was doing. You somehow got to the depth of the tragedy. I'd never cared about her so much before.'

'Heavens.' Kate felt uncomfortable. As she always did in the presence of a True Fan. She didn't know what to say. Suddenly stifled by the clingy intense atmosphere she became distant, awkward, formal. 'Well, thanks.' She had to get away.

'I'd really like to talk about it one day.'

'Yes, that would be nice. Bit late tonight. Well, lovely to meet you. See you again, I hope.' Lying.

'Oh. Yes. Sorry.'

'No, thanks for being so nice–'

'Anyway, I live just down here. So...' The girl hovered, not knowing what gesture to make. Did they shake hands or what? Kate thrust out her hand and the girl took it. A good firm handshake. Kate felt remorse. 'Look, I'm sorry. You must think I'm really rather rude. It's just I never know what to say.'

'Oh, I understand.'

'And just now. You know. This Alison business. It's hard to think about anything else.'

'Yes. One never knows whether to speak. But if I never met you except this once and I hadn't said–'

'Yes. I really would like to discuss *Hedda* some time. It's full of fascinating problems. Just bad timing.'

Margaret looked at her in silence. 'Bad timing. Yes. Well, thank you, anyway.'

'For what?'

'For not dismissing me as just another Fan.'

'I did, initially.'

'I know.'

'Thanks for not minding.'

They grinned in the moonlight and

parted, Margaret down Pylle Hill Crescent, Kate up the steep Richmond Street. Kate felt lightened by the encounter, indeed oddly blessed.

27

BRIGHT TAKES THE RAP

'I let her go in there, knowing she was a rookie kid. I could at least have organised someone on watch at the back.'

'You didn't have anyone. I couldn't spare anyone. This is not under your jurisdiction, if you remember.'

'Anyone would have done. Didn't have to be a copper. Anyone can make a citizen's arrest.'

'I knew you were not on to the right bloke anyway.' Ryan towered over him.

'You're wrong.' Hoarse with hangover – scotch then wine was par for the course – the three grappas were the big mistake. 'You're wrong, Ryan.'

Ryan was unmoved. 'This Mark Leighton was in London when the body was being left on the hill. He didn't get back till the next morning.'

'Have you checked?'

'Of course I've checked! He had his train ticket. He produced it. We've seen it.'

'He had *a* train ticket. Doesn't mean he was on a train.'

'Where did he get it then?'

'A ticket's easy enough to come by. He could have picked one up at Temple Meads on the way up to get his car. He told you there was no one collecting tickets at the barrier. Someone coming off the London train coulda dropped one. He just has to pick it up.'

'Far-fetched, John.'

'Anyone see him in London? Or on the train? Or getting off it?' Every word he spoke hammered a nail in his skull.

'We didn't check because there was no reason to suspect him. Only the vivid imagination of little Goldilocks.'

'So why's he done a runner?'

'It's what I'd do in the circumstances. A police officer turning up to flirt with me all dressed up in her frilly frock.'

'No you wouldn't. You'd ring up the officer in charge and complain of police entrapment.'

'You know the public don't react like that.'

'He left an invalid mother behind, Ryan. Do the public react like that?'

Ryan sat, a brooding presence. He seemed to overflow his desk. He put a big hand up to scratch his big nose. 'Yes, that's odd, sure enough.'

Bright laughed. It hurt the bones in his face. 'It's more than odd, Ryan.'

'He's not exactly your macho man. These

fellas can be scared off easy. And maybe there's something he didn't want us to know. Something nothing to do with this, but that he wouldn't like to come out. That happens in cases like this, you know that. All sorts of stones get turned over and some nasty creepy-crawlies are found underneath. I'm not saying anything necessarily criminal but something he mightn't like his mother to know.'

Big brawny Ryan would assume that such a slim pretty lad was queer. 'Should check out the gay clubs if that's the way you're thinking.'

'All I've got is his name. No photo. No fingerprints.'

'You'll get a good photofit from Goldie's description.'

Ryan scowled.

'Have you run a check on him for previous?'

'Same thing applies.'

'Just don't blame that nice girl Goldie, Ryan. Blame me.'

'Listen, mate, I know the man I want is that git with the ringlets.'

'Dave Fowler.' Bright groaned.

'I know it's him, I feel it in my big policeman's bones. So, you screwed up, sure. My respect for your reputation is now zilch, okay? But you have not screwed up my investigation, believe me. You'd be better employed hanging out round that Dave if you feel like giving me a leg-up.'

Bright grimaced.

'Yeah, he's a mate of a mate of yours. But you're a copper, John. And he's a feckin' paedophile or something close to it. I don't like him. I want him caught.'

Bright hadn't the strength to give him an argument. 'Are you running a check on Mark Leighton's activities in London? As you're so sure he went there.' He stood. The headache rolled like a boulder from over the left eye to over the right. He winced.

Ryan gave a cruel grin. 'I'll bring it up at morning prayers.' He looked at his watch. 'Where I'm meant to be in five minutes. The IO's a stickler.'

Crossing the tarmac yard, Ryan said, 'We did check Mark Leighton's story as a matter of fact. They do have a flat in London like he said. And it did look quite tidy. Like he could have been there and cleaned it up.'

'But he wasn't seen there, right?'

Ryan shrugged. 'You know what London's like. No one sees anything. You all walk round with your eyes shut there.'

28

GOING TO WORK

Kate stood white-faced in the kitchen. Maisie hovered, anxious. Lizzie whirl-winded round them: 'I drank too much. I never drink too much. I'm not used to it. I was awake all night. I'm going to be late.' She swallowed scalding coffee, insisted on washing up the cup.

'Just go, mum.'

'Where's my handbag?'

'Ankate? You're sitting on it.'

'Oh yes.'

'For heaven's sake, Kate, what is the matter with you? You weren't nearly as drunk as me last night.'

'She's nervous, mum.'

'Nervous? What about?'

'It's her first day of rehearsal.'

'Oh, that. Well, you shouldn't have got yourself a hangover, should you?'

'The hangover will probably help. The more brain-dead the better.'

Lizzie pulled up short. 'Oh, God, Maisie, you'll be alone here today.'

'I'll be all right.'

'Don't go out on your own.'

'I won't. Don't worry, mum.'

'Of course I'll worry.'

'John Bright's meeting me at the theatre at lunchtime,' Kate said. 'We'll drop in here.'

'I'll make lunch for you.'

'Thanks, Maisie. If we're facing food by then.'

'Go on, mum, or you really will be late.'

'Sarah-next-door is blowing her horn.' Kate waved from the window. Sarah gestured at her wrist-watch with a frantic finger. Maisie kissed Lizzie and pushed her out of the door. 'Phew!' she said.

Kate walked down to the theatre. To get some oxygen to her brain. She wasn't hungover. She was sick with nerves. *I can't go through this again. It's too hard on the nervous system. I can't do it any more. I've forgotten how to act on the stage. Anyway, the part's beyond me. I don't know what makes Rosalind tick. I don't know what I'm doing. That will be obvious to everyone. Colum will realise he should have cast someone else. He probably knows that already. I was probably a last resort anyway. For Christsake, you'd think you'd never done this before. Why doesn't it get easier? Why does it get worse?*

Maureen was still the stage door keeper. 'Comforting that some things don't change,' Kate said.

'Nice to see you back, Kate. It's great you're doing Rosalind. You must be looking forward to it.'

'Are you joking?'

'Ah, you'll be great.'

'Ha.'

She climbed the stairs to the rehearsal room. Sun beating already through the high windows. A table a mile long. Hundreds of people, it seemed. Alan Tate hugged her, saying into her ear, 'This is the reason I do movies, I've just realised. You think it's too late to pull out?'

'No. Let's go now.'

'Kate!' Colum's face was a little more lined than last year, the only sign he might be more than fourteen years old. A lanky Derry lad with a chrysanthemum of curly brown hair, he didn't look like a director. 'Oh, Kate!' Beaming, he threw open spider arms. 'I'm so glad to see you.' He whispered in her ear, 'I'm shitting bricks actually.'

Kate laughed but felt no better. This time she was going to be found out. She smiled, sickly, at ten people she didn't know huddled round the coffee table, spilling milk and sugar, scalding mouths, till the DSM called them to order.

Some sidled up to the table, eyeing those already seated. Should you sit next to the actor you'd be working most with in the play? Should you just for safety sit next to the only actor you already knew? Should you in order to seem in control of things sit confidently any old where? Should you hide down the end of the table farthest from the director, hoping not to be noticed?

And then the reading itself. What was the form? Go for it or hold back? Perform or mumble? Commit yourself or wait to see what others were doing? Or make no decision at all, just go with the flow and see how it comes out?

Lots of arranging of things: the script, the pencil, the polystyrene cup, the cigarettes. Kate sat close to Colum for protection. A little dark girl hovered close by. Kate smiled at her. 'Hi, I'm Kate.'

'I'm Gemma. I'm playing Celia.'

'I suspected as much. Sit next to me? Since we're together in nearly every scene.'

Gemma sat, grateful to be asked. Kate hadn't dared speak to the Orlando. He was too young and beautiful by far, made her shy. Then she saw him too hovering, poor thing, not knowing what to do. She bravely smiled at him. 'Sit with us?'

He actually blushed, nodded gruffly, frowning, and sat opposite. Ian McLean, fatter than ever these days, puffed along next to him. 'A nice s-slim little thing like you,' he said, 'can surely f-fit me in?' The boy looked scared then laughed. 'After all we're f-family,' Ian said. 'Us c-city folk.'

She suddenly in a rush began to feel good. In here no young girls had been abducted, no one's father was under suspicion, no one's niece was in possible danger. This was real life. This was where the real thing lived. Between these walls between the hours of ten and six life was going to be okay.

Colum began his introductions. He started with Orlando on his left: 'Rupert Angel' - Ian murmured, 'So aptly named' - and finished with Kate on his right. Gave a little speech in his attractive flat Derry tones. 'I'm not going to say much. Just I'm really glad to see you all. It's a tremendous play. You know me, I keep things open, I haven't got a firm concept. I can feel all the big themes, I expect you all can, but I don't want to say, Oh this play is categorically about this or that, because I think we're smaller than Shakespeare and I think he'll show us the amazing connections as we go along. I don't want to set up in the audience's expectation something smaller than the play is. I think if we go for the truth we'll find out some amazing things. Sandy and I agree we should set it in the present day, just because we can signal more immediate messages that way, especially to young audiences. And, listen, I do just think this one thing: this is a *young* people's play. It's *about* young people, young people falling in love, and doing other reckless things, and how badly the grown-ups treat them, the shit place the adults have made the world. But that's not all it's about. I mean, the townees' attitude to the country. It's just awful the way they treat the country people, isn't it? Well, I won't go on. As usual, a really cogent well-thought-out speech. This is the longest one you'll hear from me. I hope. It's you doing the talking from now on. Okay?'

The reading began. Kate was blind and deaf with nerves for fifteen minutes and then she started flying. And taking in what was going on around her. Alan Tate had a real line on Jaques, not just a cynic but a man with a tragic longing not to be. She watched the faces round the table aghast at Ian McLean's stammer. She'd worked with him before, so knew that it disappeared the minute he got his performance right. Even with the stammer he got laughs, not so easy with Shakespeare's clowns. And Celia too was funny. Impossible to tell about the Orlando, Rupert. He was a mumbler, too scared to commit himself. Kate always went for it, hook, line and sinker, at the read-through. Took big risks, making mental notes. After this, pull back and explore the murky emotional depths, but fly here this once, get an idea of the speed and the trajectory of the flight.

Big laughter at coffee break, relief at

having got the blocks off, tested the water. 'I feel worn out,' Alan Tate said. 'You're sparkling.'

'Oh, I love it. I forget how much. Each time I forget.'

He poured himself a coffee, murmured, 'Your sister's rather a stunner, isn't she?'

'Oh, is she? I thought you were just giving her the treatment.'

He gave his wolfish grin. 'She's a bit of a challenge, I admit.'

'She's no pushover, Alan.'

'Will she be around much?' he said in a casual tone.

'You may see her from time to time.'

'Hmm.'

Getting up from his third coffee in the front of house bar, John Bright raised an eyebrow. 'What set you on fire?'

Kate laughed. 'Relief. Listen, do you mind going up to Totterdown for lunch? Maisie's alone. Just to check. You know.'

'Sure. Anything for a sight of that little cracker. I'm seriously in love.'

'She's amazing, isn't she?'

In the car he said, 'How could that long-haired git Dave walk away from Maisie? You understand that?'

'Come on, John. Life's complicated. You know. Anyway, it was Lizzie he walked away from. Marriage. Being a family man.'

'He walked away from growing up. He's still walking.'

'Yes, well...'

'Maybe this business will shake him up a bit.'

'They don't still suspect him, do they?'

Bright didn't reply. She turned to look at him. Eyes on the road, he didn't glance her way.

'Do they?' she said again.

'Ryan doesn't like him. But that's not evidence. That's all I can say.'

'Are you in big trouble there?'

'Not nearly as bad as I thought. Thanks to Dave.'

'Thanks to Dave how?'

'Ryan doesn't believe the bloke I lost is the bloke he's looking for.'

'So he does think it's Dave?'

'I did not say that.' He still would not look at her.

They got out of the car. Kate hunted in every pocket and the depths of her bag.

Bright said, 'What is this with you and keys?'

'I have only a tenuous connection with all my belongings.'

'Tenuous, is it?' He rang the bell. 'Maisie'll let us in.'

Kate scrabbled a little more, at last found the key folded in her script. Maisie had still not answered the bell. They went in.

'Maisie? We're back!' Kate walked through to the kitchen. Bright followed. 'Not here.' She looked down into the garden. No one there. 'She must be in the loo.' Kate ran up the stairs. Bright followed. They pushed open the door of each bedroom then of the bathroom.

Maisie wasn't there.

29

DESPERATELY SEEKING MAISIE

Kate started to shake. She shook so that her mouth would not form words and she could not hold on to things. Bright said, 'What's Lizzie's number at work?'

Kate could only shake her head. At last she got out: 'Not Lizzie. Not yet.'

'Maisie might be *with* Lizzie.'

A gasp came out of Kate. She scrambled through her Filofax for the number, showed it to him. He asked for Lizzie. Said to Kate, 'She's gone out for lunch,' and into the phone, 'Was her daughter with her?' Pause. 'And she hasn't been there this morning? You sure? Tell Lizzie to phone home the minute she gets back. Thanks.'

'Dave,' Kate whispered.

He was already dialling. 'Dave? John Bright here. Is Maisie with you? And she hasn't been with you this morning? She's not in the house. And she's not with Lizzie. That's right. Might be a good idea.'

Kate's brain had gone into paralysis. She could only think: *Maisie promised. There was no one she would have gone with. Nowhere she*

227

would have gone. She promised. She promised not to go out.

'Neighbours.' Bright opened the front door. 'You take this side of the street. I'll take the houses opposite.'

A mysterious person rented Lizzie's basement. He came and went. They barely knew him, even by sight. She scrambled down the stone steps and banged on the door. She looked through the window, and through the letter box. Piles of bills and junk mail on the mat. He wasn't there. Sarah-next-door was out at work with Lizzie. And Laura, the nice girl in Sarah's basement, gardened for the council. She'd be out. Kate rang anyway. No answer there either. The man at the off-licence with the beer crates outside said he hadn't seen Maisie. But he hadn't opened up till late. Eleven or so, he said.

The old couple opposite had been in their garden out back all morning. The people either side were away on holiday. Bright and Kate stood in the street. Bright got the Alison incident room on his mobile. 'It might be a false alarm but another girl is not where she should be.' He gave succinct details and rang off.

Kate's brain was back in gear. 'Alison's family live in Stevens Crescent.' They ran down the hill, turned the corner by the little mosque, crossed the road, and ran uphill again to half-way along the crescent. Stevens Crescent was more upmarket than William Street: a man was painting his house Mediterranean blue. Several families of West Indian origin lived up here.

The curtains were closed at the house. Flowers were piled against the low brick wall. Kate said, 'I've never met the mother,' as she rang the bell. A black woman opened the door, clearly Alison's mother. The same proud head, the same grace. But the woman's skin had a matt grey look, the eyes red-veined with grief. 'Yes?'

'I'm sorry to bother you. I'm Kate. Maisie's my niece. This is John Bright. We just wondered if– Is Maisie here?'

'Maisie? No. She comes most days but she's not here today. What happened?'

Kate explained. The woman put her hands up to her face. 'Oh no. Oh no. It's a curse, it's a curse.'

'What's the matter, Louie?' A deep voice. Little trace of West Indies in the accent. Alison's father came to the door. No resemblance at all, except for his height. A tall square-shouldered man with a slightly severe face. Like his wife he said, 'Oh no. Oh no. Who is doing this?'

Bright said, 'We're not sure yet that anything bad has happened. Don't let's jump to conclusions. Where do you think she could have gone?'

229

They looked at each other. Mrs Holt said, 'There's only the school. That's where the girls hang out. It's a place for them to be, you know?'

'The school!' Suddenly Kate had hope. If one of the girls had come by– It was possible, it was! She said to Bright, 'Will you go back to the house? Someone should be there.'

'No. I'll go down the school. Give me directions. I'll walk.'

'Down there, straight over the hill, over that way, to the railway side. You'll pass the place where–' She stopped, seeing the faces of Alison's parents in front of her.

'Where our daughter was found,' Mrs Holt said.

Mr Holt said, 'Through the barrier, and the school is right there on your left.'

Bright took off, running.

The house was as she had left it. Empty. Silent. She stood in the hallway desperate. Then the doorbell rang. Dave stood there, dishevelled, dismayed. 'Any news?'

Kate shook her head.

'What can we do, Kate?'

'Nothing except think. John Bright's gone down to the school. You could go down too. The girls hang out there, you know? Just a place to be.' She repeated the words of Alison's mother.

230

'I could search the streets.'

'Which streets?'

'I could do what the police call a house-to-house.'

'We've done the immediate neighbours.'

'I could go to meet Lizzie.'

'Lizzie.' Kate wrapped her arms round her stomach and groaned.

Dave called the pottery in Clifton. They told him Lizzie was on her way home. Kate remembered she should be back at work in a minute. She called the theatre office. It only occurred to her then that maybe Maisie had taken it into her head to go down to the theatre for lunch. So first she asked cautiously if anyone had seen this slim tall blonde girl, fragile with a lot of frizzed-out hair, fifteen years old, very pretty. 'Your niece?' the secretary asked.

'Yes!'

'She was at the opening night of *Hedda*. She and her friend used to come to all the shows. Theatre mad. Her friend's the one who—'

'Yes.'

'Is your niece all right, Kate?'

'We don't know.' Kate started to cry.

'Don't worry. If she's been anywhere round the theatre today we'll let you know. I'll ring you as soon as I know.'

Kate managed to give her the number. 'And please tell Colum I can't be there the

231

rest of the day. I'm so sorry. I'm so sorry.'

Lizzie got out of the taxi and ran up the steps. The driver shouted something. Kate ran down and paid him. Lizzie stopped in her tracks at the sight of Dave.

'Lizzie–'

She ran on, all round the house, making sure for herself. She wrenched open the kitchen door and ran down the steps into the garden. She ran up again peering at the surrounding gardens. The dogs penned in the cage four gardens down howled and yelped. That would go on for hours now. She came back into the hallway. 'Where are the police?'

'John phoned them. They'll be on their way.'

'Why aren't you doing something?' She accused Dave.

'He wanted to run down to the school. John had already gone. He should be back soon.'

The phone rang. Kate grabbed it. The nice secretary from the theatre. Nobody had seen Maisie anywhere near the theatre that morning or at lunchtime. She had asked everyone. But they would continue to look. They would keep their eyes peeled. Everyone. As Kate put the phone down it rang again. 'John?'

'Yeah, me. Any sign of her?'

'No.'

'She's not at the school and hasn't been seen there. A few of the girls have been there since nine this morning keeping a vigil. They haven't seen her. I'm dropping in to Alison's house again, on my way back. See you soon.'

Kate put the phone down. She shook her head. There was no need to speak. Lizzie looked as though she might never speak again. Her eyes were wild. Even her hair, normally neat and sleek, seemed to stand out from her head as though electrified. Dave stood like a tree suddenly deprived of water, foliage withered, branches drooping dead.

He stepped towards Lizzie and she moved as though about to fall forward. He put his arms round her, not in his usual come-to-Mr-Powerful-he-will-take-care-of-you way; they came together like two crash survivors. She clung round his neck. He round her waist. Kate sat on the stairs. The fridge stopped making a noise. There was no sound in the house. None.

30

MAKING CONNECTIONS

'Mr Holt, is there anyone at work, a colleague or an employee that you've had trouble with? Sacked maybe? Or just had cause to reprimand? Someone you've had a difficult time with? Someone—'

'Mr Bright, I've thought and thought about this, don't you think I haven't? I told the police. There's no one. Truly. Is there, Louie?'

'And you, Mrs Holt?'

'I'm a teacher, Mr Bright. There's always little things going on. With little kids there's always something. Their parents come up to the school or whatever but it's all over quick and everybody's happy again. There's never been anything serious. No.'

'You never got promoted over anyone who might have borne a grudge?'

'Mr Bright, that would be the day.'

He heard the bitterness of a life of racial discrimination and didn't pursue it. He turned to Holt. 'And you?'

'Strangely I have been promoted regularly in accordance with Civil Service rules. This

234

is not a racial thing, Mr Bright. I've said so from the start and at last that's proved at least.' He answered his wife's look: 'If Maisie has gone too, that means this is not a racial thing, Louie. Maisie is as white as the driven snow.'

She moaned and rocked back and forth. 'Don't say that, Desmond. Don't speak like that.'

'The police thought it was a racial thing,' he explained to Bright. 'But racial things are generally cruder. In my experience.'

'A-ha.'

'This killer has extreme finesse. This is not a normal person. This is a sick person. Sick.' The man got up. He walked fast up and down the room, shaking his fists in a fast rhythm and controlling his breath.

Bright waited, then said, 'Is there anyone you used to be close to and then you stopped being close with?'

Mr Holt gave him a sharp look. Bright's squint intensified so you couldn't tell where he was looking: at you, beyond you or to the side of you. If he were a dog his ears would be cocked.

'You mean at work?' Holt said.

'Wherever.'

An odd expression crossed Holt's face. He began to speak, stopped, then began again: 'There was a young man at work. He was very good. Keen. He asked my advice a lot.

He was a bit too keen actually. Worked too hard. I told him to cool it. He clung to me a bit. I didn't mind but colleagues started to comment. You know, he was always there at lunch and breaktimes. I got a little bit fed up with it myself once I started to notice it. So I started to avoid him a bit. Nothing that he would notice, I hope. I didn't want to hurt his feelings. And then he got transferred to another department, so the thing was solved.'

It was clear to Bright that this person was not the one who had first come to Mr Holt's mind. The person who had first come to his mind was someone he did not wish to discuss in front of his wife. But this could wait. Bright shot an arrow into the air: 'Was his name Mark Leighton?'

Both the Holts looked stunned, horrified. Holt nodded slowly. 'Yes. Why?'

'His name is on the suspect list. I knew he worked in the same department as you for a bit. It doesn't mean anything.'

'No.' Holt's head shook from side to side. His wife stared into his eyes. 'No. No,' he said.

Bright watched as a new light began to surround this person from the past. A person of previously blameless character. The light of suspicion.

'He couldn't.' Holt's deep confident voice had lost all resonance. 'He was a – he was a

236

nice young man – he was – okay. I didn't – do anything bad to him. I didn't do anything he could want to – take that kind of revenge for. Kill my daughter? Kill Alison? No. Not Mark.'

Mrs Holt said, 'Why not? I can think anything of anybody now. Everyone I see, I wonder, could it be you? Life was simple before this. There's no way to know what anybody is. My neighbours. My own relations. You can't tell. I don't trust anybody now.'

Holt pulled his wits together. 'Mr Bright. Even if Mark did – even if he is the one – why Maisie? He has some quarrel with Maisie's folks too?'

'That's what I have to find out. Can you think of any connection?'

'He did his degree at Bristol University.'

'Oh, did he?'

'Maisie's father is a lecturer there.'

'A-ha. I know.'

'Does he know Mark?'

'I don't think he's been asked. Up to now.'

The Holts stared at each other. She reached out her hands. Her husband took them.

'Mam?' The door at the back of the room opened and two small faces looked in. 'Can we come in now? We can't think of no more things to play.'

'Come in, love.' Mrs Holt looked at John

Bright. 'Will you find out who did it, Mr Bright?'

'Have they put you in charge?' Mr Holt assumed he was the big gun sent from Scotland Yard.

Bright didn't disabuse him. 'I've been helping out on an informal basis up to now. But that might change. Believe me, if I can find this bastard, informally or formally, I will.'

'Will they question him? Mark Leighton?'

'You bet they will.' If *they ever find him again,* Bright thought but did not say. It was possible Mark had returned and was even now in the clutches of Ryan. It was possible and as unlikely as hell.

Kate opened the door. Lizzie and Dave now sat on the stairs, hands locked together. They stood when Bright came in. He said, 'Dave, before Ryan gets here, do you remember teaching a Mark Leighton? Maybe seven years ago?'

'Mark Leighton?' Dave looked blank.

'About five foot ten, slim but strong apparently, longish hair well, it is nowadays, curly, mid-brown. Nice neck, I'm told. I've never seen the guy, don't have a picture, this is just hearsay. Scruffy stylish clothes.'

'Mark Leighton.'

They stared at Dave as at the oracle.

'Has this man got Maisie?'

'It's a possibility.'

Dave put both hands over his face. They waited. He took his hands away and shook his head. Tears came out of his eyes. He wailed, 'I can't remember him!'

Then Ryan arrived. Came in the house like a mammoth. Huge. Filled the hall space. Looked at no one but Dave. 'Shouldn't have let you go, should I, Mr Fowler? This is a warrant to search your premises. You'll come with us, please, make sure everything is done by the book.'

Hearing this, Lizzie said, 'I'm coming too.'

'Sorry, Mrs – er...'

'It's our daughter who is missing, Mr Ryan.'

'We'll find her, Mrs...'

'My name is Creech. Maisie's name is Creech. And I'm not *Mrs* anything.'

'I'm sorry. Get Mr Fowler over there quick. Now, Mrs Creech. We've already started a house-to-house in the neighbourhood. Every house in this part of Totterdown will be visited by one of my officers. We've pulled men off other cases. This is priority. Time is of the essence. It's unusual for a disappearance to be reported so quickly. Normally people wait a few days or even longer before contacting us. But we know about this right away. It will be on all the news bulletins this afternoon. Do you have a recent photo of Maisie that we can borrow now?'

Lizzie's shaking hands went through the recent snaps, fumbling them, dropping them. She handed one over, Maisie in her wispy frock, the one she had worn to the first night of *Hedda Gabler*. Standing next to Alison.

'Is this a good likeness?' Ryan asked.

They all simply looked at it.

They had him by the arms, one on either side. They almost ran him up the stairs. The place was swarming with police. Turning it over. They shook pillows out of their cases, they heaved the mattresses up and over, they pulled out drawers, shook out the contents and left the lot on the floor, turned out cupboards, mess spilling everywhere. Papers, photographs, clothes, books opened and shaken, some left open with their spines bent back. Lizzie watched dead-eyed.

They started to throw stuff off the sleeping platform. They said, 'Bring him up here.' Dave went up the ladder, a policeman in front and one behind. Lizzie followed. The platform was maybe ten foot by twelve, half of it covered with mattress. Bedding had been thrown off, pillows and cushions flung about. One mattress stood up against the wall, the other had been lifted off the floor and two policemen were holding it up. On the floor where the mattress had lain was a small polythene bag containing brown powder, and another polythene bag containing a dried greenish herbal material.

'Just to confirm that you witnessed us finding this, Mr Fowler,' Ryan said.

'I didn't.' Dave said the words but they lacked hope.

'You didn't?'

'No. I came up here and saw the stuff on the floor. I did not see anyone lift the mattress and discover it. I did not put it there and you know I didn't.'

'This is your premises and the stuff was found here.'

Dave didn't bother to reply. Lizzie couldn't.

'David Fowler, I am arresting you on suspicion of dealing in illegal substances. You do not have to say anything...'

They went backwards down the ladder. Two policemen took Dave out to a car. Lizzie watched from the dark doorway. Ryan said, 'Can we drop you back home, Mrs Creech?'

Lizzie said, 'He didn't do this. He didn't do any of this. You should be searching somewhere else.'

Dave didn't even look back at her as they drove him away. She walked home. She walked home by way of a million streets. Looking for Maisie. She went by waste ground searching the rough grass.

31

EXCERPT FROM A DIARY

vii

Well, it was so easy. I knocked on the door and said I had just been at Dave's. She has seen me of course a few times at Dave's. So she invited me in. She was lonely. And bored. And grieving with no relief. She said she wanted to visit Alison's parents. She has seen them every day since Alison went missing. And since the death she takes the children out. She takes them to the playground on Windmill Hill. It gives them all something to do. She loves the children. They are heartbroken and the little one can't understand that Alison is never coming back. 'I can't understand it myself, come to that,' Maisie said. (She has a most attractive Bristol accent) in her light little husky voice. She takes them to the school sometimes. They go the long route over the hill, behind the school and then round. So as to avoid the site (and the sight of the site) of Alison's laying-out. The children like that, she said. And she's very worried that this morning they'll be at a loss without her. But she promised her mother she wouldn't go out.

'I'd go with you,' I said.

She looked doubtful, as well she might. But I'm used to dealing with distrust. I get over it, round it and through it several times every day in my job. I said, 'Well, let's phone Dave then. He could come over and take you.'

That convinced her I must be above board. She did not call my bluff. Though if she had it would only have put this off to another time. She was bashful too at seeming not to trust me. A respectable person such as I, youngish, not at all dangerous or villainous, must surely be okay. It's awfully insulting after all to suspect a person you know of doing the things I have done. I said, 'You could leave a note for your mother to say where you have gone.'

'No,' she said, 'it's okay. I'll be back before lunchtime and Ankate will be here then with John Bright. He's a detective inspector from London.' She spoke with pride. And a slight hint of my-dad's-a-policeman defiance. I adore her. She is ravishing. I can't wait to have her to myself. I can't wait.

So out we walked into the sun and into my car. Oh yes, of course I have another car. The grey Renault is my cover in every sense.

And when in the car I suddenly said, 'Oh, Lord, I forgot my asthma inhaler, do you mind if we go via my place?' although she became a little alarmed she was too well brought up to show it. And when we got to my place, though she sensibly got out of the car so as to be able to make a run for it if I should attempt anything, when I from inside my doorway cried out, 'Ouch! Oh God!' or words to that effect, pretending to have injured myself, she called out, 'What's the matter?' and came running into my arms. Well, not literally into my arms. Just into my domain. When I locked the door behind her she was simply astonished.

The things that happen to young girls simply because they are too polite. People spend their whole lives teaching children to say yes, when the major thing they should teach them is to say no. No, no and no. To all adults. They pretend to children that adults are for the most part kind and good. This is a lie. Most adults are corrupt, cowardly, cruel, bullies who will abuse any creature weaker or smaller than themselves, and who lie and cheat. Men particularly. Because the most important thing to most men is their image. The image they have of themselves that must be upheld at all costs. People sacrifice their lives, whole nations have sacrificed themselves, to preserve one man's image of himself.

Some children of course are corrupted almost right away. They accept the adults' picture of the world and the adults' picture of themselves. Lies are wicked, say the adults, lying themselves all the time about everything. Most children accept the picture: yes lying is wrong wink wink now let's lie to our heart's content. But some children believe the adults, and have a hard time reconciling the picture they present with the reality that the child's clear eyes see. Some children never reconcile the image with the reality and they go mad. Others add it all up eventually and remain sad and disillusioned, never able to trust that they will not be betrayed. Some, like Alison, like Maisie, shine like moons in a black night, gliding above corruption. BUT THEY WILL BE BROUGHT LOW. THEIR LIGHT WILL BE EXTIN-GUISHED. AND THEIR CORRUPTION WILL BE THE WORSE BECAUSE THEY SHONE SO BRIGHT. I will not live or let them live to see that happen. The drugs, the sex games, the power games, the pros-titution to employment and worldly power and to worldly goods. These will not be allowed to bargain for the souls of these bright children. They have the best. They have been the best. Flights of angels sing them to their rest. The rest is silence. Who can be sad at Hamlet's death? Or Ophelia's?

They were pure. They were the good and the pure. They were truly not for this world. Death is not tragedy. Death is triumph. I shall convince Maisie of this.

I shall tell Maisie the truth from the start. She will know what I mean to do. I tried to deceive Alison but she guessed. She was nobody's fool. Maisie too is intelligent and perspicacious. She deserves nothing less than the truth. I shall discuss my theories with her. I have never discussed my position with another human being. I have never dared. Perhaps Maisie will raise telling arguments that will shift me from my position. Who knows? I believe that by now my position is too entrenched, too solid to admit of argument. But you never can tell.

Do you like my quotations from plays? Dropped in here and there for your eyes? What do you think of my theories? Do you suspect that I envy you, and that my actions are a kind of revenge on you for the gifts that you have and that I lack? Please do not think that of me. I have seen in your work a wide and profound understanding of the ways of human beings, even the human beings that horrify the general run of human beings. Your Medea, your Hedda, your Clytemnestra. These are all people who killed from a powerful belief that death was better than a corrupt life. You have depicted powerfully for the world the motives for these actions. You have brought understanding to dull minds. If only for the duration of the play they have understood and sympathised with a human being whom in life they would condemn and vilify. You are their interpreter to the world. And when you present these notes, this account for publication, you will do so again, in a different role.

I had meant to send you my diary in instalments but that was, I now realise, a rash decision made when I was in an exalted state. I have no doubt the forensic experts, infinitely more competent than the dummkopf constabulary, would trace the pages somehow back to me. But I beg you to publish this account after I am gone. I really do beg. The only desire for which I have ever begged. I need the world to understand. Its understanding is always limited. But occasionally a crack appears into which light penetrates if only for a brief flash. Out out brief candle and all that. And none of that she-should-have-died-hereafter stuff. Most people should die BEFORE they do, not after. Withered old leaves that the poor old tree of life can't shake off. Clinging on for grim life.

I know you understand. I know that, though you will feel pain, you will see that this is the best time for Maisie to die. Now while she is perfect and uncorrupted. Now before she starts to decline. Into physical and moral degradation. I know you understand.

Well, enough of this polemic. Maisie is here, safe and well. For the moment she is unfortunately blindfolded and gagged and her hands are tied. I did this as gently as possible. She fought of course, that's only natural, but I am strong and have now had experience. This whole thing has been easier than it was with Alison.

I asked Maisie to sit down while I explained things to her. She did so. I taped her hands behind her before she knew what I was doing. She screamed and lifted the chair with her and thrashed about. I managed to tape her mouth. I'm sorry to say I did this cruelly. I'm afraid I slightly hurt her neck on the back of the chair. I had to. I would not have chosen to. The gag will be removed later. But not before she is introduced to her own special room, you understand: I cannot allow her to shout and scream. Also, I cannot reveal to you the location of her special room, in case my whereabouts are discovered. After the gagging, blindfolding her was relatively easy.

The idea of the special room came to me some years ago. I was in the sixth form at school. A group of us doing Media Studies were taken to London. One of our visits was to a Radio Studio at Broadcasting House. A production of *Cymbeline* was being rehearsed /recorded. You were giving one of your award-winning performances as Imogen. You will recall that, I'm sure. Just as I am sure that you will not recall meeting me. Though naturally I do remember meeting you.

One area of the radio studio was called the DEAD ROOM. I was overcome with the symbolic significance of the name, naturally. This room had padded walls and ceiling. Conical stalactites of foam rubber, covered with a greyish muslin, protruded inward and downward as though the dead all round were trying to punch their way through. No, that is fanciful. The padding was to deaden the sound. Kill the sound.

The open air (mountain, garden, forest, street), it was explained to us, reduces the resonance of the human voice, thinning it, 'deadening' it (you of course know this), so scenes set in the open air are played in the Dead Room. (You indeed were recording the Milford Haven scene, begging Pisanio to kill you – *the lamb entreats the butcher – where's thy knife?* I was greatly affected by this scene. By your playing of it. And also by your speaking of the dirge to the innocent dead: *Fear no more the heat of the sun...*) But enough of fond reminiscence. Thus my Dead Room is padded, not just the walls and ceiling but the floor too. The padding kills sound. So the inhabitant can make as much din as she likes. No one will ever hear.

I have spent much time myself in this room and have observed a curious phenomenon. This deadening or thinning of the voice has a strange effect. Speaking becomes a less than pleasurable experience. I discover that all of us literally enjoy the sound of our own voice. When we are robbed of that sound we become disorientated, lost, afraid. We force our voices to make more sound, but although we shout at the top of our lungs we cannot hear ourselves any better. (The aural equivalent of drowning, perhaps, or of looking into a mirror and seeing – nothing.) We are filled with a kind of despair, as though perhaps we are ceasing to exist. Whether this effect contributes to the choice of death over life I do not know. Alison in fact died in my Dead Room. And she died willingly. And so, I hope, will Maisie. She will die painlessly, peacefully, and she will be reconciled to her death. You must not worry about her. You must be glad for her. I may decide to die with her. If I decide that, through you, sufficient understanding of my motives will be reached, disseminated – *broadcast* if you like – then my work will be completed and it will be time for me to die also.

32

CHANGING ALLEGIANCES

Kate rang Colum to tell him what had happened. He made a harsh intake of breath like a sob. 'Oh God, Kate, what are you going to do?'

'We're helpless, Colum, helpless. We sit here. Then we go out. We roam the streets. People watch from their windows. They all know. They gaze sympathetically. They don't dare speak to Lizzie. No one can speak to her. I can't, myself.'

'Are you pulling out of the play?'

'I don't know, I don't know.'

'Don't decide yet. There's time.'

'The show must go on?'

'Well, it must actually. Yes.'

'It seems obscene to be acting make believe when this horror is happening in real life.'

'This play is more than make believe.'

'No, Colum, it's not.'

'What else would you be doing?'

'Sitting helplessly next to Lizzie staring into space waiting for news.'

'You can get news at the theatre.'

'Yes.' Kate was not convinced.

Strangely, the only person Lizzie could bear to have around was John Bright. He brought her cups of coffee and tea, placed them in her hands and made her drink them. He cooked spaghetti and made her eat, at least a forkful or two. He found some Mogadon in her bedside cabinet and made her take one so that for a few hours she might sleep.

At 2 a.m., when they had put her to bed, he and Kate sat in the living room. He said, 'This is my fault. I know who did this and I forced his hand. I blew it. Don't interrupt. If they'll have me I'm going to try to get leave to join the team.'

'Will they–?'

'I might be able to swing it if Ryan puts in a word with the IO.'

'The what?'

'Investigating Officer.'

'I thought that was Ryan.'

'No. He's just one of the two DCIs on the team. He heads one of the shifts. If the IO gives the say-so I'll be in. I'll do it voluntary, just use my leave. I'll get her out alive. I will, Kate.'

Kate looked up. Lizzie was standing in the doorway in her dressing-gown. She and John Bright stared at each other for a long time. She nodded several times. So did he.

Then she turned round and went back upstairs.

Kate's mouth made a movement that resembled a smile. Bright just looked desperate. 'Some way to get your sister to tolerate me,' he said.

'Where do you begin to look for this person?' Kate whispered.

'His mother's house.'

'But he left—'

'The trail starts there. Even if all we find is a picture to circulate. His history. What the mother has to say about him. See, Ryan is fixated on Dave. The whole team is. You can see why.'

Kate made the same noise Colum had made on the phone, an inward-breathing sob, an ugly grunting sound. 'Dave didn't Dave didn't—'

'No.' Bright's expression was grim. 'Dave didn't.'

'So...'

'So if I get on the team I'll get them to let me pursue this line. See, the guy has a link to this area. He's visited families round here. I can start with them. They're still doing the house-to-house. I can get them to ask.' Bright started to pace, bouncing on the balls of his feet, rattling the change in his pockets.

Kate kept still. She did not share her sister's faith. She felt the way she had felt sitting in her kitchen that day clutching her heart. When she had heard about the missing Bristol schoolgirl and known it was Maisie. She had lost Maisie now. She had lost Maisie because she had gone to the theatre to rehearse a play instead of staying with Maisie, her niece, whom she knew to be in danger. They had all done the same. Maisie's mother, and her father too. But it was no use telling herself that. She was responsible. One great love had lost her another. She felt utter despair.

'Here. You take a Moggie as well. You got to sleep.' He pulled her to her feet. 'Ah, Kate.'

'Yup.'

'What's going on?'

'How do you mean?'

'In your head?'

'Same as you. Only I can't do anything. Nothing I can do.'

'You be with Lizzie.'

'She doesn't want me. The sight of me is anathema to her. Haven't you noticed? It's terrible.'

'Is that right?'

'Yes. She only has eyes for you, dear.'

'Is that right?'

'Yup. She believes in you.'

'And you don't.'

Kate looked at him.

'A-ha,' he said.

'Not just not in you. Not in anything.'

'Go back to work then. Do the play.'

'How can I do the fucking play with this going on?'

'Here.' He handed her a Mogadon and a glass of water.

They were all awake and in the jolly kitchen at seven in the morning. Bright had the merry clown teapot in one hand and the mobile phone in the other. 'A-ha,' he said, 'a-ha.' Then, 'Ryan, listen–' He put down the pot and went out into the hall. Kate poured tea. Lizzie drank hers in one ravenous gulp burning her mouth.

The sun shone like yesterday, like all the days, the sun gentler at this time of morning than it would be later. Kate went out on to the steps. Sarah-next-door was in her garden. She silently mouthed to Kate: Any news? Kate shook her head. Sarah wiped her eyes with her skirt hem. Kate went down the steps. Sarah whispered, 'How is she?'

Kate did not need to speak.

'Would she like me to come round?'

Lizzie appeared at the top of the steps. She saw Sarah and came down slowly. Sarah said, 'Oh Lizzie. Shall I come into yours? I can't see me going to work somehow.'

Lizzie nodded. Sarah disappeared up her own steps. Lizzie went back inside. Kate followed, after looking round at all the gardens lower down the hill. As though Maisie might suddenly appear: *Hi, I'm here, gave you all a fright, didn't I?* Then she followed Lizzie. The bell rang. Bright opened the door. Sarah came in. Lizzie walked into her arms and they stood there locked in support. Kate looked on. Bright caught her eye. His unmoving mask expressing – she could not have said how sympathy, irony, solidarity.

Lizzie and Sarah went into the kitchen. Bright said, 'Is she going to stay with Lizzie?'

Kate nodded.

'Go to work, Kate.'

'What does Ryan say?'

'He's been on to the IO. The IO's a bit startled. It's unprecedented, apparently. But he's getting on to my guv'nor now. If my guv'nor goes for it he'll ring me. Then it'll be settled.'

'How can they spare you?'

He gave her a look. 'I've got leave due. And luckily we've just closed a case. And I'm more dispensable than you are.'

''Fraid not. The show will go on with or without me. There are probably thirty actresses out of work at this moment who could play Rosalind as well as me.'

'Go to work.'

She went into the kitchen. Sarah and Lizzie sat at the table. Lizzie held Sarah's hand. Sarah said, 'I'm staying, Kate.'

Kate smiled at her. 'Good. Shall I phone the pottery for you?'

'No, I'll do it.' She went to the living room to phone.

Kate said, 'What can I do, Lizzie?'

Lizzie did not look at her or reply. Bright came in shoving down the aerial on his mobile. Lizzie looked at him as a dog looks at its beloved master. 'I'm on the case,' he said.

Lizzie covered her face with her hands.

'I'll be at the station for an hour or so probably. And this is my mobile number if you need me.' He wrote it on the kitchen message board. The previous message had been written by Maisie: *Mum. We need bread and milk.*

Lizzie said, 'Thank you.'

Going out of the front door he said to Kate, 'Go to work.'

'You seem to have learned that line. You're delivering it quite well. Could you move on to the next one now?'

'I'll call you later. At the theatre.' Before he was down the steps he was on his mobile again. She heard: 'Permission to pursue this line of investigation...'

She sat round the house. She hoovered. She washed up. Lizzie ignored her. Sarah tried to compensate by making conversation. In the afternoon she went to the theatre.

257

33

BRIGHT GOES HIS OWN WAY

'Bright, we have the stations watched, the motorways, the ferries. Feckin' Eurostar. Coach stations. The guy did a runner.'

'I need to get in the house. Question the mother.'

'It's no use questioning the mother. She doesn't speak.'

'And I'd like to take Helen Goldie with me.'

'You're supposed to be helping us, Bright.'

'A-ha.'

'Hear you're a good interviewer. Question Dave Fowler for me first.'

'Can't do that.'

'Why not?'

'Couldn't be objective, mate. Friend of the family.'

'Little gobshite.'

'Who? Me or him?'

'Take your pick.'

'I'll take Goldilocks. To see Mother Bear.'

'Get the hell out and get back here for the briefing at five.'

Bright sprinted to the incident room.

A plump woman in navy blue opened the door and let them in. 'She's sleeping just at the moment.'

'We'll wait.'

The hallway gleamed with the same civilised brilliance as yesterday. Was it yesterday? No. The day before. Seemed a year ago. The flowers were still alive, twisted stems, feathery ruffs, purple, crimson, ultramarine, scarlet, faces with hairy grasping black middles. 'Are they anenomes?' Helen asked.

The woman said, 'Enemies? Who?'

'Er – no – the flowers.'

'Anemones,' John Bright said.

'I thought you meant Mrs Leighton and her son. Enemies, I thought you said.'

'*Are* they enemies?' Bright said.

'Well, she looks frightened if you mention him.'

'Frightened of him or frightened for him?'

'Oh. I don't know. I can't tell.'

'But you thought Helen said enemies.'

But the nurse thought she had said enough. 'Wait in here, please. I'll let you know when she wakes up.'

Bright took out a hankie and slid open drawers in the sideboard: perfectly arranged canteens of cutlery, napkins, cruets. In the desk perfectly arranged wedges of writing paper, envelopes, folders of bills paid on

259

time. The signature on the bills was not Mark's. Bright presumed it was the mother's. The initial was E. Cheque-book stubs showed only the payments of these bills, no other items. Mark's stuff must be elsewhere in the house, in his own quarters. Helen, on watch at the door, signalled the return of the nurse. Bright pocketed the hankie and stood at the window.

'She's just woken up. She's a nervous type. Don't upset her, will you?'

'Don't worry.' Helen was conciliatory. 'We'll be careful.' She let Bright go ahead into the room. She murmured to the nurse, 'What actually is the matter with her, do you know?'

The nurse made a face. 'Well, she doesn't get out of bed. Her legs appear to be paralysed. There's the most amazing arrangements. She's got a commode and she can lever herself out on to that. She has a Teasmade thing and an electric ring and a wheelchair. So she's not confined to bed. She can get about.'

'But only on this floor?'

'That's right. Not much of a life, is it?' The nurse was settling in for a good old chin-wag. Helen smiled and slipped into the room after Bright.

The curtains did not quite meet. A stiletto of sunshine sliced between them and cut across the bed. But the room had a rosy dimness. The colours were faded and dim too, the worn Persian carpet, the soft Indian cotton quilt, the curtains themselves a rosy velvet faded in strips by the sun.

Mark Leighton's mother sat supported by pillows. She wore a pale grey fine jersey top with a silk scarf at the neck. She had a noble face, pale indoor skin. She was younger than either of them had imagined. No more than forty-five. She must have had Mark when she was very young.

She shrank back when Helen came in. 'It's okay,' Bright said. 'This is Helen. She's a friend of mine. I was just saying to Mrs Leighton—'

The woman shook her hand in a shooing motion to correct him.

'I'm sorry – Miss Leighton – she must have been only a girl when Mark was born.'

'I was a child. I was a schoolgirl. I was seduced by the father of my dearest friend while a guest in his house. I lost everything. I lost all my friends. I lost my family. I lost everything.' She recited this like a litany.

'But you gained your son,' Bright said.

A strange expression crossed the woman's face. She held the quilt with both hands, drawing it closer to her chin.

'Where is Mark now, Miss Leighton?'

Helen couldn't believe the way his nasal South London croak transformed itself into a catlike purr. This frightened weird woman seemed to trust him. But not that much. 'Has he gone?' she said.

'He's gone, but he hasn't told us where. Is there somewhere he goes when he goes away?'

She whispered, 'We have a little flat in London.'

'A-ha, I know. He hasn't gone there.'

'I don't know where it is he goes. Mark is very good to me. Very good.'

'A-ha. I know that, I can see that. He's a good son. When do you expect him back?'

'Back?'

'Did he tell you when he's coming home?'

'No, no. He never says. I'm all right here. You see I have everything I need.'

The room was wonderfully equipped, a small fridge, a pretty little sink and cupboard, the simple cooking arrangements.

'For a few days, yes.'

'Oh, I'm never alone for longer than a few days. I have never been.'

'I believe you have a daughter in Ireland.'

'In Ireland?'

'That's what Mark said.'

'Is she in Ireland?'

'He didn't tell you?'

'I didn't think she was so far away.'

'Doesn't she keep in touch with you?'

'She comes to see me.'

'Often?'

'Not often, no.' The woman's voice was mournful.

'Don't her and Mark get on?'

The woman looked bewildered for a moment. 'We miss her,' she said.

'But you've got her address?'

'No.'

'You don't have your daughter's address? You don't write to her? She doesn't write?'

Miss Leighton stared at him all this time, not responding to the questions in any way, as though trying to work out what they might mean.

'Did you quarrel with her? How many years ago? What happened?'

Miss Leighton's expression didn't change. But her eyes changed their focus so that though they seemed to rest on Bright's face as before, in fact they looked inward or far off. He was not going to get an answer, he could see that. He was stumped. He squinted at Helen fast then away with an expression that almost made her laugh aloud. He said, 'Could we have a look at Mark's room? Would that be okay by you?'

She looked away a moment towards the window. A hiatus. They waited. It was not clear whether she would bother to reply. Or even whether she had heard. Then she said, 'Yes. I think you may,' in a voice that sounded as though she had leapt a chasm.

'Where is it, Miss Leighton?'

'Nurse?'

The nurse's head came round the door, looking for trouble. 'Yes?'

'Will you show these people Mark's room?'

The nurse looked nonplussed. 'I don't know where it is.'

'It is on the floor above. Will you show them to it?'

Only the upper classes, Bright thought, could give people orders in quite that way, make their wishes clear without saying a word that could cause offence. The order was: accompany these people and keep an eye on them so they don't overstep the mark or steal the silver. The nurse was not accustomed to this mode of address. It took time for the penny to drop. 'Oh yes,' she said at last. 'Of course. All right.'

This was a narrower staircase but graceful. A long window on the half-landing gave them the whole city and the hills around and the river shining and winding here and there. The shimmer of heat over the distance. Helen said, 'Wow.'

'Not bad, is it?' Bright stood a moment near her and smelled a light perfume. She turned her face to him and he moved on up. There were three rooms up here, a bathroom at the head of the stairs and two rooms interconnecting by double doors.

Fitted coir carpet. White walls. Narrow bed in the back room. White bed cover. White curtains on all windows. Ikea desk, in the front room, lap-top computer, good laser printer. Apart from the computer, with closed lid, the desk top was clear. No papers, notebooks, photos, pens. Both rooms were obsessively neat.

Bright said to the nurse, 'The son has gone missing. I'm going to have to search the drawers. She said it was okay. I just want you to make sure we don't do anything out of order. Right?'

'Oh.' She was worried and reassured in one. 'Yes. Very well then.'

'You're a witness, you see, that Miss Leighton gave us permission and that we don't overstep the mark.'

'Yes.'

'No pun intended.'

The nurse looked blank and again Helen felt a desire to laugh. For some reason Bright cheered her up. She knew he was in a state about the missing girl, but she could see that here, doing something about it, doing his job, he was in his element. She could see he had this finesse about him that wasn't like any of the other coppers she'd worked with up to now. And then, watching him, his hands had this precision and delicacy, the way they went through things—

'Come here, Helen.'

Startled, she went across to him. He held open the pine chest of drawers: one drawer socks, one vests, one underpants, one sweaters. Neatly lined with white paper. The cupboard held shirts on hangers, jeans on hangers, jackets on hangers. The upper shelf had two travel bags. Bright lifted them down. They zipped them open, felt inside. Nothing at all, not even an old plane ticket or gum wrapper. They replaced them carefully, Bright standing on a chair and feeling across the whole shelf just in case: lined also, and clean. Under the bed, not even a scrap of fluff. 'Clean guy,' Bright said to the nurse in passing. 'Unusual.'

'Most men...' the nurse said, and rolled her eyes.

'A-ha. Bit funny, you think?'

'Well, not for me to say. But he is a mother's boy, isn't he? You can see the way he takes care of her.'

'A-ha.' While the nurse talked he had started on the desk drawers. One side two filing cabinet drawers, the other four ordinary small drawers. 'You take that side,' he said to Helen. She opened a small drawer. 'Surprise surprise,' he groaned: neatly stacked paper, envelopes, pens, pencils, instruction manuals for the computer, the software, the printer. 'Don't miss anything though.' He was warning her.

He went through the files. No bills with

266

Mark's signature. Nothing with his handwriting. A receipt or two, for clothes or computer stuff, all paid in cash. No credit card receipts. No cheque-book. No cheque-book stubs. He put those on one side. No address book. No diary. No photographs. A letter informing him he had got a job with the social services department. A letter saying they were transferring him to another department. This letter friendly in tone and signed by Mr Holt. Alison's father Mr Holt. No letters from the sister or from any family member or friend. Some theatre programmes. Bright stopped dead. Helen felt him stop breathing.

A picture of Kate. The programme for *Hedda Gabler.* Bright went through the others. Kate's Mask Play. The programme for the Bristol Old Vic Studio and also for the Donmar Warehouse where the play moved to in London. Kate. Maisie. Dave. Maisie. Mr Holt. Alison. Maisie. Alison. The guy had left his story here. The bare bones but a story. It was like he'd left it on purpose. This was the story he wanted to tell. Was that right? Was Bright being too clever, thinking this way?

The rest of the damn drawer was empty, nothing slipped out of a file, no photos. Nothing. He opened the lower drawer. White as the driven snow. Virgin. Zilch. He stood up and looked round. One bookshelf.

Mostly plays: Becket, Chekhov, Pinter, Shakespeare, Shaw, and some Bright had never heard of, foreign names, in strict alphabetical order, naturally. He dutifully opened them and shook them out, one by one, not expecting results. 'Thank Christ there's only one shelf.' And there behind a book by a geezer called Grotowski, stood three photographs.

Bright picked up the photographs and looked at them. He said to the nurse, 'I'll be taking these. With his mother's permission of course. Right?'

'Oh. Yes, Well, fine.'

'Get copies. I don't know how many. A lot. Ryan'll sign the order.' He was on his way out of the incident room.

'Where are you going now?'

'Why?'

'Don't I get to come?'

He looked at her. His mask look. The unfocused squint. She suddenly knew he liked her. She hadn't been sure before. She usually was sure, to her fingertips. It was intriguing not to be sure. She took a risk: 'Would you like to have a drink tonight? Forget all this?'

'No.'

Oops. She'd got it wrong. 'Oh. Sorry.'

'It's okay. I'm off the booze, that's all.'

She knew this was not the reason. But

there was no use arguing. He turned fast and went, with the file of evidence from the Leighton house in his hand.

He slapped the file on to Ryan's desk. 'This is the story, Ryan! He is connected to every area of this case.'

Ryan slowly finished filling an interview form. Slowly pulled the file to him and opened it. Sighed heavily. Slowly turned over the items one by one. Theatre programmes from four shows featuring Kate. A snap of Kate at the microphone in a radio studio holding a script. The two letters from Desmond Holt. Three pictures. The first two portraits. The third a Polaroid: grass, and sitting on the grass Dave with two young girls. Standing, gesticulating and laughing, a young man, slim, curly brown longish hair, jeans and torn sweater.

'Mark Leighton,' Bright said. 'Helen Goldie gives a positive ID.'

'Mr Guru Man Dave Fowler?'

'Looks like they were friends, right? Dave has totally forgotten him. No recollection now.'

'Says Dave.'

'No reason for him to lie.'

'No reason that we know of.'

'Okay, Ryan. You show this colour snap to Dave. See if he remembers the guy.'

'Oh, I will, I will.'

'And Desmond Holt. Look! Look at the letter. I told you what Holt said. They used to be friends too. Then Holt virtually sacked him. Both blokes reject him. He abducts Holt's daughter. He abducts Dave's daughter. Mark Leighton is giving us the story on a plate.'

'You're the one giving us the story.'

'What's that mean?'

'Too feckin' clever by half.'

'So what? We don't have another story that holds up.'

'It's no better than my Mr Guru Man theory.'

'The boy *is* clever. That's why you've got nothing on him, can't trace him. He's cleverer than us.'

'Speak for yourself.'

'I am doing.'

'What's this with your actress friend?'

'He doesn't know her personally. He's just a theatre buff.'

'Unless *she's* forgotten him as well.' Ryan laid on the sarcasm thick.

But Bright stopped pacing a moment. 'You might have something there, Ryan.'

'Well, God forbid there could be a hole in the perfect theory now.'

'Kate's connected to Maisie, for Christ's sake. Maisie's her niece. Kate's known Dave for nearly twenty years. She could have known this lad when he was friends

270

with Dave.'

'Oh, I see, right, there is no hole in the perfect theory after all.'

'Come on, Ryan. You should at least get a look at that house. The guy's seriously weird. No one keeps things that neat. There's nothing there except what he wanted us to find.'

'According to the perfect theory.'

'There's something wrong about the set-up. The mother. Everything!' Bright buzzed round the room.

Ryan got bigger, more stolid, more fixed, his eyes grey, cold, like frozen shards of winter sea. He sat back and looked at his watch. He stood up. 'Time for the briefing,' he said.

But at the briefing he passed out copies of the pictures, with Helen Goldie's description. A young DC asked was this the prime suspect.

'No.' Ryan looked at Bright. 'The prime suspect, David Fowler, is still in custody. We're processing him, as you know, at the moment on possession with intention to deal, but we are accumulating evidence. This photograph, as you see, has him with two young girls considerably younger than himself.'

'They're not missing, are they, guv?' It was Helen who asked with an innocent face.

Ryan's not so innocent face flushed purple. But he spoke with perfect control: 'Perhaps you'd like to look into that, constable.'

'Yes, guv. Okay.' She caught Bright's eye – which eye she couldn't say – and again had this wild desire to laugh.

Coming out of the briefing, Bright said, 'You be careful. Don't get carried away. You're a brave girl but don't push it. You've got no clout yet. Watch it, okay? I want you on the case.' He held her eye for only a moment – no squint, she could swear – then walked off. He said without turning round, 'See you tomorrow.'

34

RETURNS

Colum said, 'I'm pathetically grateful, though I think it'll be good for you as well as us.'

Alan Tate gave her his heavy-lidded look: 'Thank Christ you came back. We were having the horrors.'

'Who could they have got to replace you at such short notice?' Ian McLean murmured. 'Hattie Jacques?'

Rupert the Angel gave her a shy pleased brief smile.

Celia/Gemma looked wild. 'Oh God, am I glad to see you!'

She was touched by their tact and their sympathy. She was depressed and uninvolved in the proceedings.

Colum said, 'As Kate is, thank God, back with us, we'll go back to the top of the play. Let's just read it quietly to each other, scene by scene, and find out what's going on.'

At the end of the afternoon of quiet reading and quiet discussion, Kate was still uninvolved, still profoundly depressed. She felt she had contributed nothing, could contribute nothing. Wasn't really there. She said, 'Colum? I don't know if I'm doing any good here.'

'What?'

'I've no idea what's going on in Rosalind. She's like a different character in this first bit of the play. She hardly speaks.'

'That's right! That's true! I hadn't realised till this afternoon.'

'She's just – nothing. Not there. I can't do anything with it.'

'You think Shakespeare just forgot to write some lines for her or what?'

Kate was dumbstruck. An idea began to form. 'She's silent for a reason? You mean her very silence is significant?'

'Well, maybe you should think along those lines.'

'Yes.' She pondered. 'Yes...'

She walked back to Lizzie's, all her mind searching for Maisie. Everywhere she looked there was Maisie. Only it never was Maisie. Each time it was a girl who could have been Maisie but wasn't. She stopped outside Dave's place. His windows were dark. No use to ring the bell. But she did. No answer. Just the sound of the echoing: Dong dong dong, just like the last time, Maisie ringing it.

She stopped on the foot-bridge and looked into the water. Crowds of people on

274

the quay outside the Ostrich Inn. Summer dresses, shorts, young men with bare chests. A picture of Rupert the Angel in the wrestling scene came into her mind. *That's when Rosalind comes to life! Then! After she falls in love. Before that she's like a space in the world, empty. Empty like I am now. With loss. With hopeless unspeakable loss. Loss! That's it. She has lost everything – her father is banished. The man who banished him, his brother, her uncle, has taken her in after purloining all his money and land. That is,* her *father,* her *money,* her *home,* her *land, her prospects for any kind of life, married or otherwise. She is tolerated only because of the love of Celia. It's Celia who is the talkative funny confident one in this part of the play because she's in every sense 'at home'. If Rosalind betrays the loathing and rage and sorrow she feels, this villain her uncle will do something worse, bump her off, use her to attack her father. Whichever way she jumps she jumps into a trap. So she doesn't jump. She stays expressionless, betrays nothing. And she loathes her position. That's the reason for her silence. She is profoundly unhappy, powerless and stuck. Like me now. With loss. Like me now.*

Kate put her head in her hands. Her skull expanded, the way it always did with rehearsal inspiration. She felt gratitude to Colum from the bottom of her heart. Such directors are rare. The releasers, the enablers. Excitement flooded her, sizzling

275

through her veins. In spite of Maisie. In spite of Maisie's abductor. In spite of her own desperation and guilt, Kate stood flooded with excitement on the little bridge. The bridge over troubled water. That's what the play might come to mean for her. The bridge from Maisie to no Maisie.

'No.' Bright's small brown eyes speared her. 'She's alive. Never forget that. Alison was alive until the night before they found her. And there was not a mark on her. She had not been harm – physically harmed, she had not been – attacked, she had not been – See? And she stayed alive for three weeks. And the search for Maisie started right away, in these cases even a day can make a difference. Look.' He took them to the window where a helicopter circled low over Totterdown and disappeared behind rooftops in the direction of Bedminster. 'The heat-seeking camera. I'm not saying we've got three weeks or anything like that. But Maisie's got staying power, know what I mean? More than Alison maybe?'

Kate looked at Lizzie. For the first time she saw a little hope. Quickly doused because hope was more painful than the effort at acceptance of loss. Lizzie looked at Sarah.

'Yes,' Sarah said. 'Allie was more, like, soft.'

Lizzie cleared her throat. 'Compliant,' she said.

'The house-to-house has come up with nothing. Nobody saw her. Nobody saw anyone come here.'

'Come here?' Lizzie sat up. 'You think someone came here? But she went out. Someone grabbed her in a car.'

'That's how you see it?' he said. 'Why would she go out when she said she wouldn't?'

Lizzie shook her head.

'No one phoned,' he said. 'We checked the phone calls. Someone persuaded her to go out. They had to come here to do that. And they must have given her a good reason. No?'

Kate said, 'Yes.'

Sarah nodded, blind faith in anything he might say.

Lizzie, in a tangled collision of fear, rage, loss, hope, despair, lifted her shoulders and shook her head.

'And it was someone she knew,' Bright said.

Lizzie stood up. 'It was not Dave. Don't you tell me it was Dave.'

Bright moved his hands to calm her. 'It was not Dave.'

'They've got Dave.' Lizzie's fervid eyes. 'They won't look for the real person. It will be the cause. It will be the cause.'

'Sit down, Lizzie.' His nasal South London voice took on a hard metallic ring. 'I'm looking for the real perpetrator. And so are the investigating team. And we'll find him.'

Shocked, Lizzie sat.

'Now listen. It was someone Maisie knew. She would not have gone with a stranger. And it was someone with a convincing message. From you, or from Dave, or maybe from Kate. Someone who knows you, or Dave or Kate. See what I mean? This is the way we've got to think. There is no other way she would have gone out.' He waited. No one spoke. 'Now, what would be a convincing reason? One of you needed her?'

'I'd never send for her because I needed her.' Lizzie spoke with scorn. 'She'd know that.'

Kate said, 'She wouldn't know that, Lizzie.'

Lizzie's eyes darted her a snake's tongue of hate that took Kate's breath away. Then she went on calmly to Bright, 'She would go somewhere for Dave. Or for her' – indicating Kate with a slight move of her head – 'but not for me. Not once I'd told her not to go out.' She turned and glared again at Kate. Her eyes said, *Don't tell me what my daughter would say or do.* As if it were Kate who had taken Maisie away.

Kate saw now that Lizzie had always

278

resented her relationship with Maisie. Their collusion, hers and Maisie's, had hurt Lizzie. And that one kind of taking away was mirrored in this physical taking away, so that, to Lizzie, Kate had become responsible for the one as for the other. And Lizzie had concealed her pain and fury until now when all her fences were down.

Bright watched this behind his expressionless mask. In the tumbling silence he put an envelope on the table. Out of it he pulled three photographs. One was a photo booth snap for a passport. One was a blurred colour print. One was a black and white portrait, amateurishly lit, shadows crossing the face like black hands. They were all of the same person. 'This,' Bright said, 'is Mark Leighton.' He passed the pictures round.

A young man. A lovely face. Dark curling hair, looking lighter in the colour snap. The colour snap taken on grass under trees with three other people. Mark has his back to the camera but his head is turned to the side. His hair is back in a short pony tail. He is in a long sweater and jeans. He is laughing. He is standing. The other people are sitting on the grass. They are looking up at him. They are, curiously, not laughing. This gives the innocent-looking snap a sinister air. One of the people sitting on the grass is Dave. The other two are young girls.

'Do you know him? Have you seen him?'

They all study the pictures closely. They look hard. They try hard. They shake their heads.

Bright said, 'Maisie probably did.'

'Is this the–?' Lizzie stopped.

'A-ha. I'm not saying it's him. But he's the one who's done a runner.'

Sarah said, 'He looks so nice.'

'I've had these printed up and handed round. Learn him off by heart, okay? He can't stay hidden. He went off with nothing, a small bag, that's all. Unless he's...'

They all looked at Bright, waiting. He got up and went to the kitchen window. He turned round, slow. He said, 'They've been checking trains, coaches, motorways, Eurostar, ferries, they've been going long distance. The clever little bastard knew they'd do that so maybe... Maybe he's round here somewhere. And if he is round here that means maybe so is Maisie.'

35

THE SINS OF THE FATHERS

Holt came to the door looking red-eyed. He'd drunk a fair amount. 'Have you found her?'

Bright shook his head. 'No. Can I come in?'

Leading the way into the living room Holt slurred, 'Wife and kids in bed. Got be quiet.'

Bright moved a miniature fire engine and sat on the couch.

'Beer?'

'Sure.' He opened the can and drank warmish carbonated stuff.

'Why you come to see me? If you haven't found her.'

'Ryan questioned you today.'

Holt shook his head. His eyes filled up. 'Again.'

'Not nice, is it?'

'Even my wife has started to think–'

'A-ha.'

The man covered his face with his hands. Then he wiped his eyes and his face. 'And you? That what you think? I killed my beautiful daughter and now I killed her best friend? You think that, Mr Bright?'

Bright looked at him. A hard stare. No squint. No doubt about where he was looking. 'You're lying though, aren't you, mate?'

'Lying?'

'Lying.'

'No. No!'

'Oh yes you are. Not about this maybe. But about something. Your wife senses it. Just like I do.'

'No!'

'Listen, it happens to all of us one time or another. We get involved. Something goes too far. Tell the truth about this. It might help. Might clear up at least your wife's mind. Even if it's something you're ashamed of.'

Holt stood there silent then said, 'I shouldn't have invited you in.'

'Yes, you should. Listen. When I was asking you about Mark Leighton–'

'I told you the truth about that. A bit of hero worship on his part. I cooled it. He got moved to another department. That was the end of it.' A moan came out of him and his hands covered his face again. 'Oh dear Lord.'

'So what really happened? Gonna tell me?'

'Give me a minute.' Holt got up. He kept his hands over his eyes. He walked round the back of his chair. He turned and put his hands on the back of his chair. His eyes down, not looking at Bright but at his own brown hands on the chair back, he said, 'My wife mustn't know this.'

'Look, mate–'

'No. You don't understand. We're members of the Pentecostal Church. We are very serious Christians. It means something. It's not like these casual Church of England people who make the rules up as they go along.'

'Okay okay. I'm not gonna run upstairs and invite your wife down to hear this, okay?'

'But no one else must know.'

Bright groaned. 'As far as I can, I'll respect this as a confidence. Whatever you like to tell me. Okay?'

'Okay.' The man's voice had nearly deserted him. 'Well...' He folded his arms across his chest. Took a deep breath. 'After I – cooled things off with Mark, he wrote me a few letters. They were weird, man. They were like – they were like letters from a woman, you know? Well, I felt – dirty. I mean, I've never been involved in anything like that. I've never been – that way inclined. I had no idea. It never occurred to me. He was just a young man I was showing the ropes, you know?'

'A-ha. I believe you, I believe you. You still got these letters?' Bright asked this knowing

283

what the answer would be.

'Are you joking? I shredded them in the office shredder.' He spoke with disgust as though contaminated by their very touch.

'And what then? He start pestering you at work, ringing you up, what?'

Holt shook his head slowly. 'His sister came to see me.'

'His sister?'

'She came to the office.'

'The one who lives in Ireland?'

'She was visiting, she said.'

'A-ha?'

'She told me Mark was in a bad way. She told me he had a tough life, looking after the mother, all that stuff. If I would just see him. He didn't want any more than that. Just to be my friend still. All this stuff.'

'Did you agree?'

'No, I said no. I put it as nicely as I could, but I said that for his own good it would be better if he moved on. I told her he needed help. You can get help on the National Health – I don't mean for being – you know – gay or whatever, but for being so – needy. I could give her the names of several therapists and so on.' Holt stopped.

'A-ha? Go on.'

Holt sighed. He came round the chair and sat down. He rubbed his face with both hands. He said, 'I don't know if I can tell you this.'

'Oh yes, you can. It's easy once you start.'

'You don't know.'

'You fell for her.'

'What?'

'Well, didn't you?'

Holt looked at him speechless.

'You fell for each other. You had long talks about it on park benches, right? Discussing what you should do? She's betraying Mark. You're betraying your wife.'

'My wife and kids, my religion. And Mark.'

'Yeah, both his beloveds in one go.'

'You talk about it cheerfully, as if it's nothing. Something that happens every day.'

'It does, mate.'

'Not to me. Not to people like us. To people on the telly, in the soaps, in the movies, yes. But to real people? No.'

'You'd be surprised.'

'And believe me, it's nothing like the soaps. They don't tell you about the real pain.'

'What's that?'

'The lying, deceiving. Pretending. Always having to think what to say when you've always been open and clear and true. It's true love I have for my wife. Good love. And for God too. I'd stand in church with all the good people not knowing how to face my God. Come home not knowing how to face my wife. I was nearly destroyed.'

'I see.'

'I doubt if you do.'

'Well, no. So what happened? Anything happen? Between you and the sister?'

'She had problems too. She'd been seduced when she was a student. By one of her lecturers. She'd never say who he was. She'd really fallen for him. She was completely innocent. She thought it was love for life. Marriage and children. All that. Apparently she went to bed with him. He deflowered her as she put it. And then he seemed to forget her!'

'Forget her? She was still a student of his?'

'Well, she meant forget about the – incident – as he would have seen it. Just one among many, apparently. A man of no morals. When she confronted him he said he wasn't ready for the sort of commitment she had in mind!'

'A-ha.' Bright sounded weary.

'This may seem a common thing in your experience. But to God-fearing people it's not, believe me. It had destroyed this girl. So she was afraid to start another relationship. And knowing I was married and so on–'

'But?' Bright sounded even wearier.

'Don't belittle this.'

'Listen, mate, I can tell you the story. There's nothing new. You have all these secret meetings, lying about where you've been and who with. You can't think about anything else. You smell her everywhere you go, like she's on your skin? Even though you haven't done anything yet, you've done plenty in your mind. And eventually one night things get a little bit out of hand, in your car? Up on the Downs? Over the other side of the Gorge, Leigh Woods maybe, less close to home? Down a lane in the back of the car? Or at her place? Anyway, you do it. The big bad deed. Live up to your expectations, did it? Yeah, probably. All that guilt and fear dresses it up a bit, doesn't it? Makes it more exciting than between your God-fearing marital sheets. Okay, so you done it. What next?'

Holt stared, dumbstruck, offended but astounded beyond offence. 'Is this really so common, so ordinary? Don't tell me that. I'm ashamed enough.'

'Nah. It's different for all of us. But the story's roughly the same.'

Holt closed his eyes. 'It has never seemed a common experience to me.'

'So what happened next? She run screaming rape? She threaten to tell your wife and insist on marriage? She get pregnant?'

Holt gave a faint smile. 'I never saw her again.'

'What?'

287

'Oh? I have managed to surprise you?'

'You never saw her again? By mutual agreement or what?'

'She wrote to me. She said she couldn't break up a marriage. And she couldn't betray her brother. She had done enough damage. It had to stop now before we destroyed more lives. Not to try to get in touch with her.'

'Still got the letter? Need I ask?'

'I kept it for months. I threw it in the river in small pieces only a few weeks ago.'

'Scattering the ashes.'

'Precisely so.'

'And did you try to get in touch with her?'

'I couldn't. The only way I knew to reach her was through her brother. That was out of the question. I didn't have a number for her. I assumed she had gone back to Ireland.'

'Directory Enquiries?'

'I tried, yes.'

'A-ha.'

'I didn't know which part of Ireland. There was no trace. There were several M. Leightons. But none of them was she.'

'What's the M stand for?'

'Margaret.' A frisson of pain passed over his face when he said the name.

'A-ha.' Bright pondered a minute. 'Did she look like him?'

'Like Mark? Well … yes, I suppose in a way

she did. But she was so unlike him in manner, in the way she thought and spoke. She had a lovely voice.'

Bright felt an inner shiver. Millie's voice. His mother: *Kate has a lovely voice. All actresses have lovely voices, ma.*

Holt said, 'He said she had a lovely face. God in his mercy lent her grace.'

'What?'

'The Lady of Shalott. Tennyson.'

'Oh. Poetry. Yeah. A-ha.'

Holt said, 'I was punished. I went on longing for her. More than before. And now I have been truly punished. By the loss of my beloved daughter. Let's hope He has lent her grace. Oh Christ, Oh Christ.' Holt bent his head and began to sob.

Bright said, 'Have you got a picture of her? Margaret, I mean.'

Holt shook his head, blowing his nose.

Bright stood up. Looked down on the dignified man so distraught. He said, 'You'll feel freer now you've told someone. People always do.'

'He won't.'

Bright looked round. The voice had come from the doorway. Holt's wife stood there in her dressing-gown. Holt raised his wet face. He said, 'Leonie.'

She said to Bright, 'I thought it was something worse. It's a relief actually.' She didn't sound relieved. Or as though she would find it easy to forgive. She sounded as hard as a woman can who has lost her daughter and thought her husband had something to do with the death.

Bright said, 'The coppers knew you were hiding something. They knew you were guilty of something. You can't hide these things if you're not a villain. If you'd told them all this, you'd have been off the hook weeks ago.'

Holt said nothing. He gazed at his wife as though an unforgiving God were about to speak through her.

Bright said, 'I'll let myself out.'

Ryan said, 'Told you he was hiding something. What do you bet it was Dave Fowler seduced the sister?'

'Give Mark a motive, wouldn't it, Ryan?'

'What, he takes revenge on two men for seducing his sister, by killing their daughters? Come off it, Bright.'

'Anyway it's more like this Margaret was taking the revenge on Holt for rejecting her brother. She seduced him if you like, then left him high and dry. The more I see of it the more I think this Margaret's a significant factor.'

'Fowler can't remember Mark. But then Mark's a bloke. Not the Guru's primary interest. Maybe he'll remember the sister better.'

36

AIDES-MÉMOIRE

'Well, Dave, remember a Margaret Leighton in your trawl through the student population of this city?'

'Margaret Leighton, like the actress?'

Ryan was nonplussed for a moment. 'I guess – yes. Though I don't imagine she shares any other characteristics with the lady. You remember a student of that name?'

Dave tried to concentrate. Miles of students like those fold-out paper dolls stretched back nearly twenty years, dancing in front of his eyes, featureless. He shook his head, despair and exasperation. His hair, normally clean and shining in waves, was lank and greasy, tied back in a knot. Ryan wanted to take the shears to it. And not just to his hair, either, the ponce. 'All one to you, are they, Fowler? Don't even remember their names?'

'I've been teaching for seventeen years. That's an awful lot of students. I can't be expected to recall every one. Was she exceptional, this Margaret Leighton?'

'No. You seduced her. I wouldn't say that

was exceptional, would you? You sick bastard.'

Dave, arms tightly crossed on his chest, stared hard at a spot on the wall. He must not allow this man to shake him. He must keep his thoughts where this man could not reach. He said, 'When is this supposed to have happened?'

'We're about to find out. We think at least six years back, if not more.'

'You asked me about another Leighton? A male student of mine. Am I supposed to have seduced him too? What is your theory exactly?'

'And you still don't remember him either.'

'I'm afraid not.'

'Here.' Ryan thrust the blurred snap under Dave's nose. 'Recognise anyone there?'

Dave took it. His fingers trembled, Ryan noted with pleasure. He studied the picture. For a long time. Ryan crossed his big legs, wagged his big feet. But he didn't speak, let the Guru take his time.

Dave said, 'Oh God.'

'What?'

'I remember him. This guy with the pony tail, is that him?'

'What about him?'

'He was my student. He was doing English and theatre studies. He fancied himself as an actor. He had some talent, but there was something weird in his nature.'

'*You* thought *he* was weird?'

Dave closed his eyes, praying for patience. 'He couldn't form relationships. He talked *at* people. *When* he talked. He'd be silent then talk in a burst. And it was way-out rap, full of references to all sorts of esoteric stuff that the other students hadn't heard of and most of the lecturers hadn't either.'

'Showed you up, did he? You wouldn't like that, would you?'

'It was disconnected. It didn't add up. It made people uneasy. You can see here in this picture he's on one of his riffs. I can't recall what it was about. But you can see he thinks it's funny and the rest of us don't; we're disturbed by it. I don't remember this specific occasion. It was one of a number.'

Dave's long fine hand came up to his face. He brushed back his hair. Ryan almost winced watching him. He'd rarely felt such antipathy, even with the worst villains he'd had to deal with and he'd dealt with a fair few. 'Well?'

Dave said in a flattened voice, 'He might have a motive. For harming me. He might have two motives. He failed his degree. Because I gave him low marks.'

'You're kidding me.'

'I assure you not, Mr Ryan.'

'And the other convenient memory return?'

293

Dave said, 'I rejected his sister.'

'Rejected,' Ryan said, sardonic, 'in what sense?'

'I turned down an offer of marriage from her.'

'What?' Ryan laughed in spite of himself. 'Now you are definitely having me on.'

Dave looked sad. 'No. She wasn't a student of mine. She wasn't a student at all as far as I know. She turned up at my place, brought by someone else, no idea who. Introduced herself. Apologised for her brother. Said he was a difficult character. She used to hang around after the others had left, waylay me on the way to work, that kind of thing. I realised she had a bit of a crush. It's a hazard of the job, nothing to do with one's personal qualities.'

'Really.' Even more sardonic. 'And?'

'I met her in the street one day. Got off my bike to walk with her because she said she had something important to ask me. That's what it was.'

'Would you marry her?'

'Yes.' Dave didn't rise to the sceptical rudeness of Ryan's tone.

'Why? She was pregnant with triplets or what?'

Dave took some time to answer.

'Well, come on, Fowler.'

'She was pregnant, yes. The man had abandoned her. He was married. She couldn't tell her mother, who was an invalid. Or her brother, who she thought was rather disturbed.'

'And what did you do?'

'I said I couldn't marry her. I was opposed to marriage.'

'Ach Jesusmaryandjoseph–'

'But I would give her some money if she needed it, either to go away somewhere or–'

'Or what? A quick private abortion, that it?'

'I offered her money if she needed it. She looked at me as if she would like to kill me.'

'Well, it wouldn't seem much to the likes of you, would it?'

'As a matter of fact I am not in favour of abortion, on all kinds of grounds, religion not being one of them. The mental health of the mother for instance, afterwards. Certain women just can't handle it. Anyway, these problems arise all the time with students. I was not responsible for her. I assumed she had sorted it out. I was too busy to think of her. Yes, if you like, Mr Ryan, I'm an unmitigated shit. So are most men. So what.'

'Don't take that tone with me, my lad.'

Dave shook his head. He said, 'Do you think that this could have given Mark Leighton a reason to take revenge on me? It seems far-fetched. But he was disturbed. He wasn't normal. I assure you he wasn't.

295

Where is he now?'

A heavy silence. Dave looked from Ryan to Bright. He addressed Bright for the first time: 'You met him, you know.'

'I met Mark Leighton? When?'

'At my place. You know the night you came with Kate and – and the girls – after the opening of *Hedda Gabler?*'

'A-ha.'

'The girls–' Dave's voice gave out. He gasped with pain. He controlled himself and said on a breath, 'The girls danced. We all stopped to watch. It was so beautiful.' Tears dropped down his face. He ignored them. 'He was – Mark was – standing next to you.'

Bright looked at Ryan and back to Dave. He remembered the young man. Enraged, ravaged at the notion of what the world could do to innocence. Their brief conversation. 'That was him?' he said.

'That was Mark.' Dave's tears had stopped. 'I hadn't seen him since his student days. He arrived with some other people. Just before you and Kate and–'

'A-ha.' Bright took the picture off the table and studied it. He shook his head. 'I can't see any resemblance.' Ryan handed him the portrait picture with the atmospheric shadows. Again Bright shook his head. 'He didn't look like this. I mean, I guess if you knew the guy you'd see it. But I damn well can't.'

296

Dave said, 'You met Margaret too.'

Bright and Ryan looked at him. There was a long pause.

Dave spoke to Bright: 'It was the night Lizzie came.'

'I was out of my skull.' Bright looked sick. 'I can't remember her.'

Dave said, 'I hadn't seen her for years. Not since–'

Bright thrust the pictures into Ryan's big fist. 'Ryan, I got to talk to you.'

Ryan managed to tangle his big foot with the leg of Dave's chair. The chair almost toppled and Dave with it. Ryan walked on without looking back, slamming the door behind him.

Outside, Bright said, 'You've got enough circumstantial now. Mark Leighton is our perpetrator. We've got to find him. He's got to be brought in.'

'We'd better find the whereabouts of this Margaret.'

'Mark might have gone to her, you think?'

'No trace of him entering the Republic but you never know. Hasn't the mother got the address?'

'She says not. We couldn't get anything out of her.'

'Try again. Ireland's not that big. But it's a great place to hide.'

'Are we in touch with the Irish police?'

'They don't like to hand people over to the Garda, over there. They believe in a Higher Justice with its own rules.'

'He's motivated. He hasn't finished with these people yet. He's still got an agenda. To do with Dave. Maybe–' Bright hesitated. 'Maybe even to do with Kate Creech.'

Ryan folded his arms across his chest. It was hard for him: giving up Dave Fowler as his prime suspect. He glowered at the floor, then from under his eyebrows at Bright.

'I don't think he's left the country.' Bright waited.

Ryan said, 'The house-to-house in Totter-down gave us nothing.'

'We didn't have a picture then. We didn't know what we were looking for.'

Ryan's beefy hand rubbed over his rough hair, down over the big forehead, the boxer's nose, and covered his mouth. He growled.

Bright said, 'He knew we'd find this stuff. He's giving us the story–'

'Stop saying that.'

'Okay okay. Look. We've got the revenge angle, right? On Holt for his sister, now on Dave, also for his sister. But I'm telling you, this bloke is hung up on innocence. He's got this thing– You know, Ryan, that night when I talked to him? That night could have been it. You know. The time and the place when he flipped. When he decided to take Alison. Take both of them. Maybe it was just

298

coincidence it was Alison first. It could have been Maisie first if it had worked out that way. Jesus, Ryan, I was there. And he knew I was a copper! How did he know that? He'd know that because of my connection with Kate. That case was in all the papers. All that Body in the Bath stuff. He's followed her career. Jesus, Ryan–'

'You not telling me he's going after Kate Creech next.'

'I've got to remember what he said to me that night. He didn't like the blokes looking at the little girls dancing. He was beside himself. We had this argument about innocence. He said they'd get – what was it – sucked in or something, something like that – sucked in, corrupted.' Bright stopped and met Ryan's eyes. For the first time the big man was listening. 'Christ, Ryan. He's killing little girls to stop them growing up?'

'To stop them getting corrupted like his sister.'

'Not just his sister, Ryan. Some upper class git seduced his mother when she was – ah Christ – fifteen.'

37

A MOTHER'S WORD

That afternoon posters were printed and placed in post offices, shops, bus shelters, railway stations. Mark Leighton's picture appeared on the front page of every newspaper, and on every television screen. In addition to that, a battalion of uniformed police distributed leaflets to every house in Totterdown, Windmill Hill and Bedminster.

All Mark's clients were questioned again. They hadn't seen him for a week or two. They were mostly vague about times. They liked him. They were fond of him. Most of them said he wouldn't hurt a soul. But nobody had seen him.

Bright said, 'Get the uniforms to report any house they couldn't gain entry to. Get them to explore every empty property. If they couldn't gain entry once, they go back again. Twice no entry, they gotta get in some other way.'

'And leave me to pick up all the complaints?'

'You'll find a way, Ryan. Come to that, I'll

find a way.'

'In the meantime I'm keeping my hands on Fowler. A suspect in the hand...'

'Margaret? I remember her!' Lizzie's face took on some life. 'She said she'd heard about me from Dave. She seemed like an old friend of his.'

'She didn't say anything about where she lived or–?'

Lizzie shook her head. 'I can't remember! I mean, it was the first time I'd been to Dave's, and we were thinking about Alison and–' She swallowed and her face settled back into grey fatigue. 'And how to get Maisie through it. I wasn't noticing much. I just thought – you know – another of his girls. Though she seemed different. Not his type. Brighter. Nicer. Dependable. Sort of – good.'

'Where is your daughter, Miss Leighton?'

She held the bedcover up to her chin. Terrified.

'Miss Leighton?' Goldie's soft Bristol voice soothed the woman's terror. 'Listen, it's okay. It's nothing you've done. And nothing Margaret's done. She's not in trouble, honestly. But she might know something that can help us.'

'Help you?'

'Well, to find Mark.'

'What has Mark done?'

Goldie looked at Bright, helpless: What do we tell her?

Bright left the room, talked to the nurse on the landing. 'What sort of state is she in?'

'She's a nervous woman.'

'Yeah but how nervous? What's her medical condition? Is she gonna have a heart attack or a nervous breakdown if we give her bad news?'

'She's on tranquillising medication. Apart from that she's physically quite strong. It's just she can't walk. She seems to function fine otherwise.'

'So it's okay if I give her some bad news?'

'Is her son dead or something?'

''Fraid not. As far as we know.'

'Miss Leighton? You still haven't heard from Mark, right?'

'No.'

'And you don't know where he might be?'

She shook her head.

'And he hasn't done this before? Run off, left no address?'

She shook her head.

'Miss Leighton, we suspect that he is implicated in the death of Alison Holt.'

Her eyes round, she began to gasp. Goldie gave her water. She drank. She said, 'Oh oh oh oh,' on a rising scale.

Bright said, 'That's enough.'

302

Shocked, she stopped. Put a trembling hand to her mouth.

'Now listen. I said we suspect; we *don't know*. But he can only clear himself if he comes forward. We also suspect him of abducting another girl, Maisie Creech.'

The woman closed her eyes. Her head flopped back on the pillows. She moaned.

Bright said, 'Stop it. That won't help. We don't want this girl to die. She's fifteen years old.'

'Fifteen,' the woman whispered.

'That's right, Miss Leighton. The age you were when–'

'Yes.' A sigh like wind in grass.

'Is it possible that–'

She began to nod, hands over her mouth. 'Yes,' she said. 'Yes, yes. Oh yes.'

Goldie looked at Bright. Bright said, '–that Mark might have–?'

'Yes.'

'Why do you think this, Miss Leighton?'

'I can't say–'

'You know but you can't say?'

She nodded, rigid little nods like a bird.

'You know for certain he's done it?'

A sighing groan: 'No. No. But...'

'But what? Come on, Miss Leighton. Help us.'

Something seemed to stiffen in the woman. 'He cares too much.'

'About what happened to his sister?'

Again she gripped the bedcover and pulled it up to her chin. She didn't speak.

'Would his sister be harbouring him, Miss Leighton? That's the thing. If he went to her would she take him in?'

She blinked. This seemed to mean assent.

'Are you sure you don't know where she is? Are you sure you do not have an address for her? Are you sure?'

Minute nods of the head.

'If you are lying, Miss Leighton, you will be prosecuted. I know it's hard. I know you want to protect your child. Your children. That's natural. But another child is in imminent danger of losing her life. Her life. Not her virginity. Or her innocence as your Mark would call it. Her life. At fifteen years of age. If you know, you've got to tell us. Where is Margaret?'

'Lost,' she said. 'Gone. A long time ago.'

'And no address? You're sure?'

She shook her head steadily from side to side. 'My fault. I favoured Mark. Margaret went away.'

'If either of them gets in touch with you, you will get in touch with us. Right away. And get an address before they hang up. If you can. Do you understand?'

'Yes.'

'Do you agree? Do you promise me?'

'He won't. He won't get in touch.'

'Stay with her. The IO's sending

304

reinforcements. They'll search the house. Don't let them frighten her. You search this room yourself. Keep the nurse with you as witness. I gotta go.'

38

EXCERPT FROM A DIARY

viii

It's rather wonderful to be free of mother at last. Margaret has been free for a long time. But I have not until now. It's as though Alison was my payment to mother. Her death has freed me from my obligations. I don't like to think that Alison's life was some kind of payment to mother. But maybe in some sense it was? It is mother who has always stressed the primacy of innocence. The wanton destruction of a young girl's innocence the Great Offence. *"'T'were better a millstone"* and all that. And she herself the living example. Always in my sight. But now I have actually lived out my duty, I am at last autonomous. At last I can act alone. For my own ideals. For my own beliefs. Ironic, isn't it? At last, I say. And it is truly at last. I don't think I've got long.

If I were not prepared to give my own life, it would not be fair to have taken someone else's. It would not be right. The only way I could justify it would be if I were to continue my crusade. I would have to be alive, I think you would agree, to do that.

It is the suitability, the perfection almost, of these two deaths, that makes them so unutterably satisfactory. Each of their fathers had ruined the innocence of those younger and purer than themselves. Neither of these fathers deserved his daughter. I do not take the lives of the girls for this reason, naturally. But it satisfies me beyond all wonder that the preserving of these two innocent souls for eternity should punish their guilty fathers their whole livelong lives.

Their mothers? Strange how I barely think of their mothers. Well, their mothers should have taken better care of them. Lock Up Your Daughters. Lock them up. You don't deserve them otherwise.

Maisie is proving not quite such a delightful companion as I had hoped. She refuses to speak to me. I have been unfailingly pleasant to her. I have made it clear that I like her very much. Admire her. Respect her. As soon as she was ensconced in the Dead Room, I removed her gag. I expected the torrent of incoherent words I had got from Alison, begging, pleading, appealing to my better nature, appealing to my worse nature. Yes, Alison even offered herself carnally to me. But in such an innocent simple way, poor child, it only increased her innocence in my eyes. It naturally did not help her cause.

But Maisie remains silent. She looks at me with a cold gaze. She does not answer me when I speak. I do not know if this is fear disguised, or simple loathing. It looks like bitter cold hatred and could hurt me badly if I allowed it to penetrate. I smile and make it clear that I am waiting, that's all.

I feel stupid now for not understanding right away. It came to me last night. I had taken in her food. A deliciously tempting little salad: avocado, cherry tomatoes, green pepper, spring onions – my version of guacamole, very pretty. It always tempted mother. Maisie said nothing. She never took her eyes off me. 'How are you feeling, Maisie? Is there anything I can get for you to make you more comfortable? A book to read perhaps? I have some books.' I listed a few of my authors. She watched me. My voice was thin. I began to think she couldn't hear me. I explained about the Dead Room. She watched me coldly while I did so. I must say my heart began to fail me. As did my voice after a while. 'You see, Maisie,' I said, 'I can't allow you to be heard, shouting or making noise of any kind. You understand I'm sure.'

Of course when I left the room, shutting the second door behind me, it came to me, the reason for her hostility: Alison! She knows me to be responsible for the death of her friend. Which in a sense I am. But only in a sense. Alison was brought kindly and skilfully to acquiesce in her own death. As I hope will Maisie be. But I can see Maisie is a more difficult task. A tougher character. She doesn't look it, with her butterfly-frail appearance. But she has great strength. You must be proud of her.

She ate the salad. But not till I left her alone. As I discovered this morning when I took in her breakfast. She has a hearty appetite, by the way, doesn't she? I kept her company a while. I don't always like to be alone. I sat and wrote my diary in her presence. I wanted her to ask, What are you writing? or Are you a writer? or Are you writing about me? To show some interest. But she did not. She ate her breakfast, as best she could with her wrists bound together, licked the spoon, and threw it into the dish. A thin clatter it makes in this acoustic. So strange. For a moment I saw in her eyes a hint of vulnerability. The loss of sound is a strangely disorientating thing. She will eventually speak to me.

This afternoon the police came visiting. Again. I went into the Dead Room with Maisie. She had not heard the knocking of course. I must make sure from now on that no lights are to be seen at night. The nights are still light till quite late and will be for some weeks yet. I shall shut myself in here after dark. With Maisie. The police must not be allowed to interfere with the inevitable course of events. I have enough food in the freezer and in my storage jars to last for months. Perhaps from now on it would be safer if I did not go out at all. Though I would miss the newspapers. The police must surely have found the trail.

They have pictures now.

I broke off there because Maisie began to perform the most extraordinary series of physical exercises, as best she can with bound ankles and wrists: back bends and somersaults and pressups. A rather intimidating exhibition. As perhaps it was meant to be. After a while I realised it was a good idea: if we can't go out, we can still keep fit. I joined in. Maisie stopped. I felt rather dispirited, explained that I had to sleep in there with her and switched off the light.

In the middle of the night I was woken by an odd sound, small, muffled but un-mistakable: crying. I listened for some time. I wanted very much to go to her and offer comfort. But I knew this would not be welcome. I pretended to sleep until she slept again. It is slightly gratifying to discover that she is at least human, to find out at least that her hard impenetrable demeanour is a front. That inside she is frightened, lonely and distressed. I was beginning to wonder. She has remarkable will. But the carapace will crack. It won't take long.

It cracked this morning, I thought: she thanked me for her breakfast! Speech at last! I was touched. I realised immediately however that she has a strategy. She is carrying out a plan. But of course I must respond as if I don't know that. She said, 'You know my Aunt Kate, then.'

I thought for a second. 'Only from her work,' I said. 'Which I admire very much.'

'Wouldn't you like to meet her?'

Good heavens, this child is patronising me. She sees me as a freak. Some kind of pathetic anorak. To be bought off by a promised meeting with the great Kate Creech. Oh no. We can't have this. 'As an exponent of her craft,' I said, 'she interests me, as I said. As a person I have no curiosity about her at all. Those artists whose work we admire never live up to our expectations in real life.'

'Aunt Kate' (her Bristol accent makes it sound like Ankate – very sweet) 'Ankate would live up to them,' she said. 'She's really straight.'

'I should have expected no less of her,' I

replied. I smiled at Maisie.

'It'll kill her if anything happens to me,' she said. 'She'll definitely think it's her fault.'

'Why should she think that?'

'She thinks everything's her fault. Her brother died when he was about my age. I think that's why.'

'Subtle psychology, Maisie, for one so young.'

'Don't patronise me,' she said. 'You sick git.'

That's what she said. I couldn't believe it. In this little tiny voice etiolated by the dead acoustic: 'You sick git.' I was amused. So much so I had to leave the room.

You sick git. Am I? Sick?

Many people would think so. Of course. I don't think so. Of course. Well, I wouldn't, would I? I think the world is sick. So sick I don't want to live in it. And I don't want perfect creatures like Alison and Maisie to live in it. I suddenly find myself moved and shaking. I will not let Maisie live in this sick world. And if she thinks that's sick: then, tough. *You sick git.* I did laugh.

Ruminations in the morning. Have they made the Margaret connection yet? Mother would never tell them where Margaret is. Even if she knew. And she hasn't known for years. Amazing how Margaret got free. Free

312

of mother. Of course mother wanted Margaret to be free. I was the one she wanted to enslave. Margaret will always come to my aid. No matter how sick she thinks I am. I can always call on her. She got free of mother. But not free of me.

Sorry, this has become rather introspective. It's a stressful time. Maisie is throwing up questions Alison didn't. Please believe me: I want to do the best for everyone. For everyone who matters, that is. You. Maisie. Margaret. There isn't anyone else.

39

EXPLORING A CHARACTER

In rehearsal Kate was surfing the strato-
sphere, flying on automatic. Rehearsing full
of anxiety and grief was like performing
when exhausted: inspirational, all the nerve
ends exposed, ready to catch any idea on the
wing. She said, 'Colum, Rosalind comes
alive when she falls in love. She's released.'

Colum said, 'Yes, that's the transition.
How do we create a moment for it?
Something the audience will immediately
grasp.'

They tried this, they tried that. Nothing
quite worked. Then like a sleepwalker she
walked alone on to the set, marked out with
tape on the rehearsal room floor. She
walked around the marked-out wrestling
ring, empty now, the wrestling match over
and Orlando gone. She looked at the
imaginary wrestling ring. A stool in the
professional wrestler's corner. A stool in
Orlando's corner. Orlando's towel still there
on the floor, hanging over the imaginary
rope. She suddenly climbed into the ring,
miming the ropes. She went to Orlando's

corner. She took his towel in her hands. She looked at it. Then she closed her eyes and brought the towel slowly to her face. The watching actors made a collective sound, a kind of sigh.

Colum said, 'That's it.'

She came back to herself. Rupert's gaze was fixed on her. She returned a long slow look. Then she smiled. She said, 'Yes but Orlando doesn't *know* I feel like that. That's the hard thing in this play, Colum. Remembering how much you don't know.'

At this moment she reached out her hand to Rupert's face, took his baseball cap and, pushing her hair up inside it, put it on her head. She said, 'Could Orlando leave his cap behind in the wrestling ring? That's what she does! Takes his cap! That's why she's determined to be the boy when they run away to the forest. She wants to be Orlando! It's a talisman.'

She couldn't stop talking. She couldn't stop discovering. It was terror transformed into creativity. If she hadn't been taking Lizzie's Mogadon at night she would never have slept. She was motoring on high octane fuel.

That evening Bright told her and Lizzie what he had found out. About Mark Leighton and his connection to Alison's father and to Dave. And about his sister. 'His sister?' Kate marvelled.

Lizzie said, 'She left at the same time as you.'

'Left where?'

'Dave's.'

Kate stared at Bright: 'That was her? That night? Margaret? Margaret is his sister?'

'You remember her?'

'Don't you?'

'Three of Renato's grappas. I was out of my box.'

'You talked to her. You asked her questions.'

'Did I?'

'She left with us.'

'Did she?'

Kate said, 'I walked all the way back here with her.'

'Here?'

'Well, up the top of the steps, down at the junction of Richmond Street and...?'

Lizzie said, 'Pylle Hill Crescent.'

'Yes? She said she lived down there.'

'Which house?'

'I didn't ask. I wasn't interested. I didn't look where she went. I said goodnight and walked on up here. I think she went off along the crescent but she could have gone back down the steps.' Kate's eyes were wild.

Bright grabbed her by the upper arms. He kissed her on the mouth then on each cheek.

She said, 'It might not be true.'

316

'Why would she lie to you?'

'If she's protecting him. Giving him sanctuary. Covering for him.'

'Why would she do that?'

'I'd do that for my brother.'

Lizzie said, 'Typical. Disgusting. Romantic rubbish.'

Bright said, 'If he'd killed a fifteen-year-old girl? Abducted Maisie?'

Kate said, 'I'd have a problem.'

Bright looked at her in a funny way. Then he phoned Ryan and told him Kate's story. He said, 'Talk to the IO. Not tomorrow, Ryan; now! Every house. I don't care how late it is. Tomorrow it could be too damn late... Right.' He shut down his phone. 'I just heard what I said. About tomorrow – I only said it–'

Lizzie said, 'I agree with you. Can we go? Now?'

'Lizzie. This might not be a good idea.'

'We're four more people.'

Sarah shook her head. 'Not me. I couldn't.'

'Okay, three more.'

Kate stood up. 'Let's do it, John, Otherwise we just sit here and wait. It's intolerable. And we know what she looks like. The police don't.'

House after house in Pylle Hill Crescent. Nobody knew Margaret. They held a discussion at the top of the steps. Lizzie said, 'If you go down the steps a bit the next crescent down is St Luke's.' Irate residents, disturbed watching the telly, became sympathetic on hearing what it was about. They tried every front door in St Luke's Crescent, every basement entrance. Not every house had a basement, because of the extraordinary slope of the street. Kate knocked at a blue front door, no basement. There was no reply. She knocked louder, though the windows were dark. She caught a glimpse at the window blind of the slightest of movements. She knocked again. She was what she called white-tired, wiped out, the ground rocking under her feet. She waited. At last the door opened. Margaret stood there.

It was a strange flat. Not what Kate would have expected. Slightly bare. A stripped wood floor. Grey walls. Mattress-ticking curtains and a black sofa. All monochrome. Like existing inside a black and white photograph. It was just one room, knocked through, with the kitchen at the back and the bathroom next to it. They were cramped, all squeezed in there. Bright had been on the mobile. Now he said, 'Where do you sleep?'

Margaret pointed at the black sofa. 'It's a sofa bed.'

'A-ha.' He looked at the garden. Rather good expensive paving that looked like York stone, wall to wall. A few big pots with yuccas and other spiky exotic plants. No flowers. In the dark, the light from the kitchen window rendered the garden monochrome too. Like a photographic negative. 'Low maintenance,' Bright said.

'I'm away a lot.'

'Ireland, right?'

She nodded.

'Write your address there, would you?' He handed her a small notebook. She wrote and handed it back. 'Beara?' he said, not sure of the pronunciation.

'It's a remote place. Not everyone in Ireland knows it. Here it's hardly known at all.'

'Is that where your brother is?'

'I haven't been there myself for a year. I sold up and came back here.'

'Why?'

'It wasn't working out. The person who helped me. Well – she left. So I became too tied to the place. I couldn't leave it to come and see my brother any more.'

'Your mother said she hadn't seen you for years.'

'A year at least.'

'You came back here but you didn't see your mother.'

'I do not get on with my mother, we are

not compatible. She has always tried to annihilate me.'

'That's heavy stuff.'

'Yes.'

Lizzie said, 'Haven't you seen him? Your brother. Don't you know where he is?'

Margaret looked at her. She shook her head. Her frank straightforward face expressed compassion. 'You're Maisie's mother,' she said. 'I saw the posters today. And the local paper.' She indicated the *Bristol Evening Post* folded at Mark's picture. 'Did you know before that it was him?'

'I don't think even now that it is him.'

'Dave Fowler told us you thought Mark was disturbed.'

'Then. Yes. Because he was doing badly on his literature course. But I believe he's better now. He loves his job. He's good at it. He helps the helpless, you know.'

'So do you,' Kate said.

Margaret looked taken aback. 'How?'

'The donkey sanctuary.'

'Oh that. Yes. But animals are easy. To help people is harder, don't you think?'

Bright said, 'Mark has done a runner. He is lying low. Has he ever done that before?'

Margaret seriously thought. 'No. He has never done that before. He has always been there to look after mother. Who is doing that now, by the way?'

'A social services nurse. Will you do it,

now you know?'

Margaret shook her head. 'No. She would find some way to blame me. My presence does not improve her quality of life.'

'Will Mark get in touch with you?'

'I hope not.'

'You hope not?'

'Because then this will become my responsibility. I can't face giving him up. Not yet. I wish I could.'

'So if he does contact you, we can't depend on you to let us know.'

'I don't know.'

Kate thought Lizzie was going to leap on the girl and shake the life out of her. 'John? I think we should go.'

Bright nodded. Kate steered Lizzie out. As they passed her, Margaret said to Kate, 'I'm ashamed to be the cause of such distress. But I love my brother as she loves – well...'

As Kate steered Lizzie down the path a girl leaped out of a car and ran towards them. She was blonde and young and a little plump. She stopped in their path. They all moved left then right then left. 'I'm sorry. I'm looking for DI John Bright?'

Kate indicated the front door. 'In there.'

The girl ran past them.

'Who's she?' Lizzie still spoke through clenched teeth.

'A policeman, I think.'

321

'This is my colleague, WPC Goldie. Helen, this is Margaret. She's Mark Leighton's sister.'

'You're his sister? Oh.' She asked no questions. Great restraint. Just one amazed glance at Bright, then her eyes wandered over Margaret and around the strangely colourless flat.

'Ms Leighton is going to let us look round. That's right, isn't it, Margaret?'

'Oh yes. Please. Whatever. Of course.'

Bright opened the kitchen cupboards one by one. Margaret sat, tucking her cotton skirt under her knees, and watched.

He went into the bathroom and tapped the panel that boxed in the bath. Opposite the bathroom door a pair of light louvre doors. Bright opened the louvre doors. The corridor of the flat had been partitioned off. It now formed a deep walk-in closet back here to hang clothes, store suitcases, vacuum cleaner, ironing board, the usual domestic junk, neatly stowed. He came back in and stood in front of Margaret. 'Come with me,' he said. She obediently stood. He led her into the little lobby between kitchen and bathroom. They stood looking into the long narrow cupboard. 'Good idea,' he said, 'doing that with the corridor. Will you empty it out for us, please, Margaret?'

Margaret looked dismayed.

'Sorry, but I can't get any sense of the size, what with the hanging rail and everything. Just want to get a proper look. You don't mind, do you?'

'Will you help me?'

'Sure. So will Helen. Won't you, Helen?'

The three of them toiled. Margaret discovered a tennis racket she had forgotten. And a box of audio cassettes. And a box of clothes belonging to her brother. 'We'll take this, if you don't mind. Helen will get you to sign a chit. All right?'

'They're just his old clothes. I was going to give them to Oxfam.'

'Well, we can do that for you. After we've finished with them.'

'Why do you want them?'

'Heard of DNA?'

'Oh. I see.'

'Up to now, see, we've only had circumstantial evidence to connect him to Alison. If these clothes had traces of her–'

'Oh, they couldn't. I took them to Ireland with me by mistake. Years ago. And again when I came back they just got packed up with the rest of my stuff. I meant to throw them away. It really isn't worth your while taking them.'

'Just sign there, okay?'

'Sorry. Of course. You have to do your job.' Margaret took the chit. Bright handed her a pen. She finished signing and said, 'You still

323

think I might be harbouring him?'

'What do you think?'

'I have never been involved in a police investigation of any kind. I don't know how you work.' Her voice, which was deep and melodious, quavered a little.

'Well, I don't know either, Ms Leighton. We'll probably discover the answer to that as we go along. But now that I've found you I'm reluctant to let you go, know what I mean?'

Helen watched him half amused, half really scared. There was something slightly manic about him. Under his dead calm exterior, she felt he wanted to tear the place apart with his bare hands.

'Okay then.' He spoke to Margaret very pleasantly. 'We're off. Sorry to leave you with this mess.'

'I expect the police often leave messes behind for civilians to clean up.' Margaret gave a sad smile which took the edge off this remark.

Outside by Helen's car Bright said, 'What did you think?'

'There was nothing in that walk-in cupboard,' she said. 'There was nothing anywhere.'

'How did that flat make you feel?'

'A bit weird, wasn't it? Sort of – colourless like?'

'A-ha. Nothing else?'

'Sort of – empty. No heart.'

'A-ha?'

She tried hard. Knew he wanted something to inspire him, something that would rip a hole in the curtain that hid Mark Leighton from him. But she couldn't think of anything. 'That Margaret seems ... Well, I dunno. Well, she's quite like him in a way. But, like, he's all clever and sort of showing off and, I dunno – gleeful? But she's sort of – like, good, isn't she? Sincere.'

'You don't think she's lying then?'

'Well ... no.'

'Okay. Good girl. Get off home. See you in the morning.'

She was going to suggest a drink, but he patted her arm, shut her car door on her, and went off up the street. Not even a backward glance.

Lizzie was in the armchair, head back, snoring. It was the first time she had slept since Maisie had gone. Impressed, Bright whispered, 'What did you do?'

Kate silently shut the door and led him to the kitchen. She held up an empty scotch bottle: 'Two large ones. She'll be awake in three hours I should think. I'll be up, keeping her company while she hates me in spades.'

'What did you think back there?'

'Curious person, isn't she, that Margaret?'

'How?'

'So calm. So nice. And what Lizzie said: somehow good. Only–'

'A-ha? Only what?'

'Well, I think the psychiatrists would call it loss of affect.'

'What's that when it's at home?'

'Are you playing ignorant copper?'

'It's Yank-speak. Don't know if I know what it means.'

'Well – lack of – reaction, emotion, the ability to be affected by things, I suppose. Too calm. Too cool. Like you could stick a pin in her and though she might feel it she wouldn't cry out.'

'And what does that mean?'

'I don't know.'

'Fat lot of help you are.'

'Thanks.'

They were lodged between the kitchen table and the stove. He crashed his body at her like a missile. They clung together. Their mouths roamed searching: eyes, ears, neck, cheeks, then mouth to mouth, mutual resuscitation. They tore at clothes fumbling, trembling. They began standing, Kate back to the kitchen table, Bright back to the cooker, and ended on the scarlet linoleum floor. A grim ecstatic coupling, silent in case Lizzie should hear and be scandalised. They stared afterwards with horror and friendship into each other's eyes. He said, 'I thought it would never happen.' She said, 'So did I.' He closed his eyes and placed his hot brow on hers. She said, 'We can't go on lying here under Lizzie's kitchen table.' He said, 'Why not?' Kate kissed him and sat up. 'She hates me enough already.' When Lizzie did open the kitchen door they were making decaf as though nothing had occurred.

40

EXCERPT FROM A DIARY

ix

Well, it happened. They came here and they did not discover the Dead Room. I am amazed and know not what to say. Isn't it incredible? Even that little cross-eyed London policeman. His eyes are like screwdrivers. I remember thinking that night at Mr Wonderful's place, his eyes could screw secrets out of the sphinx. He's the first real test this place has had. It passed with flying colours. Good old Margaret. Her open candid face, her calmness and goodness. They work every time. I owe everything to her. It was meant to be the other way around. I was meant to be the one who fought the battles, stood up for the so-called weaker sex. Well, over the years, I guess we have complemented each other. Sometimes she has defended me. Sometimes I have defended her.

I debated whether to tell Maisie they had been here - her mother, her 'Ankate', her friend the policeman. I decided to keep it for a future occasion when she has really annoyed me. I don't like to think of her in this antagonistic way, but she really is recalcitrant. I would like to shake her sometimes. I do not, I have to admit, like her thinking me 'sick'. It causes me a curious shaking anger in the pit of my stomach. I have several times had to leave the room, afraid of what I might do.

This seems crazy, I know, when my whole aim is that Maisie should die. But I do not want my motives to be mixed. I want this to be a perfect act: a pure end to a pure life. I must summon all my resources of patience and logic to bring her to an understanding and appreciation of my motives. My aims.

This resolve was good, it appears. She asked me at lunchtime if she could have pen and paper. 'With what in mind?' I asked.

'Writing actually,' she replied. Then she smiled, for the first time since I brought her here. She has a wonderful childlike smile. This took the edge off her sarcasm and pleased me. 'Writing what?' I said patiently.

'My experiences here. My thoughts.'

'I am here. You can speak your thoughts.'

'You're going to kill me. I want to leave a record. I got the idea from you. Writing in your diary every day. We can compare notes if you like.'

'How do you know I'm going to kill you?'

'You killed Alison.'

'Alison died voluntarily.'

'I don't believe you.'

'I can't prove it. But there wasn't a mark on her, was there?'

'Alison never would. She wanted to have six kids. She loved her mum and dad. She loved her little brothers. She never would.'

'You don't have to believe me.' I shrugged.

'It must've been because you sapped her will. It must've. You must've made her believe– You must have given her drugs or something–' She stopped herself saying more. She changed her tone. She said, 'Okay then. You explain it to me.'

She was humouring me, the sweet child. I decided to indulge her. 'You see, Maisie, you and Alison possess something precious, the most precious thing there is. Do you know what it is? No, you don't. It is innocence.' I waited. Maisie screwed up her eyes and looked at me as though from a great distance. She didn't reply. 'Yes,' I said, 'it is a rare quality these days, rarer and rarer. The world, you see, is corrupt. Most of the people in it have become degraded, compromised, before they are even old enough to know what has happened to them. Somehow you and Alison managed to escape that. But you were both on the brink, on the cusp. You were both ripe for the–' I heard myself and stopped. I was in danger myself of corrupting the mind of the child.

What was I thinking of?

'On the cusp of what? Not being virgins any more? Is that what you mean?' Maisie waited and watched me to see how I would take this.

I was shocked, I admit. But quickly apprehended what she was trying to do. I smiled. 'You are trying to shock me, Maisie.'

'I'm not. That's what you mean, isn't it? How would the human race go on if people didn't lose their virginity? Are you a virgin? Is that your problem? You can't lose yours so you don't want anyone else to lose theirs, that what it is? I tell you what. I'd rather lose my virginity than lose my life, if that's the choice I've got. And Alison would say the same. I know.'

This child came out with this stuff. Her innocent sweet mouth spat forth this worldly claptrap. The hackneyed nature of her thoughts only served to reveal her true innocence. 'You know not of what you speak,' I said. 'You have not experienced such a choice.'

'You don't have to experience everything to know about it,' she averred.

'Oh yes,' I corrected her, 'you do.'

'You don't!' she said. 'My Ankate–'

Ah, she is going to quote her other guru. I waited with bored expression and bated breath.

'My Ankate says that we have all

331

experienced everything by the age of five. You can't learn anything more, you can only remember. And imagine.' She saw my bored expression and her voice faltered a little: 'Well, that's what she says. I wouldn't know, myself. Not yet.'

'In this field,' I replied, 'you can only speak for yourself.'

'You're not giving me any choice,' she says, changing tack. 'Do you think that's right?'

'But I am! That's what you're going to understand. I am going to convince you that it is better to lose your life than lose your precious innocence. You see, I am not talking just about physical integrity but moral integrity. Moral simplicity. Innocence of mind. I talk in this way because I think you are able to understand.'

At this point Maisie gave me a look. You know those looks. She knew I was talking up to her in order to talk down to her. She is unusually subtle, isn't she? A worthy opponent.

By this time I had talked so much I had strained my voice. The effect of the Dead Room. When you can't hear your voice you start to think you are not there. You can't hear yourself breathing either. The sense of one's own presence is literally vital. You know this. I know this. Before, I have seen its effect. This time I was experiencing it for

332

myself. I admit to a sense of panic.

The Dead Room acoustic, or lack of acoustic rather, contributed greatly to Alison's desire for death. I know she became disorientated. She became terrified. And when I explained that she could choose either to stay with me for ever in there, or to die, she did not hesitate long.

Maisie has raised a doubt in me. I have to admit. I get out of the Dead Room, I come and go as I please. But to be in there continuously day and night is the worst kind of sensory deprivation. Not to hear your own breath, is to experience a kind of death. With Alison this did not seem unfair. My sense of mission, my knowledge of the path awaiting her, were stronger than– Oh, I see what is happening here: Maisie is seducing me. She is bringing me round to her point of view, I am seeing through her eyes. Clever child. She is also aware of the effect of talking in the Dead Room. She is talking little to make me talk too much. I see! It won't work. She may have to be dispatched more quickly than Alison and possibly even without her consent. I must be on my guard.

You have a wonderful niece. When she is gone you will appreciate her more, not less. She will remain as you know her now. Perfect. Unsullied. Pure. That's better than seeing her grow up, grow away from you, turn into the usual ambitious tart, making the right career moves, being taken by this man, then that, then possibly having children, growing older and plainer and sadder while her man goes off plying other young girls with his attentions and she sinks into grey middle age. Is that what you want for her? Well, that's what you'll get if she lives. That's life. And that's why I am intervening in her life's inevitable course. And nobody will talk me out of that.

I must stop for tonight. It has been a nerve-racking day. Resolution: I must not talk so much. Confine my thoughts to these pages, don't waste my energy on Maisie. Let things take their course.

Next Day.

I took off the night-gag and Maisie screamed. Her mouth opened, she screwed up her eyes, but I heard no sound. She closed her mouth, looked at me cheekily and started to eat her breakfast.

When I recovered from the shock I saw she was playing a joke on me. A bitter joke about the effect of the Dead Room. She was also letting me know she was not going to waste her breath on me. Her voice on me. I smiled at her. She smiled back, like a little cat. She licked her spoon and put it in the cereal bowl. She sat back and stared at me. I looked away first. I pretended I found her defiance tedious, beneath my consideration. She knew that was not the case.

When I came out into the outer room I was shaken. I know the difference here. Alison did not take me seriously. She did not believe I would actually take her life, or keep her for ever. To convince her, I told her about her father. What he had done to Mark. And to Margaret. I allowed my hatred of her father to show. To interfere with my pure motives. I told her I had kidnapped her to blackmail her father. I told her he had refused to pay the ransom. I now believe this was the reason Alison co-operated in her own death. She despaired. At the time I felt this was another sin on the head of her father. But no. I refused to admit it at the time, but it was my fault for not telling her the truth. I will not make this mistake with Maisie.

But Maisie knows that Alison died. She knows from the start it's serious. She is ready for me. She is a match for me. I have met my match. These everyday expressions. Match can mean opponent, or mate. A perfect match. A match made in heaven.

41

GOING BEHIND THEIR BACKS

'You got me out in the middle of my dinner to toil up and down that feckin' hill. For what? The sister's place is clean. And she's a nice young woman. She said she wouldn't give him up, but believe me, after I talked to her she saw that there was no other way. That it's for his own good. If he gets in touch with her now she'll let us know all right. Believe me, she will.'

Bright stood silent. Ryan looked at him: 'What's up with you?'

'Meaning what?'

'You're not arguing with me.'

'Oh. Right. Yeah. No. A-ha. That's right.'

'Are you quite well?'

'I'm not sure, Ryan. Ask me when I've got my hands on Mark Leighton. Ask me when I've got Maisie back unharmed. I'll tell you then.'

But Rosalind's joy filled Kate like helium. So much joy, so much delight, so much fear, so much excitement, and so much incomparable language to express it: O *wonderful*,

wonderful, and yet more wonderful, and after that, out of all whooping!

After one of the mock-love-mock-quarrel scenes Kate took off the baseball cap and threw it in the air, terrifying Celia. Her mass of hair fell loose and she felt freedom, experienced her womanhood, longed to be able to show herself to Orlando as she really was. Then rehearsals stopped for lunch.

Rupert sat with her. He was getting braver, like a bird she was taming. She felt the tenderness for him that she would feel for such a creature. He asked her how things were. She told him about the visit to Margaret. He said, 'You must go to see her again.'

'You think?'

'It's the only way to find out anything. What else have you got?'

She looked at him with narrowed eyes. She'd thought him too beautiful and too young to be this sharp, this direct in his thinking. Blinded by his extreme beauty and his youth she hadn't expected a mind at all.

Sandy came in at teatime to discuss costume. Today Rupert was wearing long loose shorts, a loose sweat shirt and Birkenstock sandals. Kate said, 'I want your clothes. I want all your clothes.'

Rupert looked horrified. 'You want me to strip off now?'

She went on without even a smile. 'Jeans is

337

no good because men and women both wear jeans and it's always quite clear which gender is which.'

Rupert nodded, serious. 'It's the bum that gives it away.'

Kate flicked him a look.

Sandy said, 'Trouble is now males and females dress so much alike.'

'In Shakespeare's day, put a bloke in a farthingale, or a girl in doublet and hose, and *voilà*!' Colum clicked his fingers. 'They'd changed gender!'

'That's an idea,' Sandy groaned. 'Let's do it in Elizabethan dress!'

'Now now. Sandy, you can do it, don't despair.'

Kate hovered light as a feather midway up the steep stone steps. The evening light laid gold over the park far below and long shadows over the streets. She could go up and see Lizzie, not a cheerful thought, or trot down St Luke's Crescent and try Margaret Leighton's door.

No one answered her knock. She waited. She was curiously tired, empty, weightless, separated from herself by events. Unable to think a coherent thought but open to impressions, the slightest pressure on mind or body would leave a bruise, a tender place. The copper-coloured sun clasped her in heat, blinded her. She sat on the low wall

338

and closed her eyes. When she opened them, turned away from the sun, Margaret was climbing the slope of the crescent with a plastic carrier.

Kate stayed where she was. She thought Margaret hesitated a second, seeing her, but then she shaded her eyes with her *Bristol Evening Post* and walked up faster, smiling. 'I thought you might be what they call a police presence.'

'No. Just me.'

'You seem tired.'

'Yes.' The young woman's sympathy might dislodge Kate's fragile control. 'Cup of tea might help. Just couldn't face the rest of the steps just yet.'

'You walked from the theatre?'

'Yes. A breath of air after the day. And before hearing there's no news. And walking, there's more chance of seeing – Well, you feel there is.'

Margaret nodded, sympathy not over-done. She got out her key and Kate followed her inside. The room was cool, airy from an open window on to the terrace at the back. 'Nice to have that,' Kate said.

'Yes, except it faces north-east. Hopeless for growing things, or sitting in the sun.'

'Some of the houses down here have basements and some don't,' Kate said.

'That's right. They all have cellars though.'

'Oh?'

'Yes. And because the ground slopes up so steeply at the back, some of the back yards are very deep down. Those ones have buildings in the yard behind the house.'

'But you don't.'

'No.' Margaret shuddered. 'Those buildings are very gloomy and sinister, like air raid shelters or something. Mostly full of rotting rubbish, and, I suspect, rats. No. This was just dusty earth. I paved it for easy maintenance. I'm no gardener. How do you take your tea?'

The front room was held in a shaft of copper light. Margaret cleared some papers off a chair. 'My pathetic efforts.'

'How are you getting on?'

'Well, I may be getting somewhere. Who knows?' She studied Kate as she sat. 'No news then. Of Maisie.'

Kate shook her head. 'Margaret. I've come here to plead with you really. I don't know what else to do. Or where else to turn. If you have any idea where your brother is. Where he might have gone. Where he might have taken – I know you don't think he did. But I know you thought he was unbalanced once, and maybe he has become unbalanced again. It can happen–'

Margaret stopped her, a cool hand on her wrist. 'If I knew, I hope I would tell you.'

'Margaret, that's not enough. I had a brother. He died young. I'd have done anything for him. So I know it's not easy. I know the struggle between loyalty to someone you love and doing the right thing for – well – society, I suppose, I know that's the toughest choice there is, probably.' Kate found herself in tears. 'I only loved two people that much. Liam and Maisie. I'm sorry–'

Margaret handed her a box of tissues and watched her as she mopped up. Her gaze was more detached than sympathetic now. Kate felt she'd blown it. 'I didn't mean to do this. I came here to plead with you but not to use emotional blackmail.'

Margaret said, 'It's not that. I have a plan, you see.'

'A plan?'

'I know that Mark will get in touch with me. When he does – assuming it is not too late to save Maisie's life – I will try to persuade him to give her up. To give her back. I will probably be able to persuade him. I have always been able to in the past.'

'But this time he has gone where you can't find him. Perhaps because he knows that and is determined that you won't persuade him.'

'Well, if that is the case, I can't help, can I?'

'No.'

'Persuading him myself will be easier than handing him over.'

'You'd let him get away to do this again?'

Margaret turned her head away. Kate waited. Margaret stood up. She came towards Kate. She spoke quietly, keeping her voice under control. 'He won't live after doing this.'

Kate could barely speak: 'What do you mean?'

'I know him. These acts. Alison's death and now abducting Maisie. These are extreme acts. The acts of a person *in extremis*. Aren't they? I know Mark. If they are his acts. If he is responsible. If he has done these things, he won't want to live afterwards. He is a good person. I know it seems strange to say that. But he does not have a sanguine view of the world.'

'We love Maisie. Lizzie, and Dave. And I. We love her. She has a life to live. It's nobody's right to take that life.'

'I feel like that about my brother.'

'Nobody is threatening his life. Except himself, if you're right.'

'They would lock him up and he would never know freedom again.'

'He must know he is taking that risk.'

They were sparring now. Kate had not intended this; only to appeal to Margaret's better nature, and also, to the True Fan in her, calling in a debt. The True Fan seemed curiously to have died in the fight for her brother.

342

'You all talk as though you're sure it's Mark. But you can't be. It could just as easily be Dave Fowler. Mr Wonderful, as Mark calls him. Or any of the people who hang out with Dave.'

'Yes.' Kate decided to agree with her, not get her back up any further. 'I seem to have blown this. Thanks for the tea.' She got up.

'No. You haven't blown it. You have shown me something. Something I hadn't imagined. Our imaginations are weak when it comes to other people's – feelings, point of view. I've been so concerned for my brother – I was even shocked last night to see Maisie's mother, to see face to face how she is feeling.'

'If only your brother could see it.'

'I don't believe my brother would unavoidably cause an innocent person to suffer.'

'I'm so sorry if I've offended you.'

'No.' Margaret covered her face for a moment. When she took her hand away she had calmed down. 'Actually I'm honoured to have you here. In other circumstances I'd be over the moon.'

Kate gave a wan smile.

'How is the play going?'

'Wonderful, I think.'

'How do you manage to act with this on your mind?'

'It's the one thing that stops me going

round the bend. When you're doing it, when you're rehearsing, there's only that. Nothing else exists. When it stops, the real world comes back. At the moment the real world is so unreal, the unreal world seems real-er.'

Margaret gave her extraordinary smile. 'I envy you.'

'So you should. So should everyone. It's the greatest thing. To be able to turn sorrow into joy. To be able to make use of the bad things to create something else.'

'Yes,' Margaret said. 'That's the true alchemy.'

'But you're a writer. You do that too.'

'Your voice takes on a hollow ring when you say that.'

Kate accepted this challenge; no point denying it. 'That's because I haven't seen your work. I don't know how good it is.'

Margaret looked at the sheaf of papers: 'You won't see it yet. No one will. I'm going to finish something before I show a word.'

'Well, if you change your mind and want an opinion – and it would only be one opinion, I don't set myself up as a judge – I'd be glad. I feel you're good.'

'Good?'

'Original.'

'Why?'

'I think you have an original mind. Cool. With a dispassionate over-view.'

Margaret's eyes filled with tears. Kate was

astonished. The girl had seemed to her strangely emotionless. Now she got herself back under control quickly with no fuss. 'Oh. What a surprise. Sorry. Never do that. But nobody before has appreciated those qualities in me. They are precisely the qualities I've always hoped – that I've striven for. Nobody has touched that – ambition – suspected it even – before. And that it should be you. I'm grateful.'

Kate trudged up the steps, as tired as if she'd been physically wrestling with a powerful opponent. And she didn't know the result. No referee. Was it a draw? Or had she been overthrown, as Rosalind says to Orlando? *Sir, you have wrestled well, and overthrown more than your enemies.*

On her left a row of cottages with country-ish front gardens, beyond them, far below on the other side of the railway cutting, the city of Bristol. Brunel's lovely railway station quite clear and small. And on her right the end house of St Luke's Crescent. She saw what Margaret had meant by the steep slope at the back. The side wall of the end house rose as steeply as the steps.

Half-way up the final flight of steps at a cobbled resting place, she stopped to get her breath. Here, at right angles to the steps, there was a narrow opening between the backs of the St Luke's Crescent houses and the houses of Pylle Hill Crescent, above. This alleyway did not look inviting. She could not see where it ended: it curved with the crescents. But down it she went.

The back yards of the St Luke's Crescent houses were on her right. The walls were too high for her to see over. But twenty yards along the alley, a wall was broken down. She looked over the jagged bricks. She could see clearly now what Margaret meant. Some of the yards were incredibly deep and dark. Some, less deep – the houses without basements, she guessed – had earth banks that sloped steeply up from the house to the end wall. In most of the deeper yards a flat-roofed building filled the entire space, its roof level with the ground floor.

The backs of these houses were not only sinister but also confusing. It was impossible to tell what level of the houses you were looking at. At the front, some of the houses appeared to have basements, some not. But at the back some had double basements, one over the other. Or did they? Her tired brain could not work it out.

She counted down to the house where Margaret lived. But she could not see into that yard. The alley came to a dead end, a gruesome dark corner, piled with black garbage bags, chewed, spilling out un-recognisable gunk, old push chairs, a car seat, tyres, a burst football. The picture of

346

her despair.

She made her way back to the steps, climbed to the top, and carried on up Richmond Street, high, airy, the houses backing on to the railway cutting painted pretty colours, with restored stonework, original windows and doors.

Bright greeted her in the hallway. She didn't know how they'd look at each other today. She'd had no time, and no room in her mind, to consider what had happened between them. They stood in Lizzie's hallway in a momentary hiatus, then pressed body to body from forehead to knees, holding tight like there was nothing else in the world to hold on to, which was the truth. 'All right?' he said.

She nodded: 'How's Lizzie?' All this in whispers.

He made a face – not good.

Lizzie sat wrecked in a chair, uncombed, in her dressing-gown. Sarah sat with her, distraught.

'Do you want to go home for a bit, Sarah? I can be here,' Kate offered. But Lizzie grabbed Sarah's arm and Sarah shrugged: 'No, Kate, thanks, I'm fine.'

In the kitchen Bright was cooking an omelette. His deft movements, his hands cracking the yellow eggs into the white bowl, his hands and the swift motions of the fork, made a calm centre in Kate's universe, just for now.

'I checked out donkey sanctuaries.' He swirled a nut of butter in the pan.

'Margaret?'

'A-ha. No donkey sanctuary in miles of here has heard of her.'

'What?'

'Except one. Near Minehead. She worked there for a month ten years ago in her school vacation.'

'Why should she lie?'

'Want to ask her?' He poured the eggs into the pan. She watched the edges become opaque, then set and curl, the middle a swirl of golden liquid. He sprinkled little stars of parsley over the yellow and, a moment before the whole thing set solid, with the spatula, folded one side over the other, enclosing the perfect slightly liquid centre under its frilly edge. She took two hot plates from the oven and he expertly chopped the omelette into two and slid them on to the white porcelain. He placed a slice of good brown bread on each plate and a spoon of salad, picked them up with a tea towel and carried them through. Then he came back to the kitchen.

'Will she eat?' Kate said.

'If she can't eat that she can't eat anything.' He poured them each a glass of wine. He sat at the table and held on to

Kate's hand. 'Margaret lied because whatever she was doing all those years, and
especially what she's been doing recently,
she doesn't want us to know.'

'Brilliant deduction.'

'Yeah, clever clogs. Now why doesn't she
want us to know? Is it something to do with
her brother? Or some secret nothing to do
with all this? We're checking out the Ireland
story. So far no one's heard of her over
there.'

'I've just been to see her.'

'On your own?' Bright was shocked.

'What do you think she would do to me?
Hit me over the head with a meat cleaver
because I want her to betray her brother?'

'You shouldn't do that. You've got to tell
me first.'

'Anyway she's a True Fan, I thought I
might have some influence because of that.'

'And have you?'

'I fear not.'

'Nah,' He rubbed his eyes.

'But there's an alleyway between the backs
of her houses and the street above. The
houses have a weird construction. Some of
them, the whole yard is filled with a
building. You come out of the back door
deep deep down, and across a narrow yard,
no more than three feet from the house, is
this flat-roofed building. The roofs are just
big concrete blocks. It's the most sinister

349

unpleasant backs of houses I've ever seen. Have those buildings in the yards been searched?'

He got up from the table and took out the mobile. 'Helen? Aha, it's me. No, don't put me through to Ryan, I don't want to get up his nose. Listen, find out something for me?' He explained then covered the receiver and spoke to Kate: 'Is there one of these buildings at the back of Margaret's place?'

'The alley doesn't go all the way. I couldn't get far enough to see.'

'From inside it looked like a paved garden, simple.'

'I know. But the kitchen units go all along the back window. You can't see straight down the back of the house without clambering on to the kitchen sink. It looks like the paving comes right up to the back wall of the house but–'

Bright was back on the phone. 'Find out if those buildings in the back yards have been searched. Ask around. Call me back.'

The sun had gone now, an orange glow low in the sky over the hill. They climbed up and over Richmond Street, Pylle Hill Crescent off to the left at the end. Down the first section of steps, to the alley. More uninviting in the gloaming. Bright took out a small torch. They peered over the broken wall. 'I see what you mean. Villains' paradise. From the inside you wouldn't suspect. I mean, even here it's hard to tell what level you're on. Completely different levels front and back. Never seen anything like it.'

Something scurried over Kate's foot. She gasped and lifted both feet. She couldn't see in the dark of the litter at the wall's base what the animal had been. She hoped cat and doubted it. Bright's warm dry hand held hers. 'Margaret's place is a bit further along, right? Two houses? Three?'

They counted their way back along the alley then continued down the steps to St Luke's Crescent. They counted the houses along to Margaret's. 'Four,' Bright said, 'from the end of the alley.' They walked on past. There was a light in the window. Margaret sat at her small desk, her head bent over her papers, writing in longhand. She looked concentrated and easy. Happy even. Bright and Kate walked on down the crescent. His phone rang. 'Yeah?'

He listened, said 'A-ha,' once or twice, then, 'Thanks, Helen. Talk to the DCI on the next shift, not Ryan, the nice guy who knows about the drug scene. Get him to institute a raid or something. The pretext doesn't matter. He's got to see the inside of every one of those buildings, okay?'

Shutting off the phone he said, 'This is dealers' paradise, apparently. The basement

flats are in big demand in certain circles.'
They were passing a house with metal
shutters over the windows. It appeared to
have no basement but there was a ventilator
grille in the front bay. 'They were doing a bit
of refining and packaging in the building
out the back. Mixing brick dust with the
browns.'

'What?'

'Heroin. They call it the browns. It's
brownish powder, looks like brick dust, so
they use brick dust to bulk it out a bit. Ten
quid a go.'

'No.'

'That's what these kids are squirting into
their veins. Cheers you up, doesn't it?'

As they reached the bottom of the street
three squad cars came round the corner. No
blue lights, no sirens, quiet and sweet.
Helen Goldie got out of the first car, with a
man in a brown sweater and casual trousers.
A nice bank manager on holiday, he looked.
Bright whispered, 'That's Pollock. He's a
good bloke. Hasn't got solid ivory between
the ears.' Two uniformed police in each car.
They spread out up the hill, four or five
houses each, up the steps to front doors or
down to basements. Bright bounced on the
balls of his feet, rattled the change in his
pockets. Kate said, 'I wish you wouldn't do
that.'

She saw his teeth in the dark. 'Finding

fault with me already?' He took his hands out of his pockets and put an arm round her. 'About last night–'

'We'll think about it later,' she said. 'Some other time. How about that?'

Doors opened, closed, oblongs of light coming and going, shadowy figures appearing on steps, disappearing. 'That's Margaret's place.' Kate moved up the hill a little. Saw Helen Goldie and Inspector Pollock go inside. Bright was bouncing again, his change rattling like mad. Kate walked down then up then in a circle, then got off the pavement to let some people pass.

'What's this then?' A mulish Bristolian voice.

Bright shrugged. 'Dunno, mate. Looks like a raid.'

'Which house they gone to then?'

'Seem to be trying them all.'

'Christ. C'm'on, less go.' The two men backed off down to Windsor Terrace then ran down to the main road. Kate could see Bright's instinct to give chase. Instead he got on his mobile and gave a description: 'Short, stocky. Blondish. Round heads, short haircuts, satin baseball jackets.' Shutting the phone down he said, 'Yeah, fits ninety per cent of the blokes round here.'

'Mulish manner,' Kate said. 'You didn't mention that.'

Bright gripped her arm. Pollock and Helen were coming out of Margaret's place. They came down the hill towards Pollock's car. Bright and Kate shrank back a bit. Before Helen got into the car she shook her head, a minimal movement easy to miss. She could have been shaking her hair back if it hadn't been back already in its neat arrangement. Bright's shoulders drooped. Pollock and Helen drove off.

42

EXCERPT FROM A DIARY

x

Well well, my sister is good, no point denying it. Such cool, such sang-froid. 'Oh, of course,' she says. 'Yes, do look. I do have a basement now I come to think of it, well, it's more a cellar. I never go down there because it's rather spooky, but by all means look.' So she goes into the broom cupboard that used to be the corridor, and she shifts a few things.

'You didn't tell us about this before,' says the little policewoman, very quiet so that the man can't hear.

'Well,' says Margaret, 'I just ignore its existence, as far as possible.' She gets out the last box and she uses the edge of a shovel to lift up the trap door. She tries not to look at the little policewoman. She doesn't want to make her feel any more foolish. 'The trap door is very hard to see,' she says. 'It used to have a handle but I took it off.'

The man says, 'Well, it would get in the

way of storing things, wouldn't it.' He's humouring Margaret, of course.

Margaret pretends she doesn't know this. 'Hold on,' she says, 'I think there's a light somewhere.' She feels around and finds the switch, and turns it on. The feeble bulb swings on that dangerous-looking wire thick with cobweb fluff, over the rickety open-tread stairs. 'More a ladder really,' Margaret says apologetically.

The man goes down first. The girl looks at Margaret closely. 'I met your brother,' she says.

'Did you?' says Margaret.

'I liked him, actually,' says the girl.

Margaret looks really touched.

'Up close, you're quite alike,' says the little policewoman – sorry – woman police officer, actually – her little Bristol voice, her charming plump soft skin. 'Aren't you?' she says.

'I've always hoped so,' Margaret says.

The little policewoman sees Margaret's too moved to say anything else. So she goes off down the cellar steps after the chap.

Margaret follows them down. They have torches and they poke about, at the brick walls thick with black rime, the slimy damp red pantiles of the floor. They turn over a pile of sacks in a corner. 'Coal,' the man says. 'These were the coal cellars in the old days. You'd have to come down here with a

356

coal scuttle three times a day, carry it all the way up the house.' They move some boxes stacked in a corner, look inside them, look behind them. Nothing there!

'I hope there's no – well – animals,' says the little policewoman. 'I'm not scared of much, but rats I just go spare.' Now there's a thought. I'd like to see her go spare, I have to admit.

She's a fine little actress, plays it so sweet with this inspector, butter wouldn't melt. She doesn't want him to know she's been here before with the little cockney one, and failed to discover the cellar. And she knows that Margaret doesn't want that known either. She really plays men on the end of her line. Though he seems oblivious. Just getting on with the job. She's wasting her time there.

They go through to the back. Margaret follows them. He shines his torch all along the back wall and finds the bricked-up doorway. Touches it. 'Yes,' – Margaret's so cool – 'I don't know when that was bricked up. A long time ago, I expect.'

The inspector says, 'What would be outside there? What level are we on here?'

'Oh, on THE level, I assure you,' says Margaret. 'Always on the level.' No she doesn't. (Oh, I wish!) She says, 'Yes, it is difficult to work out. Some of the houses have deep yards depending on the slope of the hill. Their basements open out on to the yard. Others like this are just earth at the back, I think. Mine was when I came here.'

'You had it paved.'

'Yes, it was unsightly and I'm no gardener.'

'You've made it nice,' the little police-woman simpers.

Margaret gives her a small smile. 'Thanks.'

The officer is still feeling along the wall. He pats it all over with the flat of his hand listening for differences in sound. But the sound is flat and dead and solid everywhere, there's no difference at all. He shines his torch closely at the brick. He shakes his head. 'Why did it have an opening in the first place?'

Margaret says, 'I thought it might have been one of those storage areas that you sometimes find under the pavement in the front area of a house. Only in this case it's the back?'

The officer shakes his head. He is exasperated. Flummoxed. In other circumstances I'd have liked to help him out: the backs of these house *are*, quite objectively, interesting. 'Let's go,' he says. 'Thanks for being so co-operative, Miss Leighton. This thing is pretty hard on you, I suppose?'

Margaret gives a deprecatory shrug, too full of feeling to speak. 'Sorry to bother you,' says the nice policeman, and up they go, up the rickety steps, up through the trap and into the nice warm dry flat. Out through the front door.

Margaret watched them. Down the short path to the pavement. They opened the bin cupboard and shone the torch. Nothing there except bins.

You need lateral thinking for police work, a type of inspiration most simple bobbies are not capable of. I can't help but despise their limited imaginations.

359

you, says the nice policeman, and up they go, up the... Kite steps up through the trap and into the nice warm fire flip. Out through the front door.

Margaret watched them. Down the short path to the front gate. They opened the big cupboard and she... watch... North... they except him.

43

SHIFTS

Bright came back with Kate to her digs. The family were in the kitchen eating. The warm glow at the end of the corridor and Thomas laughing helplessly at some story Luke was telling him. Normal life. Everyone safe. A rush of emotion to Kate's throat. Bright put a hand on her back. They went upstairs quietly, so as not to disturb that secure life.

Now he cooked an omelette for Kate and himself. They drank more red wine. Helen Goldie called. She gave him a full report. He looked fit to be tied as he shut off the phone.

He told Kate about the cellar. 'Why didn't she show us before if there's nothing to hide? There's got to be something there! Why that street?' he said to Kate. 'I've been, up and down those streets, round and round that little hill. That street is weird. Why does Margaret live there? She could live in a nice street. She's not short of a bob or two, and anyway, nowhere up that bit of Totterdown is expensive. Why there?'

'I'll ask her.' Kate reached for his phone.

Bright put his hand over hers and a plate in front of her. 'Eat.'

She realised she was trembling with hunger, light in the head. 'Okay.'

They didn't bother opening the sofa bed out. They lay on the rug in front of the coal effect gas fire. 'Are we always going to make love on the floor?' she said.

He covered her up with the duvet and clung close to her. His legs circled her legs, his arms circled her back. His body was warm, dry, he smelt like autumn grass. They didn't talk. No future. No past. Just now. Just them. Before she slept Maisie's face looked right at her out of the dark. She opened her eyes and he was watching her. 'It's okay,' he said. 'It's going to be okay.'

She decided to suspend disbelief, and sleep.

She never left the rehearsal room except for lunch or the loo. She watched avidly the production come together. She watched with unusual attention the process whereby an actor makes himself a conduit through which the character can be expressed, a vessel the character can inhabit, a medium for the message. She found the process unusually moving. Particularly as the actor is largely unaware of the metamorphosis, the chrysalis stage a frustrating head-banging time, the actor thinking he's getting nowhere, while in fact the character is entering, him imperceptibly, infiltrating him bone, sinew and skin.

Today she watched Rupert. There couldn't be a more perfect Orlando, so young, a fledgling. All the wildness, truth and passion of a fledgling. Because he was so serious, he was heartbreakingly funny. She was too old for him surely? Wouldn't it show?

Before lunch, Ian sidled up to Colum. 'C-Colum, I have an idea f-for the interval. May I show you after lunch?'

At lunch Kate said to Rupert, 'I'm too old for you.'

He looked appalled. 'Of course you're not!' He blushed and laughed. 'You're not.'

She shrugged, unconvinced, but glad at least he hadn't immediately agreed. A silence and some unspoken thought elapsed between them. He overcame his shyness to ask, 'Did you visit the sister?'

Kate told him the story. 'Hopeless, I think. If she knows where he is she'll never say.'

'You have to keep in touch with her.'

'I know. I don't like her, I realise. She's a True Fan, a bit embarrassing. Earnest. Not great on humour. She Wants to Write. The only time I got through to her was when I flattered her about being a writer. She seemed really touched.'

'Get her to show you her stuff.'

362

'Maybe I will.' She looked at him. You could drown in those puppy-like honest intelligent eyes. What was she thinking of? She found herself blushing too.

After lunch Ian made his entrance. Sandy sidled in in his wake to watch. He'd dressed his pear-shaped body in perfect Boy Scout uniform from the Mounties' hat to the big khaki shorts and knee-socks. He carried an enormous rucksack. He had found the perfect metaphor for the dyed-in-the-wool townee off on a jaunt to the country. He was an ineffably comic sight.

While they laughed he seriously un-shouldered his back-pack, knelt and opened it up. Out came a series of creature comforts, alarm clock, radio, magazines, a torch, food, food, and more food. Then out came a bundle of cloth. He unravelled this to reveal it as a small tent. He proceeded to erect this tent, giving members of the cast ropes to hold. The tent up, he at last disappeared inside. The tent bulged and heaved while he settled himself to sleep. The cast applauded. Ian poked his head out with an enquiring expression. 'Brilliant.' Colum got up. 'You've decided me where to have the interval. Now look.' Colum and Ian went into deep confabulation. Ian clenched a fist and grinned. 'Right, let's try it.'

'Rupert, Ian will stay in his tent right

through the interval. We'll start the second half with the sonnets on trees scene. Want to try it now?' Colum had a few quiet words with Rupert, who nodded, dead earnest, then he sat down near Kate, to watch.

Ian squeezed back into his tent while Rupert rehearsed his sweetly crazy love scene, pinning poems addressed to Rosalind on tree after tree. Running off at the end of the scene, Rupert tripped on a tent rope. The tent collapsed and Ian was revealed reading *Playboy* by torchlight. In a state of wounded dignity he gathered up his collapsed belongings and removed himself, a heap of wobbling flesh. 'I th-thought I'd get a member of the audience to h-help with the tent.'

Kate cried with laughter and knew this was the whole point of the exercise, of their job: to fly people out of their troubles however bad, just for a minute, just for an hour. You didn't suspend just disbelief, you suspended your life, you put your problems on hold. She thought how Maisie would laugh, how she and Alison would be crazy about Rupert, how she and Alison–

Gemma scraped her up off the floor of the loo. Kate wept in her arms. And even while she did so she thought, This is how Celia would have comforted Rosalind. At the start of the play, this is how it would be. Her sister Lizzie had no such release. No use she could make of her sorrow, her horror. Nothing she could do. And nothing Kate could do for her, her real sister, in their real life.

After rehearsal Alan Tate sidled up in the long striped scarf he had decided to wear for Jaques. 'How's your sister bearing up?'

'Badly. Well. I don't know. She doesn't speak to me.'

'No?'

'She thinks it's all my fault.'

He blinked. 'Why?'

She sighed. 'How far back do you want to go?'

'I see. Family history.'

'Habit. Anyway, it *is* my fault.'

'Oh dear dear, no.'

'Want to come up and see her?'

Nothing so revealing as a blush had invaded his perfect poise for years, but a kind of frisson passed over his face. 'Oh, she wouldn't want – erm...'

'I'm going now.'

He seemed too tall and stately for the little house. But Lizzie for the first time actually looked somewhere other than within. She was unembarrassed by her dishevelled appearance, because she was unaware of it, though he was shocked.

Sarah looked grateful to take a break. In

365

the kitchen she said, 'Oh Kate, I feel dreadful sorry for her, but I'll have to get away for a bit or I'll go crazy.'

'That's okay, Sarah. I'll stay here.' Kate made tea in the mocking clown's-head teapot.

'Your policeman comes round regular. She's pleased to see him even when he's got no news.'

'He had no news today then?'

'Said he'd be round about seven. I need an evening off. I feel awful saying that.'

'You've been amazing.'

'Well, she's got Sir with her now.'

Kate smiled. 'Alan would like that. He does have the air of a Knight of the The-at-ah.'

'I'd just like a night in my own bed.'

Kate for a moment thought she said knight. They collapsed in hysterical mirth, crying tears of laughter, then crying tears of fear and grief. For the second time Kate found herself clinging to another human being, unusual for her, so undemonstrative, so contained, so independent. For a moment she felt strapped to a raft in a sea so stormy that survival was not a possibility.

She gave Sarah a tea towel to wipe her eyes. Sarah said, 'Kate? What will you do if—?'

Kate said, 'I can't imagine wanting to go on. I can't imagine Lizzie wanting to go on.'

366

'Doesn't make any sense, does it?'

Bright was standing in the doorway. 'I see His Nibs has come to visit. That'll do her good. Go home, Sarah. Have a drink. Have a lie-down. Go to the pictures. Get away from this. We'll be here.'

Sarah said, 'D'you know, I never thought I could get to like a policeman?'

They stood with their arms round each other at the kitchen window.

'Anything new today?'

'Pollock, the DCI on the late shift? He's persuaded the IO to put twenty-four-hour surveillance on Margaret's flat.'

'Is she hiding him there? Her brother?'

'Don't look hopeful, Kate. It doesn't look likely, does it? We've searched twice. But if he goes anywhere near, they won't miss him. And if she goes anywhere near him, we won't miss that either.'

'She's being followed?'

'Under observation, as we say.'

Kate shivered.

'Apart from that, they smoked out a little heroin factory further down the street. Doesn't help us much but Pollock's pleased. That's his speciality. Small-time drugs and thieving. He's not used to good-quality crime.'

'Good-quality crime?'

'A-ha. Murder. High-class burglary. Fraud.'

'That's what you call it?'

'A-ha. Doesn't come better quality than this.'

When Kate went into the front room with food, Alan Tate was, perched imposingly on an armchair. Though physically uneasy he seemed oddly at home. And Lizzie, miracle of miracles, was talking. She shut up when Kate arrived, naturally. But outside the door Kate heard her start up again, the occasional murmur from Alan prompting her on.

Bright was off to keep a rendezvous with Helen Goldie. He crept by the front room: the murmur of Lizzie's voice, Lizzie crying, Tate's resonant comforting tones. He raised his eyebrows at Kate. 'Didn't figure him as the sympathetic type.'

'I'm amazed,' Kate said.

'See you later?'

'Here's the keys to my digs. But I expect to be here tonight.'

'We really looked everywhere. There wasn't any way there could be a place below, or a place at the back. There was nothing there, John!' It was the first time she'd called him John. It had slipped out of her secret mind. She blushed.

'Then there's got to be another place in that street. Otherwise why is Margaret there?'

'I don't think she knows where he is. That's just her place, that's all.'

'Nah. Maybe you're right. Any news from Ireland?'

'No. But Pollock's going to start using Anna Kappa on Margaret. I got him interested. He's started going back in months, not minutes. Where was Margaret before she turned up here?'

'He got anywhere?'

'He's starting with his shift tonight.'

Bright nodded, staccato small movements of his head. 'I want to talk to the mother again.'

'She's so–'

'I know she's a bit barmy, but there's method in it somewhere. Do you believe she never knew where her daughter was all that time?'

'Well, if they don't get on very well–'

'If you fell out with your folks would you just not let them know where you were?'

'Lots of people do it. You know that.'

'Get back in to see her. Try and get me in.'

'John–'

'I know it's hard, I'm really grateful. I am. Sorry. It's knocking me to hell, all this. Should never get involved with friends' cases, but what can I do? We've got to get to Maisie before–'

'It's okay.'

'If there is a before. If it isn't already after.'

He left her outside her door and drove up to Kingsdown Parade. Caroline greeted him in the hall with Thomas in her arms. 'I just can't get him to sleep. He's always restless when Luke's out. He must pick up some vibes from me.'

Bright sat in her kitchen with them, drinking tea till midnight. Kate didn't come in. He slept wrapped in the duvet on her floor. Her perfume surrounded him. It wasn't Millie's perfume, it was just Kate's.

Kate went out at midnight. She found herself walking the streets of Totterdown. Round and round the hill, and over and over the hill. She went down the steps and along the alley behind St Luke's Terrace, shivering with fear and a kind of sickness. Margaret's place was in darkness, so far as she could see. She stood there in the dark, hoping there would be no rustling in the garbage at her feet. She pulled herself up on to the wall hoping for a better view. No good. One or two windows in other houses dimly glowed. But it was hard to tell if she was even looking at the right house at this distance.

Alan Tate was closing the door gently behind him when. Kate arrived back. He whispered, 'She's sleeping.'

'Alan! I don't think she's slept for over a week.'

'Ah, darling, all you need is one performance from me – send anyone to sleep.'

Kate kissed him. 'Thanks.'

But Kate didn't sleep. She lay on Maisie's bed holding the teddy bear she'd bought for Maisie's first Christmas. She thought about Liam, her lost brother, Dave alienated from his family, Margaret Leighton alienated from her mother, then all the dysfunctional families in As *You Like It,* all the brothers alienated, missing, exiled, plotted against. Celia takes the name Aliena when she goes to the forest. She is alienated from her father. The love of Rosalind and Orlando rises from a dunghill of hate and revenge. Her work her saviour. She floated into harried searching dreams way after dawn.

Bright caught her at the stage door before she went into work and gave her Helen's update.

'What's Anna Kappa?' She looked as bleary as he felt.

'It's this island. I forget where. South Seas or somewhere. Weather conditions. Lots of mist swirling around. It appears and disappears. Well, it's a methodology by time.'

'I'm mystified.'

'Well, you take the point of the crime.'

371

'The crime?'

'In this case, because of Alison, they're taking the point of disappearance, near as they can. Maisie's disappearance. They make a line backwards and forwards from that, and along that line they place events.'

'Like Mark Leighton disappearing?'

'A-ha. And Pollock's placing Margaret in the frame. Just to see. See if her movements add up in terms of Mark's, or Maisie's. It's an outside chance but you never know.'

'How did you persuade Pollock?'

'He's a good bloke. Didn't like the Margaret set-up. He'll have a hard job persuading Ryan, though. Gonna bring it up at morning prayers.'

Kate was bewildered. 'Prayers?'

'The morning conference. The two DCIs off each shift, and the Investigating Officer, decide on the actions to be taken, allocate personnel to the actions. The IO's more sympathetic to Ryan than Pollock.' Bright looked troubled. His shoulders sagged.

'What? Something new?'

'No, nothing new, that's the thing. Kate–'

'What?'

'They got no leads, it's not going anywhere. It's a question of resources, manpower. There's other crimes. And Maisie's disappearance isn't even a definite crime yet. It's getting on for a week. If there's no leads in forty-eight hours the heat goes out of it. It goes cold. That's the problem.'

'Oh Christ.' Kate covered her face with her hands.

'Helen and me are gonna try and get to see Mark's mother again. We'll do it on our own time, after our shift.'

'It's a risk for her?'

'A-ha. Pollock's sympathetic but she could get in trouble.'

'So could you.'

'Ach.' He dismissed this.

'Well, please thank her from us.'

They were at the stage door. Kate was going to be late. They clung together in a fierce quick embrace. 'I missed you last night,' he said.

'Yup.'

That day Alan rehearsed his Seven Ages of Man speech. The rich modulated despairing voice had the power of the Last Post played on a single bugle over fields of the dead. Astonishingly towards the end Jaques the arch cynic cried. There was no hint of crying in his voice but tears ran down his cheeks. An extraordinary silence hovered over the rehearsal room, astonished, shocked, illuminated. No one had ever done it like this before.

The sense of awe stretched even over the coffee break. Alan gave Kate a sidelong look. Embarrassment, she thought. He said in a rich-toned mumble, 'I didn't intend that.'

'It's wonderful.'

'Oh no. You think?'

Colum approached and put a hand on Alan's shoulder. 'Is it likely to occur again?'

'Oh, you guessed it wasn't meant.'

'It was astonishing. I've never known you take the emotional route.'

'Do you think I should take it again?'

'I think it would be wonderful but don't try for it.'

'Ah yes, we all know the pitfalls of trying to repeat an effect.'

Later Kate and Rupert worked on the play's greatest, longest, disguised-love scene, Rosalind like mercury, like fireworks. like an electric storm, like a cooing dove. For Kate the piercing joy of Rosalind's love was fuelled by the piercing despair of Maisie's absence, both passions equally intense, equally acute. At the end of the day Colum looked at her with concern. 'Be careful, Kate. Don't get there too soon. Can you hold back a bit? I think you're frightening Rupert.'

'Am I frightening you, Rupert?'

'I feel a clodhopping mutt.'

Colum's eyes lit up. 'Maybe that's how Orlando feels? And he's confused too, because he's having these sexy tender feelings for a boy. We have to define those moments of confusion, make them work for us.'

Rupert groaned.

Kate took him for a drink in the theatre bar. He gazed at her with eyes full of love. He seemed almost about to make a declaration. Oh no, Kate thought, not this. I don't have time or room for this, it's the wrong time and the wrong place, *it's a lovely face but it's the wrong face...* With Rupert, a woman in her position would have to make the first move, and such a thing was beyond Kate, so far out of character as to be impossible. If she could ever do it she'd make a hash of it. *Of course, Rosalind has precisely that problem and finds a way around it...* She was off again. Work as displacement activity. Work as anaesthetic.

Alan Tate stopped by their table. 'I'm going to cook your sister my incomparable spaghetti this evening. No need to rush back.' He sailed on, a proud ship, through the bar.

Helen stepped down to the stone floor of the Coronation Tap. Bright sat looking at the *Bristol Evening Post,* not reading it. He looked up. Seeing her, his dead brown eyes took on their metallic points of light. 'What'll you have?'

375

'Scrumpy.'

'You sure?'

'It's nice here, the cider. Out of the barrel.'

'Any news?'

'They've let Dave Fowler go.'

'Christ.'

'The superintendent said it was getting embarrassing. Fowler's lawyer's been getting really tough. Pollock had this big argument with Ryan, apparently. Well, that's the story going round.'

'So now they haven't got anyone in the frame.'

'Well, Pollock's got them to definitely put Mark in it. And now we've started concentrating on his sister.'

'Thank Christ for that. Cheers.'

'I rang the nurse and asked if I could visit the mother. She said it would be okay. You'll be late for Ryan's shift.'

'Yup. I'll spin him a tale. Keep you out of it.' She looked at her watch on the smooth plump wrist. Bright found himself with a sudden urgent desire to touch that smooth baby flesh. What was happening here? Cured by Kate of a three-year paralysing obsession, turned on by Kate not just to her but to all women? Helen was young enough to be his– He buried his nose in his pint.

'We've got ten minutes,' Helen said.

'A-ha. Good. Right.'

376

The house did not have the shine, the gleam, it had had when Mark was there. The smell was different. Sadder. A slight cabbagey odour drifted up from the kitchen. The nurse wiped her hands on her apron.

'Sorry to bother you. I can see you're busy.' Bright's most tomcat-like purr.

The nurse tucked a lock of grey hair behind her ear. 'I'm cooking her supper.'

'That's all right, love. We know the way.' He started up the stairs after Helen.

The nurse looked harassed. 'Mind if I get on?'

'You go ahead. I'll ask you a few things later, okay? Nothing heavy. You take your time.' Her footsteps could be heard clomping off to the kitchen as they reached the first landing. Bright looked out at the back yard. Not the only time in this hilly city a basement had had him fooled. Just the first. He started to follow this thought. Had the basement here given Mark the idea? Had he got Margaret to take the flat in St Luke's Crescent because of its deceptive levels? No, that was no good. Margaret's basement had been searched now. Nothing there. He wished he could have searched it himself. He might do that – Helen was knocking on the door of Miss Leighton's room. There was no reply. Bright gave Helen the nod and followed her in.

'Hello, Miss Leighton?' Helen's voice soothed with its softest Bristolian inflection. She was learning from Bright. 'We've come to see you again. Are you awake?'

Mark's mother had not moved since their entrance. She was no more than a hump in the bed in the dusky room. Helen went to the window and pulled back the curtain. A shaft of evening sun cut across the bed. The woman was asleep, it seemed, head back almost off the pillow. Then Bright saw her eyes were open. He'd been in rooms before where death had got there ahead of him Helen turned from the window. Her face stiffened with shock, comic, almost. She recovered to say, 'Is she dead?'

Bright knelt by the bed. A small chenille cushion had landed on the rug there. Knocked off in a struggle? Or simply used and then carelessly thrown down? He had a quick look at the woman's fingernails. There had been no struggle.

Though it was obvious there wouldn't be one, Helen felt for a pulse. Then she called for the nurse. The nurse sang up cheerfully, 'I'm coming. Won't be a mo!'

Bright said, 'She's a witness I was here. No point making a run for it. Sorry, Helen.'

'Oh, well.' She made her report into the mobile phone. Bright circled the room like a cat, sniffing in detail, minute observations: closed curtains middle of the day, someone might have noticed that. Someone had been here. When? How did they get in?

The smell of cabbage ascended with the nurse. She carried a bowl of overcooked-vegetable soup on a tray. Helen raised a hand to stop her in the doorway. It was strange to Bright to do nothing in this situation, to have no place, no clout. Helen shut down her phone. 'Put down the tray, please.'

The nurse looked taken aback, no more. Puzzled, anxious, she put the tray on a washstand in the hall. 'What is it? Has she been taken ill?'

'When were you last up here?'

'Oh... Oh dear, I didn't come up at lunchtime. Her daughter came. She brought the lunch up instead of me.'

'Her daughter? You're sure?'

'Yes. Well, she said she was her daughter. She *was* her daughter. She came once before and Miss Leighton recognised her all right. She didn't seem to like her much.'

'She brought the lunch up and you—'

'I stayed downstairs to eat my own lunch in peace. Then I went out for a few things, just to the village. The daughter – Margaret, is she called? - yes. Margaret said it would be okay, she'd be here till I came back.'

'And was she?'

'Yes.'

'Yes?' Helen looked at Bright. He raised an eyebrow.

'I'd been back about ten minutes, must have been four o'clock or so. She called out from the hall, Don't worry, I'll let myself out. Mother's fine, she's asleep, don't disturb her. Don't bother taking her tea. That's what she said.' The nurse's face went quite blank for a moment. 'Oh my God,' she said. 'She's died, hasn't she? Oh my God.'

Bright stopped her from going into the room. He didn't want her to touch anything in there, though her prints must already be over everything. She sat on a stair with her head between her knees. 'It's your nightmare,' she said to Bright. 'If you're a nurse. It's your nightmare they'll die on you. I haven't neglected her, I really haven't.'

'No, no. No one thinks you have.'

'Oh.'

'You're sure it was the daughter who came?'

'Margaret. Yes.'

'Not the son?'

'Mark? No! What are you–? Is there something fishy about it, then? Is that why you're asking–?'

'Well, we won't know till they've done the PM. But, well, it looks like it.'

'Oh no.' It was almost a whimper and her hands started to tremble.

'Listen, love, it wasn't your fault, right? Keep cool 'cause you're going be needed round here. You're the only one so far who saw the daughter here.'

'It couldn't have been her who did it. She's so nice. She's so calm.'

'But Miss Leighton here didn't like her, right?'

'No. That's right. She always looked a bit alarmed when I mentioned her. The son now, that's a different matter. She seemed to be keener on him. Why has he stayed away so long? she kept asking me. That police guard on the house, that was watching out for him, wasn't it?'

Bright didn't answer this. When Mark first did a runner there had been surveillance. It had been transferred to Margaret's place. There's only ever so much manpower to go around. But surely someone must have followed Margaret up here, at least. The ruthlessness of this killing. The smooth way it had been done. Margaret was involved, in some way. He felt it. He knew it. And he knew it would not be possible to prove.

He led the nurse down to the basement. The back door was open. He said, 'Did you leave this open?'

She had both hands pressed flat to her chest. She shook her head, swallowing. She whispered, 'I never open it. Last time I saw it it was bolted shut.'

'When was the last time you saw it?'

'I keep the vegetables down here, it's such a small fridge in the kitchen. I came down to get onions and carrots for the soup. That was this morning about ten o'clock.'

'And it was bolted then?'

She nodded her head, then shook it, then said, 'I never noticed if it was bolted. I didn't look. But it wasn't open, I can tell you that.' She had started to rally. Outrage, the sense of invasion, of being tricked, got the blood moving in her veins again. 'He was hiding somewhere then? All the time. He could have been watching me even.' She suddenly spat out, 'The little shit.'

'You're sure Margaret left by the front door?'

'Yes.'

'You saw her go? Or she just called out, or what?'

'Oh. Oh God. Hang on. She called out to me. I was busy in the kitchen. I poked my head round the door. She said goodbye. She opened the front door. I came back down here. I heard the door close.'

'You didn't see her actually go out?'

'Oh God. Margaret? You're not saying Margaret– Are you saying Margaret let him in?'

'I'm not saying anything, love. Just repeat to the officer who comes what you said to me. Great observation. Good as a copper.'

'It's the training. We're taught to look for signs.'

The noise of arrival broke out upstairs.

Ryan would be spitting blood to know he was here. Bright held the door open with a tea towel, threw the towel to the nurse and went out. Into the yard. Into the mews. Deserted. The garage men had long gone home. Out into the wide street. Great long shadows everywhere, stretching over everything, like fingers.

44

BLOOD OUT OF STONE

He found himself with no breath, like he'd been running up the hills, not driving. He ran now past three parked cars and down the path to her door. She opened the door and gave her shy composed smile.

'Can I come in? Thanks.' He said this like one word and slid inside in one movement, fast on his feet, smooth as an alley-cat. She had no chance to stop him. Not that she seemed to want to. She looked a little taken aback but nothing more. Not guilty, not scared, not even alarmed. He said, 'You went to see your mother this afternoon?'

'How did you know?'

'I've just been visiting too.'

'Why?'

'To ask a few more questions about Mark.'

'And about me, I suppose.'

'How was your mother?'

'She's weak. She's gone to pieces since Mark went. She misses him. Well, he did everything for her. I felt almost guilty. I even wondered should I move back in? But that wouldn't work. It never did. And the nurse seems good. Conscientious anyway.'

Was the girl talking more than usual? Her nice modulated voice laved calm over everything, but she was talking a lot, wasn't she? 'She was okay, though? Your mother?'

Margaret's brow creased slightly. 'Yes. I mean, as well as— Why are you asking this?'

I ask the questions, Bright thought, but did not say. *Mustn't alienate the girl. Not yet. Bird in the hand. Don't scare it off.* 'Did you see Mark when you were there?'

'Mark?'

'Your missing brother Mark, a-ha.'

'You're saying Mark was there?'

'You didn't see him? You didn't arrange to meet him there? You didn't open the door to let him in, let him out?'

'Mark was there?' She put her long hands up to her face. 'How do you know? Have you seen him? Have they – have they arrested him? Oh no.'

This was all spoken in this tranquil unhurried voice, the way she said everything. He couldn't work out whether this gave an air of utter falsehood or utter truth. He was having a job working out anything. His brain seemed to have come off its tracks. He said, 'Look, love, sit down a minute, all right?' He sat himself opposite her. That felt better. He must not break the news of the mother's death, much as he wanted to; he had to wait for the local force. Pollock or Ryan would come in person for this. They should get her reaction fresh.

'Tell me what happened,' he said. 'From the moment you got there. Hang on. Why did you go? You don't like your mother. Did you get a call from Mark?'

She looked at him level, enquiring. 'I went because Mark isn't around, not because he is. If Mark were there, I wouldn't need to go. But it appears to be my duty just to look in. It's not the first time I've been.'

'No?'

'I went about a week ago, just after—'

'A-ha.'

'She's never pleased to see me. She makes me feel bad. Really bad. You know? A bad person, I mean. She doesn't mean to, but that's how it is. I stayed a while. To give the nurse a break.'

'What did you talk about?'

She tried to avoid his eye but something in that concentrated squint — was it focused on her? was it not? — forced words out of her. At last she said, 'All right. I went there to see if she knew where Mark was, okay? That's the reason I went both times. Not to see my mother. I can't believe he wouldn't have been in touch with her. But she said she knew nothing. She's heard nothing. He hasn't even phoned.' Her voice disappeared a second. She cleared her throat, and her

386

emotion with it.

'Was she worried about him?'

'She was worried he might not come back to look after her. Her. Her. That's all she worries about. All she ever has worried about. I'm sorry to sound so bitter. But if Mark has by any chance done the dreadful things you suspect him of, it will be my mother's fault, not his. And I want to go on record now as saying that.'

You'll be on record soon enough, Bright thought. He suddenly found himself saying, 'We found your mother dead.'

Margaret stood. She backed away. She pressed her whole body back against the wall, even the palms of her hands. Her eyes were shut. Then she bent forwards, her hair ends touched her feet, her hands hung. She went down on her hands and knees. Then she sat back on her heels. It was an astonishing series of movements, carried out in utter silence. She breathed out long breaths like she was doing yoga.

Bright said, 'I'm asking you again: did you let Mark in?'

She shook her head from side to side.

'Did you let Mark out?'

Again she shook her head: no.

'Did you see Mark?'

'No.'

'Did you know he was there?'

'No.'

387

'Then I think you're going to be arrested for your mother's murder.'

'In that case I wish I had killed her. It would make it all worth while.'

45

EXCERPT FROM A DIARY

xi

When Margaret decided to go up to the house I was disturbed. She said she was worried about mother, but Margaret stopped worrying about mother years ago. I never like it when Margaret lies or starts to get clever. It's not like her. It churns me up. I do not like her taking action on her own. I refused to go with her.

I am really not sure what happened. She must have done things coolly, slowly, she was there for hours. And mother did not struggle. I believe she gave mother some of her sleeping pills and just waited, watching her.

Margaret has never taken action like this alone before. I could always call on her when I needed her, but apart from that she kept away. I needed her to abduct Maisie. Because of what had happened to Alison, Maisie would never have left her house alone that day with a man. So I had to send Margaret to get her and bring her here. And since then, to give me time, I have had to use her to talk to the police etc. She has had to have a high profile. It's I who have had to disappear. This way she has got back into my life. She has got too close to me. Things are getting confused between us. Blurred. I don't like this.

Margaret walked back in here, so cool. She wanted to go in to look at Maisie. I would not let her. I know that for Margaret mother's death is a liberation. A triumph. A necessity. I suppose she had always known this and that is why she went away. And if she had not been hounded and chased into this corner she would not have taken such a revenge. I don't believe she meant to do this when she went up there. I believe she was overcome, taken by surprise.

I do not want that to happen to me. I waited a good while before going in to Maisie myself.

Maisie knew at once that something big had happened. She said, 'What's going on?' and I realised I had taken her no food or drink for some time and that she was scared I was going to leave her here to starve. She was more scared than she has been before and I was sorry to see that. I told her I would not let her die like that. I would not let her die till she agreed. 'I'm hungry,' she said. I brought her food. She said, 'Aren't you eating?' I shook my head and I told her what had happened. It was only then it became real to me. I realised I had lost my mother and now there is nothing in my life to cling to. Nobody who needs me. Margaret doesn't need me any more. She has freed herself from both of us. It doesn't matter, I told myself, because I'm going to die when Maisie does, but just the same I did feel utterly desolate.

I knew once again I had talked too much in the Dead Room and that this had added to my despair. Maisie strangely enough looked compassionately upon me. When I stopped crying she said, 'Now you know how I feel about my mother. Why don't you let me go to her, and just stop all this?' She said it as though she did not expect me to reply. And I didn't. She thinks it would be hard for me to send her back because of Alison. But that's not the reason.

I am writing my diary in the Dead Room with her tonight because I am afraid to be alone. I'm afraid of Margaret.

46

GOING SOLO

Bright thought Ryan might burst a blood vessel finding him at Margaret's. He slipped out, leaving him to pull in Margaret on his own, but the damage was done. The interview later in his office was short. Bright knew he'd overstepped the mark. Ryan threatened to make a report to Bright's superintendent at Kentish Town. The superintendent was new, he didn't know Bright yet. It could mean disaster. 'Don't do that, Ryan. I'll go quietly, okay?'

On his way out he had a word with Pollock. Pollock said he'd do what he could. 'Sorry you're off the team.'

'Thanks. Not as sorry as I am.'

He managed a short meet with Helen late that night. Not at the police station bar; it wouldn't do Helen's prospects much good to be seen with him. They were in the Coronation Tap again. Bright liked the feel of the place, it had become his home from home. 'They took Margaret's fingerprints,' Helen said. 'They're all round the mother's room, and on the front door, the banister

392

rail, all over the house. But they would be, wouldn't they?'

'Why would they?'

'Well—'

'She hasn't spent time there for years, she says.'

'No, but she'd have gone all over the place, wouldn't she? Her first visit home and that? You explore, don't you?'

'What about the back door downstairs?'

'Only Margaret's prints and the nurse's.'

'No others?'

'Well, a few smudgy ones. But we never got Mark's to compare, did we? 'Cause Ryan – well – Mark wasn't a suspect, was he, till he did a runner?'

Bright groaned. 'They got the nurse in the frame?'

'They're not ruling her out.'

'She's helping them with their enquiries.'

'Yes.'

'Waste of time. She's got nothing to do with it.' Bright gulped a mouthful of scotch, a double, neat, one cube of ice. 'I've pissed off Ryan all right.'

'Why did you stay at Margaret's till he came?'

'I couldn't scarper once I'd told her about her mother, could I? She could have done a runner too. Could've told her brother. If he's killed his mother, it means he's gone right off the rails. It doesn't look good for

393

Maisie. It doesn't look good.'

'We've let her go.'

'The nurse? Sure.'

'Margaret.'

He put down his scotch. 'Let Margaret go?'

'I *thought* you'd be surprised.'

'Why?'

'The mother was alive when she left. Forensic confirm it. She died at least an hour later.'

'Cause of death?'

'Barbiturates, then suffocation.'

'Same as Alison.'

Bright slowly sipped the scotch. He swirled the ice around. He stared at it, swirling. He said, 'She gave the mother the sleeping pills. She opened the back door for Mark. She left. He did the suffocation. They're working together. Can you get anyone to see that?' He looked at her. A raw recruit. Eager to get into CID. Imaginative. Ambitious. But just a kid. He was too low tonight even to fancy her. He swallowed the ice cube and drained the glass. 'I shouldn't be here. I'm doing nobody any good.'

Lizzie's had a different atmosphere. He felt it outside the front door. He heard the mighty rumble of the voice of Alan Tate. But when he got inside he saw Dave. Dave looked bad. In custody he'd grown a beard.

He looked like Rip Van Winkle. He'd come out of the mountain into a different world. He shook Bright's hand.

'How're you feeling?' Bright said.

'I somehow thought they'd let me out when they found Maisie. Only they haven't found Maisie. Why did they let me go? Nobody would say.'

'Mark Leighton's mother was found dead early this evening.'

Dave looked blank. 'And? She was an invalid, wasn't she?'

'She'd been helped on her way.'

'Are we talking euthanasia here?'

'Doesn't look like it, no.'

A succession of thoughts slowly crossed Dave's face. 'So now Mark Leighton's their prime suspect?'

'Been mine all along.'

'Thanks.'

'You're welcome. I'm no closer to catching him. The sister's in cahoots with him, I'm sure she is, but she comes across pure as the driven snow, and she'll never give him up. They've let her go. All I can do is keep a close watch on her.'

'Can I help?'

'More help here, aren't you?'

Dave's gaunt face expressed a rueful sense of loss. He opened the door to the front room. Silence fell. Lizzie was dressed and had combed her hair. Her face was dead tired, white, its severe expression wiped out by anxiety and grief. She nodded at Bright and Dave. Alan Tate stood up. 'Well, I must be on my way, as they say.' He crossed to Lizzie. 'Don't get up, Lizzie. I'll drop in tomorrow, if I may?'

Lizzie nodded. He lightly touched her hair, and left. Bright went into the kitchen to see Kate. She looked wild, her hair, her eyes, like something bad was chasing her. He sat close to her. 'There's something I'm not getting. Something dead simple. I know that girl Margaret is aiding and abetting him, covering for him. She knows where he is. She knows where Maisie is.'

Kate said, 'I'm going to see her again.'

'I'll go with you when you go.'

'You're in trouble enough,' she said.

'I'll keep out of sight. But I'll be around.'

'You think I'm in danger from her?'

'I think she helped him to kill his mother.'

'*Her* mother too.'

'She told me she wished she'd killed her.'

'John.'

'A-ha.'

A shiver ran through Kate. All the tiredness she'd been holding at bay fell suddenly on her like an avalanche.

Bright said, 'Don't go and see her tonight. Go home and go to bed. Take a sleeping pill. I'll be keeping an eye on Margaret's place, just in case. I might take Dave with me to

396

watch the back. Keep him occupied.'

But strolling up St Luke's Crescent, Bright recognised one of the uniforms from Broadbury Road police station, slumped in an unmarked car in plain clothes just across from Margaret's place. He climbed the steps at the end of the street to the back yard wall level, the mouth of the alleyway. Two young blokes lounged there, smoking. He knew them too, from the police station bar. He nodded and went on up the steps.

Dave and Lizzie were asleep on the couch in each other's arms, babes in the wood. He covered them with a duvet from upstairs. They didn't stir. He left the house. He walked the streets.

Helen told him next day what he already knew – that a constant watch was being kept on Margaret. He said, 'What's the matter with them? They could have pulled her in yesterday.'

'What for?'

'A crime was committed, she was there, her fingerprints were found at the scene, come on! *What for?*'

'But then she couldn't lead them to Mark.'

'No, but at least they could search her place without a warrant. PACE section eighteen: searches.'

'But Inspector Pollock already searched. I

397

was with him.'

'Mark's there, Helen. I know he's there. He's living in that flat in St Luke's Crescent with that mad sister.'

'You think she's mad?'

'A-ha. And you think I am.'

Helen blushed. 'We really did search. Honestly there was nothing there.'

'A-ha.'

She was irritated that she couldn't convince him. He was wild, couldn't sit still, got out of the car. Paced up and down. Up here on the edge of the Downs, that amazing bridge, the river below, the lovely Georgian houses, all air and grace, and there was Maisie somewhere, in some prison, kept by a maniac capable of killing not just a young girl on the brink of life, Alison, but his own mother whom he'd looked after for twenty years. He felt like he was in one of those dreams where everything's calm on the surface and underneath something boils and ticks and you can't get hold of it.

He went to see Kate at lunchtime. He felt weird round the theatre, no business there, spare prick at the wedding. She said, 'That's how *I* feel when I'm not working. You only feel okay here when you've got a job to do.'

His small brown eyes had this desperate burn to them today. She knew he knew time was running out. The mother's death was a sign the guy had flipped. She took him to the Arnolfini. They got a sandwich and sat at a table on the grey cobbles by the water. The smart young things of Bristol milled around, eating and drinking and flirting and laughing. The sun shone. And there were they, enclosed by darkness in the sun. He said, 'He's cleverer than we are.'

'I don't believe he's cleverer than you.'

That made him more desperate, he felt like grinding his teeth. He groaned. He couldn't eat. Fed his posh sandwich to the gulls. Kate said, 'Look, we've got the theatre just for this afternoon. We're having a stagger-through. Why don't you come?' Normally she'd die rather than let someone in before she was ready. But this time there were more important things than the performance. He looked appalled. She said, 'What else are you going to do?'

'I can't do a blind thing. They got Margaret pinned down. She can't take a piss without they'll know. That's what *they* think. She's got a phone, hasn't she?'

'Won't they be tracing her calls?'

'She'll have a way. She's abetting him. I know she is.'

A juddering roar above. They looked up. A helicopter circled low over the warehouses opposite, not yet turned into fashionable loft apartments, over where Dave lived.

'The heat-seeking camera,' he said.

Kate too threw her sandwich to the gulls. 'I'm praying, nonstop, all the time, to something I don't believe in.'

He looked at her. He'd been talking to her as if she was a colleague on the case. But she loved Maisie. She gazed at him, pleading. She said, 'Come and see the run-through.'

He looked at the helicopter twinkling away over Bedminster way, then at her poor face, white like Lizzie's face, with feverish eyes. He nodded. 'Okay.'

'Providing the others agree.'

They took a vote to let him stay. Colum said, 'Sit by me and tell me what's wrong with it.' But Bright declined. Sat towards the back, scrunched down in his seat, in case the actors could see him. He dreaded catching anyone's eye. He was nervous. He was going to be shown up. He wasn't going to understand a word.

First surprise: he understands everything. That poor kid Orlando. His brother's doing him out of his inheritance, but he's a good-hearted lad, looking after this old servant bloke. Then Rosalind and Celia come on, Rosalind's dead depressed. He thinks at first, *It's Kate, she's in such a state about Maisie she can't lift herself out of it,* but then she wasn't Kate, she was changed, not outwardly but from within somehow. So it's

400

Rosalind who's depressed about her dad who's been given the push by her uncle. Here's another wicked brother doing dirty deeds. Then they do this wrestling match. Good as the real thing. The lad throws this big tough guy. And Rosalind falls in love and this joy invades Kate, she lights up. She dresses up like the lad and they go off to the forest.

Suddenly he remembers it from school. It hadn't seemed like this then. He actually finds himself laughing when Touchstone, this little fat guy, comes on in full Scout regalia. And then the lad pinning these poems on the trees. The whole thing had been about evil and sadness and loss and now suddenly it's about love. Everyone's falling in love and it's a bit mad, because they're all out of their depth in this forest, and all that evil stuff is still there in the background. But they forget it, and so do you, except when that old misery Jaques wanders in reminding everyone. The lad gallops off to pin up his next poem and down comes Touchstone's tent and there he is reading *Playboy* by the light of a torch. He gathers everything up, mortified. Bright's laughing. He wouldn't have thought it possible an hour ago.

And then come these amazing love scenes. The girl's flying. Only she's a boy and the real boy is getting confused because he's got these feelings for this Ganymede and how can he be getting the hots for this kid when he's in love with Rosalind? And she's enjoying herself so much she's almost crazy. That nice little Celia is getting really upset. Who can blame her? It's wicked. She says to Rosalind, 'We must have your doublet and hose plucked over your head and show the world what the bird hath done to her own nest!' and Rosalind takes off her cap and throws it in the air and all her hair comes tumbling out so she's a girl again and she says, 'That thou didst know how many fathom deep I am in love!' And Bright knew.

He knew why only Margaret's fingerprints were at the scene. He knew why Maisie had gone in the first place. He knew where Maisie was. He knew who was holding her. He didn't know why. But he knew who. He stood up. Colum turned, shocked: *the show was that bad?* Nearly out of the back doors Bright stopped. He pulled out his notebook and wrote a note for Kate, not getting her hopes up, but saying he had to go.

47

EXCERPT FROM A DIARY

xii

Margaret behaved with total cool at the police station. She was incredible but I know when she gets like that, the stress is building up. Margaret is beginning to frighten me.

Maisie can see I'm frightened. Maisie whispers to me in the Dead Room. Whispering is horrible in there. But not as worrying as hearing one's own voice so thin and distant. I whispered to Maisie about our lives, Margaret's and mine. How Margaret had struggled to be herself all her life. How I had given in and become what mother wanted. 'Don't be a girl,' mother said. 'Look at *me:* this is what happens to girls.' She did not want a girl. She wanted an invulnerable, strong, male person. Sometimes she would say, *'You'll* make sure Margaret comes to no harm. You'll keep her safe. You will protect her.' She dressed Margaret in my clothes. She called Margaret Mark. She sent Margaret to school as Mark. It was fine when we were small. It seemed a joke. It made mother happy, it made us laugh. It was when Margaret started to become a woman that things went wrong. She came in one day dressed much as she dresses now, in a simple cotton frock, with just a faint tasteful trace of makeup, and mother behaved as though she had committed a heinous crime. 'Take that off. Take that off. Get out of here. Get out.'

I'm losing it. I have to try to keep control. I don't want Margaret to take over. I don't want her to win. I know in a sense Margaret and mother are the same. Both of them ruthless and cruel, and they've manipulated me between them. I've been there for them and yet because of me Margaret could never be herself, never have lovers or children or a decent life. No. Not because of me. Because of mother. But I have never been able to blame mother. I can only blame the man who did what he did to her when she was fifteen and innocent. Margaret blamed mother for passing that hurt on. When I told Maisie this, she said, 'That's what you're doing too. Just like your mother. You're passing it on. That's why you're killing young girls, you're doing the same thing the man did to your mother and your mother did to Margaret.' She said, 'Why don't you stop?' She became a little bit agitated and she had the sense to stop talking. Her small hands were trembling a little today. And I took my decision.

She's weak, from fear at being left alone so much, from revulsion at her chemical toilet which had not been emptied while Margaret was in custody. And from hunger of course. She's very hungry. I did not want it to be quite like this. But sometimes we don't have a choice. While her stomach is empty is a good time. I prepared her cocktail.

When I said to her, Here, have a drink, it will cheer you up, she said, 'Is this it then? This what you gave Alison?'

'Alison accepted it,' I said. 'She understood.'

'*I* understand,' Maisie said. 'I understand you're not going to let me out of here whatever happens. But I'm not going to take your drugs.'

I tried to persuade her. Then I gave up. I said, 'Oh all right then,' and gave her some food. It was one of my delicious curries. A mixed vegetable dish called Niramish. The barbiturates were in that. Maisie was so hungry she never suspected. And in some strange way she trusts me. I really love her. I'd like to die with her, but unfortunately I have to make sure she is really gone first. I don't have to leave her on the hillside. That cockney policeman, the one with the screwdriver voice, the icicle sharp eyes, he'll find us. I knew as soon as he came here that

405

our time was short.

You will publicise this diary, won't you? You will try to make people understand. You will understand, yourself? That I have done everything from the purest of motives, even when pushed to my limits. And I do admit limits, at last. Don't miss Maisie. Remember her as she was. Perfect. Unsullied. Her own self. She and Alison.

They shall not see corruption.

48

THEY WHO HAVE EYES TO SEE

He phoned the incident room on the way. He was lucky, it was Pollock's shift. He told Pollock what he knew. Pollock said, 'You're barking mad.' Bright said, 'Think about it. Think through what you've got and why you haven't got more. And then speak to the IO and then get your arse down there and pull Leighton in. On any pretext, doesn't matter, just do it. You know I'm right, Pollock.'

He was just driving under the railway bridge. Even if Pollock went along, the IO would think it was a mad idea. Bright had to get there himself, and fast, and bugger the consequences. He shot along by the side of the green hill where Alison's beautiful body had been laid out by this freak, he zoomed round the corner into steep Windsor Terrace, shot left into steeper St Luke's Crescent, squealed to a stop outside Margaret's place, jumped out and hurtled up the path. He rang the bell, not too hard, not too long. He waited. Rang again and knocked. Nothing. He broke a pane of glass and opened the door.

The place was silent. Empty. Now one of the uniforms from the surveillance car was on his back: 'What you think you're doing?' Then the lad recognised him and didn't know what to do.

'It's okay, mate. DCI Pollock'll be down here any minute. I was in the vicinity. Maisie Creech is in here. She's somewhere in this building.'

The second uniform ran upstairs. Bright moved, light on his feet, through to the kitchen at the back, looking, listening, sniffing the air, feeling his way, a tracker dog with its tail up. 'DCI Pollock says the way down to the cellar is through the big cupboard.' Swift, silent, they moved away the brooms and stuff, and there was the trap door. Bright knew that was no good. He knew it for certain in his bones. Margaret had taken them down there. She wouldn't do that if–

'Sir?' The uniform who'd gone upstairs panted in. 'Sir, I just noticed something. You can't see it from down here. Come and look.' The lad climbed on to the sink unit. Bright followed. 'Look, sir.' The lad pointed down. From here, pressed up against the window, looking straight down, you could see: the York-stone paving of Margaret's smart garden did not come right up to the house as it had seemed to. It stopped about two feet away and the space between the

408

house and the paving was roofed over. There was a ventilator fan in this strip of roof.

Bright silently got off the sink unit, followed by the lad. 'What's your name?'

'Peters, sir.'

'They should make you sergeant tomorrow. Now how would you get down there?'

'Through the cellar.'

'Too obvious for this freak. And it's been searched. So has this damn kitchen. I searched these cupboards myself. But then I was looking for Mark Leighton, not for a way down to a prison.' Bright opened the cupboards under the sink and the work surface. The lad cottoned on, pulled out all the stuff. They felt round the edges of the cupboard floors. Nothing. Bright opened the tall narrow cupboard in the corner. Took out a mop and bucket. Pulled at the floor. It came up, hinged at one side. A ladder led down the side wall, metal rungs down into light. A nice little kitchen area. Mark Leighton's clothes on a hanging rail, so instantly recognisable it might have been him hanging there. Margaret's cotton dress too. And a door.

Bright pulled the big metal handle. The door didn't budge. He put more effort and with a deep-throated *pfluck*, the thing threw him back on his heels. Immediately inside was a second door. He pulled. No good. He

409

pushed. The door opened.

Leighton knelt over Maisie. Only, without the scruffy long sweater, it was suddenly clear that this was a woman's body, not a man's. Maisie's head was inside a plastic bag. Leighton turned. The face was made up, a little tasteful lipstick and eye shadow, nothing too much.

It took both uniforms to restrain her. She was screaming. 'You don't understand. Let me finish. I've got to finish what I've begun!'

Bright got the bag off Maisie's head. He began to pump at her lungs. She was far gone and fading. He could hear the uniforms calling for back-up. It might not get here in time. He knew he shouldn't move her but he had to get her some air. He picked her up and put her in a fireman's lift over his shoulder while he climbed the ladder. As he flung her over his shoulder he felt her start to heave. By the time he got her outside she had certainly thrown up, all down his back. The squad car was going off down the crescent, Leighton's face pressed to the window, he/she/it still screaming, silenced by glass.

Bright laid Maisie down. Her delicate limbs. She was so light. A crowd was forming, and no back-up yet. A woman gave him a blanket. He wrapped Maisie in it. Though she'd thrown up, her breathing was fragile. She was in big trouble, he could feel her slipping away. He pumped at her back. He turned her over. He wiped her mouth and held her nose and brought his mouth to hers, he'd give his life for her, to her, his breath for hers.

The ambulance howled up the hill as Lizzie and Dave ran along from the steps at the other end of the street. Bright watched them get in the back, together. The family united.

The murmuring crowd stayed in the street. Pollock arrived. Bright was finding it hard to speak. He showed the poor DCI what he'd missed. Now they looked at this weird padded room. It was the worst thing Bright had ever seen. Worse than the discovery under the shed floor of that pervert on the estate in Kentish Town. This was elaborate, prepared. This was expensive. This padded cave. He noticed that talking in there thinned your voice like talking on a mountain in a high wind. It made you feel lost. He and Pollock got out of there fast. Outside, Pollock shivered. 'Bloody hell,' he said.

Up in the flat, going through the desk, Pollock found this thick wodge of A4 paper in a white folder. On the front it said, DIARY. Pollock opened it. The top page was blank except for the words: *Dear Kate Creech. From one who admires dedication and excellence, a fellow perfectionist. This is for you. You will understand.*

Pollock turned to page one. Over his shoulder Bright read: *2 a.m. A moonless night. I crouched in the car listening...*

Maisie was on oxygen and a drip. They'd pumped her out. But the barbiturates were in her bloodstream. She was way gone. Out of it. Not out of danger, but taking a rest from life. They told Lizzie and Dave she'd live. Looking at her, nothing but a junction box for all the lines going into her and out of her, this was hard to believe.

The casualty department was non-stop. This was the middle of the night. Kate's shaking hands turned the pages. 'How did you–?'

'Helen smuggled me a copy.'

Something about the way he said Helen told her something. She'd think about it later. She didn't care. She didn't care about anything in the world, just having Maisie back again.

This Large Print Book for the partially sighted, who cannot read normal print, is published under the auspices of

THE ULVERSCROFT FOUNDATION